The Wind's
Twelve Quarters

The Wind's Twelve Quarters

Short Stories by
URSULA K. LE GUIN

HARPER & ROW, PUBLISHERS
New York, Evanston
San Francisco, London

"SEMLEY'S NECKLACE" originally appeared under the title "THE DOWRY OF THE ANGYAR" in *Amazing*, 1964.
"APRIL IN PARIS" originally appeared in *Fantastic*, 1962.
"THE MASTERS" and "DARKNESS BOX" originally appeared in *Fantastic*, 1963.
"THE WORD OF UNBINDING" and "THE RULE OF NAMES" originally appeared in *Fantastic*, 1964.
"WINTER'S KING" originally appeared in *Orbit 5*, 1969.
"THE GOOD TRIP" originally appeared in *Fantastic*, 1970.
"NINE LIVES" originally appeared in *Playboy*, 1969.
"THINGS" originally appeared under the title "THE END" in *Orbit 6*, 1970.
"A TRIP TO THE HEAD" originally appeared in *Quark 1*, 1970.
"VASTER THAN EMPIRES AND MORE SLOW" originally appeared in *New Dimensions 1*, 1971.
"THE STARS BELOW" originally appeared in *Orbit 12*, 1973.
"THE FIELD OF VISION" originally appeared in *Galaxy*, 1973.
"DIRECTION OF THE ROAD" originally appeared in *Orbit 14*, 1974.
"THE ONES WHO WALK AWAY FROM OMELAS" originally appeared in *New Dimensions 3*, 1973.
"THE DAY BEFORE THE REVOLUTION" originally appeared in *Galaxy*, 1974.
Excerpt from A. E. Housman's *A Shropshire Lad* reprinted by permission of Cambridge University Press.

FIRST EDITION

Designed by Janice Stern

Library of Congress Cataloging in Publication Data

Le Guin, Ursula K.
 The wind's twelve quarters.
 CONTENTS: Semley's necklace. —April in Paris. —The masters. —Darkness box. [etc.]
 I. Title.
PZ4.L518Wi [PS3562.E42] 813'.5'4 75-6372
ISBN 0-06-012562-4

75 76 77 78 79 10 9 8 7 6 5 4 3 2 1

From far, from eve and morning
 And yon twelve-winded sky,
The stuff of life to knit me
 Blew hither; here am I.

Now—for a breath I tarry
 Nor yet disperse apart—
Take my hand quick and tell me,
 What have you in your heart.

Speak now, and I will answer;
 How shall I help you, say;
Ere to the wind's twelve quarters
 I take my endless way.

A. E. Housman: *A Shropshire Lad*

CONTENTS

FOREWORD

This collection is what painters call a retrospective; it gives a roughly chronological survey of my short stories during the first ten years after I broke into print, belated but undaunted, at the age of thirty-two. They appear here very roughly in the order in which they were written, so that the development of the artist may become part of the interest of the book. I have not been rigid about the chronology (it is impossible; stories may be written in one year, not published until two or three years later, and then possibly revised, and which date do you use?) but there are no severe displacements.

It is by no means a complete collection of my stories. One early story is left out because I don't much like it; fiction which doesn't fit under the headings Fantasy or Science Fiction is not included; and most of my stories published in the last few years are not in this book, because the anthologies in which they first appeared are still in print. The last two in the volume, however, appeared in 1973 and 1974, so the seventeen stories do cover the last ten or a dozen years.

The relation between short story and novel, inside the writer's head, is interesting. "Semley's Necklace," though a complete story in itself, was the germ of a novel. I had done with Semley when I finished it, but there was a minor character, a mere by-

stander, who did not sink back obediently into obscurity when the story was done, but who kept nagging me. "Write *my* story," he said. "I'm Rocannon. I want to explore my world. . . . " So I obeyed him. You really can't argue with these people.

"Winter's King" was another such germinal story, and so were "The Word of Unbinding" and "The Rule of Names," though all of them gave me the place, rather than the person, for the novels to come. The last story in the book is not a germinal but an autumnal one. It came after the novel, a final gift, received with thanksgiving.

Most of the straight narrative stories in this volume are in fact connected with my novels, in that they fit more or less well into the rather erratic "future history" scheme which all my science fiction books follow. Those that don't fit in are the early fantasies, and then later the ones I call psychomyths, more or less sur-realistic tales, which share with fantasy the quality of taking place outside any history, outside of time, in that region of the living mind which—without invoking any consideration of immortality—seems to be without spatial or temporal limits at all.

Collectors might want to know that the titles used in this volume are my own choice, in some cases varying from previous publications:

"Semley's Necklace" first appeared as "Dowry of the Angyar" (a grammatical error by the editor, who didn't speak Angyo fluently);

"Things" appeared as "The End";

"The Field of Vision" appeared as "Field of Vision."

The only stories that have been revised, beyond an occasional one-word or one-sentence change and restitution of cuts and errors in the published versions, are:

"Winter's King" (see note to the story);

"Vaster than Empires and More Slow" (a cut in the first pages);

"Nine Lives" (see note to the story).

SEMLEY'S NECKLACE

This story, written in 1963, published as "Dowry of the Angyar" in 1964 and as the Prologue of my first novel, Rocannon's World, *in 1966, was actually the eighth story I got printed; but it opens the book because I think it's the most characteristic of my early science fiction and fantasy works, the most romantic of them all. The progress of my style has been away from open romanticism, slowly and steadily, from this story to the last one in the volume, written in 1972. It has been a progress. I am still a romantic, no doubt about that, and glad of it, but the candor and simplicity of "Semley's Necklace" have gradually become something harder, stronger, and more complex.*

How can you tell the legend from the fact on these worlds that lie so many years away?—planets without names, called by their people simply The World, planets without history, where the past is the matter of myth, and a returning explorer finds his own doings of a few years back have become the gestures of a god. Unreason darkens that gap of time bridged by our lightspeed ships, and in the darkness uncertainty and disproportion grow like weeds.

In trying to tell the story of a man, an ordinary League scientist, who went to such a nameless half-known world not many years ago, one feels like an archaeologist amid millennial ruins, now

struggling through choked tangles of leaf, flower, branch and vine to the sudden bright geometry of a wheel or a polished cornerstone, and now entering some commonplace, sunlit doorway to find inside it the darkness, the impossible flicker of a flame, the glitter of a jewel, the half-glimpsed movement of a woman's arm.

How can you tell fact from legend, truth from truth?

Through Rocannon's story the jewel, the blue glitter seen briefly, returns. With it let us begin, here:

Galactic Area 8, No. 62: FOMALHAUT II.
High-Intelligence Life Forms: Species Contacted:
Species I.

A. Gdemiar (singular Gdem): Highly intelligent, fully hom-inoid nocturnal troglodytes, 120–135 cm. in height, light skin, dark head-hair. When contacted these cave-dwellers possessed a rigidly stratified oligarchic urban society modified by partial colonial telepathy, and a technologically oriented Early Steel culture. Technology enhanced to Industrial, Point C, during League Mission of 252–254. In 254 an Automatic Drive ship (to-from New South Georgia) was presented to oligarchs of the Kiriensea Area community. Status C–Prime.

B. Fiia (singular Fian): Highly intelligent, fully hominoid, diurnal, av. ca. 130 cm. in height, observed individuals generally light in skin and hair. Brief contacts indicated village and no-madic communal societies, partial colonial telepathy, also some indication of short-range TK. The race appears a-technological and evasive, with minimal and fluid culture-patterns. Currently untaxable. Status E–Query.

Species II.
Liuar (singular Liu): Highly intelligent, fully hominoid, di-urnal, av. height above 170 cm., this species possesses a fortress/

village, clan-descent society, a blocked technology (Bronze), and feudal-heroic culture. Note horizontal social cleavage into 2 pseudo-races: (a) Olgyior, "midmen," light-skinned and dark-haired; (b) Angyar, "lords," very tall, dark-skinned, yellow-haired—

"That's her," said Rocannon, looking up from the *Abridged Handy Pocket Guide to Intelligent Life-forms* at the very tall, dark-skinned, yellow-haired woman who stood halfway down the long museum hall. She stood still and erect, crowned with bright hair, gazing at something in a display case. Around her fidgeted four uneasy and unattractive dwarves.

"I didn't know Fomalhaut II had all those people besides the trogs," said Ketho, the curator.

"I didn't either. There are even some 'Unconfirmed' species listed here, that they never contacted. Sounds like time for a more thorough survey mission to the place. Well, now at least we know what she is."

"I wish there were some way of knowing *who* she is. . . ."

She was of an ancient family, a descendant of the first kings of the Angyar, and for all her poverty her hair shone with the pure, steadfast gold of her inheritance. The little people, the Fiia, bowed when she passed them, even when she was a barefoot child running in the fields, the light and fiery comet of her hair brightening the troubled winds of Kirien.

She was still very young when Durhal of Hallan saw her, courted her, and carried her away from the ruined towers and windy halls of her childhood to his own high home. In Hallan on the mountainside there was no comfort either, though splendor endured. The windows were unglassed, the stone floors bare; in coldyear one might wake to see the night's snow in long, low

drifts beneath each window. Durhal's bride stood with narrow bare feet on the snowy floor, braiding up the fire of her hair and laughing at her young husband in the silver mirror that hung in their room. That mirror, and his mother's bridal-gown sewn with a thousand tiny crystals, were all his wealth. Some of his lesser kinfolk of Hallan still possessed wardrobes of brocaded clothing, furniture of gilded wood, silver harness for their steeds, armor and silver mounted swords, jewels and jewelry—and on these last Durhal's bride looked enviously, glancing back at a gemmed coronet or a golden brooch even when the wearer of the ornament stood aside to let her pass, deferent to her birth and marriage-rank.

Fourth from the High Seat of Hallan Revel sat Durhal and his bride Semley, so close to Hallanlord that the old man often poured wine for Semley with his own hand, and spoke of hunting with his nephew and heir Durhal, looking on the young pair with a grim, unhopeful love. Hope came hard to the Angyar of Hallan and all the Western Lands, since the Starlords had appeared with their houses that leaped about on pillars of fire and their awful weapons that could level hills. They had interfered with all the old ways and wars, and though the sums were small there was terrible shame to the Angyar in having to pay a tax to them, a tribute for the Starlords' war that was to be fought with some strange enemy, somewhere in the hollow places between the stars, at the end of years. "It will be your war too," they said, but for a generation now the Angyar had sat in idle shame in their revel-halls, watching their double swords rust, their sons grow up without ever striking a blow in battle, their daughters marry poor men, even midmen, having no dowry of heroic loot to bring a noble husband. Hallanlord's face was bleak when he watched the fair-haired couple and heard their laughter as they drank bitter wine and joked together in the cold, ruinous, resplendent fortress of their race.

Semley's own face hardened when she looked down the hall and saw, in seats far below hers, even down among the halfbreeds and the midmen, against white skins and black hair, the gleam and flash of precious stones. She herself had brought nothing in dowry to her husband, not even a silver hairpin. The dress of a thousand crystals she had put away in a chest for the wedding-day of her daughter, if daughter it was to be.

It was, and they called her Haldre, and when the fuzz on her little brown skull grew longer it shone with steadfast gold, the inheritance of the lordly generations, the only gold she would ever possess. . . .

Semley did not speak to her husband of her discontent. For all his gentleness to her, Durhal in his pride had only contempt for envy, for vain wishing, and she dreaded his contempt. But she spoke to Durhal's sister Durossa.

"My family had a great treasure once," she said. "It was a necklace all of gold, with the blue jewel set in the center—sapphire?"

Durossa shook her head, smiling, not sure of the name either. It was late in warmyear, as these Northern Angyar called the summer of the eight-hundred-day year, beginning the cycle of months anew at each equinox; to Semley it seemed an outlandish calendar, a midmannish reckoning. Her family was at an end, but it had been older and purer than the race of any of these north-western marchlanders, who mixed too freely with the Olgyior. She sat with Durossa in the sunlight on a stone windowseat high up in the Great Tower, where the older woman's apartment was. Widowed young, childless, Durossa had been given in second marriage to Hallanlord, who was her father's brother. Since it was a kinmarriage and a second marriage on both sides she had not taken the title of Hallanlady, which Semley would some day bear; but she sat with the old lord in the High Seat and ruled with him

his domains. Older than her brother Durhal, she was fond of his young wife, and delighted in the bright-haired baby Haldre.

"It was bought," Semley went on, "with all the money my forebear Leynen got when he conquered the Southern Fiefs—all the money from a whole kingdom, think of it, for one jewel! Oh, it would outshine anything here in Hallan, surely, even those crystals like koob-eggs your cousin Issar wears. It was so beautiful they gave it a name of its own; they called it the Eye of the Sea. My great-grandmother wore it."

"You never saw it?" the older woman asked lazily, gazing down at the green mountainslopes where long, long summer sent its hot and restless winds straying among the forests and whirling down white roads to the seacoast far away.

"It was lost before I was born."

"No, my father said it was stolen before the Starlords ever came to our realm. He wouldn't talk of it, but there was an old mid-woman full of tales who always told me the Fiia would know where it was."

"Ah, the Fiia I should like to see!" said Durossa. "They're in so many songs and tales; why do they never come to the Western Lands?"

"Too high, too cold in winter, I think. They like the sunlight of the valleys of the south."

"Are they like the Clayfolk?"

"Those I've never seen; they keep away from us in the south. Aren't they white like midmen, and misformed? The Fiia are fair; they look like children, only thinner, and wiser. Oh, I wonder if they know where the necklace is, who stole it and where he hid it! Think, Durossa—if I could come into Hallan Revel and sit down by my husband with the wealth of a kingdom round my neck, and outshine the other women as he outshines all men!"

Durossa bent her head above the baby, who sat studying her

own brown toes on a fur rug between her mother and aunt. "Semley is foolish," she murmured to the baby; "Semley who shines like a falling star, Semley whose husband loves no gold but the gold of her hair. . . ."

And Semley, looking out over the green slopes of summer toward the distant sea, was silent.

But when another coldyear had passed, and the Starlords had come again to collect their taxes for the war against the world's end—this time using a couple of dwarfish Clayfolk as interpreters, and so leaving all the Angyar humiliated to the point of rebellion—and another warmyear too was gone, and Haldre had grown into a lovely, chattering child, Semley brought her one morning to Durossa's sunlit room in the tower. Semley wore an old cloak of blue, and the hood covered her hair.

"Keep Haldre for me these few days, Durossa," she said, quick and calm. "I'm going south to Kirien."

"To see your father?"

"To find my inheritance. Your cousins of Harget Fief have been taunting Durhal. Even that halfbreed Parna can torment him, because Parna's wife has a satin coverlet for her bed, and a diamond earring, and three gowns, the dough-faced black-haired trollop! while Durhal's wife must patch her gown—"

"Is Durhal's pride in his wife, or what she wears?"

But Semley was not to be moved. "The Lords of Hallan are becoming poor men in their own hall. I am going to bring my dowry to my lord, as one of my lineage should."

"Semley! Does Durhal know you're going?"

"My return will be a happy one—that much let him know," said young Semley, breaking for a moment into her joyful laugh; then she bent to kiss her daughter, turned, and before Durossa could speak, was gone like a quick wind over the floors of sunlit stone.

Married women of the Angyar never rode for sport, and Semley had not been from Hallan since her marriage; so now, mounting the high saddle of a windsteed, she felt like a girl again, like the wild maiden she had been, riding half-broken steeds on the north wind over the fields of Kirien. The beast that bore her now down from the hills of Hallan was of finer breed, striped coat fitting sleek over hollow, buoyant bones, green eyes slitted against the wind, light and mighty wings sweeping up and down to either side of Semley, revealing and hiding, revealing and hiding the clouds above her and the hills below.

On the third morning she came to Kirien and stood again in the ruined courts. Her father had been drinking all night, and, just as in the old days, the morning sunlight poking through his fallen ceilings annoyed him, and the sight of his daughter only increased his annoyance. "What are you back for?" he growled, his swollen eyes glancing at her and away. The fiery hair of his youth was quenched, grey strands tangled on his skull. "Did the young Halla not marry you, and you've come sneaking home?"

"I am Durhal's wife. I came to get my dowry, father."

The drunkard growled in disgust; but she laughed at him so gently that he had to look at her again, wincing.

"Is it true, father, that the Fiia stole the necklace Eye of the Sea?"

"How do I know? Old tales. The thing was lost before I was born, I think. I wish I never had been. Ask the Fiia if you want to know. Go to them, go back to your husband. Leave me alone here. There's no room at Kirien for girls and gold and all the rest of the story. The story's over here; this is the fallen place, this is the empty hall. The sons of Leynen all are dead, their treasures are all lost. Go on your way, girl."

Grey and swollen as the web-spinner of ruined houses, he turned and went blundering toward the cellars where he hid from daylight.

Leading the striped windsteed of Hallan, Semley left her old

home and walked down the steep hill, past the village of the mid-men, who greeted her with sullen respect, on over fields and pastures where the great, wing-clipped, half-wild herilor grazed, to a valley that was green as a painted bowl and full to the brim with sunlight. In the deep of the valley lay the village of the Fiia, and as she descended leading her steed the little, slight people ran up toward her from their huts and gardens, laughing, calling out in faint, thin voices.

"Hail Halla's bride, Kirienlady, Windborne, Semley the Fair!"

They gave her lovely names and she liked to hear them, minding not at all their laughter; for they laughed at all they said. That was her own way, to speak and laugh. She stood tall in her long blue cloak among their swirling welcome.

"Hail Lightfolk, Sundwellers, Fiia friends of men!"

They took her down into the village and brought her into one of their airy houses, the tiny children chasing along behind. There was no telling the age of a Fian once he was grown; it was hard even to tell one from another and be sure, as they moved about quick as moths around a candle, that she spoke always to the same one. But it seemed that one of them talked with her for a while, as the others fed and petted her steed, and brought water for her to drink, and bowls of fruit from their gardens of little trees. "It was never the Fiia that stole the necklace of the Lords of Kirien!" cried the little man. "What would the Fiia do with gold, Lady? For us there is sunlight in warmyear, and in coldyear the remembrance of sunlight; the yellow fruit, the yellow leaves in end-season, the yellow hair of our lady of Kirien; no other gold."

"Then it was some midman stole the thing?"

Laughter rang long and faint about her. "How would a midman dare? O Lady of Kirien, how the great jewel was stolen no mortal knows, not man nor midman nor Fian nor any among the Seven Folk. Only dead minds know how it was lost, long ago when

Kireley the Proud whose great-granddaughter is Semley walked alone by the caves of the sea. But it may be found perhaps among the Sunhaters."

"The Clayfolk?"

A louder burst of laughter, nervous.

"Sit with us, Semley, sunhaired, returned to us from the north." She sat with them to eat, and they were as pleased with her graciousness as she with theirs. But when they heard her repeat that she would go to the Clayfolk to find her inheritance, if it was there, they began not to laugh; and little by little there were fewer of them around her. She was alone at last with perhaps the one she had spoken with before the meal. "Do not go among the Clayfolk, Semley," he said, and for a moment her heart failed her. The Fian, drawing his hand down slowly over his eyes, had darkened all the air about them. Fruit lay ash-white on the plate; all the bowls of clear water were empty.

"In the mountains of the far land the Fiia and the Gdemiar parted. Long ago we parted," said the slight, still man of the Fiia. "Longer ago we were one. What we are not, they are. What we are, they are not. Think of the sunlight and the grass and the trees that bear fruit, Semley; think that not all roads that lead down lead up as well."

"Mine leads neither down nor up, kind host, but only straight on to my inheritance. I will go to it where it is, and return with it."

The Fian bowed, laughing a little.

Outside the village she mounted her striped windsteed, and, calling farewell in answer to their calling, rose up into the wind of afternoon and flew southwestward toward the caves down by the rocky shores of Kiriensea.

She feared she might have to walk far into those tunnel-caves to find the people she sought, for it was said the Clayfolk never came out of their caves into the light of the sun, and feared even the Greatstar and the moons. It was a long ride; she landed once

to let her steed hunt tree-rats while she ate a little bread from her saddle-bag. The bread was hard and dry by now and tasted of leather, yet kept a faint savor of its making, so that for a moment, eating it alone in a glade of the southern forests, she heard the quiet tone of a voice and saw Durhal's face turned to her in the light of the candles of Hallan. For a while she sat daydreaming of that stern and vivid young face, and of what she would say to him when she came home with a kingdom's ransom around her neck: "I wanted a gift worthy of my husband, Lord. . . ." Then she pressed on, but when she reached the coast the sun had set, with the Greatstar sinking behind it. A mean wind had come up from the west, starting and gusting and veering, and her windsteed was weary fighting it. She let him glide down on the sand. At once he folded his wings and curled his thick, light limbs under him with a thrum of purring. Semley stood holding her cloak close at her throat, stroking the steed's neck so that he flicked his ears and purred again. The warm fur comforted her hand, but all that met her eyes was grey sky full of smears of cloud, grey sea, dark sand. And then running over the sand a low, dark creature—another—a group of them, squatting and running and stopping.

She called aloud to them. Though they had not seemed to see her, now in a moment they were all around her. They kept a distance from her windsteed; he had stopped purring, and his fur rose a little under Semley's hand. She took up the reins, glad of his protection but afraid of the nervous ferocity he might display. The strange folk stood silent, staring, their thick bare feet planted in the sand. There was no mistaking them: they were the height of the Fiia and in all else a shadow, a black image of those laughing people. Naked, squat, stiff, with lank hair and grey-white skins, dampish-looking like the skins of grubs; eyes like rocks.

"You are the Clayfolk?"

"Gdemiar are we, people of the Lords of the Realms of Night." The voice was unexpectedly loud and deep, and rang out pompous

through the salt, blowing dusk; but, as with the Fiia, Semley was not sure which one had spoken.

"I greet you, Nightlords. I am Semley of Kirien, Durhal's wife of Hallan. I come to you seeking my inheritance, the necklace called Eye of the Sea, lost long ago."

"Why do you seek it here, Angya? Here is only sand and salt and night."

"Because lost things are known of in deep places," said Semley, quite ready for a play of wits, "and gold that came from earth has a way of going back to the earth. And sometimes the made, they say, returns to the maker." This last was a guess; it hit the mark.

"It is true the necklace Eye of the Sea is known to us by name. It was made in our caves long ago, and sold by us to the Angyar. And the blue stone came from the Clayfields of our kin to the east. But these are very old tales, Angya."

"May I listen to them in the places where they are told?"

The squat people were silent a while, as if in doubt. The grey wind blew by over the sand, darkening as the Greatstar set; the sound of the sea loudened and lessened. The deep voice spoke again: "Yes, lady of the Angyar. You may enter the Deep Halls. Come with us now." There was a changed note in his voice, wheedling. Semley would not hear it. She followed the Claymen over the sand, leading on a short rein her sharp-taloned steed.

At the cave-mouth, a toothless, yawning mouth from which a stinking warmth sighed out, one of the Claymen said, "The air-beast cannot come in."

"Yes," said Semley.

"No," said the squat people.

"Yes. I will not leave him here. He is not mine to leave. He will not harm you, so long as I hold his reins."

"No," deep voices repeated; but others broke in, "As you will,"

and after a moment of hesitation they went on. The cave-mouth seemed to snap shut behind them, so dark was it under the stone. They went in single file, Semley last.

The darkness of the tunnel lightened, and they came under a ball of weak white fire hanging from the roof. Farther on was another, and another; between them long black worms hung in festoons from the rock. As they went on these fire-globes were set closer, so that all the tunnel was lit with a bright, cold light.

Semley's guides stopped at a parting of three tunnels, all blocked by doors that looked to be of iron. "We shall wait, Angya," they said, and eight of them stayed with her, while three others unlocked one of the doors and passed through. It fell to behind them with a clash.

Straight and still stood the daughter of the Angyar in the white, blank light of the lamps; her windsteed crouched beside her, flicking the tip of his striped tail, his great folded wings stirring again and again with the checked impulse to fly. In the tunnel behind Semley the eight Claymen squatted on their hams, muttering to one another in their deep voices, in their own tongue.

The central door swung clanging open. "Let the Angya enter the Realm of Night!" cried a new voice, booming and boastful. A Clayman who wore some clothing on his thick grey body stood in the doorway, beckoning to her. "Enter and behold the wonders of our lands, the marvels made by hands, the works of the Nightlords!"

Silent, with a tug at her steed's reins, Semley bowed her head and followed him under the low doorway made for dwarfish folk. Another glaring tunnel stretched ahead, dank walls dazzling in the white light, but, instead of a way to walk upon, its floor carried two bars of polished iron stretching off side by side as far as she could see. On the bars rested some kind of cart with metal wheels. Obeying her new guide's gestures, with no hesitation and

no trace of wonder on her face, Semley stepped into the cart and made the windsteed crouch beside her. The Clayman got in and sat down in front of her, moving bars and wheels about. A loud grinding noise arose, and a screaming of metal on metal, and then the walls of the tunnel began to jerk by. Faster and faster the walls slid past, till the fireglobes overhead ran into a blur, and the stale warm air became a foul wind blowing the hood back off her hair.

The cart stopped. Semley followed the guide up basalt steps into a vast anteroom and then a still vaster hall, carved by ancient waters or by the burrowing Clayfolk out of the rock, its darkness that had never known sunlight lit with the uncanny cold brilliance of the globes. In grilles cut in the walls huge blades turned and turned, changing the stale air. The great closed space hummed and boomed with noise, the loud voices of the Clayfolk, the grinding and shrill buzzing and vibration of turning blades and wheels, the echoes and re-echoes of all this from the rock. Here all the stumpy figures of the Claymen were clothed in garments imitating those of the Starlords—divided trousers, soft boots, and hooded tunics—though the few women to be seen, hurrying servile dwarves, were naked. Of the males many were soldiers, bearing at their sides weapons shaped like the terrible light-throwers of the Starlords, though even Semley could see these were merely shaped iron clubs. What she saw, she saw without looking. She followed where she was led, turning her head neither to left nor right. When she came before a group of Claymen who wore iron circlets on their black hair her guide halted, bowed, boomed out, "The High Lords of the Gdemiar!"

There were seven of them, and all looked up at her with such arrogance on their lumpy grey faces that she wanted to laugh.

"I come among you seeking the lost treasure of my family, O Lords of the Dark Realm," she said gravely to them. "I seek Leynen's prize, the Eye of the Sea." Her voice was faint in the racket of the huge vault.

"So said our messengers, Lady Semley." This time she could pick out the one who spoke, one even shorter than the others, hardly reaching Semley's breast, with a white, fierce face. "We do not have this thing you seek."

"Once you had it, it is said."

"Much is said, up there where the sun blinks."

"And words are borne off by the winds, where there are winds to blow. I do not ask how the necklace was lost to us and returned to you, its makers of old. Those are old tales, old grudges. I only seek to find it now. You do not have it now; but it may be you know where it is."

"It is not here."

"Then it is elsewhere."

"It is where you cannot come to it. Never, unless we help you."

"Then help me. I ask this as your guest."

"It is said, *The Angyar take; the Fiia give; the Gdemiar give and take.* If we do this for you, what will you give us?"

"My thanks, Nightlord."

She stood tall and bright among them, smiling. They all stared at her with a heavy, grudging wonder, a sullen yearning.

"Listen, Angya, this is a great favor you ask of us. You do not know how great a favor. You cannot understand. You are of a race that will not understand, that cares for nothing but wind-riding and crop-raising and sword-fighting and shouting together. But who made your swords of the bright steel? We, the Gdemiar! Your lords come to us here and in the Clayfields and buy their swords and go away, not looking, not understanding. But you are here now, you will look, you can see a few of our endless marvels, the lights that burn forever, the car that pulls itself, the machines that make our clothes and cook our food and sweeten our air and serve us in all things. Know that all these things are beyond your understanding. And know this: we, the Gdemiar, are the friends of those you call the Starlords! We came with them to Hallan, to

Reohan, to Hul-Orren, to all your castles, to help them speak to you. The lords to whom you, the proud Angyar, pay tribute, are our friends. They do us favors as we do them favors! Now, what do your thanks mean to us?"

"That is your question to answer," said Semley, "not mine. I have asked my question. Answer it, Lord."

For a while the seven conferred together, by word and silence. They would glance at her and look away, and mutter and be still. A crowd grew around them, drawn slowly and silently, one after another till Semley was encircled by hundreds of the matted black heads, and all the great booming cavern floor was covered with people, except a little space directly around her. Her windsteed was quivering with fear and irritation too long controlled, and his eyes had gone very wide and pale, like the eyes of a steed forced to fly at night. She stroked the warm fur of his head, whispering, "Quietly now, brave one, bright one, windlord. . . ."

"Angya, we will take you to the place where the treasure lies." The Clayman with the white face and iron crown had turned to her once more. "More than that we cannot do. You must come with us to claim the necklace where it lies, from those who keep it. The air-beast cannot come with you. You must come alone."

"How far a journey, Lord?"

His lips drew back and back. "A very far journey, Lady. Yet it will last only one long night."

"I thank you for your courtesy. Will my steed be well cared for this night? No ill must come to him."

"He will sleep till you return. A greater windsteed you will have ridden, when you see that beast again! Will you not ask where we take you?"

"Can we go soon on this journey? I would not stay long away from my home."

"Yes. Soon." Again the grey lips widened as he stared up into her face.

What was done in those next hours Semley could not have retold; it was all haste, jumble, noise, strangeness. While she held her steed's head a Clayman stuck a long needle into the golden-striped haunch. She nearly cried out at the sight, but her steed merely twitched and then, purring, fell asleep. He was carried off by a group of Clayfolk who clearly had to summon up their courage to touch his warm fur. Later on she had to see a needle driven into her own arm—perhaps to test her courage, she thought, for it did not seem to make her sleep; though she was not quite sure. There were times she had to travel in the rail-carts, passing iron doors and vaulted caverns by the hundred and hundred; once the rail-cart ran through a cavern that stretched off on either hand measureless into the dark, and all that darkness was full of great flocks of herilor. She could hear their cooing, husky calls, and glimpse the flocks in the front-lights of the cart; then she saw some more clearly in the white light, and saw that they were all wingless, and all blind. At that she shut her eyes. But there were more tunnels to go through, and always more caverns, more grey lumpy bodies and fierce faces and booming boasting voices, until at last they led her suddenly out into the open air. It was full night; she raised her eyes joyfully to the stars and the single moon shining, little Heliki brightening in the west. But the Clayfolk were all about her still, making her climb now into some new kind of cart or cave, she did not know which. It was small, full of little blinking lights like rushlights, very narrow and shining after the great dank caverns and the starlit night. Now another needle was stuck in her, and they told her she would have to be tied down in a sort of flat chair, tied down head and hand and foot.

"I will not," said Semley.

But when she saw that the four Claymen who were to be her

guides let themselves be tied down first, she submitted. The others left. There was a roaring sound, and a long silence; a great weight that could not be seen pressed upon her. Then there was no weight; no sound; nothing at all.

"Am I dead?" asked Semley.

"Oh no, Lady," said a voice she did not like.

Opening her eyes, she saw the white face bent over her, the wide lips pulled back, the eyes like little stones. Her bonds had fallen away from her, and she leaped up. She was weightless, bodiless; she felt herself only a gust of terror on the wind.

"We will not hurt you," said the sullen voice or voices. "Only let us touch you, Lady. We would like to touch your hair. Let us touch your hair. . . ."

The round cart they were in trembled a little. Outside its one window lay blank night, or was it mist, or nothing at all? One long night, they had said. Very long. She sat motionless and endured the touch of their heavy grey hands on her hair. Later they would touch her hands and feet and arms, and once her throat: at that she set her teeth and stood up, and they drew back.

"We have not hurt you, Lady," they said. She shook her head.

When they bade her, she lay down again in the chair that bound her down; and when light flashed golden, at the window, she would have wept at the sight, but fainted first.

"Well," said Rocannon, "now at least we know what she is."

"I wish there were some way of knowing *who* she is," the curator mumbled. "She wants something we've got here in the Museum, is that what the trogs say?"

"Now, don't call 'em trogs," Rocannon said conscientiously; as a hilfer, an ethnologist of the High Intelligence Life-forms, he was supposed to resist such words. "They're not pretty, but they're Status C Allies. . . . I wonder why the Commission picked them

to develop? Before even contacting all the HILF species? I'll bet the survey was from Centaurus—Centaurans always like nocturnals and cave dwellers. I'd have backed Species II, here, I think."

"The troglodytes seem to be rather in awe of her."

"Aren't you?"

Ketho glanced at the tall woman again, then reddened and laughed. "Well, in a way. I never saw such a beautiful alien type in eighteen years here on New South Georgia. I never saw such a beautiful woman anywhere, in fact. She looks like a goddess." The red now reached the top of his bald head, for Ketho was a shy curator, not given to hyperbole. But Rocannon nodded soberly, agreeing.

"I wish we could talk to her without those tr—Gdemiar as interpreters. But there's no help for it." Rocannon went toward their visitor, and when she turned her splendid face to him he bowed down very deeply, going right down to the floor on one knee, his head bowed and his eyes shut. This was what he called his All-Purpose Intercultural Curtsey, and he performed it with some grace. When he came erect again the beautiful woman smiled and spoke.

"She say, Hail, Lord of Stars," growled one of her squat escorts in Pidgin-Galactic.

"Hail, Lady of the Angyar," Rocannon replied. "In what way can we of the Museum serve the lady?"

Across the troglodytes' growling her voice ran like a brief silver wind.

"She say, Please give her necklace which treasure her blood-kin-forebears long long."

"Which necklace?" he asked, and understanding him, she pointed to the central display of the case before them, a magnificent thing, a chain of yellow gold, massive but very delicate in workmanship, set with one big hot-blue sapphire. Rocannon's eyebrows

went up, and Ketho at his shoulder murmured, "She's got good taste. That's the Fomalhaut Necklace—famous bit of work."

She smiled at the two men, and again spoke to them over the heads of the troglodytes.

"She say, O Starlords, Elder and Younger Dwellers in House of Treasures, this treasure her one. Long long time. Thank you."

"How did we get the thing, Ketho?"

"Wait; let me look it up in the catalogue. I've got it here. Here. It came from these trogs—trolls—whatever they are: Gdemiar. They have a bargain-obsession, it says; we had to let 'em buy the ship they came here on, an AD-4. This was part payment. It's their own handiwork."

"And I'll bet they can't do this kind of work anymore, since they've been steered to Industrial."

"But they seem to feel the thing is hers, not theirs or ours. It must be important, Rocannon, or they wouldn't have given up this time-span to her errand. Why, the objective lapse between here and Fomalhaut must be considerable!"

"Several years, no doubt," said the hilfer, who was used to starjumping. "Not very far. Well, neither the *Handbook* nor the *Guide* gives me enough data to base a decent guess on. These species obviously haven't been properly studied at all. The little fellows may be showing her simple courtesy. Or an interspecies war may depend on this damn sapphire. Perhaps her desire rules them, because they consider themselves totally inferior to her. Or despite appearances she may be their prisoner, their decoy. How can we tell? . . . Can you give the thing away, Ketho?"

"Oh, yes. All the Exotica are technically on loan, not our property, since these claims come up now and then. We seldom argue. Peace above all, until the War comes. . . ."

"Then I'd say give it to her."

Ketho smiled. "It's a privilege," he said. Unlocking the case, he

lifted out the great golden chain; then, in his shyness, he held it out to Rocannon, saying, "You give it to her."

So the blue jewel first lay, for a moment, in Rocannon's hand.

His mind was not on it; he turned straight to the beautiful, alien woman, with his handful of blue fire and gold. She did not raise her hands to take it, but bent her head, and he slipped the necklace over her hair. It lay like a burning fuse along her golden-brown throat. She looked up from it with such pride, delight, and gratitude in her face that Rocannon stood wordless, and the little curator murmured hurriedly in his own language, "You're welcome, you're very welcome." She bowed her golden head to him and to Rocannon. Then, turning, she nodded to her squat guards— or captors?—and, drawing her worn blue cloak about her, paced down the long hall and was gone. Ketho and Rocannon stood looking after her.

"What I feel . . ." Rocannon began.

"Well?" Ketho inquired hoarsely, after a long pause.

"What I feel sometimes is that I . . . meeting these people from worlds we know so little of, you know, sometimes . . . that I have as it were blundered through the corner of a legend, or a tragic myth, maybe, which I do not understand. . . ."

"Yes," said the curator, clearing his throat. "I wonder . . . I wonder what her name is."

Semley the Fair, Semley the Golden, Semley of the Necklace. The Clayfolk had bent to her will, and so had even the Starlords in that terrible place where the Clayfolk had taken her, the city at the end of the night. They had bowed to her, and given her gladly her treasure from amongst their own.

But she could not yet shake off the feeling of those caverns about her where rock lowered overhead, where you could not tell who spoke or what they did, where voices boomed and grey hands

reached out— Enough of that. She had paid for the necklace; very well. Now it was hers. The price was paid, the past was the past.

Her windsteed had crept out of some kind of box, with his eyes filmy and his fur rimed with ice, and at first when they had left the caves of the Gdemiar he would not fly. Now he seemed all right again, riding a smooth south wind through the bright sky toward Hallan. "Go quick, go quick," she told him, beginning to laugh as the wind cleared away her mind's darkness. "I want to see Durhal soon, soon. . . ."

And swiftly they flew, coming to Hallan by dusk of the second day. Now the caves of the Clayfolk seemed no more than last year's nightmare, as the steed swooped with her up the thousand steps of Hallan and across the Chasmbridge where the forests fell away for a thousand feet. In the gold light of evening in the flightcourt she dismounted and walked up the last steps between the stiff carven figures of heroes and the two gatewards, who bowed to her, staring at the beautiful, fiery thing around her neck.

In the Forehall she stopped a passing girl, a very pretty girl, by her looks one of Durhal's close kin, though Semley could not call to mind her name. "Do you know me, maiden? I am Semley, Durhal's wife. Will you go tell the Lady Durossa that I have come back?"

For she was afraid to go on in and perhaps face Durhal at once, alone; she wanted Durossa's support.

The girl was gazing at her, her face very strange. But she murmured, "Yes, Lady," and darted off toward the Tower.

Semley stood waiting in the gilt, ruinous hall. No one came by; were they all at table in the Revel-hall? The silence was uneasy. After a minute Semley started toward the stairs to the Tower. But an old woman was coming to her across the stone floor, holding her arms out, weeping.

"O Semley, Semley!"

She had never seen the grey-haired woman, and shrank back.

"But Lady, who are you?"

"I am Durossa, Semley."

She was quiet and still, all the time that Durossa embraced her and wept, and asked if it were true the Clayfolk had captured her and kept her under a spell all these long years, or had it been the Fiia with their strange arts? Then, drawing back a little, Durossa ceased to weep.

"You're still young, Semley. Young as the day you left here. And you wear round your neck the necklace. . . ."

"I have brought my gift to my husband Durhal. Where is he?"

"Durhal is dead."

Semley stood unmoving.

"Your husband, my brother, Durhal Hallanlord was killed seven years ago in battle. Nine years you had been gone. The Starlords came no more. We fell to warring with the Eastern Halls, with the Angyar of Log and Hul-Orren. Durhal, fighting, was killed by a midman's spear, for he had little armor for his body, and none at all for his spirit. He lies buried in the fields above Orren Marsh."

Semley turned away. "I will go to him, then," she said, putting her hand on the gold chain that weighed down her neck. "I will give him my gift."

"Wait, Semley! Durhal's daughter, your daughter, see her now, Haldre the Beautiful!"

It was the girl she had first spoken to and sent to Durossa, a girl of nineteen or so, with eyes like Durhal's eyes, dark blue. She stood beside Durossa, gazing with those steady eyes at this woman Semley who was her mother and was her own age. Their age was the same, and their gold hair, and their beauty. Only Semley was a little taller, and wore the blue stone on her breast.

"Take it, take it. It was for Durhal and Haldre that I brought

it from the end of the long night!" Semley cried this aloud, twisting and bowing her head to get the heavy chain off, dropping the necklace so it fell on the stones with a cold, liquid clash. "O take it, Haldre!" she cried again, and then, weeping aloud, turned and ran from Hallan, over the bridge and down the long, broad steps, and, darting off eastward into the forest of the mountainside like some wild thing escaping, was gone.

APRIL IN PARIS

This is the first story I ever got paid for; the second story I ever got published; and maybe the thirtieth or fortieth story I wrote. I had been writing poetry and fiction ever since my brother Ted, tired of having an illiterate five-year-old sister around, taught me to read. At about twenty I began sending things off to publishers. Some of the poetry got printed, but I didn't get systematic about sending out the fiction till I was getting on to thirty. It kept systematically coming back.

"April in Paris" was the first "genre" piece—recognizably fantasy or science fiction—that I had written since 1942, when I wrote an Origin-of-Life-on-Earth story for Astounding, which for some inconceivable reason rejected it (I never did synch with John Campbell). At age twelve I was very pleased to get a genuine printed rejection slip, but by age thirty-two I was very pleased to get a check. "Professionalism" is no virtue; a professional is simply one who gets paid for doing what an amateur does for love. But in a money economy, the fact of being paid means your work is going to be circulated, is going to be read; it's the means to communication, which is the artist's goal. Cele Goldsmith Lalli, who bought this story in 1962, was as enterprising and perceptive an editor as the science fiction magazines have ever had, and I am grateful to her for opening the door to me.

Professor Barry Pennywither sat in a cold, shadowy garret and stared at the table in front of him, on which lay a book and a breadcrust. The bread had been his dinner, the book had been his lifework. Both were dry. Dr. Pennywither sighed, and then shivered. Though the lower-floor apartments of the old house were quite elegant, the heat was turned off on April 1st, come what may; it was now April 2nd, and sleeting. If Dr. Pennywither raised his head a little he could see from his window the two square towers of Notre Dame de Paris, vague and soaring in the dusk, almost near enough to touch: for the Island of Saint-Louis, where he lived, is like a little barge being towed downstream behind the Island of the City, where Notre Dame stands. But he did not raise his head. He was too cold.

The great towers sank into darkness. Dr. Pennywither sank into gloom. He stared with loathing at his book. It had won him a year in Paris—publish or perish, said the Dean of Faculties, and he had published, and been rewarded with a year's leave from teaching, without pay. Munson College could not afford to pay unteaching teachers. So on his scraped-up savings he had come back to Paris, to live again as a student in a garret, to read fifteenth-century manuscripts at the Library, to see the chestnuts flower along the avenues. But it hadn't worked. He was forty, too old for lonely garrets. The sleet would blight the budding chestnut flowers. And he was sick of his work. Who cared about his theory, the Pennywither Theory, concerning the mysterious disappearance of the poet François Villon in 1463? Nobody. For after all his Theory about poor Villon, the greatest juvenile delinquent of all time, was only a theory and could never be proved, not across the gulf of five hundred years. Nothing could be proved. And besides, what did it matter if Villon died on Montfaucon gallows or (as Pennywither thought) in a Lyons brothel on the way to Italy? Nobody cared. Nobody else loved Villon enough. Nobody loved Dr. Pennywither, either;

not even Dr. Pennywither. Why should he? An unsocial, un-married, underpaid pedant, sitting here alone in an unheated attic in an unrestored tenement trying to write another unreadable book. "I'm unrealistic," he said aloud with another sigh and another shiver. He got up and took the blanket off his bed, wrapped himself in it, sat down thus bundled at the table, and tried to light a Gauloise Bleue. His lighter snapped vainly. He sighed once more, got up, fetched a can of vile-smelling French lighter fluid, sat down, rewrapped his cocoon, filled the lighter, and snapped it. The fluid had spilled around a good bit. The lighter lit, so did Dr. Pennywither, from the wrists down. "Oh hell!" he cried, blue flames leaping from his knuckles, and jumped up batting his arms wildly, shouting "Hell!" and raging against Destiny. Nothing ever went right. What was the use? It was then 8:12 on the night of April 2nd, 1961.

A man sat hunched at a table in a cold, high room. Through the window behind him the two square towers of Notre Dame loomed in the Spring dusk. In front of him on the table lay a hunk of cheese and a huge, iron-latched, handwritten book. The book was called (in Latin) *On the Primacy of the Element Fire over the Other Three Elements*. Its author stared at it with loathing. Nearby on a small iron stove a small alembic simmered. Jehan Lenoir mechanically inched his chair nearer the stove now and then, for warmth, but his thoughts were on deeper problems. "Hell!" he said finally (in Late Mediaeval French), slammed the book shut, and got up. What if his theory was wrong? What if water were the primal element? How could you prove these things? There must be some way—some method—so that one could be sure, absolutely sure, of one single fact! But each fact led into others, a monstrous tangle, and the Authorities conflicted, and anyway no one would read his book, not even the wretched

pedants at the Sorbonne. They smelled heresy. What was the use? What good this life spent in poverty and alone, when he had learned nothing, merely guessed and theorized? He strode about the garret, raging, and then stood still. "All right!" he said to Destiny. "Very good! You've given me nothing, so I'll take what I want!" He went to one of the stacks of books that covered most of the floor-space, yanked out a bottom volume (scarring the leather and bruising his knuckles when the overlying folios avalanched), slapped it on the table and began to study one page of it. Then, still with a set cold look of rebellion, he got things ready: sulfur, silver, chalk. . . . Though the room was dusty and littered, his little workbench was neatly and handily arranged. He was soon ready. Then he paused. "This is ridiculous," he muttered, glancing out the window into the darkness where now one could only guess at the two square towers. A watchman passed below calling out the hour, eight o'clock of a cold clear night. It was so still he could hear the lapping of the Seine. He shrugged, frowned, took up the chalk and drew a neat pentagram on the floor near his table, then took up the book and began to read in a clear but self-conscious voice: "Haere, haere, audi me . . . " It was a long spell, and mostly nonsense. His voice sank. He stood bored and embarrassed. He hurried through the last words, shut the book, and then fell backwards against the door, gap-mouthed, staring at the enormous, shapeless figure that stood within the pentagram, lit only by the blue flicker of its waving, fiery claws.

Barry Pennywither finally got control of himself and put out the fire by burying his hands in the folds of the blanket wrapped around him. Unburned but upset, he sat down again. He looked at his book. Then he stared at it. It was no longer thin and grey and titled *The Last Years of Villon: an Investigation of Possibilities*. It was thick and brown and titled *Incantatoria Magna*. On his

table? A priceless manuscript dating from 1407 of which the only extant undamaged copy was in the Ambrosian Library in Milan. He looked slowly around. His mouth dropped slowly open. He observed a stove, a chemist's workbench, two or three dozen heaps of unbelievable leatherbound books, the window, the door. His window, his door. But crouching against his door was a little creature, black and shapeless, from which came a dry rattling sound.

Barry Pennywither was not a very brave man, but he was rational. He thought he had lost his mind, and so he said quite steadily, "Are you the Devil?"

The creature shuddered and rattled.

Experimentally, with a glance at invisible Notre Dame, the professor made the sign of the Cross.

At this the creature twitched; not a flinch, a twitch. Then it said something, feebly, but in perfectly good English—no, in perfectly good French—no, in rather odd French: "Mais vous estes de Dieu," it said.

Barry got up and peered at it. "Who are you?" he demanded, and it lifted up a quite human face and answered meekly, "Jehan Lenoir."

"What are you doing in my room?"

There was a pause. Lenoir got up from his knees and stood straight, all five foot two of him. "This is *my* room," he said at last, though very politely.

Barry looked around at the books and alembics. There was another pause. "Then how did I get here?"

"I brought you."

"Are you a doctor?"

Lenoir nodded, with pride. His whole air had changed. "Yes, I'm a doctor," he said. "Yes, I brought you here. If Nature will yield me no knowledge, then I can conquer Nature herself, I can work a miracle! To the Devil with science, then. I was a scientist—"

he glared at Barry. "No longer! They call me a fool, a heretic, well by God I'm worse! I'm a sorcerer, a black magician, Jehan the Black! Magic works, does it? Then science is a waste of time. Ha!" he said, but he did not really look triumphant. "I wish it hadn't worked," he said more quietly, pacing up and down between folios.

"So do I," said the guest.

"Who are you?" Lenoir looked up challengingly at Barry, though there was nearly a foot difference in their heights.

"Barry A. Pennywither, I'm a professor of French at Munson College, Indiana, on leave in Paris to pursue my studies of Late Mediaeval Fr—" He stopped. He had just realized what kind of accent Lenoir had. "What year is this? What century? Please, Dr. Lenoir—" The Frenchman looked confused. The meanings of words change, as well as their pronunciations. "Who rules this country?" Barry shouted.

Lenoir gave a shrug, a French shrug (some things never change). "Louis is king," he said. "Louis the Eleventh. The dirty old spider."

They stood staring at each other like wooden Indians for some time. Lenoir spoke first. "Then you're a man?"

"Yes. Look, Lenoir, I think you—your spell—you must have muffed it a bit."

"Evidently," said the alchemist. "Are you French?"

"No."

"Are you English?" Lenoir glared. "Are you a filthy Goddam?"

"No. No. I'm from America. I'm from the—from your future. From the twentieth century A.D." Barry blushed. It sounded silly, and he was a modest man. But he knew this was no illusion. The room he stood in, his room, was new. Not five centuries old. Unswept, but new. And the copy of Albertus Magnus by his knee was new, bound in soft supple calfskin, the gold lettering gleaming. And there stood Lenoir in his black gown, not in costume, at home. . . .

"Please sit down, sir," Lenoir was saying. And he added, with the fine though absent courtesy of the poor scholar, "Are you tired from the journey? I have bread and cheese, if you'll honor me by sharing it."

They sat at the table munching bread and cheese. At first Lenoir tried to explain why he had tried black magic. "I was fed up," he said. "Fed up! I've slaved in solitude since I was twenty, for what? For knowledge. To learn some of Nature's secrets. They are not to be learned." He drove his knife half an inch into the table, and Barry jumped. Lenoir was a thin little fellow, but evidently a passionate one. It was a fine face, though pale and lean: intelligent, alert, vivid. Barry was reminded of the face of a famous atomic physicist, seen in newspaper pictures up until 1953. Somehow this likeness pompted him to say, "Some are, Lenoir; we've learned a good bit, here and there. . . ."

"What?" said the alchemist, skeptical but curious.

"Well, I'm no scientist—"

"Can you make gold?" He grinned as he asked.

"No, I don't think so, but they do make diamonds."

"How?"

"Carbon—coal, you know—under great heat and pressure, I believe. Coal and diamond are both carbon, you know, the same element."

"Element?"

"Now as I say, I'm no—"

"Which is the primal element?" Lenoir shouted, his eyes fiery, the knife poised in his hand.

"There are about a hundred elements," Barry said coldly, hiding his alarm.

Two hours later, having squeezed out of Barry every dribble of the remnants of his college chemistry course, Lenoir rushed out into the night and reappeared shortly with a bottle. "O my master," he

cried, "to think I offered you only bread and cheese!" It was a pleasant burgundy, vintage 1477, a good year. After they had drunk a glass together Lenoir said, "If somehow I could repay you . . . "

"You can. Do you know the name of the poet François Villon?"

"Yes," Lenoir said with some surprise, "but he wrote only French trash, you know, not in Latin."

"Do you know how or when he died?"

"Oh, yes; hanged at Montfaucon here in '64 or '65, with a crew of no-goods like himself. Why?"

Two hours later the bottle was dry, their throats were dry, and the watchman had called three o'clock of a cold clear morning. "Jehan, I'm worn out," Barry said, "you'd better send me back." The alchemist was too polite, too grateful, and perhaps also too tired to argue. Barry stood stiffly inside the pentagram, a tall bony figure muffled in a brown blanket, smoking a Gauloise Bleue. "Adieu," Lenoir said sadly. "Au revoir," Barry replied. Lenoir began to read the spell backwards. The candle flickered, his voice softened. "Me audi, haere, haere," he read, sighed, and looked up. The pentagram was empty. The candle flickered. "But I learned so little!" Lenoir cried out to the empty room. Then he beat the open book with his fists and said, "And a friend like that—a real friend— " He smoked one of the cigarettes Barry had left him— he had taken to tobacco at once. He slept, sitting at his table, for a couple of hours. When he woke he brooded a while, relit his candle, smoked the other cigarette, then opened the *Incantatoria* and began to read aloud: "Haere, haere . . . "

"Oh, thank God," Barry said, stepping quickly out of the pentagram and grasping Lenoir's hand. "Listen, I got back there —this room, this same room, Jehan! but old, horribly old, and empty, you weren't there—I thought, my God, what have I done? I'd sell my soul to get back there, to him—What can I do with

what I've learned? Who'll believe it? How can I prove it? And who the devil could I tell it to anyhow? Who cares? I couldn't sleep, I sat and cried for an hour— "

"Will you stay?"

"Yes. Look, I brought these—in case you did invoke me." Sheepishly he exhibited eight packs of Gauloises, several books, and a gold watch. "It might fetch a price," he explained. "I knew paper francs wouldn't do much good."

At sight of the printed books Lenoir's eyes gleamed with curiosity, but he stood still. "My friend," he said, "you said you'd sell your soul . . . you know . . . so would I. Yet we haven't. How— after all—how did this happen? That we're both men. No devils. No pacts in blood. Two men who've lived in this room . . . "

"I don't know," said Barry. "We'll think that out later. Can I stay with you, Jehan?"

"Consider this your home," Lenoir said with a gracious gesture around the room, the stacks of books, the alembics, the candle growing pale. Outside the window, grey on grey, rose up the two great towers of Notre Dame. It was the dawn of April 3rd.

After breakfast (bread crusts and cheese rinds) they went out and climbed the south tower. The cathedral looked the same as always, though cleaner than in 1961, but the view was rather a shock to Barry. He looked down upon a little town. Two small islands covered with houses; on the right bank more houses crowded inside a fortified wall; on the left bank a few streets twisting around the college; and that was all. Pigeons chortled on the sun-warmed stone between gargoyles. Lenoir, who had seen the view before, was carving the date (in Roman numerals) on a parapet. "Let's celebrate," he said. "Let's go out into the country. I haven't been out of the city for two years. Let's go clear over there— " he pointed to a misty green hill on which a few huts and

a windmill were just visible— "to Montmartre, eh? There are some good bars there, I'm told."

Their life soon settled into an easy routine. At first Barry was a little nervous in the crowded streets, but, in a spare black gown of Lenoir's, he was not noticed as outlandish except for his height. He was probably the tallest man in fifteenth-century France. Living standards were low and lice were unavoidable, but Barry had never valued comfort much; the only thing he really missed was coffee at breakfast. When they had bought a bed and a razor—Barry had forgotten his—and introduced him to the landlord as M. Barrie, a cousin of Lenoir's from the Auvergne, their housekeeping arrangements were complete. Barry's watch brought a tremendous price, four gold pieces, enough to live on for a year. They sold it as a wondrous new timepiece from Illyria, and the buyer, a Court chamberlain looking for a nice present to give the king, looked at the inscription—Hamilton Bros., New Haven, 1881—and nodded sagely. Unfortunately he was shut up in one of King Louis's cages for naughty courtiers at Tours before he had presented his gift, and the watch may still be there behind some brick in the ruins of Plessis; but this did not affect the two scholars. Mornings they wandered about sightseeing the Bastille and the churches, or visiting various minor poets in whom Barry was interested; after lunch they discussed electricity, the atomic theory, physiology, and other matters in which Lenoir was interested, and performed minor chemical and anatomical experiments, usually unsuccessfully; after supper they merely talked. Endless, easy talks that ranged over the centuries but always ended here, in the shadowy room with its window open to the Spring night, in their friendship. After two weeks they might have known each other all their lives. They were perfectly happy. They knew they would do nothing with what they had learned from each other. In 1961 how could Barry ever prove his knowledge of old Paris, in 1482 how could

Lenoir ever prove the validity of the scientific method? It did not bother them. They had never really expected to be listened to. They had merely wanted to learn.

So they were happy for the first time in their lives; so happy, in fact, that certain desires always before subjugated to the desire for knowledge, began to awaken. "I don't suppose," Barry said one night across the table, "that you ever thought much about marrying?"

"Well, no," his friend answered, doubtfully. "That is, I'm in minor orders . . . and it seemed irrelevant. . . . "

"And expensive. Besides, in my time, no self-respecting woman would want to share my kind of life. American women are so damned poised and efficient and glamorous, terrifying creatures. . . . "

"And women here are little and dark, like beetles, with bad teeth," Lenoir said morosely.

They said no more about women that night. But the next night they did; and the next; and on the next, celebrating the successful dissection of the main nervous system of a pregnant frog, they drank two bottles of Montrachet '74 and got soused. "Let's invoke a woman, Jehan," Barry said in a lascivious bass, grinning like a gargoyle.

"What if I raised a devil this time?"

"Is there really much difference?"

They laughed wildly, and drew a pentagram. "Haere, haere," Lenoir began; when he got the hiccups, Barry took over. He read the last words. There was a rush of cold, marshy-smelling air, and in the pentagram stood a wild-eyed being with long black hair, stark naked, screaming.

"Woman, by God," said Barry.

"Is it?"

It was. "Here, take my cloak," Barry said, for the poor thing now stood gawping and shivering. He put the cloak over her

shoulders. Mechanically she pulled it round her, muttering, "Gratias ago, domine."

"Latin!" Lenoir shouted. "A woman speaking Latin?" It took him longer to get over that shock than it did Bota to get over hers. She was, it seemed, a slave in the household of the Sub-Prefect of North Gaul, who lived on the smaller island of the muddy island town called Lutetia. She spoke Latin with a thick Celtic brogue, and did not even know who was emperor in Rome in her day. A real barbarian, Lenoir said with scorn. So she was, an ignorant, taciturn, humble barbarian with tangled hair, white skin, and clear grey eyes. She had been waked from a sound sleep. When they convinced her that she was not dreaming, she evidently assumed that this was some prank of her foreign and all-powerful master the Sub-Prefect, and accepted the situation without further question. "Am I to serve you, my masters?" she inquired timidly but without sullenness, looking from one to the other.

"Not me," Lenoir growled, and added in French to Barry, "Go on; I'll sleep in the store-room." He departed.

Bota looked up at Barry. No Gauls, and few Romans, were so magnificently tall; no Gauls and no Romans ever spoke so kindly. "Your lamp" (it was a candle, but she had never seen a candle) "is nearly burnt out," she said. "Shall I blow it out?"

For an additional two sols a year the landlord let them use the store-room as a second bedroom, and Lenoir now slept alone again in the main room of the garret. He observed his friend's idyll with a brooding, unjealous interest. The professor and the slave-girl loved each other with delight and tenderness. Their pleasure over-lapped Lenoir in waves of protective joy. Bota had led a brutal life, treated always as a woman but never as a human. In one short week she bloomed, she came alive, evincing beneath her gentle passiveness a cheerful, clever nature. "You're turning out a regular Parisienne," he heard Barry accuse her one night (the

attic walls were thin). She replied, "If you knew what it is for me not to be always defending myself, always afraid, always alone . . . "

Lenoir sat up on his cot and brooded. About midnight, when all was quiet, he rose and noiselessly prepared the pinches of sulfur and silver, drew the pentagram, opened the book. Very softly he read the spell. His face was apprehensive.

In the pentagram appeared a small white dog. It cowered and hung its tail, then came shyly forward, sniffed Lenoir's hand, looked up at him with liquid eyes and gave a modest, pleading whine. A lost puppy . . . Lenoir stroked it. It licked his hands and jumped all over him, wild with relief. On its white leather collar was a silver plaque engraved, "Jolie. Dupont, 36 rue de Seine, Paris VIe."

Jolie went to sleep, after gnawing a crust, curled up under Lenoir's chair. And the alchemist opened the book again and read, still softly, but this time without self-consciousness, without fear, knowing what would happen.

Emerging from his store-room-bedroom-honeymoon in the morning, Barry stopped short in the doorway. Lenoir was sitting up in bed, petting a white puppy, and deep in conversation with the person sitting on the foot of the bed, a tall red-haired woman dressed in silver. The puppy barked. Lenoir said, "Good morning!" The woman smiled wondrously.

"Jumping Jesus," Barry muttered (in English). Then he said, "Good morning. When are you from?" The effect was Rita Hayworth, sublimated—Hayworth plus the Mona Lisa, perhaps?

"From Altair, about seven thousand years from now," she said, smiling still more wondrously. Her French accent was worse than that of a football-scholarship freshman. "I'm an archaeologist. I was excavating the ruins of Paris III. I'm sorry I speak the language so badly; of course we know it only from inscriptions."

"From Altair? The star? But you're human—I think— "

"Our planet was colonized from Earth about four thousand years

ago—that is, three thousand years from now." She laughed, most wondrously, and glanced at Lenoir. "Jehan explained it all to me, but I still get confused."

"It was a dangerous thing to try it again, Jehan!" Barry accused him. "We've been awfully lucky, you know."

"No," said the Frenchman. "Not lucky."

"But after all it's black magic you're playing with— Listen—I don't know your name, madame."

"Kislk," she said.

"Listen, Kislk," Barry said without even a stumble, "your science must be fantastically advanced—is there any magic? Does it exist? Can the laws of Nature really be broken, as we seem to be doing?"

"I've never seen nor heard of an authenticated case of magic."

"Then what goes on?" Barry roared. "Why does that stupid old spell work for Jehan, for us, that one spell, and here, nowhere else, for nobody else, in five—no, eight—no, fifteen thousand years of recorded history? Why? Why? And where did that damn puppy come from?"

"The puppy was lost," Lenoir said, his dark face grave. "Somewhere near this house, on the Île Saint-Louis."

"And I was sorting potsherds," Kislk said, also gravely, "in a house-site, Island 2, Pit 4, Section D. A lovely Spring day, and I hated it. Loathed it. The day, the work, the people around me." Again she looked at the gaunt little alchemist, a long, quiet look. "I tried to explain it to Jehan last night. We have improved the race, you see. We're all very tall, healthy, and beautiful. No fillings in our teeth. All skulls from Early America have fillings in the teeth. . . . Some of us are brown, some white, some gold-skinned. But all beautiful, and healthy, and well-adjusted, and aggressive, and successful. Our professions and degree of success are pre-planned for us in the State Pre-School Homes. But there's an occasional genetic flaw. Me, for instance. I was trained as an archaeol-

ogist because the Teachers saw that I really didn't like people, live people. People bored me. All like me on the outside, all alien to me on the inside. When everything's alike, which place is home? . . . But now I've seen an unhygienic room with insufficient heating. Now I've seen a cathedral not in ruins. Now I've met a living man who's shorter than me, with bad teeth and a short temper. Now I'm home, I'm where I can be myself, I'm no longer alone!"

"Alone," Lenoir said gently to Barry. "Loneliness, eh? Loneliness is the spell, loneliness is stronger. . . . Really it doesn't seem unnatural."

Bota was peering round the doorway, her face flushed between the black tangles of her hair. She smiled shyly and said a polite Latin good-morning to the newcomer.

"Kislk doesn't know Latin," Lenoir said with immense satisfaction. "We must teach Bota some French. French is the language of love, anyway, eh? Come along, let's go out and buy some bread. I'm hungry."

Kislk hid her silver tunic under the useful and anonymous cloak, while Lenoir pulled on his moth-eaten black gown. Bota combed her hair, while Barry thoughtfully scratched a louse-bite on his neck. Then they set forth to get breakfast. The alchemist and the interstellar archaeologist went first, speaking French; the Gaulish slave and the professor from Indiana followed, speaking Latin, and holding hands. The narrow streets were crowded, bright with sunshine. Above them Notre Dame reared its two square towers against the sky. Beside them the Seine rippled softly. It was April in Paris, and on the banks of the river the chestnuts were in bloom.

THE MASTERS

"The Masters" was my first published genuine authentic real virgin-wool science fiction story, by which I mean a story in which or to which the existence and the accomplishments of science are, in some way, essential. At least that is what I mean by science fiction on Mondays. On Tuesdays sometimes I mean something else.

Some science-fiction writers detest science, its spirit, method, and works; others like it. Some are anti-technology, others are technology-worshippers. I seem to be rather bored by complex technology, but fascinated by biology, psychology, and the speculative ends of astronomy and physics, insofar as I can follow them. The figure of the scientist is a quite common one in my stories, and most often a rather lonely one, isolated, an adventurer, out on the edge of things.

The theme of this story is one I returned to later, with considerably better equipment. It has a good sentence in it, though: "He had been trying to measure the distance between the earth and God."

In darkness a man stood alone, naked, holding a smoking torch. The reddish glow lit air and ground for only a few feet; beyond that was the darkness, the immeasurable. From moment to moment there was a rush of wind, a half-glimpsed glitter of eyes, a vast muttering: "Hold it higher!" The man obeyed, though the torch

shook in his shaking hands. He raised it clear above his head, while the darkness rushed and jabbered around him, closing in. The wind blew colder, the red flame guttered. His rigid arms began to quiver, then to jerk a little; his face was oily with sweat; he barely heard the soft, huge jabbering, "Hold it up, up, hold it up. . . ." The current of time had stopped; only the whispering grew and grew till it was a howling, and still, horribly, nothing touched him, nothing came within the circle of light. "Now walk!" the great voice howled. "Walk forward!"

The torch above his head, he stepped forward on the ground he could not see. It was not there. With a scream for help, he fell, darkness and thunder about him, the torch he would not let go flaming backward into his eyes.

Time . . . time, and light, and pain, they had all started again. He was crouching in some kind of ditch, on all fours in the mud. His face stung and his eyes, in this bright light, were full of fog. He looked up from his mud-blotched nakedness to a blurred, radiant figure standing above him. Light fell in glory on white hair, the long folds of a white cloak. The eyes gazed at Ganil, the voice spoke to him: "You lie in the Grave. You lie in the Grave of Knowledge. So lie your forefathers forever beneath the ashes of the fires of Hell." The voice swelled out: "O fallen Man, arise!" Ganil managed to get to his feet. The white figure was pointing: "That is the Light of Human Reason. It guided you to the grave. Drop it." Ganil realized he was still holding a mud-sodden black stick, the torch; he let it fall. "Now rise," the white figure cried in a slow exaltation, "rise from darkness and walk in the Light of Common Day!" Hands reached to Ganil, helping and hauling him up. Men knelt offering him basins and sponges, others towelled him, rubbed him down till he stood clean and warm, a grey cloak round his shoulders, amid the chatting and laughter, coming and going, in the bright spacious hall. A bald man clapped his shoulder. "Come on, time for the Oath."

"Did I—did I do all right?"

"Fine! Only you held up that damn fool torch so long. Thought you'd keep us growling around in the dark all day. Come on." They led him over black pavement and under the very lofty, white-beamed ceiling, to a curtain that dropped, pure white, in a few straight folds, thirty feet from roof to floor. "Curtain of Mystery," somebody said to Ganil in a matter-of-fact tone. Laughing and talking had died away; they stood all round him, silent. In silence the white curtain parted. Ganil stared foggily at what was revealed: a high altar, a long table, and an old man in white.

"Postulant, will you swear our Oath with us?"

Somebody nudged Ganil, whispering, "I will." "I will," Ganil stuttered.

"Swear then, Masters of the Rite!" The old man raised up a shape of silver: an X-cross, supported by an iron shaft. "Under the Cross of the Common Day I swear never to reveal the rites and mysteries of my Lodge—"

"Under the Cross . . . I swear . . . the rites . . ." muttered all the men around Ganil, and propelled by another nudge he muttered with them.

"To live well, to work well, to think well—" As Ganil finished repeating this a voice whispered in his ear, "Don't swear."

"To avoid all heresies, to betray all necromancers to the Courts of College, and to obey the High Masters of my Lodge from now forth till my death—" Mutter, mutter. Some seemed to be repeating the long passage, some not; Ganil, confused, muttered a word or two and then stood silent. "And I swear never to teach the Mysteries of Machinery to any gentile. I swear this beneath the Sun." A grating rumble almost drowned their voices. Slowly, crankily, a section of the roof was swinging back to reveal the yellow-grey, cloud-covered sky of summer. "Behold the Light of Common Day!" the old man in white cried out, triumphant, and Ganil stared up at

it. The machinery apparently stuck before the skylight was fully open; there was a loud clanking of gears, then silence. The old man came forward, kissed Ganil on both cheeks, and said, "Welcome, Master Ganil, to the Inner Rite of the Mystery of the Machine." The initiation was over. Ganil was a Master of his Lodge.

"Mean burn you got there," the bald fellow said as they all walked back down the hall. Ganil put up his hand and found that his left cheek and temple were raw and sore. "Lucky it missed your eye."

"Just missed being blinded by the light of Reason, eh?" said a soft voice. Glancing round Ganil saw a fair man, with brown hair and blue eyes, actually blue, like those of an albino cat or a blind horse. He looked away from the deformity at once, but the fair man went on in his soft voice, the voice that had whispered "Don't swear" during the taking of the Oath, "I'm Mede Fairman. I'll be your Co-Master in Lee's shop. Feel like getting a beer when we're out of here?"

The dank beer-dreggy warmth of the tavern was a queer change from all the terror and ceremony of the day. Ganil felt dizzy. Mede Fairman drank off half a tankard, wiped foam pleasurably off his mouth, and inquired, "What d'you think of the initiation?"

"It was—it was— "

"Humbling?"

"Yes," Ganil agreed. "Really humbling."

"Humiliating, even," the blue-eyed man suggested.

"Yes. A—a great mystery." Perplexed, Ganil stared down into his beer. Mede smiled and said in his soft voice, "I know. Drink up, now. I think you ought to have an Apothecary look at that burn." Ganil obediently followed him out into the evening, into the narrow streets thronged with pedestrians, horse-carts, ox-carts, chuffing motor-carts. In the Merchantsplace the booths of the artisans were being closed for the night, and down High Street the

great doors of the Shops and Lodges were already barred. Here and there the overhung, elbowing houses were parted by the blank yellow façade of a temple, marked with one plain circle of polished brass. In the dull, brief summer twilight under the unmoving clouds the black-haired, bronze-skinned people of the Common Day crowded and idled and pushed and talked and cursed and laughed, and Ganil, dizzy from fatigue and pain and strong beer, kept close beside Mede as if, for all his own new Masterhood, this blue-eyed stranger were his only guide.

"XVI plus IXX," Ganil said impatiently, "what the devil, boy, can't you add?" The apprentice flushed red. "Isn't it XXXVI, then, Master Ganil?" he asked feebly. For answer Ganil jammed one of the rods the boy had been machining into its place in the steam engine that was being repaired; it was too long by an inch.

"It's because my rule of thumb's so long, sir," the boy said, displaying his knobby hands. The distance between first and second thumb-joint was in fact unusually long. "So it is," Ganil said. His dark face darkened. "Very interesting. But it doesn't matter how long your inch is so long as you use it consistently. And what matters, you blockhead, is that XVI and IXX don't make XXXVI, never have, never can, never will till the world ends—you incompetent gentile!"

"Yes, sir. It's so hard to remember, sir."

"It's intended to be hard to remember, Wanno Prentice," said a deep voice: Lee the Shopmaster, a fat deep-chested man with bright black eyes. "Come over here a minute, Ganil." Leading him to a quieter corner of the great workshop, Lee went on cheerfully, "You're a bit impatient, Master Ganil."

"Wanno should know his addition-tables."

"Even Masters forget an addition now and then, you know." Lee patted Ganil's shoulder in a fatherly way. "Why, you sounded for

a moment there as if you expected him to compute it!" He laughed aloud, a fine bass laugh through which his eyes gleamed merrily and with infinite shrewdness. "Take it easy, that's all. . . . I understand you're coming for dinner next Altarday Eve?"

"I took the liberty—"

"Fine, fine! More power to you. Wish she'd take on a good steady fellow like you. But I give you fair warning. My daughter's a willful hussy." Again the Master laughed, and Ganil grinned, a little ruefully. The Shopmaster's daughter Lani had not only most of the young men of the Shop, but also her father, twisted right round her little finger. A clever, quicksilver girl, she had at first rather scared Ganil. It took him a while to notice that she spoke, to him only, with a certain shyness, a hint almost of pleading. He had finally got up courage to ask a dinner invitation from her mother, the recognized first step of a courtship. He stood now where Lee had left him, thinking of Lani's smile.

"Ganil, have you ever seen the Sun?"

It was a low voice, dry and easy. He turned, meeting his friend's blue eyes.

"The Sun? Yes, of course I have."

"When was the last time?"

"Let's see, I was twenty-six; four years ago. Weren't you here in Edun then? It came out in late afternoon, and that night there were stars. I counted eighty-one, I remember, before the sky closed."

"I was up north in Keling then in my first Mastership." Mede leaned against the wooden guard rail of the model heavy steam engine as he spoke. His light eyes looked away from the busy shop, out the windows at the fine, steady rain of late autumn. "Heard you telling off young Wanno just now . . . 'What matters is that XVI and IXX don't make XXXVI. . . .' 'When I was twenty-six, four years ago . . . I counted eighty-one stars. . . .' A little more and you'd be computing, Ganil."

Ganil frowned, unconsciously rubbing the whitish scar on his temple. "Well, hell, Mede! even gentiles know IV from XXX!"

Mede smiled faintly. He had his Comparing Stick in his hand, and lowering it he drew on the dusty floor a round shape. "What's that?" he asked.

"The Sun."

"Right. It's also a . . . a figure. A number. The figure for Nothing."

"The figure for Nothing?"

"Yes. You could use it in the subtraction-tables, for instance. I from II leaves I, right? But what does II from II leave?" A pause. He tapped the circle with his stick. "That."

"Yes, of course." Ganil stared down at the circle, the sacred image of the Sun, the Hidden Light, the Face of God. "Is that priest-knowledge?"

"No." Mede drew an X-cross over the circle. "That is."

"Then what—whose knowledge is the—the figure for Nothing?"

"No one's. Anyone's. It's not a mystery." Ganil frowned in surprise at this statement. They spoke in low voices, standing close as if discussing a measurement on Mede's Comparing Stick. "Why did you count the stars, Ganil?"

"I . . . I wanted to know. I've always liked counting, numbers, the tables. That's why I'm a Mechanic."

"Yes. You're thirty, aren't you, you've been a Master for four months now. Did you ever think, Ganil, that to be a Master means you have learned everything your trade can teach? From now on until your death you'll learn nothing more. There is no more."

"But the Shopmasters—"

"Shopmasters learn some secret signals and passwords," Mede said in his soft, dry voice, "and of course they have power. But they know no more than you. . . . You thought perhaps they were allowed to compute, didn't you? They aren't."

Ganil was silent.

"And yet there are things to be learned, Ganil."

"Where?"

"Outside."

There was a long pause.

"I can't listen to this, Mede. Don't speak of it again. I won't betray you." Ganil turned and walked away, his face harsh with anger. With all his will he turned that confused and struggling anger against Mede, a man as deformed of mind as of body, an evil counsellor, a lost friend.

It had been a pleasant evening: Lee jovial, his fat wife motherly, and Lani shy and radiant. Ganil's youthful gravity made her tease him, but even in her teasing was that pleading, yielding note; another moment, it seemed, and all her verve would turn to tenderness. Passing a dish at table once her hand had for an instant touched his. He still knew exactly where, there, the side of his right hand near the wrist, one soft touch. He moaned luxuriously as he lay in bed in his room over the Shop in the utter blackness of the city night. O Lani, soft touch of a hand, of lips—O Lord, Lord! Courtship was a long business, eight months at least, going from step to step as one must with a Master's daughter. Ganil had to get his mind off this unendurable sweetness. Think of nothing, he told himself firmly, go to sleep. Think of nothing. . . . And he thought of nothing. The circle. The round empty circle. What was I times 0? The same as II times 0. What if you put I beside 0, what would that figure be, I0?

Mede Fairman sat up in bed, brown hair lank over groggy blue eyes, and tried to focus on the person crashing around his room. The first dirty-yellow light of dawn showed at the window. "This is Altarday," he growled, "go away, I'm sleepy." The vague figure resolved into Ganil, the crashing into a whisper. "Mede!" Ganil

kept whispering, "look!" He stuck a slate under Mede's nose. "Look, look what you can do with that figure for Nothing—"

"Oh, that," said Mede. He pushed Ganil and the slate away, went and dunked his head in the basin of icy water on his clothes-chest, and kept it there a while. He returned dripping to sit on the bed. "Let's see."

"See, you can use any number for a base, I used XII because it's handy. XII becomes I–0, see, and XIII is I–I, then when you get up to XXIV—"

"Sh."

Mede studied the slate. Finally he said, "Will you remember this?" and at Ganil's nod, wiped the neat crowded figures off the slate with a rub of his sleeve. "I hadn't realized that one could use any base. . . . But look, use the base X, I'll tell you why in a minute, and here's a device that makes it easier. Now X will be I0, and XI will be II, but for XII, write this," and he wrote on the slate, 12.

Ganil stared at the figure. At last he said in a peculiar struggling voice, "Isn't that one of the black numbers?"

"Yes, it is. All you've done, Ganil, is to come at the black numbers by the back door."

Ganil sat beside him, silent.

"What's CXX times MCC?" Mede inquired.

"The tables don't go that high."

"Watch." Mede wrote on the slate:

$$\begin{array}{r} 1200 \\ 120 \\ \hline \end{array}$$

and then as Ganil watched,

$$\begin{array}{r} 0000 \\ 2400 \\ 1200 \\ \hline 144000 \end{array}$$

Another long pause. "Three Nothings . . . XII times itself . . . Give me the slate," Ganil muttered. Then after a silence broken only by the patter of rain and the squeak of chalk on slate, "What's the black number for VIII?"

By twilight of that cold Altarday they had gone as far as Mede could take Ganil. Indeed Ganil had gone farther than Mede could follow him. "You must meet Yin," the fair man said. "He can teach you what you need. Yin works with angles, triangles, measurements. He can measure the distance between any two points, points you can't reach, using his triangles. He is a great Learner. Numbers are the heart of this knowledge, the language of it."

"And my own language."

"Yes, it is. Not mine. I don't love numbers for themselves. I want to use them. To explain things . . . For instance, if you throw a ball, what makes the ball move?"

"Your throwing it." Ganil grinned. White as a sheet—much whiter than Mede's sheets—his head ringing with sixteen straight hours of mathematics minus meals or sleep, he had lost all fear, all humility. His smile was that of a king come home from exile.

"Fine," said Mede. "Why does it *keep on* moving?"

"Because . . . because the air holds it up?"

"Then why does it ever fall? Why does it follow a curve? What kind of curve is it? Do you see how I need your numbers?" It was Mede who now looked like a king, an angry king with an empire too immense to control. "And they talk about Mysteries," he snorted, "in their little shuttered shops! —Here, come on, let's get some dinner and go see Yin."

Built right up against the city wall, the tall old house peered from leaded windows at the two young Masters down in the street. Sulfurous late-autumn twilight hung over the steep slate roofs shining with rain. "Yin was a Machine-Master like us," Mede told Ganil as they waited at the iron-barred door, "retired now, you'll

see why. Men from all the Lodges come here, apothecaries, weavers, masons. Even some artisans. One butcher. He cuts up dead cats." Mede spoke with amused tolerance, as physicists generally speak of biologists. Now the door swung open, and a servant took them upstairs to a room where logs glowed on a great hearth, and a man rose from a high-backed oaken chair to greet them.

Ganil thought at once of the Overmaster of his Lodge, the figure that had cried down to him in his grave, "Arise." Yin too was old and tall, and wore the white cloak of the High Masters. But he stooped, and his face was creased and weary as an old hound's. He held out his left hand to greet them. His right arm ended in a long healed, shiny stump at the wrist.

"This is Ganil," Mede was saying. "He invented the duodecimal system last night. Get him working on the mathematics of curves for me, Master Yin."

Yin laughed, an old man's short, soft laugh. "Welcome, Ganil. From now on, come here when you please. We're all necromancers here, we practice the black arts. Or try to . . . Come freely, day or night. And go freely. If we're betrayed, so be it. We must trust one another. Mystery belongs to no man; we're not keeping a secret, but practicing an art. Does that make sense to you?"

Ganil nodded. Words never came easily to him, only numbers. And he found himself very moved, which embarrassed him. This was no solemn symbolic Initiation and Oath, but only an old man talking quietly.

"Good," said Yin, as if Ganil's nod had been quite sufficient. "Some wine, young Masters, or ale? My dark ale came out first-rate this year. So you like numbers, do you, Ganil?"

In early spring Ganil stood in the shop supervising Wanno as the prentice took measurements onto his Comparing Stick from the model of the hauling-cart engine. Ganil's face was grim. He had

changed over these few months, looked older, more resolute, harder. Four hours' sleep a night plus the invention of algebra might well change a man.

"Master Ganil?" said a shy voice.

"Repeat that measurement," he told Wanno, and then turned questioningly to the girl. Lani too had changed. Her face looked a little cross, a little forlorn, and she spoke to Ganil with real timidity. He had taken the second step of courtship, the three evening calls, and then becoming absorbed in his work with Yin, had gone no further. No man had ever dropped Lani in the middle of a courtship. No man had ever looked right through her, as he was doing now. What was it he saw, when he looked through her? She was wild to know that, to get at his secret, to get at him. In a vague, unquantifiable way he knew this, and was sorry for Lani, and a little afraid of her.

She was watching Wanno. "Do they . . . do you ever change those measurements?" she asked, trying to make conversation.

"To change a Model is the heresy of Invention."

That ended that. "My father wanted me to tell you the Shop will be shut tomorrow."

"Shut? Why's that?"

"The College has announced there's a west wind rising, and the Sun may come out tomorrow."

"Good! A good beginning for the spring, eh? Thanks." And he turned back to the model.

The Priests of the College had for once been right. Weather prediction, on which they spent most of their waking hours, was a thankless task. But once in ten tries or so they caught a Sun, and this was one of the times. By noon the rains had ceased and the cloud-cover was paling, beginning to boil and flow slowly eastward. By mid-afternoon all the people of Edun were out on the streets and squares, on chimneypots and roof-trees, on the wall and the

fields beyond the wall, watching; the Priests of the College had begun their ceremonial dance, bowing and interweaving on the great forecourt of the College; priests stood ready in every temple to pull chains that would open the roofs so that the Sun's light might strike the altar-stones. And in late afternoon at last the sky opened. Between ragged smoking edges of yellow-grey appeared a streak of blue. A sigh, a soft tremendous murmur rose up from the streets, squares, windows, roofs, walls of the city of Edun: "Heaven, heaven . . ."

The rent in the sky widened. A shower of rain spattered over the city, blown aslant on the fresh wind, and suddenly the raindrops glittered, as at night in torchlight; but this glory they reflected was the glory of the Sun. To westward it stood, all alone in heaven, blinding.

Ganil stood with the others, face lifted. On his face, on the scar of his burn, he felt the heat of the Sun. He stared at it till his eyes swam with tears, the Circle of Fire, the face of God. . . .

"What is the Sun?"

That was Mede's soft voice, remembered. A cold midwinter night, he and Mede and Yin and the others talking before the fire in Yin's house. "Is it a circle, or a sphere? Why does it cross the sky? And how big is it—how far away is it? Ah, to think that once all a man had to do to see the Sun was lift up his head. . . ."

Flutes and drums throbbed, a gay faint sound, away off at the College. Sometimes cloud-fragments blew across the intolerable face and the world turned grey and chill again, the flutes stopped; but the west wind blew, the clouds passed and the Sun reappeared, always a little lower. Just before it sank into the heavy cloud-rack in the west it was growing red and one could look at it without pain. In those moments it certainly looked to Ganil's eyes not like a disk but like an enormous, haze-warped, slowly falling ball.

It fell, was gone.

Overhead through the torn sky glimpses of heaven still shone, clear and deep, blue-green. Then westward near where the Sun had set, at the edge of a mounting cloud, gleamed one bright point: the evening star. "Look!" Ganil cried, but few turned to look. The Sun was set, what did stars matter. The yellowish haze, part of the single windingsheet of cloud that had covered earth with its mantle of dust and rain ever since Hellfire fourteen generations ago, moved up over the star, erased it. Ganil sighed, rubbed his neck that was stiff with craning, and started home along with all the other people of the Common Day.

He was arrested that night. From guards and fellow-prisoners (all his shop was in jail with him except the Shopmaster Lee) he learned that his crime was that of knowing Mede Fairman. Mede stood accused of heresy. He had been seen out on the fields pointing an instrument at the Sun, a device, they said, for measuring distances. He had been trying to measure the distance between the earth and God.

The prentices were soon let go. On the third day guards came for Ganil, bringing him out into one of the enclosed courts of the College, into the soft, fine rain of early spring. Priests lived almost wholly out of doors, and the great complex of Edun College was only a series of meager barracks surrounding the roofless sleeping-courts, writing-courts, prayer-courts, eating-courts, and courts of law. Into one of these they brought Ganil, forcing him on between the ranks of men robed in white and yellow that filled it, until he stood in front of them all. He saw a clear space, an altar, a long table shining wet with rain, and behind it a priest in the golden robe of the High Mystery. At the far end of the table was another man who like Ganil was flanked by guards. This man was looking at Ganil, a straight look, cold and blank; yet they were blue eyes, the same blue as heaven above the clouds.

"Ganil Kalson of Edun, you are suspect as an acquaintance of

Mede Fairman, accused of the heresies of Invention and Computation. You were this man's friend?"

"We were Co-Masters— "

"Yes. Did he ever speak to you of measurements made without Comparing Sticks?"

"No."

"Of black numbers?"

"No."

"Of the black arts?"

"No."

"Master Ganil, you've answered No three times. Do you know the Order of the Priest-Masters of the Mystery of the Law concerning suspects in heresy?"

"No, I don't— "

"The Order says: 'If the suspect shall deny the questions four times, the questions may be repeated with use of the handpress until answered.' I shall now repeat, unless you wish to retract one of your denials."

"No," Ganil said, confused, looking round him at the crowded blank faces, the high walls. When they had brought out a squat wooden machine of some kind and had locked his right hand into it, he was still more confused than scared. What was all this mumbo-jumbo? It was like his initiation, when they had worked so hard to frighten him; that time they had succeeded.

"As a Mechanic," the golden priest was saying, "you know the use of the lever, Master Ganil. Will you retract?"

"No," Ganil said, frowning a little. He had noticed that his right arm now seemed to end at the wrist, like Yin's.

"Very well." One of the guards put his hands on the lever sticking out of the wooden box, and the golden priest said, "Were you a friend of Mede Fairman?"

"No," Ganil said. He said No to each question even after he had

ceased to hear the priest's voice; he went on saying No till he heard his own voice mixed with the clapping echo from the walls above the courtyard, No, no, no, no.

The light came and went, the rain fell cold on his face and ceased, somebody kept trying to help him stand up. His grey cloak stank, he had been sick with pain. At the thought, he was sick again. "Take it easy, now," a guard was whispering to him. The motionless white and yellow ranks were still crowded there, the faces set, the eyes staring . . . but not at him now.

"Heretic, do you know this man?"

"He is my Co-Master."

"Did you speak to him of the black arts?"

"Yes."

"Did you teach him the black arts?"

"No. I tried to." The voice cracked a little; even in the silence of the courtyard, over only the whisper of the rain, it was hard to hear Mede speak. "He was too stupid. He dared not and could not learn. He'll make a fine Shopmaster." The cold blue eyes looked straight at Ganil without pity or appeal.

The golden priest turned to face the court again. "There is no evidence against the suspect Ganil. You may go, suspect. Come here at noon tomorrow to witness the execution of judgment. Failure to come will be taken as proof of your guilt." Before he understood, the guards had led Ganil out of the courtyard. They left him at a side door of the College, barring the door behind him with a clang. He stood there a while, then crouched down on the pavement, pressing his blackened, blood-caked hand against his side under his cloak. Rain whispered around him. No one passed. It was not till dusk that he pulled himself up and walked, street by street, house by house, step by step, across the city to Yin's house.

In the shadows of the doorway a shadow moved, spoke: "Ganil!" He stopped. "Ganil, I don't care if you're suspect. It's all right.

Come back home with me. My father will take you back into the shop. He will if I ask him."

Ganil was silent.

"Come with me. I waited for you, I knew you'd come here, I've followed you before." Her nervous, jubilant laugh died away.

"Let me by, Lani."

"No. Why do you come to old Yin's house? Who lives here? Who is she? Come back with me, you have to, my father won't take a suspect back into his shop, unless I— "

Yin's door was never locked. Ganil brushed past her and went in, shutting it behind him. No servant came; the house was dark, silent. They had all been taken, all the Learners, they would all be questioned and tortured and killed.

"Who's that?"

Yin stood on the stair-landing, lamplight bright on his white hair. He came to Ganil and helped him up the stairs. Ganil spoke very fast: "I was followed here, a girl from the shop, Lee's daughter, if she tells him he'll recognize your name, he'll send the guards here— "

"I sent the others away three days ago." At the sound of Yin's voice Ganil stopped, stared at the old man's creased, quiet face, and then said childishly, "Look," holding out his right hand, "look, like yours."

"Yes. Come sit down, Ganil."

"They condemned him. Not me, they let me go. He said he couldn't teach me, I couldn't learn. To save me— "

"And your mathematics. Come here now, sit down."

Ganil got control of himself, and obeyed. Yin made him lie down, then did what he could about cleaning and bandaging his hand. Then, sitting down between Ganil and the glowing fire, he gave a wheezy sigh. "Well," he said, "now you're a heresy suspect. I've been one for twenty years. You get used to it. . . . Don't worry

about our friends. But if the girl tells Lee and your name gets linked with mine . . . We'd better leave Edun. Separately. But tonight."

Ganil said nothing. To leave his shop without the Overmaster's permission meant excommunication, the loss of his Mastership. He would be barred from his own trade. What could he do, with his crippled hand, where could he go? He had never been out of Edun in his life.

The silence of the house spread out above and below them. Ganil strained to hear sounds down in the street, the tramping of a troop of guards come to re-arrest him. He had to get out, to get away, tonight— "I can't," he said abruptly. "I have to be—to be at the College tomorrow, at noon."

Yin knew what he meant. Again the silence closed round them. The old man's voice was very dry and weary when he finally spoke. "That's the condition of your release, eh? All right; go do it; you don't want them hunting you through the Forty Towns as a condemned heretic. A suspect isn't hunted, merely outcast. It's preferable. Get some sleep now, Ganil. Before I go I'll tell you where to meet me. Leave as soon as you can; and travel light. . . ."

When Ganil left the house late in the morning, however, he carried something with him, a roll of papers hidden under his cloak, each sheet covered edge to edge with Mede Fairman's clear writing: "Trajectories," "Speed of Falling Bodies," "The Nature of Motion . . ." Yin had left before daybreak, jogging calmly out of town on a grey donkey. "I'll see you in Keling" had been his only parting with Ganil. Ganil had seen none of the other Learners. Only serfs, servants, beggars, truant schoolboys, and women with their nursemaids and whining children stood with him now in the dull light of noon on the great forecourt of the College. Only riffraff and the idle gathered to see a heretic die. A priest had ordered Ganil to stand at the very front of the crowd. Many people glanced curiously at him, standing there alone in his Master's cloak.

On the other side of the square, in the front of the crowd, he saw a girl in a violet gown. He was not sure it was Lani. Why would she be here to see Mede die? She did not know what it was she hated; or what it was she loved. Love that wants only to get, to possess, is a monstrous thing, Ganil thought. She loved him, she stood separated from him only by the width of that square. She would never be willing to see that she was separated from him by her own act, by ignorance, by exile, by death.

They brought Mede out just before noon. Ganil glimpsed his face; it was very white, all his deformity exposed, the atavistic pallor of skin, hair, eyes. There was no drawing-out of the scene; a gold-robed priest raised his crossed arms in invocation to the Sun that stood, unseen, at noon behind the pall of clouds, and as he lowered his arms torches were set to the stacks of wood round the stake. Smoke curled up, the same grey-yellow as the clouds. Ganil stood with his injured hand in its sling pressed hard against the roll of papers under his cloak, repeating silently, "Let the smoke suffocate him first. . . ." But the wood was dry and caught quickly. He felt the heat on his face, on his fire-scarred temple. Beside him a young priest tried to draw back, could not because of the pressing, staring, sighing crowd, and stood still, swaying a little and breathing in gasps. The smoke was thick now, hiding the flames and the figure among them. But Ganil could hear his voice, not soft now, loud, very loud. He heard it, he forced himself to hear it, but at the same time he listened in his spirit to a steady voice, soft, continuing: "What is the Sun? Why does it cross the sky? . . . Do you see how I need your numbers? . . . For XII, write 12. . . . This is also a figure, the figure for Nothing."

The screaming had stopped, but the soft voice had not.

Ganil raised his head. The crowd was drifting away; the young priest knelt on the pavement by him, praying and sobbing aloud.

Ganil glanced up at the heavy sky and then set off alone through the streets of the city and out through the city gate, northward, into exile and towards his home.

DARKNESS BOX

∽∽∽∽∽
∽∽∽

When my daughter Caroline was three she came to me with a small wooden box in her small hands and said, "Guess fwat is in this bockus!" I guessed caterpillars, mice, elephants, etc. She shook her head, smiled an unspeakably eldritch smile, opened the box slightly so that I could just see in, and said: "Darkness."

Hence this story.

On soft sand by the sea's edge a little boy walked leaving no footprints. Gulls cried in the bright sunless sky, trout leaped from the saltless ocean. Far off on the horizon the sea serpent raised himself a moment in seven enormous arches and then, bellowing, sank. The child whistled but the sea serpent, busy hunting whales, did not surface again. The child walked on casting no shadow, leaving no tracks on the sand between the cliffs and the sea. Ahead of him rose a grassy headland on which stood a four-legged hut. As he climbed a path up the cliff the hut skipped about and rubbed its front legs together like a lawyer or a fly; but the hands of the clock inside, which said ten minutes of ten, never moved.

"What's that you've got there, Dicky?" asked his mother as she added parsley and a pinch of pepper to the rabbit stew simmering in an alembic.

"A box, Mummy."

"Where did you find it?"

Mummy's familiar leaped down from the onion-festooned rafters and, draping itself like a foxfur round her neck, said, "By the sea."

Dicky nodded. "That's right. The sea washed it up."

"And what's inside it?"

The familiar said nothing, but purred. The witch turned round to look into her son's round face. "What's in it?" she repeated.

"Darkness."

"Oh? Let's see."

As she bent down to look the familiar, still purring, shut its eyes. Holding the box against his chest, the little boy very carefully lifted the lid a scant inch.

"So it is," said his mother. "Now put it away, don't let it get knocked about. I wonder where the key got to. Run wash your hands now. Table, lay!" And while the child worked the heavy pump-handle in the yard and splashed his face and hands, the hut resounded with the clatter of plates and forks materializing.

After the meal, while his mother was having her morning nap, Dicky took down the water-bleached, sand-encrusted box from his treasure shelf and set out with it across the dunes, away from the sea. Close at his heels the black familiar followed him, trotting patiently over the sand through the coarse grass, the only shadow he had.

At the summit of the pass Prince Rikard turned in the saddle to look back over the plumes and pennants of his army, over the long falling road, to the towered walls of his father's city. Under the sunless sky it shimmered there on the plain, fragile and shadowless as a pearl. Seeing it so he knew it could never be taken, and his heart sang with pride. He gave his captains the signal for quick march and set spurs to his horse. It reared and broke into a gallop, while his gryphon swooped and screamed overhead. She teased the

white horse, diving straight down at it clashing her beak, swerving aside just in time; the horse, bridleless, would snap furiously at her snaky tail or rear to strike out with silver hoofs. The gryphon would cackle and roar, circle back over the dunes and with a screech and swoop play the trick all over. Afraid she might wear herself out before the battle, Rikard finally leashed her, after which she flew along steadily, purring and chirping, by his side.

The sea lay before him; somewhere beneath the cliffs the enemy force his brother led was hidden. The road wound down growing sandier, the sea appearing to right or left always nearer. Abruptly the road fell away; the white horse leaped the ten-foot drop and galloped out over the beach. As he came out from between the dunes Rikard saw a long line of men strung out on the sand, and behind them three black-prowed ships. His own men were scrambling down the drop, swarming over the dunes, blue flags snapping in the sea wind, voices faint against the sound of the sea. Without warning or parley the two forces met, sword to sword and man to man. With a great shrilling scream the gryphon soared up, jerking the leash from Rikard's hand, then dropped like a falcon, beak and claws extended, down on a tall man in grey, the enemy leader. But the tall man's sword was drawn. As the iron beak snapped on his shoulder, trying to get the throat, the iron sword jabbed out and up, slashing the gryphon's belly. She doubled up in air and fell, knocking the man down with the sweep of her great wing, screaming, blackening the sand with blood. The tall man staggered up and slashed off her head and wings, turning half blinded with sand and blood only when Rikard was almost on him. Without a word he turned, lifting his steaming sword to parry Rikard's blow. He tried to strike at the horse's legs, but got no chance, for the beast would back and rear and run at him, Rikard's sword slashing down from above. The tall man's arms began to grow heavy, his breath came in gasps. Rikard gave no quarter. Once more the tall man

raised his sword, lunged, and took the whizzing slash of his brother's sword straight across his uplifted face. He fell without a word. Brown sand fell over his body in a little shower from the white stallion's hoofs as Rikard spurred back to the thick of the fight.

The attackers fought on doggedly, always fewer of them, and those few being pushed back step by step towards the sea. When only a knot of twenty or so remained they broke, sprinting desperately for the ships, pushing them off chest-deep in the breakers, clambering aboard. Rikard shouted to his men. They came to him across the sand, picking their way among hacked corpses. The badly wounded tried to crawl to him on hands and knees. All that could walk gathered in ranks in a hollow behind the dune on which Rikard stood. Behind him, out on deep water, the three black ships lay motionless, balanced on their oars.

Rikard sat down, alone on the dune-top among the rank grass. He bowed his head and put his hands over his face. Near him the white horse stood still as a horse of stone. Below him his men stood silent. Behind him on the beach the tall man, his face obliterated in blood, lay near the body of the gryphon, and the other dead lay staring at the sky where no sun shone.

A little gust of wind blew by. Rikard raised his face, which though young was very grim. He signalled his captains, swung up into the saddle, and set off round the dunes and back towards the city at a trot, not waiting to see the black ships steer in to shore where their soldiers could board them, or his own army fill up its ranks and come marching behind him. When the gryphon swooped screaming overhead he raised his arm, grinning at the great creature as she tried to perch on his gloved wrist, flapping her wings and screeching like a tomcat. "You no-good gryphon," he said, "you hen, go home to your chicken coop!" Insulted, the monster yawped and sailed off eastward towards the city. Behind him his

army wound upward through the hills, leaving no track. Behind them the brown sand lay smooth as silk, stainless. The black ships, sails set, already stood out well to sea. In the prow of the first stood a tall, grim-faced man in grey.

Taking an easier road homeward, Rikard passed not far from the four-legged hut on the headland. The witch stood in the doorway, hailing him. He galloped over, and, drawing rein right at the gate of the little yard, he looked at the young witch. She was bright and dark as coals, her black hair whipped in the sea wind. She looked at him, white-armored on a white horse.

"Prince," she said, "you'll go to battle once too often."

He laughed. "What should I do—let my brother lay siege to the city?"

"Yes, let him. No man can take the city."

"I know. But my father the king exiled him, he must not set foot even on our shore. I'm my father's soldier, I fight as he commands."

The witch looked out to sea, then back at the young man. Her dark face sharpened, nose and chin peaking crone-like, eyes flashing. "Serve and be served," she said, "rule and be ruled. Your brother chose neither to serve nor rule. . . . Listen, prince, take care." Her face warmed again to beauty. "The sea brings presents this morning, the wind blows, the crystals break. Take care."

Gravely he bowed his thanks, then wheeled his horse and was gone, white as a gull over the long curve of the dunes.

The witch went back into the hut, glancing about its one room to see that everything was in place: bats, onions, cauldrons, carpets, broom, toad-stones, crystal balls (cracked through), the thin crescent moon hung up on the chimney, the Books, the familiar— She looked again, then hurried out and called "Dicky!"

The wind from the west was cold now, bending the coarse grass down.

"Dicky! . . . Kitty, kitty kitty!"

The wind caught the voice from her lips, tore it into bits and blew it away.

She snapped her fingers. The broom came zooming out the door, horizontal and about two feet off the ground, while the hut shivered and hopped about in excitement. "Shut up!" the witch snapped, and the door obediently slammed. Mounting the broom she took off in a long gliding swoop southwards down the beach, now and then crying out, "Dicky! . . . Here, kitty, kitty, kitty!"

The young prince, rejoining his men, had dismounted to walk with them. As they reached the pass and saw the city below them on the plain, he felt a tug at his cloak.

"Prince—"

A little boy, so little he was still fat and round-cheeked, stood with a scared look, holding up a battered, sandy box. Beside him a black cat sat smiling broadly. "The sea brought this—it's for the prince of the land, I know it is—please take it!"

"What's in it?"

"Darkness, sir."

Rikard took the box and after a slight hesitation opened it a little, just a crack. "It's painted black inside," he said with a hard grin.

"No, prince, truly it's not. Open it wider!"

Cautiously Rikard lifted the lid higher, an inch or two, and peered in. Then he shut it quickly, even as the child said, "Don't let the wind blow it out, prince!"

"I shall take this to the king."

"But it's for you, sir—"

"All seagifts are the king's. But thank you for it, boy." They looked at each other for a moment, the little round boy and the hard splendid youth; then Rikard turned and strode on, while Dicky wandered back down the hills, silent and disconsolate. He heard

his mother's voice from far away to the south, and tried to answer; but the wind blew his call landwards, and the familiar had disappeared.

The bronze gates of the city swung open as the troop approached. Watchdogs bayed, guards stood rigid, the people of the city bowed down as Rikard on his horse clattered at full gallop up the marble streets to the palace. Entering, he glanced up at the great bronze clock on the bell-tower, the highest of the nine white towers of the palace. The moveless hands said ten minutes of ten.

In the Hall of Audience his father awaited him: a fierce grey-haired man crowned with iron, his hands clenched on the heads of iron chimaeras that formed the arms of the throne. Rikard knelt and with bowed head, never looking up, reported the success of his foray. "The Exile was killed, with the greater part of his men; the rest fled in their ships."

A voice answered like an iron door moving on unused hinges: "Well done, prince."

"I bring you a seagift, Lord." Still with head bowed, Rikard held up the wooden box.

A low snarl came from the throat of one of the carven monsters of the throne.

"That is mine," said the old king so harshly that Rikard glanced up for a second, seeing the teeth of the chimaeras bared and the king's eyes glittering.

"Therefore I bring it to you, Lord."

"That is mine—I gave it to the sea, I myself! And the sea spits back my gift." A long silence, then the king spoke more softly. "Well, keep it, prince. The sea doesn't want it, nor do I. It's in your hands. Keep it—locked. Keep it locked, prince!"

Rikard, on his knees, bowed lower in thanks and consent, then rose and backed down the long hall, never looking up. As he came out into the glittering anteroom, officers and noblemen gathered

round him, ready as usual to ask about the battle, laugh, drink, and chatter. He passed among them without a word or glance and went to his own quarters, alone, carrying the box carefully in both hands.

His bright, shadowless, windowless room was decorated on every wall with patterns of gold inset with topazes, opals, crystals, and, most vivid of all jewels, candle flames moveless on golden sconces. He set the box down on a glass table, threw off his cloak, unbuckled his swordbelt, and sat down sighing. The gryphon loped in from his bedroom, talons rasping on the mosaic floor, stuck her great head onto his knees and waited for him to scratch her feathery mane. There was also a cat prowling around the room, a sleek black one; Rikard took no notice. The palace was full of animals, cats, hounds, apes, squirrels, young hippogriffs, white mice, tigers. Every lady had her unicorn, every courtier had a dozen pets. The prince had only one, the gryphon which always fought for him, his one unquestioning friend. He scratched the gryphon's mane, often glancing down to meet the loving golden gaze of her round eyes, now and then glancing too at the box on the table. There was no key to lock it.

Music played softly in a distant room, a ceaseless interweaving of notes like the sound of a fountain.

He turned to look at the clock on the mantle, an ornate square of gold and blue enamel. It was ten minutes of ten: time to rise and buckle on his sword, call up his men, and go to battle. The Exile was returning, determined to take the city and reclaim his right to the throne, his inheritance. His black ships must be driven back to sea. The brothers must fight, and one must die, and the city be saved. Rikard rose, and at once the gryphon jumped up lashing her tail, eager for the fight. "All right, come along!" Rikard told her, but his voice was cold. He took up his sword in the pearl-encrusted sheath and buckled it on, and the gryphon whined with excitement and rubbed her beak on his hand. He did not respond.

He was tired and sad, he longed for something—for what? To hear music that ceased, to speak to his brother once before they fought . . . he did not know. Heir and defender, he must obey. He set the silver helmet on his head and turned to pick up his cloak, flung over a chair. The pearly sheath slung from his belt clattered against something behind him; he turned and saw the box, lying on the floor, open. As he stood looking at it with the same cold, absent look, a little blackness like smoke gathered about it on the floor. He stooped and picked it up, and darkness ran out over his hands.

The gryphon backed away, whining.

Tall and white-armored, fair-haired, silver-capped in the glittering shadowless room, Rikard stood holding the open box, watching the thick dusk that dripped slowly from it. All around his body now, below his hands, was twilight. He stood still. Then slowly he raised the box up, clear up over his head, and turned it upside down.

Darkness flowed over his face. He looked about him, for the distant music had stopped and things were very silent. Candles burned, dots of light picking out flecks of gold and flashes of violet from walls and ceiling. But all the corners were dark, behind each chair lay darkness, and as Rikard turned his head his shadow leapt along the wall. He moved then, quickly, dropping the box, for in one of the black corners he had glimpsed the reddish glow of two great eyes. —The gryphon, of course. He held out his hand and spoke to her. She did not move, but gave a queer metallic cry.

"Come on! Are you afraid of the dark?" he said, and then all at once was afraid himself. He drew his sword. Nothing moved. He took a step backward towards the door; and the monster jumped. He saw the black wings spread across the ceiling, the iron beak, the talons; her bulk was on him before he could stab upwards. He wrestled, the great beak snapping at his throat and the talons tearing at his arms and chest, till he got his sword-arm free and could slash down, pull away and slash again. The second blow

half severed the gryphon's neck. She dropped off, lay writhing in the shadows among splinters of glass, then lay still.

Rikard's sword dropped clattering on the floor. His hands were sticky with his own blood, and he could hardly see; the beating of the gryphon's wings had blown out or knocked over every candle but one. He groped his way to a chair and sat down. After a minute, though he still gasped for breath, he did as he had done on the dune-top after battle: bowed his head and hid his face in his hands. It was completely silent. The one candle flickered in its sconce, mirrored feebly in a cluster of topazes on the wall behind it. Rikard raised his head.

The gryphon lay still. Its blood had spread out in a pool, black as the first spilt darkness from the box. Its iron beak was open, its eyes open, like two red stones.

"It's dead," said a small soft voice, as the witch's cat came picking its way delicately among the fragments of the smashed table. "Once and for all. Listen, prince!" The cat sat down curling its tail neatly round its paws. Rikard stood motionless, blank-faced, till a sudden sound made him start: a little ting! nearby. Then from the tower overhead a huge dull bell-stroke reverberated in the stone of the floor, in his ears, in his blood. The clocks were striking ten.

There was a pounding at his door, and shouts echoed down the palace corridors mixed with the last booming strokes of the bell, screams of scared animals, calls, commands.

"You'll be late for the battle, prince," said the cat.

Rikard groped among blood and shadow for his sword, sheathed it, flung on his cloak and went to the door.

"There'll be an afternoon today," the cat said, "and a twilight, and night will fall. At nightfall one of you will come home to the city, you or your brother. But only one of you, prince."

Rikard stood still a moment. "Is the sun shining now, outside?"

"Yes, it is—now."

"Well, then, it's worth it," the young man said, and opened the door and strode on out into the hubbub and panic of the sunlit halls, his shadow falling black behind him.

THE WORD OF UNBINDING

The two stories that follow were my first approach to and exploration of the "secondary world" of Earthsea, about which I later wrote three novels. I didn't know much about the place at first, and readers familiar with the trilogy will notice that trolls became extinct in Earthsea at some point, and that the history of the dragon Yevaud is somewhat obscure. (He must have been on Sattins Island some decades or centuries before Ged found him, and bound him, on the Isle of Pendor.) But this is only to be expected of dragons, who do not submit to the unidirectional, causal requirements of history, being myths, and neither timebinding nor timebound.

"The Rule of Names" first explores an essential element of how magic works in Earthsea. "The Word of Unbinding" foreshadows the end of the last book of the trilogy, The Farthest Shore, *in its imagery of the world of the dead. It also reveals a certain obsession with trees, which, once you notice them, keep cropping up throughout my work. I think I am definitely the most arboreal science fiction writer. It's all right for the rest of you who climbed down, and developed opposable thumbs, and erect posture, and all that. There's a few of us still up here swinging.*

Where was he? The floor was hard and slimy, the air black and stinking, and that was all there was. Except a headache. Lying flat

on the clammy floor Festin moaned, and then said, "Staff!" When his alderwood wizard's staff did not come to his hand, he knew he was in peril. He sat up, and not having his staff with which to make a proper light, he struck a spark between finger and thumb, muttering a certain Word. A blue will o' the wisp sprang from the spark and rolled feebly through the air, sputtering. "Up," said Festin, and the fireball wobbled upward till it lit a vaulted trapdoor very high above, so high that Festin projecting into the fireball momentarily saw his own face forty feet below as a pale dot in the darkness. The light struck no reflections in the damp walls; they had been woven out of night, by magic. He rejoined himself and said, "Out." The ball expired. Festin sat in the dark, cracking his knuckles.

He must have been overspelled from behind, by surprise; for the last memory he had was of walking through his own woods at evening talking with the trees. Lately, in these lone years in the middle of his life, he had been burdened with a sense of waste, of unspent strength; so, needing to learn patience, he had left the villages and gone to converse with trees, especially oaks, chestnuts, and the grey alders whose roots are in profound communication with running water. It had been six months since he had spoken to a human being. He had been busy with essentials, casting no spells and bothering no one. So who had spellbound him and shut him in this reeking well? "Who?" he demanded of the walls, and slowly a name gathered on them and ran down to him like a thick black drop sweated out from pores of stone and spores of fungus: "Voll."

For a moment Festin was in a cold sweat himself.

He had heard first long ago of Voll the Fell, who was said to be more than wizard yet less than man; who passed from island to island of the Outer Reach, undoing the works of the Ancients, enslaving men, cutting forests and spoiling fields, and sealing in underground tombs any wizard or Mage who tried to combat him.

Refugees from ruined islands told always the same tale, that he came at evening on a dark wind over the sea. His slaves followed in ships; these they had seen. But none of them had ever seen Voll. . . . There were many men and creatures of evil will among the Islands, and Festin, a young warlock intent on his training, had not paid much heed to these tales of Voll the Fell. "I can protect this island," he had thought, knowing his untried power, and had returned to his oaks and alders, the sound of wind in their leaves, the rhythm of growth in their round trunks and limbs and twigs, the taste of sunlight on leaves or dark groundwater around roots. — Where were they now, the trees, his old companions? Had Voll destroyed the forest?

Awake at last and up on his feet, Festin made two broad motions with rigid hands, shouting aloud a Name that would burst all locks and break open any man-made door. But these walls impregnated with night and the name of their builder did not heed, did not hear. The name re-echoed back, clapping in Festin's ears so that he fell on his knees, hiding his head in his arms till the echoes died away in the vaults above him. Then, still shaken by the backfire, he sat brooding.

They were right; Voll was strong. Here on his own ground, within this spell-built dungeon, his magic would withstand any direct attack; and Festin's strength was halved by the loss of his staff. But not even his captor could take from him his powers, relative only to himself, of Projecting and Transforming. So, after rubbing his now doubly aching head, he transformed. Quietly his body melted away into a cloud of fine mist.

Lazy, trailing, the mist rose off the floor, drifting up along the slimy walls until it found, where vault met wall, a hairline crack. Through this, droplet by droplet, it seeped. It was almost all through the crack when a hot wind, hot as a furnace-blast, struck at it, scattering the mist-drops, drying them. Hurriedly the mist sucked itself

back into the vault, spiralled to the floor, took on Festin's own form and lay there panting. Transformation is an emotional strain to introverted warlocks of Festin's sort; when to that strain is added the shock of facing unhuman death in one's assumed shape, the experience becomes horrible. Festin lay for a while merely breathing. He was also angry with himself. It had been a pretty simple-minded notion to escape as a mist, after all. Every fool knew that trick. Voll had probably just left a hot wind waiting. Festin gathered himself into a small black bat, flew up to the ceiling, retransformed into a thin stream of plain air, and seeped through the crack.

This time he got clear out and was blowing softly down the hall in which he found himself towards a window, when a sharp sense of peril made him pull together, snapping himself into the first small, coherent shape that came to mind—a gold ring. It was just as well. The hurricane of arctic air that would have dispersed his air-form in unrecallable chaos merely chilled his ring-form slightly. As the storm passed he lay on the marble pavement, wondering which form might get out the window quickest.

Too late, he began to roll away. An enormous blank-faced troll strode cataclysmically across the floor, stopped, caught the quick-rolling ring and picked it up in a huge limestone-like hand. The troll strode to the trapdoor, lifted it by an iron handle and a muttered charm, and dropped Festin down into the darkness. He fell straight for forty feet and landed on the stone floor—clink.

Resuming his true form he sat up, ruefully rubbing a bruised elbow. Enough of this transformation on an empty stomach. He longed bitterly for his staff, with which he could have summoned up any amount of dinner. Without it, though he could change his own form and exert certain spells and powers, he could not transform or summon to him any material thing—neither lightning nor a lamb chop.

"Patience," Festin told himself, and when he had got his breath

he dissolved his body into the infinite delicacy of volatile oils, becoming the aroma of a frying lamb chop. He drifted once more through the crack. The waiting troll sniffed suspiciously, but already Festin had regrouped himself into a falcon, winging straight for the window. The troll lunged after him, missed by yards, and bellowed in a vast stony voice, "The hawk, get the hawk!" Swooping over the enchanted castle towards his forest that lay dark to westward, sunlight and sea-glare dazzling his eyes, Festin rode the wind like an arrow. But a quicker arrow found him. Crying out, he fell. Sun and sea and towers spun around him and went out.

He woke again on the dank floor of the dungeon, hands and hair and lips wet with his own blood. The arrow had struck his pinion as a falcon, his shoulder as a man. Lying still, he mumbled a spell to close the wound. Presently he was able to sit up, and recollect a longer, deeper spell of healing. But he had lost a good deal of blood, and with it, power. A chill had settled in the marrow of his bones which even the healing-spell could not warm. There was darkness in his eyes, even when he struck a will o' the wisp and lit the reeking air: the same dark mist he had seen, as he flew, overhanging his forest and the little towns of his land.

It was up to him to protect that land.

He could not attempt direct escape again. He was too weak and tired. Trusting his power too much, he had lost his strength. Now whatever shape he took would share his weakness, and be trapped.

Shivering with cold, he crouched there, letting the fireball sputter out with a last whiff of methane—marsh gas. The smell brought to his mind's eye the marshes stretching from the forest wall down to the sea, his beloved marshes where no men came, where in fall the swans flew long and level, where between still pools and reed-islands the quick, silent, seaward streamlets ran. Oh, to be a fish in one of those streams; or better yet to be farther upstream, near the

springs, in the forest in the shadow of the trees, in the clear brown backwater under an alder's roots, resting hidden . . .

This was a great magic. Festin had no more performed it than has any man who in exile or danger longs for the earth and waters of his home, seeing and yearning over the doorsill of his house, the table where he has eaten, the branches outside the window of the room where he has slept. Only in dreams do any but the great Mages realize this magic of going home. But Festin, with the cold creeping out from his marrow into nerves and veins, stood up between the black walls, gathered his will together till it shone like a candle in the darkness of his flesh, and began to work the great and silent magic.

The walls were gone. He was in the earth, rocks and veins of granite for bones, groundwater for blood, the roots of things for nerves. Like a blind worm he moved through the earth westward, slowly, darkness before and behind. Then all at once coolness flowed along his back and belly, a buoyant, unresisting, inexhaustible caress. With his sides he tasted the water, felt current-flow; and with lidless eyes he saw before him the deep brown pool between the great buttress-roots of an alder. He darted forward, silvery, into shadow. He had got free. He was home.

The water ran timelessly from its clear spring. He lay on the sand of the pool's bottom letting running water, stronger than any spell of healing, soothe his wound and with its coolness wash away the bleaker cold that had entered him. But as he rested he felt and heard a shaking and trampling in the earth. Who walked now in his forest? Too weary to try to change form, he hid his gleaming trout-body under the arch of the alder root, and waited.

Huge grey fingers groped in the water, roiling the sand. In the dimness above water vague faces, blank eyes loomed and vanished, reappeared. Nets and hands groped, missed, missed again, then

caught and lifted him writhing up into the air. He struggled to take back his own shape and could not; his own spell of home-coming bound him. He writhed in the net, gasping in the dry, bright, terrible air, drowning. The agony went on, and he knew nothing beyond it.

After a long time and little by little he became aware that he was in his human form again; some sharp, sour liquid was being forced down his throat. Time lapsed again, and he found himself sprawled face down on the dank floor of the vault. He was back in the power of his enemy. And, though he could breathe again, he was not very far from death.

The chill was all through him now; and the trolls, Voll's servants, must have crushed the fragile trout-body, for when he moved, his ribcage and one forearm stabbed with pain. Broken and without strength, he lay at the bottom of the well of night. There was no power in him to change shape; there was no way out, but one.

Lying there motionless, almost but not quite beyond the reach of pain, Festin thought: Why has he not killed me? Why does he keep me here alive?

Why has he never been seen? With what eyes can he be seen, on what ground does he walk?

He fears me, though I have no strength left.

They say that all the wizards and men of power whom he has defeated live on sealed in tombs like this, live on year after year trying to get free. . . .

But if one chose not to live?

So Festin made his choice. His last thought was, If I am wrong, men will think I was a coward. But he did not linger on this thought. Turning his head a little to the side he closed his eyes, took a last deep breath, and whispered the word of unbinding, which is only spoken once.

This was not transformation. He was not changed. His body, the long legs and arms, the clever hands, the eyes that had liked to look on trees and streams, lay unchanged, only still, perfectly still and full of cold. But the walls were gone. The vaults built by magic were gone, and the rooms and towers; and the forest, and the sea, and the sky of evening. They were all gone, and Festin went slowly down the far slope of the hill of being, under new stars.

In life he had had great power; so here he did not forget. Like a candle flame he moved in the darkness of the wider land. And remembering he called out his enemy's name: "Voll!"

Called, unable to withstand, Voll came towards him, a thick pale shape in the starlight. Festin approached, and the other cowered and screamed as if burnt. Festin followed when he fled, followed him close. A long way they went, over dry lava-flows from the great extinct volcanoes rearing their cones against the unnamed stars, across the spurs of silent hills, through valleys of short black grass, past towns or down their unlit streets between houses through whose windows no face looked. The stars hung in the sky; none set, none rose. There was no change here. No day would come. But they went on, Festin always driving the other before him, till they reached a place where once a river had run, very long ago: a river from the living lands. In the dry streambed, among boulders, a dead body lay: that of an old man, naked, flat eyes staring at the stars that are innocent of death.

"Enter it," Festin said. The Voll-shadow whimpered, but Festin came closer. Voll cowered away, stooped, and entered in the open mouth of his own dead body.

At once the corpse vanished. Unmarked, stainless, the dry boulders gleamed in starlight. Festin stood still a while, then slowly sat down among the great rocks to rest. To rest, not sleep; for he must keep guard here until Voll's body, sent back to its grave, had turned to dust, all evil power gone, scattered by the wind and

washed seaward by the rain. He must keep watch over this place where once death had found a way back into the other land. Patient now, infinitely patient, Festin waited among the rocks where no river would ever run again, in the heart of the country which has no seacoast. The stars stood still above him; and as he watched them, slowly, very slowly he began to forget the voice of streams and the sound of rain on the leaves of the forests of life.

THE RULE OF NAMES

Mr. Underhill came out from under his hill, smiling and breathing hard. Each breath shot out of his nostrils as a double puff of steam, snow-white in the morning sunshine. Mr. Underhill looked up at the bright December sky and smiled wider than ever, showing snow-white teeth. Then he went down to the village.

"Morning, Mr. Underhill," said the villagers as he passed them in the narrow street between houses with conical, overhanging roofs like the fat red caps of toadstools. "Morning, morning!" he replied to each. (It was of course bad luck to wish anyone a *good* morning; a simple statement of the time of day was quite enough, in a place so permeated with Influences as Sattins Island, where a careless adjective might change the weather for a week.) All of them spoke to him, some with affection, some with affectionate disdain. He was all the little island had in the way of a wizard, and so deserved respect—but how could you respect a little fat man of fifty who waddled along with his toes turned in, breathing steam and smiling? He was no great shakes as a workman either. His fireworks were fairly elaborate but his elixirs were weak. Warts he charmed off frequently reappeared after three days; tomatoes he enchanted grew no bigger than canteloupes; and those rare times when a strange ship stopped at Sattins Harbor, Mr. Underhill always stayed under his hill—for fear, he explained, of the evil eye. He was, in other words, a wizard the way walleyed Gan was a

carpenter: by default. The villagers made do with badly-hung doors and inefficient spells, for this generation, and relieved their annoyance by treating Mr. Underhill quite familiarly, as a mere fellow-villager. They even asked him to dinner. Once he asked some of them to dinner, and served a splendid repast, with silver, crystal, damask, roast goose, sparkling Andrades '639, and plum pudding with hard sauce; but he was so nervous all through the meal that it took the joy out of it, and besides, everybody was hungry again half an hour afterward. He did not like anyone to visit his cave, not even the anteroom, beyond which in fact nobody had ever got. When he saw people approaching the hill he always came trotting out to meet them. "Let's sit out here under the pine trees!" he would say, smiling and waving towards the fir grove, or if it was raining, "Let's go have a drink at the inn, eh?" though everybody knew he drank nothing stronger than well-water.

Some of the village children, teased by that locked cave, poked and pried and made raids while Mr. Underhill was away; but the small door that led into the inner chamber was spell-shut, and it seemed for once to be an effective spell. Once a couple of boys, thinking the wizard was over on the West Shore curing Mrs. Ruuna's sick donkey, brought a crowbar and a hatchet up there, but at the first whack of the hatchet on the door there came a roar of wrath from inside, and a cloud of purple steam. Mr. Underhill had got home early. The boys fled. He did not come out, and the boys came to no harm, though they said you couldn't believe what a huge hooting howling hissing horrible bellow that little fat man could make unless you'd heard it.

His business in town this day was three dozen fresh eggs and a pound of liver; also a stop at Seacaptain Fogeno's cottage to renew the seeing-charm on the old man's eyes (quite useless when applied to a case of detached retina, but Mr. Underhill kept trying), and finally a chat with old Goody Guld, the concertina-maker's widow.

Mr. Underhill's friends were mostly old people. He was timid with
the strong young men of the village, and the girls were shy of
him. "He makes me nervous, he smiles so much," they all said,
pouting, twisting silky ringlets round a finger. "Nervous" was a
newfangled word, and their mothers all replied grimly, "Nervous
my foot, silliness is the word for it. Mr. Underhill is a very respect-
able wizard!"

After leaving Goody Guld, Mr. Underhill passed by the school,
which was being held this day out on the common. Since no one
on Sattins Island was literate, there were no books to learn to read
from and no desks to carve initials on and no blackboards to erase,
and in fact no schoolhouse. On rainy days the children met in the
loft of the Communal Barn, and got hay in their pants; on sunny
days the schoolteacher, Palani, took them anywhere she felt like.
Today, surrounded by thirty interested children under twelve and
forty uninterested sheep under five, she was teaching an important
item on the curriculum: the Rules of Names. Mr. Underhill, smiling
shyly, paused to listen and watch. Palani, a plump, pretty girl of
twenty, made a charming picture there in the wintry sunlight, sheep
and children around her, a leafless oak above her, and behind her
the dunes and sea and clear, pale sky. She spoke earnestly, her
face flushed pink by wind and words. "Now you know the Rules
of Names already, children. There are two, and they're the same
on every island in the world. What's one of them?"

"It ain't polite to ask anybody what his name is," shouted a fat,
quick boy, interrupted by a little girl shrieking, "You can't never
tell your own name to nobody my ma says!"

"Yes, Suba. Yes, Popi dear, don't screech. That's right. You never
ask anybody his name. You never tell your own. Now think about
that a minute and then tell me why we call our wizard Mr. Under-
hill." She smiled across the curly heads and the woolly backs at
Mr. Underhill, who beamed, and nervously clutched his sack of
eggs.

" 'Cause he lives under a hill!" said half the children.

"But is it his truename?"

"No!" said the fat boy, echoed by little Popi shrieking, "No!"

"How do you know it's not?"

" 'Cause he came here all alone and so there wasn't anybody knew his truename so they couldn't tell us, and *he* couldn't— "

"Very good, Suba. Popi, don't shout. That's right. Even a wizard can't tell his truename. When you children are through school and go through the Passage, you'll leave your childnames behind and keep only your truenames, which you must never ask for and never give away. Why is that the rule?"

The children were silent. The sheep bleated gently. Mr. Underhill answered the question: "Because the name is the thing," he said in his shy, soft, husky voice, "and the truename is the true thing. To speak the name is to control the thing. Am I right, Schoolmistress?"

She smiled and curtseyed, evidently a little embarrassed by his participation. And he trotted off towards his hill, clutching his eggs to his bosom. Somehow the minute spent watching Palani and the children had made him very hungry. He locked his inner door behind him with a hasty incantation, but there must have been a leak or two in the spell, for soon the bare anteroom of the cave was rich with the smell of frying eggs and sizzling liver.

The wind that day was light and fresh out of the west, and on it at noon a little boat came skimming the bright waves into Sattins Harbor. Even as it rounded the point a sharp-eyed boy spotted it, and knowing, like every child on the island, every sail and spar of the forty boats of the fishing fleet, he ran down the street calling out, "A foreign boat, a foreign boat!" Very seldom was the lonely isle visited by a boat from some equally lonely isle of the East Reach, or an adventurous trader from the Archipelago. By the time the boat was at the pier half the village was there to greet it, and fishermen were following it homewards, and cowherds and clam-

diggers and herb-hunters were puffing up and down all the rocky hills, heading towards the harbor.

But Mr. Underhill's door stayed shut.

There was only one man aboard the boat. Old Seacaptain Fogeno, when they told him that, drew down a bristle of white brows over his unseeing eyes. "There's only one kind of man," he said, "that sails the Outer Reach alone. A wizard, or a warlock, or a Mage . . ."

So the villagers were breathless hoping to see for once in their lives a Mage, one of the mighty White Magicians of the rich, towered, crowded inner islands of the Archipelago. They were disappointed, for the voyager was quite young, a handsome black-bearded fellow who hailed them cheerfully from his boat, and leaped ashore like any sailor glad to have made port. He introduced himself at once as a sea-peddlar. But when they told Seacaptain Fogeno that he carried an oaken walking-stick around with him, the old man nodded. "Two wizards in one town," he said. "Bad!" And his mouth snapped shut like an old carp's.

As the stranger could not give them his name, they gave him one right away: Blackbeard. And they gave him plenty of attention. He had a small mixed cargo of cloth and sandals and piswi feathers for trimming cloaks and cheap incense and levity stones and fine herbs and great glass beads from Venway—the usual peddlar's lot. Everyone on Sattins Island came to look, to chat with the voyager, and perhaps to buy something—"Just to remember him by!" cackled Goody Guld, who like all the women and girls of the village was smitten with Blackbeard's bold good looks. All the boys hung round him too, to hear him tell of his voyages to far, strange islands of the Reach or describe the great rich islands of the Archipelago, the Inner Lanes, the roadsteads white with ships, and the golden roofs of Havnor. The men willingly listened to his tales; but some of them wondered why a trader should sail alone, and kept their eyes thoughtfully upon his oaken staff.

But all this time Mr. Underhill stayed under his hill.

"This is the first island I've ever seen that had no wizard," said Blackbeard one evening to Goody Guld, who had invited him and her nephew and Palani in for a cup of rushwash tea. "What do you do when you get a toothache, or the cow goes dry?"

"Why, we've got Mr. Underhill!" said the old woman.

"For what that's worth," muttered her nephew Birt, and then blushed purple and spilled his tea. Birt was a fisherman, a large, brave, wordless young man. He loved the schoolmistress, but the nearest he had come to telling her of his love was to give baskets of fresh mackerel to her father's cook.

"Oh, you do have a wizard?" Blackbeard asked. "Is he invisible?"

"No, he's just very shy," said Palani. "You've only been here a week, you know, and we see so few strangers here. . . ." She also blushed a little, but did not spill her tea.

Blackbeard smiled at her. "He's a good Sattinsman, then, eh?"

"No," said Goody Guld, "no more than you are. Another cup, nevvy? keep it in the cup this time. No, my dear, he came in a little bit of a boat, four years ago was it? just a day after the end of the shad run, I recall, for they was taking up the nets over in East Creek, and Pondi Cowherd broke his leg that very morning— five years ago it must be. No, four. No, five it is, 'twas the year the garlic didn't sprout. So he sails in on a bit of a sloop loaded full up with great chests and boxes and says to Seacaptain Fogeno, who wasn't blind then, though old enough goodness knows to be blind twice over, 'I hear tell,' he says, 'you've got no wizard nor warlock at all, might you be wanting one?' 'Indeed, if the magic's white!' says the Captain, and before you could say cuttlefish Mr. Underhill had settled down in the cave under the hill and was charming the mange off Goody Beltow's cat. Though the fur grew in grey, and 'twas an orange cat. Queer-looking thing it was after that. It died last winter in the cold spell. Goody Beltow took on so at that cat's

death, poor thing, worse than when her man was drowned on the Long Banks, the year of the long herring-runs, when nevvy Birt here was but a babe in petticoats." Here Birt spilled his tea again, and Blackbeard grinned, but Goody Guld proceeded undismayed, and talked on till nightfall.

Next day Blackbeard was down at the pier, seeing after the sprung board in his boat which he seemed to take a long time fixing, and as usual drawing the taciturn Sattinsmen into talk. "Now which of these is your wizard's craft?" he asked. "Or has he got one of those the Mages fold up into a walnut shell when they're not using it?"

"Nay," said a stolid fisherman. "She's oop in his cave, under hill."

"He carried the boat he came in up to his cave?"

"Aye. Clear oop. I helped. Heavier as lead she was. Full oop with great boxes, and they full oop with books o' spells, he says. Heavier as lead she was." And the stolid fisherman turned his back, sighing stolidly. Goody Guld's nephew, mending a net nearby, looked up from his work and asked with equal stolidity, "Would ye like to meet Mr. Underhill, maybe?"

Blackbeard returned Birt's look. Clever black eyes met candid blue ones for a long moment; then Blackbeard smiled and said, "Yes. Will you take me up to the hill, Birt?"

"Aye, when I'm done with this," said the fisherman. And when the net was mended, he and the Archipelagan set off up the village street towards the high green hill above it. But as they crossed the common Blackbeard said, "Hold on a while, friend Birt. I have a tale to tell you, before we meet your wizard."

"Tell away," says Birt, sitting down in the shade of a live-oak.

"It's a story that started a hundred years ago, and isn't finished yet—though it soon will be, very soon. . . . In the very heart of the Archipelago, where the islands crowd thick as flies on honey, there's

a little isle called Pendor. The sealords of Pendor were mighty men, in the old days of war before the League. Loot and ransom and tribute came pouring into Pendor, and they gathered a great treasure there, long ago. Then from somewhere away out in the West Reach, where dragons breed on the lava isles, came one day a very mighty dragon. Not one of those overgrown lizards most of you Outer Reach folk call dragons, but a big, black, winged, wise, cunning monster, full of strength and subtlety, and like all dragons loving gold and precious stones above all things. He killed the Sealord and his soldiers, and the people of Pendor fled in their ships by night. They all fled away and left the dragon coiled up in Pendor Towers. And there he stayed for a hundred years, dragging his scaly belly over the emeralds and sapphires and coins of gold, coming forth only once in a year or two when he must eat. He'd raid nearby islands for his food. You know what dragons eat?"

Birt nodded and said in a whisper, "Maidens."

"Right," said Blackbeard. "Well, that couldn't be endured forever, nor the thought of him sitting on all that treasure. So after the League grew strong, and the Archipelago wasn't so busy with wars and piracy, it was decided to attack Pendor, drive out the dragon, and get the gold and jewels for the treasury of the League. They're forever wanting money, the League is. So a huge fleet gathered from fifty islands, and seven Mages stood in the prows of the seven strongest ships, and they sailed towards Pendor. . . . They got there. They landed. Nothing stirred. The houses all stood empty, the dishes on the tables full of a hundred years' dust. The bones of the old Sealord and his men lay about in the castle courts and on the stairs. And the Tower rooms reeked of dragon. But there was no dragon. And no treasure, not a diamond the size of a poppyseed, not a single silver bead . . . Knowing that he couldn't stand up to seven Mages, the dragon had skipped out. They tracked him, and found he'd flown to a deserted island up north called

Udrath; they followed his trail there, and what did they find? Bones again. His bones—the dragon's. But no treasure. A wizard, some unknown wizard from somewhere, must have met him single-handed, and defeated him—and then made off with the treasure, right under the League's nose!"

The fisherman listened, attentive and expressionless.

"Now that must have been a powerful wizard and a clever one, first to kill a dragon, and second to get off without leaving a trace. The lords and Mages of the Archipelago couldn't track him at all, neither where he'd come from nor where he'd made off to. They were about to give up. That was last spring; I'd been off on a three-year voyage up in the North Reach, and got back about that time. And they asked me to help them find the unknown wizard. That was clever of them. Because I'm not only a wizard myself, as I think some of the oafs here have guessed, but I am also a descendant of the Lords of Pendor. That treasure is mine. It's mine, and knows that it's mine. Those fools of the League couldn't find it, because it's not theirs. It belongs to the House of Pendor, and the great emerald, the star of the hoard, Inalkil the Greenstone, knows its master. Behold!" Blackbeard raised his oaken staff and cried aloud, "Inalkil!" The tip of the staff began to glow green, a fiery green radiance, a dazzling haze the color of April grass, and at the same moment the staff tipped in the wizard's hand, leaning, slanting till it pointed straight at the side of the hill above them.

"It wasn't so bright a glow, far away in Havnor," Blackbeard murmured, "but the staff pointed true. Inalkil answered when I called. The jewel knows its master. And I know the thief, and I shall conquer him. He's a mighty wizard, who could overcome a dragon. But I am mightier. Do you want to know why, oaf? Because I know his name!"

As Blackbeard's tone got more arrogant, Birt had looked duller

and duller, blanker and blanker; but at this he gave a twitch, shut his mouth, and stared at the Archipelagan. "How did you . . . learn it?" he asked very slowly.

Blackbeard grinned, and did not answer.

"Black magic?"

"How else?"

Birt looked pale, and said nothing.

"I am the Sealord of Pendor, oaf, and I will have the gold my fathers won, and the jewels my mothers wore, and the Greenstone! For they are mine. —Now, you can tell your village boobies the whole story after I have defeated this wizard and gone. Wait here. Or you can come and watch, if you're not afraid. You'll never get the chance again to see a great wizard in all his power." Blackbeard turned, and without a backward glance strode off up the hill towards the entrance to the cave.

Very slowly, Birt followed. A good distance from the cave he stopped, sat down under a hawthorn tree, and watched. The Archipelagan had stopped; a stiff, dark figure alone on the green swell of the hill before the gaping cave-mouth, he stood perfectly still. All at once he swung his staff up over his head, and the emerald radiance shone about him as he shouted, "Thief, thief of the Hoard of Pendor, come forth!"

There was a crash, as of dropped crockery, from inside the cave, and a lot of dust came spewing out. Scared, Birt ducked. When he looked again he saw Blackbeard still standing motionless, and at the mouth of the cave, dusty and dishevelled, stood Mr. Underhill. He looked small and pitiful, with his toes turned in as usual, and his little bowlegs in black tights, and no staff—he never had had one, Birt suddenly thought. Mr. Underhill spoke. "Who are you?" he said in his husky little voice.

"I am the Sealord of Pendor, thief, come to claim my treasure!"

At that, Mr. Underhill slowly turned pink, as he always did when people were rude to him. But he then turned something else. He turned yellow. His hair bristled out, he gave a coughing roar—and was a yellow lion leaping down the hill at Blackbeard, white fangs gleaming.

But Blackbeard no longer stood there. A gigantic tiger, color of night and lightning, bounded to meet the lion. . . .

The lion was gone. Below the cave all of a sudden stood a high grove of trees, black in the winter sunshine. The tiger, checking himself in mid-leap just before he entered the shadow of the trees, caught fire in the air, became a tongue of flame lashing out at the dry black branches. . . .

But where the trees had stood a sudden cataract leaped from the hillside, an arch of silvery crashing water, thundering down upon the fire. But the fire was gone. . . .

For just a moment before the fisherman's staring eyes two hills rose—the green one he knew, and a new one, a bare, brown hillock ready to drink up the rushing waterfall. That passed so quickly it made Birt blink, and after blinking he blinked again, and moaned, for what he saw now was a great deal worse. Where the cataract had been there hovered a dragon. Black wings darkened all the hill, steel claws reached groping, and from the dark, scaly, gaping lips fire and steam shot out.

Beneath the monstrous creature stood Blackbeard, laughing.

"Take any shape you please, little Mr. Underhill!" he taunted. "I can match you. But the game grows tiresome. I want to look upon my treasure, upon Inalkil. Now, big dragon, little wizard, take your true shape. I command you by the power of your true name—Yevaud!"

Birt could not move at all, not even to blink. He cowered, staring whether he would or not. He saw the black dragon hang there in

the air above Blackbeard. He saw the fire lick like many tongues from the scaly mouth, the steam jet from the red nostrils. He saw Blackbeard's face grow white, white as chalk, and the beard-fringed lips trembling.

"Your name is Yevaud!"

"Yes," said a great, husky, hissing voice. "My truename is Yevaud, and my true shape is this shape."

"But the dragon was killed—they found dragon-bones on Udrath Island—"

"That was another dragon," said the dragon, and then stooped like a hawk, talons outstretched. And Birt shut his eyes.

When he opened them the sky was clear, the hillside empty, except for a reddish-blackish trampled spot, and a few talon-marks in the grass.

Birt the fisherman got to his feet and ran. He ran across the common, scattering sheep to right and left, and straight down the village street to Palani's father's house. Palani was out in the garden weeding the nasturtiums. "Come with me!" Birt gasped. She stared. He grabbed her wrist and dragged her with him. She screeched a little, but did not resist. He ran with her straight to the pier, pushed her into his fishing-sloop the *Queenie,* untied the painter, took up the oars and set off rowing like a demon. The last that Sattins Island saw of him and Palani was the *Queenie*'s sail vanishing in the direction of the nearest island westward.

The villagers thought they would never stop talking about it, how Goody Guld's nephew Birt had lost his mind and sailed off with the schoolmistress on the very same day that the peddlar Blackbeard disappeared without a trace, leaving all his feathers and beads behind. But they did stop talking about it, three days later. They had other things to talk about, when Mr. Underhill finally came out of his cave.

Mr. Underhill had decided that since his truename was no longer a secret, he might as well drop his disguise. Walking was a lot harder than flying, and besides, it was a long, long time since he had had a real meal.

WINTER'S KING

When I wrote this story, a year before I began the novel The Left
Hand of Darkness, I did not know that the inhabitants of the planet
Winter or Gethen were androgynes. By the time the story came out
in print, I did, but too late to emend such usages as "son," "mother,"
and so on.

Many feminists have been grieved or aggrieved by The Left
Hand of Darkness because the androgynes in it are called "he"
throughout. In the third person singular, the English generic pro-
noun is the same as the masculine pronoun. A fact worth reflecting
upon. And it's a trap, with no way out, because the exclusion of
the feminine (she) and the neuter (it) from the generic/masculine
(he) makes the use of either of them more specific, more unjust, as
it were, than the use of "he." And I find made-up pronouns, "te"
and "heshe" and so on, dreary and annoying.

In revising the story for this edition, I saw a chance to redress
that injustice slightly. In this version, I use the feminine pronoun
for all Gethenians—while preserving certain masculine titles such
as King and Lord, just to remind one of the ambiguity. This may
drive some nonfeminists mad, but that's only fair.

The androgyny of the characters has little to do with the events
of this story, but the pronoun change does make it clear that the
central, paradoxical relationship of parent and child is not, as it may
have seemed in the other version, a kind of reverse Oedipus twist,

*but something less familiar and more ambiguous. Evidently my
unconscious mind knew about the Gethenians long before it saw
fit to inform me. It's always doing things like that.*

When whirlpools appear in the onward run of time and history
seems to swirl around a snag, as in the curious matter of the Suc-
cession of Karhide, then pictures come in handy: snapshots, which
may be taken up and matched to compare the parent to the child,
the young king to the old, and which may also be rearranged and
shuffled till the years run straight. For despite the tricks played by
instantaneous interstellar communication and just-sub-lightspeed
interstellar travel, time (as the Plenipotentiary Axt remarked) does
not reverse itself; nor is death mocked.

Thus, although the best-known picture is that dark image of a
young king standing above an old king who lies dead in a corridor
lit only by mirror-reflections of a burning city, set it aside a while.
Look first at the young king, a nation's pride, as bright and fortu-
nate a soul as ever lived to the age of twenty-two; but when this
picture was taken the young king had her back against a wall. She
was filthy, she was trembling, and her face was blank and mad,
for she had lost that minimal confidence in the world which is
called sanity. Inside her head she repeated, as she had been repeat-
ing for hours or years, over and over, "I will abdicate. I will abdi-
cate. I will abdicate." Inside her eyes she saw the red-walled rooms
of the Palace, the towers and streets of Erhenrang in falling snow,
the lovely plains of the West Fall, the white summits of the Kargav,
and she renounced them all, her kingdom. "I will abdicate," she
said not aloud and then, aloud, screamed as once again the person
dressed in red and white approached her saying, "Majesty! A plot
against your life has been discovered in the Artisan School," and
the humming noise began, softly. She hid her head in her arms

and whispered, "Stop it, please stop it," but the humming whine grew higher and louder and nearer, relentless, until it was so high and loud that it entered her flesh, tore the nerves from their channels and made her bones dance and jangle, hopping to its tune. She hopped and twitched, bare bones strung on thin white threads, and wept dry tears, and shouted, "Have them— Have them— They must— Executed— Stopped— Stop!"

It stopped.

She fell in a clattering, chattering heap to the floor. What floor? Not red tiles, not parquetry, not urine-stained cement, but the wood floor of the room in the tower, the little tower bedroom where she was safe, safe from her ogre parent, the cold, mad, uncaring king, safe to play cat's cradle with Piry and to sit by the fireside on Borhub's warm lap, as warm and deep as sleep. But there was no hiding, no safety, no sleep. The person dressed in black had come even here and had hold of her head, lifted it up, lifted on thin white strings the eyelids she tried to close.

"Who am I?"

The blank, black mask stared down. The young king struggled, sobbing, because now the suffocation would begin: she would not be able to breathe until she said the name, the right name— "Gerer!"—She could breathe. She was allowed to breathe. She had recognized the black one in time.

"Who am I?" said a different voice, gently, and the young king groped for that strong presence that always brought her sleep, truce, solace. "Rebade," she whispered, "tell me what to do. . . ."

"Sleep."

She obeyed. A deep sleep, and dreamless, for it was real. Dreams came at waking, now. Unreal, the horrible dry red light of sunset burned her eyes open and she stood, once more, on the Palace balcony looking down at fifty thousand black pits opening and shutting. From the pits came a paroxysmic gush of sound, a shrill,

rhythmic eructation: her name. Her name was roared in her ears as a taunt, a jeer. She beat her hands on the narrow brass railing and shouted at them, "I will silence you!" She could not hear her voice, only their voice, the pestilent mouths of the mob that hated her, screaming her name. "Come away, my king," said the one gentle voice, and Rebade drew her away from the balcony into the vast, red-walled quiet of the Hall of Audience. The screaming ceased with a click. Rebade's expression was as always composed, compassionate. "What will you do now?" she said in her gentle voice.

"I will— I will abdicate— "

"No," Rebade said calmly. "That is not right. What will you do now?"

The young king stood silent, shaking. Rebade helped her sit down on the iron cot, for the walls had darkened as they often did and drawn in all about her to a little cell. "You will call . . ."

"Call up the Erhenrang Guard. Have them shoot into the crowd. Shoot to kill. They must be taught a lesson." The young king spoke rapidly and distinctly in a loud, high voice. Rebade said, "Very good, my lord, a wise decision! Right. We shall come out all right. You are doing right. Trust me."

"I do. I trust you. Get me out of here," the young king whispered, seizing Rebade's arm: but her friend frowned. That was not right. She had driven Rebade and hope away again. Rebade was leaving now, calm and regretful, though the young king begged her to stop, to come back, for the noise was softly beginning again, the whining hum that tore the mind to pieces, and already the person in red and white was approaching across a red, interminable floor. "Majesty! A plot against your life has been discovered in the Artisan School— "

Down Old Harbor Street to the water's edge the street lamps burned cavernously bright. Guard Pepenerer on her rounds glanced

down that slanting vault of light expecting nothing, and saw something staggering up it towards her. Pepenerer did not believe in porngropes, but she saw a porngrope, sea-beslimed, staggering on thin webbed feet, gasping dry air, whimpering.... Old sailors' tales slid out of Pepenerer's mind and she saw a drunk or a maniac or a victim staggering between the dank grey warehouse walls. "Now then! Hold on there!" she bellowed, on the run. The drunk, half naked and wild-eyed, let out a yell of terror and tried to dodge away, slipped on the frost-slick stones of the street and pitched down sprawling. Pepenerer got out her gun and delivered a half-second of stun, just to keep the drunk quiet; then squatted down by her, wound up her radio and called the West Ward for a car.

Both the arms, sprawled out limp and meek on the cold cobbles, were blotched with injection marks. Not drunk; drugged. Pepenerer sniffed, but got no resinous scent of orgrevy. She had been drugged, then; thieves, or a ritual clan-revenge. Thieves would not have left the gold ring on the forefinger, a massive thing, carved, almost as wide as the fingerjoint. Pepenerer crouched forward to look at it. Then she turned her head and looked at the beaten, blank face in profile against the paving-stones, hard lit by the glare of the street lamps. She took a new quarter-crown piece out of her pouch and looked at the left profile stamped on the bright tin, then back at the right profile stamped in light and shadow and cold stone. Then, hearing the purr of the electric car turning down from the Longway into Old Harbor Street, she stuck the coin back in her pouch, muttering to herself, "Damn fool."

King Argaven was off hunting in the mountains, anyhow, and had been for a couple of weeks; it had been in all the bulletins.

"You see," said Hoge the physician, "we can assume that she was mindformed; but that gives us almost nothing to go on. There are too many expert mindformers in Karhide, and in Orgoreyn for that matter. Not criminals whom the police might have a lead on, but

respectable mentalists or physicians. To whom the drugs are legally available. As for getting anything from her, if they had any skill at all they will have blocked everything they did to rational access. All clues will be buried, the trigger-suggestions hidden, and we simply cannot guess what questions to ask. There is no way, short of brain-destruction, of going through everything in her mind; and even under hypnosis and deep drugging there would be no way now to distinguish implanted ideas or emotions from her own autonomous ones. Perhaps the Aliens could do something, though I doubt their mindscience is all they boast of; at any rate it's out of reach. We have only one real hope."

"Which is?" Lord Gerer asked, stolidly.

"The king is quick and resolute. At the beginning, before they broke her, she may have known what they were doing to her, and so set up some block or resistance, left herself some escape route...."

Hoge's low voice lost confidence as she spoke, and trailed off in the silence of the high, red, dusky room. She drew no response from old Gerer who stood, black-clad, before the fire.

The temperature of that room in the King's Palace of Erhenrang was 12° C where Lord Gerer stood, and 5° midway between the two big fireplaces; outside it was snowing lightly, a mild day only a few degrees below freezing. Spring had come to Winter. The fires at either end of the room roared red and gold, devouring thigh-thick logs. Magnificence, a harsh luxury, a quick splendor; fireplaces, fireworks, lightning, meteors, volcanoes; such things satisfied the people of Karhide on the world called Winter. But, except in Arctic colonies above the 35th parallel, they had never installed central heating in any building in the many centuries of their Age of Technology. Comfort was allowed to come to them rare, welcome, unsought: a gift, like joy.

The king's personal servant, sitting by the bed, turned towards the physician and the Lord Councillor, though she did not speak.

Both at once crossed the room. The broad, hard bed, high on gilt pillars, heavy with a finery of red cloaks and coverlets, bore up the king's body almost level with their eyes. To Gerer it appeared a ship breasting, motionless, a swift vast flood of darkness, carrying the young king into shadows, terrors, years. Then with a terror of her own the old councillor saw that Argaven's eyes were open, staring out a half-curtained window at the stars.

Gerer feared lunacy; idiocy; she did not know what she feared. Hoge had warned her: "The king will not behave 'normally,' Lord Gerer. She has suffered thirteen days of torment, intimidation, exhaustion, and mindhandling. There may be brain damage, there will certainly be side- and after-effects of drugs." Neither fear nor warning parried the shock. Argaven's bright, weary eyes turned to Gerer and paused on her blankly a moment; then saw her. And Gerer, though she could not see the black mask reflected, saw the hate, the horror, saw her young king, infinitely beloved, gasping in imbecile terror and struggling with the servant, with Hoge, with her own weakness in the effort to get away, to get away from Gerer.

Standing in the cold midst of the room where the prowlike head of the bedstead hid her from the king, Gerer heard them pacify Argaven and settle her down again. Argaven's voice sounded reedy, childishly plaintive. So the Old King, Emran, had spoken in her last madness with a child's voice. Then silence, and the burning of the two great fires.

Korgry, the king's bodyservant, yawned and rubbed her eyes. Hoge measured something from a vial into a hypodermic. Gerer stood in despair. My child, my king, what have they done to you? So great a trust, so fair a promise, lost, lost. . . . So the one who looked like a lump of half-carved black rock, a heavy, prudent, rude old courtier, grieved and was passion-racked, her love and service of the young king being the world's one worth to her.

Argaven spoke aloud: "My child—"

Gerer winced, feeling the words torn out of her own mind; but Hoge, untroubled by love, comprehended and said softly to Argaven, "Prince Emran is well, my liege. She is with her attendants at Warrever Castle. We are in constant communication. All is well there."

Gerer heard the king's harsh breathing, and came somewhat closer to the bed, though out of sight still behind the high headboard.

"Have I been sick?"

"You are not well yet," the physician said, bland.

"Where—"

"Your own room, in the Palace, in Erhenrang."

But Gerer, coming a step closer, though not in view of the king, said, "We do not know where you have been."

Hoge's smooth face creased with a frown, though, physician as she was and so in her way ruler of them all, she dared not direct the frown at the Lord Councillor. Gerer's voice did not seem to trouble the king, who asked another question or two, sane and brief, and then lay quiet. Presently the servant Korgry, who had sat with her ever since she had been brought into the Palace (last night, in secret, by side doors, like a shameful suicide of the last reign, but all in reverse), Korgry committed lèse-majesté: huddled forward on her high stool, she let her head droop on the side of the bed, and slept. The guard at the door yielded place to a new guard, in whispers. Officials came and received a fresh bulletin for public release on the state of the king's health, in whispers. Stricken by symptoms of fever while vacationing in the High Kargav, the king had been rushed to Erhenrang, and was now responding satisfactorily to treatment, etc. Physician Hoge rem ir Hogeremme at the Palace has released the following statement, etc., etc. "May the Wheel turn for our king," people in village houses said solemnly as they lit the fire on the altarhearth, to which elders sitting near the fire remarked, "It comes of her roving around the city at night

and climbing mountains, fool tricks like that," but they kept the radio on to catch the next bulletin. A very great number of people had come and gone and loitered and chatted this day in the square before the Palace, watching those who went in and out, watching the vacant balcony; there were still several hundred down there, standing around patiently in the snow. Argaven XVII was loved in her domain. After the dull brutality of King Emran's reign that had ended in the shadow of madness and the country's bankruptcy, she had come: sudden, gallant, young, changing everything; sane and shrewd, yet magnanimous. She had the fire, the splendor that suited her people. She was the force and center of a new age: one born, for once, king of the right kingdom.

"Gerer."

It was the king's voice, and Gerer hastened stiffly through the hot and cold of the great room, the firelight and dark.

Argaven was sitting up. Her arms shook and the breath caught in her throat; her eyes burned across the dark air at Gerer. By her left hand, which bore the Sign-Ring of the Harge dynasty, lay the sleeping face of the servant, derelict, serene. "Gerer," the king said with effort and clarity, "summon the Council. Tell them, I will abdicate."

So crude, so simple? All the drugs, the terrorizing, the hypnosis, parahypnosis, neurone-stimulation, synapse-pairing, spotshock that Hoge had described, for this blunt result? But reasoning must wait. They must temporize. "My liege, when your strength returns—"

"Now. Call the Council, Gerer!"

Then she broke, like a bowstring breaking, and stammered in a fury of fear that found no sense or strength to flesh itself in; and still her faithful servant slept beside her, deaf.

In the next picture things are going better, it appears. Here is King Argaven XVII in good health and good clothes, finishing a

large breakfast. She talks with the nearer dozen of the forty or fifty people sharing or serving the meal (singularity is a king's prerogative, but seldom privacy), and includes the rest in the largesse of her courtesy. She looks, as everyone has said, quite herself again. Perhaps she is not quite herself again, however; something is missing, a youthful serenity, a confidence, replaced by a similar but less reassuring quality, a kind of heedlessness. Out of it she rises in wit and warmth, but always subsides to it again, that darkness which absorbs her and makes her heedless: fear, pain, resolution?

Mr Mobile Axt, Ambassador Plenipotentiary to Winter from the Ekumen of the Known Worlds, who had spent the last six days on the road trying to drive an electric car faster than 50 kph from Mishnory in Orgoreyn to Erhenrang in Karhide, overslept breakfast, and so arrived in the Audience Hall prompt, but hungry. The old Chief of the Council, the king's cousin Gerer rem ir Verhen, met the Alien at the door of the great hall and greeted him with the polysyllabic politeness of Karhide. The Plenipotentiary responded as best he could, discerning beneath the eloquence Gerer's desire to tell him something.

"I am told the king is perfectly recovered," he said, "and I heartily hope this is true."

"It is not," the old Councillor said, her voice suddenly blunt and toneless. "Mr Axt, I tell you this trusting your confidence; there are not ten others in Karhide who know the truth. She is not recovered. She was not sick."

Axt nodded. There had of course been rumors.

"She will go alone in the city sometimes, at night, in common clothes, walking, talking with strangers. The pressures of kingship . . . She is very young." Gerer paused a moment, struggling with some suppressed emotion. "One night six weeks ago, she did not come back. A message was delivered to me and the Second Lord,

at dawn. If we announced her disappearance, she would be killed; if we waited a half-month in silence she would be restored unhurt. We kept silent, lied to the Council, sent out false news. On the thirteenth night she was found wandering in the city. She had been drugged and mindformed. By which enemy or faction we do not yet know. We must work in utter secrecy; we cannot wreck the people's confidence in her, her own confidence in herself. It is hard: she remembers nothing. But what they did is plain. They broke her will and bent her mind all to one thing. She believes she must abdicate the throne."

The voice remained low and flat; the eyes betrayed anguish. And the Plenipotentiary turning suddenly saw the reflection of that anguish in the eyes of the young king.

"Holding my audience, cousin?"

Argaven smiled but there was a knife in it. The old Councillor excused herself stolidly, bowed, left, a patient ungainly figure diminishing down a long corridor.

Argaven stretched out both hands to the Plenipotentiary in the greeting of equals, for in Karhide the Ekumen was recognized as a sister kingdom, though not a living soul had seen it. But her words were not the polite discourse that Axt expected. All she said, and fiercely, was, "At last!"

"I left as soon as I received your message. The roads are still icy in East Orgoreyn and the West Fall, I couldn't make very good time. But I was very glad to come. Glad to leave, too." Axt smiled saying this, for he and the young king enjoyed each other's candor. What Argaven's welcome implied, he waited to see, watching, with some exhilaration, the mobile, beautiful, androgynous face.

"Orgoreyn breeds bigots as a corpse breeds worms, as one of my ancestors remarked. I'm glad you find the air fresher here in Karhide. Come this way. Gerer told you that I was kidnapped, and so forth? Yes. It was all according to the old rules. Kidnapping is a

quite formal art. If it had been one of the anti-Alien groups who
think your Ekumen intends to enslave the earth, they might have
ignored the rules; I think it was one of the old clan-factions hoping
to regain power through me, the power they had in the last reign.
But we don't know, yet. It's strange, to know that one has seen
them face to face and yet can't recognize them; who knows but
that I see those faces daily? Well, no profit in such notions. They
wiped out all their tracks. I am sure only of one thing. *They* did not
tell me that I must abdicate."

She and the Plenipotentiary were walking side by side up the
long, immensely high room toward the dais and chairs at the far
end. The windows were little more than slits, as usual on this cold
world; fulvous strips of sunlight fell from them diagonally to the
red-paved floor, dusk and dazzle in Axt's eyes. He looked up at the
young king's face in that somber, shifting radiance. "Who then?"

"I did."

"When, my lord, and why?"

"When they had me, when they were remaking me to fit their
mold and play their game. Why? So that I can't fit their mold and
play their game! Listen, Lord Axt, if they wanted me dead they'd
have killed me. They want me alive, to govern, to be king. As such
I am to follow the orders imprinted in my brain, gain their ends
for them. I am their tool, their machine, waiting for the switch
to be thrown. The only way to prevent that, is to . . . discard the
machine."

Axt was quick of understanding, that being a minimal qualifica-
tion of a Mobile of the Ekumen; besides, the manners and affairs
of Karhide, the stresses and seditions of that lively kingdom, were
well known to him. Remote though Winter was, both in space
and in the physiology of its inhabitants, from the rest of the human
race, yet its dominant nation, Karhide, had proved a loyal member
of the Ekumen. Axt's reports were discussed in the central councils

of the Ekumen eighty lightyears away; the equilibrium of the Whole rests in all its parts. Axt said, as they sat down in the great stiff chairs on the dais before the fire, "But they need not even throw switches, if you abdicate."

"Leaving my child as heir, and a Regent of my own choice?"

"Perhaps," Axt said with caution, "they chose your Regent for you."

The king frowned. "I think not," she said.

"Whom had you thought of naming?"

There was a long pause. Axt saw the muscles of Argaven's throat working as she struggled to get a word, a name, up past a block, a harsh constriction; at last she said, in a forced, strangled whisper, "Gerer."

Axt nodded, startled. Gerer had served as Regent for a year after Emran's death and before Argaven's accession; he knew her honesty and her utter devotion to the young king. "Gerer serves no faction!" he said.

Argaven shook her head. She looked exhausted. After a while she said, "Could the science of your people undo what was done to me, Lord Axt?"

"Possibly. In the Institute on Ollul. But if I sent for a specialist tonight, he'd get here twenty-four years from now. . . . You're sure, then, that your decision to abdicate was—" But a servant, coming in a side door behind them, set a small table by the Plenipotentiary's chair and loaded it with fruit, sliced bread-apple, a silver tankard of ale. Argaven had noticed that her guest had missed his breakfast. Though the fare on Winter, mostly vegetable and that mostly uncooked, was dull stuff to Axt's taste, he set to gratefully; and as serious talk was unseemly over food, Argaven shifted to generalities. "Once you said, Lord Axt, that different as I am from you, and different as my people are from yours, yet we are blood kin. Was that a moral fact, or a material one?"

Axt smiled at the very Karhidish distinction. "Both, my lord. As far as we know, which is a tiny corner of dusty space under the rafters of the Universe, all the people we've run into are in fact human. But the kinship goes back a million years and more, to the Fore-Eras of Hain. The ancient Hainish settled a hundred worlds."

"We call the time before my dynasty ruled Karhide 'ancient.' Seven hundred years ago!"

"So we call the Age of the Enemy 'ancient,' and that was less than six hundred years ago. Time stretches and shrinks; changes with the eye, with the age, with the star; does all except reverse itself—or repeat."

"The dream of the Ekumen, then, is to restore that truly ancient commonalty; to regather all the peoples of all the worlds at one hearth?"

Axt nodded, chewing bread-apple. "To weave some harmony among them, at least. Life loves to know itself, out to its furthest limits; to embrace complexity is its delight. Our difference is our beauty. All these worlds and the various forms and ways of the minds and lives and bodies on them—together they would make a splendid harmony."

"No harmony endures," said the young king.

"None has ever been achieved," said the Plenipotentiary. "The pleasure is in trying." He drained his tankard, wiped his fingers on the woven-grass napkin.

"That was my pleasure as king," said Argaven. "It is over."

"Should— "

"It is finished. Believe me. I will keep you here, Lord Axt, until you believe me. I need your help. You are the piece the game-players forgot about! You must help me. I cannot abdicate against the will of the Council. They will refuse my abdication, force me to rule, and if I rule, I serve my enemies! If you will not help me, I will have to kill myself." She spoke quite evenly and reasonably; but Axt knew

what even the mention of suicide, the ultimately contemptible act, cost a Karhider.

"One way or the other," said the young king.

The Plenipotentiary pulled his heavy cloak closer round him; he was cold. He had been cold for seven years, here. "My lord," he said, "I am an alien on your world, with a handful of aides, and a little device with which I can converse with other aliens on distant worlds. I represent power, of course, but I have none. How can I help you?"

"You have a ship on Horden Island."

"Ah. I was afraid of that," said the Plenipotentiary, sighing. "Lord Argaven, that ship is set for Ollul, twenty-four lightyears away. Do you know what that means?"

"My escape from my time, in which I have become an instrument of evil."

"There is no escape," said Axt, with sudden intensity, "No, my lord. Forgive me. It is impossible. I could not consent— "

Icy rain of spring rattled on the stones of the tower, wind whined at the angles and finials of the roof. The room was quiet, shadowy. One small shielded light burned by the door. The nurse lay snoring mildly in the bed, the baby was head down, rump up in the crib. Argaven stood beside the crib. She looked around the room, or rather saw it, knew it wholly, without looking. She too had slept here as a little child. It had been her first kingdom. It was here that she had come to suckle her child, her first-born, had sat by the fireplace while the little mouth tugged at her breast, had hummed to the baby the songs Borhub had hummed to her. This was the center, the center of everything.

Very cautiously and gently she slipped her hand under the baby's warm, damp, downy head, and put over it a chain on which hung a massive ring carved with the token of the Lords of Harge. The

chain was far too long, and Argaven knotted it shorter, thinking that it might twist and choke the child. So allaying that small anxiety, she tried to allay the great fear and wretchedness that filled her. She stooped down till her cheek touched the baby's cheek, whispering inaudibly, "Emran, Emran, I have to leave you, I can't take you, you have to rule for me. Be good, Emran, live long, rule well, be good, Emran. . . ."

She straightened up, turned, ran from the tower room, the lost kingdom.

She knew several ways of getting out of the Palace unperceived. She took the surest, and then made for the New Harbor through the bright-lit, sleet-lashed streets of Erhenrang, alone.

Now there is no picture: no seeing her. With what eye will you watch a process that is one hundred millionth percent slower than the speed of light? She is not now a king, nor a human being; she is translated. You can scarcely call fellow-mortal one whose time passes seventy thousand times slower than yours. She is more than alone. It seems that she is not, any more than an uncommunicated thought is; that she goes nowhere, any more than a thought goes. And yet, at very nearly but never quite the speed of light, she voyages. She is the voyage. Quick as thought. She has doubled her age when she arrives, less than a day older, in the portion of space curved about a dustmote named Ollul, the fourth planet of a yellowish sun. And all this has passed in utter silence.

With noise now, and fire and meteoric dazzle enough to satisfy a Karhider's lust for splendor, the clever ship makes earthfall, settling down in flame in the precise spot it left from some fifty-five years ago. Presently, visible, unmassive, uncertain, the young king emerges from it and stands a moment in the exitway, shielding her eyes from the light of a strange, hot sun.

Axt had of course sent notice of her coming, by instantaneous

transmitter, twenty-four years ago, or seventeen hours ago, depending on how you look at it; and aides and agents of the Ekumen were on hand to greet her. Even pawns did not go unnoticed by those players of the great game, and this Gethenian was, after all, a king. One of the agents had spent a year of the twenty-four in learning Karhidish, so that Argaven could speak to someone. She spoke at once: "What news from my country?"

"Mr Mobile Axt and his successor have sent regular summaries of events, and various private messages for you; you'll find all the material in your quarters, Mr Harge. Very briefly, the regency of Lord Gerer was uneventful and benign; there was a depression in the first two years, during which your Arctic settlements were abandoned, but at present the economy is quite stable. Your heir was enthroned at eighteen, and has ruled now for seven years."

"Yes. I see," said the person who had kissed that year-old heir last night.

"Whenever you see fit, Mr Harge, the specialists at our Institute over in Belxit—"

"As you wish," said Mr Harge.

They went into her mind very gently, very subtly, opening doors. For locked doors they had delicate instruments that always found the combination; and then they stood aside, and let her enter. They found the person in black, who was not Gerer, and compassionate Rebade, who was not compassionate; they stood with her on the Palace balcony, and climbed the crevasses of nightmare with her up to the room in the tower; and at last the one who was to have been first, the person in red and white, approached her saying, "Majesty! A plot against your life—" And Mr Harge screamed in abject terror, and woke up.

"Well! That was the trigger. The signal to begin tripping off the other instructions and determine the course of your phobia. An induced paranoia. Really beautifully induced, I must say. Here, drink

this, Mr Harge. No, it's just water! You might well have become a remarkably vicious ruler, increasingly obsessed by fear of plots and subversions, increasingly disaffected from your people. Not overnight, of course. That's the beauty of it. It would have taken several years for you to become a real tyrant; though they no doubt planned some boosts along the way, once Rebade wormed his way—her way—a way into your confidence. . . . Well, well, I see why Karhide is well spoken of, over at the Clearinghouse. If you'll pardon my objectivity, this kind of skill and patience is quite rare. . . ." So the doctor, the mindmender, the hairy, greyish, one-sexed person from somewhere called the Cetians, went rambling on while the patient recovered herself.

"Then I did right," said Mr Harge at last.

"You did. Abdication, suicide, or escape were the only acts of consequence which you could have committed of your own volition, freely. They counted on your moral veto on suicide, and your Council's vote on abdication. But being possessed by ambition themselves, they forgot the possibility of abnegation, and left one door open for you. A door which only a strong-minded person, if you'll pardon my literalness, could choose to go through. I really must read up on this other mindscience of yours, what do you call it, Foretelling? Thought it was some occultist trash, but quite evidently . . . Well, well, I expect they'll be wanting you to look in at the Clearinghouse soon, to discuss your future, now that we've put your past where it belongs, eh?"

"As you wish," said Mr Harge.

She talked with various people there in the Clearinghouse of the Ekumen for the West Worlds, and when they suggested that she go to school, she assented readily. For among those mild persons, whose chief quality seemed a cool, profound sadness indistinguishable from a warm, profound hilarity—among them, the ex-king of Karhide knew herself a barbarian, unlearned and unwise.

She attended Ekumenical School. She lived in barracks near the Clearinghouse in Vaxtsit City, with a couple of hundred other aliens, none of whom was either androgynous or an ex-king. Never having owned much that was hers alone, and never having had much privacy, she did not mind barracks life; nor was it so bad as she had expected to live among single-sexed people, although she found their condition of perpetual kemmer tiresome. She did not mind anything much, getting through the works and days with vigor and competence but always a certain heedlessness, as of one whose center is somewhere else. The only discomfort was the heat, the awful heat of Ollul that rose sometimes to 35° C in the blazing interminable season when no snow fell for two hundred days on end. Even when winter came at last she sweated, for it seldom got more than ten degrees below freezing outside, and the barracks were kept sweltering—she thought—though the other aliens wore heavy sweaters all the time. She slept on top of her bed, naked and thrashing, and dreamed of the snows of the Kargav, the ice in Old Harbor, the ice scumming one's ale on cool mornings in the Palace, the cold, the dear and bitter cold of Winter.

She learned a good deal. She had already learned that the Earth was, here, called Winter, and that Ollul was, here, called the Earth: one of those facts which turn the universe inside out like a sock. She learned that a meat diet causes diarrhea in the unaccustomed gut. She learned that single-sexed people, whom she tried hard not to think of as perverts, tried hard not to think of her as a pervert. She learned that when she pronounced Ollul as Orrur some people laughed. She attempted also to unlearn that she was a king. Once the School took her in hand she learned and unlearned much more. She was led, by all the machines and devices and experiences and (simplest and most demanding) words that the Ekumen had at its disposal, into an intimation of what it might be to understand the nature and history of a kingdom that was over a million years old and trillions of miles wide. When she had begun to guess the

immensity of this kingdom of humanity and the durable pain and monotonous waste of its history, she began also to see what lay beyond its borders in space and time, and among naked rocks and furnace-suns and the shining desolation that goes on and on she glimpsed the sources of hilarity and serenity, the inexhaustible springs. She learned a great many facts, numbers, myths, epics, proportions, relationships, and so forth, and saw, beyond the borders of what she had learned, the unknown again, a splendid immensity. In this augmentation of her mind and being there was great satisfaction; yet she was unsatisfied. They did not always let her go on as far as she wanted into certain fields, mathematics, Cetian physics. "You started late, Mr Harge," they said, "we have to build on the existing foundations. Besides, we want you in subjects which you can put to use."

"What use?"

They—the ethnographer Mr Mobile Gist represented Them at the moment, across a library table—looked at her sardonically. "Do you consider yourself to be of no further use, Mr Harge?"

Mr Harge, who was generally reserved, spoke with sudden fury: "I do."

"A king without a country," said Gist in his flat Terran accent, "self-exiled, believed to be dead, might feel a trifle superfluous. But then, why do you think we're bothering with you?"

"Out of kindness."

"Oh, kindness . . . However kind we are, we can give you nothing that would make you happy, you know. Except . . . Well. Waste is a pity. You were indubitably the right king for Winter, for Karhide, for the purposes of the Ekumen. You have a sense of balance. You might even have unified the planet. You certainly wouldn't have terrorized and fragmented the country, as the present king seems to be doing. What a waste! Only consider our hopes and needs, Mr Harge, and your own qualifications, before you despair of

being useful in your life. Forty or fifty more years of it you have to live, after all. . . ."

The last snapshot taken by alien sunlight: erect, in a Hainish-style cloak of grey, a handsome person of indeterminate sex stands, sweating profusely, on a green lawn beside the chief Agent of the Ekumen in the West Worlds, the Stabile, Mr Hoalans of Alb, who can meddle (if he likes) with the destinies of forty worlds.

"I can't order you to go there, Argaven," says the Stabile. "Your own conscience—"

"I gave up my kingdom to my conscience, twelve years ago. It's had its due. Enough's enough," says Argaven Harge. Then she laughs suddenly, so that the Stabile also laughs; and they part in such harmony as the Powers of the Ekumen desire between human souls.

Horden Island, off the south coast of Karhide, was given as a freehold to the Ekumen by the Kingdom of Karhide during the reign of Argaven XV. No one lived there. Yearly generations of seawalkies crawled up on the barren rocks, and laid and hatched their eggs, and raised their young, and finally led them back in long single file to the sea. But once every ten or twenty years fire ran over the rocks and the sea boiled on the shores, and if any seawalkies were on the island then they died.

When the sea had ceased to boil, the Plenipotentiary's little electric launch approached. The starship ran out a gossamer-steel gangplank to the deck of the launch, and one person started to walk up it as another one started to walk down it, so that they met in the middle, in midair, between sea and land, an ambiguous meeting.

"Ambassador Horrsed? I'm Harge," said the one from the starship, but the one from the launch was already kneeling, saying aloud, in Karhidish, "Welcome, Argaven of Karhide!"

As he straightened up the Ambassador added in a quick whisper, "You come as yourself— Explain when I can— " Behind and below him on the deck of the launch stood a sizable group of people, staring up intently at the newcomer. All were Karhiders by their looks; several were very old.

Argaven Harge stood for a minute, two minutes, three minutes, erect and perfectly motionless, though her grey cloak tugged and riffled in the cold sea wind. She looked then once at the dull sun in the west, once at the grey land north across the water, back again at the silent people grouped below her on the deck. She strode forward so suddenly that Ambassador Horrsed had to squeeze out of the way in a hurry. She went straight to one of the old people on the deck of the launch. "Are you Ker rem ir Kerheder?"

"I am."

"I knew you by the lame arm, Ker." She spoke clearly; there was no guessing what emotions she felt. "I could not know your face. After sixty years. Are there others of you I knew? I am Argaven."

They were all silent. They gazed at her.

All at once one of them, one scored and scarred with age like wood that has been through fire, stepped forward one step. "My liege, I am Bannith of the Palace Guard. You served with me when I was Drillmaster and you a child, a young child." And the grey head bowed down suddenly, in homage, or to hide tears. Then another stepped forward, and another. The heads that bowed were grey, white, bald; the voices that hailed the king quavered. One, Ker of the crippled arm, whom Argaven had known as a shy page of thirteen, spoke fiercely to those who still stood unmoving: "This is the king. I have eyes that have seen, and that see now. This is the king!"

Argaven looked at them, face after face, the bowed heads and the unbowed.

"I am Argaven," she said. "I was king. Who reigns now in Karhide?"

"Emran," one answered.

"My child Emran?"

"Yes, my liege," old Bannith said; most of the faces were blank; but Ker said in her fierce shaking voice, "Argaven, Argaven reigns in Karhide! I have lived to see the bright days return. Long live the king!"

One of the younger ones looked at the others, and said resolutely, "So be it. Long live the king!" And all the heads bowed low.

Argaven took their homage unperturbed, but as soon as a moment came when she could address Horrsed the Plenipotentiary alone she demanded, "What is this? What has happened? Why was I misled? I was told I was to come here to assist you, as an aide, from the Ekumen—"

"That was twenty-four years ago," said the Ambassador, apologetically. "I've only lived here five years, my lord. Things are going very ill in Karhide. King Emran broke off relations with the Ekumen last year. I don't really know what the Stabile's purpose in sending you here was at the time he sent you; but at present, we're losing Winter. So the Agents on Hain suggested to me that we might move out our king."

"But I am *dead*," Argaven said wrathfully. "I have been dead for sixty years!"

"The king is dead," said Horrsed. "Long live the king."

As some of the Karhiders approached, Argaven turned from the Ambassador and went over to the rail. Grey water bubbled and slid by the ship's side. The shore of the continent lay now to their left, grey patched with white. It was cold: a day of early winter in the Ice Age. The ship's engine purred softly. Argaven had not heard that purr of an electric engine for a dozen years now, the only kind

of engine Karhide's slow and stable Age of Technology had chosen to employ. The sound of it was very pleasant to her.

She spoke abruptly without turning, as one who has known since infancy that there is always someone there to answer: "Why are we going east?"

"We're making for Kerm Land."

"Why Kerm Land?"

It was one of the younger ones who had come forward to answer. "Because that part of the country is in rebellion against the—against King Emran. I am a Kermlander: Perreth ner Sode."

"Is Emran in Erhenrang?"

"Erhenrang was taken by Orgoreyn, six years ago. The king is in the new capital, east of the mountains—the Old Capital, actually, Rer."

"Emran lost the West Fall?" Argaven said, and then turning full on the stout young noble, "Lost the West Fall? Lost Erhenrang?"

Perreth drew back a step, but answered promptly, "We've been in hiding behind the mountains for six years."

"The Orgota are in Erhenrang?"

"King Emran signed a treaty with Orgoreyn five years ago, ceding them the Western Provinces."

"A shameful treaty, your majesty," old Ker broke in, fiercer and shakier than ever. "A fool's treaty! Emran dances to the drums of Orgoreyn. All of us here are rebels, exiles. The Ambassador there is an exile, in hiding!"

"The West Fall," Argaven said. "Argaven I took the West Fall for Karhide seven hundred years ago— " She looked round on the others again with her strange, keen, unheeding gaze. "Emran— " she began, but halted. "How strong are you in Kerm Land? Is the Coast with you?"

"Most Hearths of the South and East are with us."

Argaven was silent a while. "Did Emran ever bear an heir?"

"No heir of the flesh, my liege," Bannith said. "She sired six."

"She has named Girvry Harge rem ir Orek as her heir," said Perreth.

"Girvry? What kind of name is that? The kings of Karhide are named Emran," Argaven said, "and Argaven."

Now at last comes the dark picture, the snapshot taken by firelight —firelight, because the power plants of Rer are wrecked, the trunk lines cut, and half the city is on fire. Snow flurries heavily down above the flames and gleams red for a moment before it melts in mid air, hissing faintly.

Snow and ice and guerrilla troops keep Orgoreyn at bay on the west side of the Kargav Mountains. No help came to the Old King, Emran, when her country rose against her. Her guards fled, her city burns, and now at the end she is face to face with the usurper. But she has, at the end, something of her family's heedless pride. She pays no attention to the rebels. She stares at them and does not see them, lying in the dark hallway, lit only by mirrors that reflect distant fires, the gun with which she killed herself near her hand.

Stooping over the body Argaven lifts up that cold hand, and starts to take from the age-knotted forefinger the massive, carved, gold ring. But she does not do it. "Keep it," she whispers, "keep it." For a moment she bends yet lower, as if she whispered in the dead ear, or laid her cheek against that cold and wrinkled face. Then she straightens up, and stands a while, and presently goes out through dark corridors, by windows bright with distant ruin, to set her house in order: Argaven, Winter's king.

THE GOOD TRIP

This story was published when the drug scene was big in the media, and one response to it was that I was trying to cash in on a hot topic. That struck me as funny, given my infallible talent for missing whatever boat all the fashionable people are on—and also in view of the fact that, in a way, the point of the little story is that Lewis doesn't take the chemical trip, but gets there on his own . . . with a little help from his friend.

But it's not an anti-drug story either. My only strong opinion about drugs (pot, hallucinogens, alcohol) is anti-prohibition and pro-education. I have to admit that people who expand their consciousness by living instead of by taking chemicals usually come back with much more interesting reports of where they've been. But I'm an addict myself (tobacco), and it would be plain silly in me to celebrate or to condemn anybody else for a similar dependence.

As he swallowed the stuff he knew he shouldn't swallow the stuff, knew it for sure, knew it as a driver knows the truck coming straight at him at 70 mph: suddenly, intimately, finally. His throat shut, his solar plexus knotted up like a sea anemone, but too late. Down the hatch it went, the bit of bitter candy, the acid-drop, the sourball, the peppy packet of power, etching a little corroded trail of terror behind it all the way down his esophagus like a poisoned

snail swallowed whole. It was the terror that was wrong. He was afraid and hadn't known it, and now it was too late. You can't afford to be afraid. Fear fouls it all up, and sends those few, those unhappy few, a very small percentage, to the loony bin to cower in corners not saying anything. . . .

You have nothing to fear but fear itself.

Yes sir. Yes sir Mr. Roosevelt sir.

The thing to do is relax. Think good thoughts. If rape inevitable—

He watched Rich Harringer open up his little packet (accurately compounded and hygienically wrapped by a couple of fellows putting themselves through grad school in chemistry by the approved American method of free enterprise, illegitimate to be sure but this is not unusual in America where so little is legal that even a baby can be illegitimate) and swallow the small sour snail with formal and deliberate enjoyment. If rape inevitable, relax and enjoy. Once a week.

But is anything inevitable besides death? Why relax, why enjoy? He would fight. He would not go on a bad trip. He would fight the drug consciously and purposefully, not in panic but with intent, and we'll see who wins. In this corner LSD/alpha, 100 micrograms, plain wrapper, the Tibetan Whirlwind; and in this corner, ladies and junglemen, L.S.D./B.A., M.A., 166 lbs., the Sonoma Sniveller, wearing white trunks, and red suitcases, and blue cheekpouches. Let me out of here, let me out of here! *Clang*.

Nothing happened.

Lewis Sidney David, the man with no last name, the Jewish Kelt, cornered in this corner, stared warily around him. His three companions all looked normal, in focus if out of touch. They did not have auras. Jim was lying on the verminous sofa-bed reading *Ramparts*, a trip to Vietnam he wanted maybe, or to Sacramento. Rich looked torpid, he always looked torpid even when serving free lunch in the park, and Alex was nitpicking around on his guitar.

The infinite satisfaction of the chord. The silver cord. Sursum corda. If he carries a guitar around why can't he play a tune on it? No. Irritability is a symptom of loss of self-control: suppress it. Suppress everything. Censor, censor. Fight, team, fight!

Lewis got up, observing with pleasure the ready ease of his responses and the perfection of his sense of balance, and filled a glass of water at the vile sink. Beard hairs, spat-out Colgate, rust and radish droppings, a sink of iniquity. A small sink, but mine own. Why did he live in this dump? Why had he asked Jim and Rich and Alex to come share their sugarlumps with him here? It was lousy enough without being an opium den too. Soon it would be littered with inert bodies, eyes dropping out like marbles and rolling under the bed to join the dust and ruin lurking there. Lewis carried the glass of water over to the window, drank half of it, and began to pour the rest gently around the roots of a seedling olive tree in a mended ten-cent pot. "Have a drink on me," he said, looking closely at the tree.

It was five inches high but looked very like an olive tree, gnarled and durable. A bonsai. Banzai! But where's satori? Where's the significance, the enhancement, all the shapes and colors and meanings, the intensification of the perception of reality? How long does it take the damned stuff to work? There sat his olive tree. No less, no more. Unenhanced, insignificant. Men cry Peace, peace, but there is no peace. Not enough olive trees to go around, due to population explosion of human species. Was that a Perception? No, any un-drugged meat-head could have perceived it. O come on, poison, poison me. Come, hallucination, come, so that I may fight you, reject you, refuse you, lose the fight and go mad, silently.

Like Isobel.

That was why he lived in this dump, and that was why he had asked Jim and Rich and Alex here, and that was why he was off on a trip with them, a pleasure-cruise, a holiday in picturesque Old

Erewhon. He was trying to catch up with his wife. What is most difficult about watching your wife go insane is that you can't go with her. Farther and farther away she walks, not looking back, a long trip down into silence. The lyre falls dumb, and the psychiatrists are liars too. You stand behind the glass wall of your sanity like one at an airport watching a crash. You shout, "Isobel!" She never heard. The plane crashed in silence. She could not hear him call her name. Nor could she speak to him. Now the walls that divided him from her were brick, very solid, and he could do what he liked with his own glass house of sanity. Throw stones. Throw alphas. Tinkle, crash.

LSD/alpha did not drive you insane, of course. It did not even unravel your chromosomes. It simply opened the door to the higher reality. So did schizophrenia, he gathered, but the trouble there was that you couldn't speak, you couldn't communicate, you couldn't say what.

Jim had lowered his *Ramparts*. He was sitting in a noticeable fashion, inhaling. He was going to get with reality the right way, like a lama, man. He was a true believer and his life now centered upon the LSD/a experience as a religious mystic's upon his mystical discipline. Could you keep it up once a week for years, though? At thirty? At forty-two? At sixty-three? There is a terrible monotony and adversity to life; you'd need a monastery. Matins, nones, vespers, silence, walls around, big solid brick walls. To keep the lower reality out.

Come on, hallucinogen, get with it. Hallucinogenate, hallucinogenize. Smash the glass wall. Take me on a trip where my wife went. Missing person, age 22, ht 5'3", wt 105 lbs, hair brown, race human, sex female. She never was a fast walker. I could catch up with her with one foot tied behind me. Take me where she walked to. . . . No.

I'll walk there by myself, said Lewis Sidney David. He finished

pouring the water in little dribbles around the roots of the olive tree, and looked up, out the window. There through smeary glass was Mount Hood, forty miles away, two miles high, a volcanic cone possessing the serene symmetry peculiar to volcanic cones, dormant but not officially extinct, full of sleepy fires and surrounded by its own atmosphere and climate different from that of lower altitudes: snow and a clear light. That was why he lived in this dump. Because when you looked out the window of it, you saw the higher reality. Eleven thousand feet higher.

"I'll be damned," Lewis said aloud, feeling that he was on the edge and verge of perceiving something really important. But he had that feeling fairly often, without chemical assistance. Meanwhile there was the mountain.

A lot of muck, freeways and disposable office buildings and high-rises and urban renewal bombsites and neon elephants washing neon cars with dotted showers of neon, lay in between him and the mountain, and the base of it was hidden along with its foothills in a pale smog, so that the peak floated.

Lewis felt a strong impulse to cry and to say his wife's name aloud. He repressed this impulse, as he had been doing for three months, ever since May when he had taken her to the sanitarium, after the silent months. In January, before the silence began, she had cried a great deal, all day long some days, and he had become frightened of tears. First tears, then silence. No good. O God get me out of this! Lewis let go, quit fighting the impalpable enemy, and begged for release. He implored the drug in his bloodstream to work, to do something, to let him cry, or see colors, or go off his rocker, anything.

Nothing happened.

He finished pouring the water in little dribbles around the roots of the olive tree, and looked up, at the room. It was a dump, but big, and it had a good view of Mount Hood, and the wisdom-

tooth crest of Mount Adams on clear days too. But nothing would happen here. This was the waiting room. He picked up his coat off a broken chair and went out.

It was a good coat, lambswool lining and a hood and all that; his sister and mother had clubbed to get it for him for Christmas, making him feel like R. R. Raskolnikov. But he was not going to murder any old pawnbrokers today. Not even a pseudocide. On the stairs he passed the painters and plasterers with their ladders and buckets, three of them, going up to do his room over, peaceful-looking, fresh-faced men in their forties and fifties. Poor bastards, what would they do with the sink? with the three alphies, Rich and Jim and Alex, who on honeydew had fed and drunk the milk of Paradise? with his notes on LeNotre, Olmsted and McLaren, with his fourteen pounds of photographs of Japanese domestic architecture, with his drawing board and fishing tackle, his *Collected Works of Theodore Sturgeon* bound in sensational cardboard, the 8′ x 10′ unfinished oil of an ataxic nude by a painter friend whose auto loan co. had attached his paintings, Alex's guitar, the olive tree, the dust and eyeballs under the bed? That was their problem. He went on down the rooming-house stairs that smelled of old tomcat, and heard his hiking boots clomping heartily. He felt that all this had happened once before.

It took him a long time to get out of the city. Since public transportation was forbidden to people in his condition, of course, he couldn't get on the Gresham bus which would have saved a lot of time, taking him through the suburbs and halfway there. But there was plenty of time. The summer evening would stay light; he could count on it. Lenient and sweet in their length are the twilights of a latitude halfway between equator and pole: no tropic monotonies, no arctic absolutes, but a winter of long shadows and a summer of long dusks: gradations and accommodations of brightness, attenuations of clarity, subtleties and leisures of the light. Children scuttered

in the green parks of Portland and down long side streets, all at one great game over all the city, the game of Young. Only here and there a kid went alone, playing Solitude, for higher stakes. Some kids are gamblers born. Bits of trash scraped along the gutters moved by a warm wind now and then. There was a great, sad sound far off over the city as if lions were roaring in cages, walking and lashing their gold sides with gold-tasselled tails and roaring, roaring. Sun set, somewhere west over roofs, but not for the mountain that still burned with a white fire away up high. As Lewis left the last of the city and went through a pleasant land, hilly and well farmed, the wind began to smell of wet earth, cool, complex, as it will as night comes on; and past Sandy there was darkness under great increasing forests on the rising slopes. But there was plenty of time. Above and ahead the peak stood white, faintly tinged with apricot, in sunlight. As he climbed the long, steep road he came out again and then again from the dark forests into gulfs of yellow clarity. He went on until he was up above the forests and up above the darkness, on heights where there was only snow and stone and air and the vast, clear, enduring light.

But he was alone.

That wasn't right. He hadn't been alone when this had happened. He had to meet with— He had been with— Where?

No skis no sled no snowshoes not even an inner tube. If I had got the commission for this landscape, God, I would have put a path along here. Sacrificing grandeur for convenience? But only a little path. No harm. Only a little crack in the Liberty Bell. Only a little leak in the dike, fuse on the bomb, maggot in the brain. O my mad girl, my silent love, my wife whom I sold into bedlam because you would not hear me speak, Isobel, come save me from yourself! I've climbed after you up above all the paths and now I stand here alone: there isn't any way to go.

Daylight died away and the white of the snow went somber. In the east, above endless darkening ranges and forests and pale, hill-enfolded lakes, Saturn shone, bright and saturnine.

Lewis did not know where the lodge was; somewhere on the timberline, but he was above timberline. He would not go down. To the heights, to the heights. Excelsior! A youth who bore mid snow and ice a banner with this strange device HELP HELP I AM A PRISONER OF THE HIGHER REALITY. He climbed. He climbed un-clomben slopes, unkempt, and as he climbed he wept. His tears crawled down over his face and he crawled up over the mountain's face.

The very high places are terrible, alone at dusk.

The light no longer stayed for him. There was no longer plenty of time. He had run out of time. Stars came out and looked at him eye to eye out of the gulfs of darkness whenever he glanced aside from the huge white uptilted plain, the higher plane he climbed. On either side of him there was a gap, with a few stars in it. But the snow kept its own cold light, and he kept climbing. He remembered the path when he came across it. God or the state or he himself had put a path there on the mountain after all. He turned right, and it was wrong. He turned left, and stood still. He did not know which way to go, and shaking with cold and fear he cried out aloud to the death-white summit above him and to the black places in between the stars his wife's name, "Isobel!"

She came along the path out of the darkness. "I began to get worried about you, Lewis."

"I went farther than I meant to," Lewis said.

"It stays light so long up here you sort of think it'll go on forever. . . ."

"Right. I'm sorry I worried you."

"Oh, I wasn't worried. You know. Lonesome. I thought maybe your leg had slowed you down. Is it a good hike?"

"Spectacular."

"Take me along tomorrow."

"Didn't you enjoy skiing?"

She shook her head. "Not without you," she muttered, shamefaced. They went leftward down the path, not very fast. Lewis was still slightly hobbled by the pulled muscle that had kept him off skis the last two days, and it was dark, and there wasn't any hurry. They held hands. Snow, starlight, stillness. Fire underfoot, darkness around; ahead of them, firelight, beer, bed. All things in their due time. Some, born gamblers, will always choose to live on the side of a volcano.

"When I was in the sanitarium," Isobel said, pausing so that he too stopped and there was no longer even the noise of their boots on the dry snow, no sound at all but the soft sound of her voice, "I had a dream like this. Awfully like this. It was the . . . most important dream I had. Yet I can't recall it clearly—I never could, even in therapy. But it was like this. This silence. Being up high. The silence above all . . . above all. It was so silent that if I said something, you would be able to hear it. I knew that. I was sure of it. And in the dream I think I said your name, and you *could* hear me—you answered me—"

"Say my name," he whispered.

She turned and looked at him. There was no sound on the mountain or among the stars. She said his name.

He answered saying hers, and then took hold of her; both of them were shaking.

"It's cold, it's cold, we've got to go down."

They went on, on their tightrope between the outer and the inner fires.

"Look at that enormous star."

"Planet. Saturn—Father Time."

"Ate his children, didn't he," she murmured, holding hard to his arm.

"All but one of them," Lewis answered. Down a long clear slope before them now they saw in grey starlight the bulk of the upper hut, the towers of the ski-lift vague and gaunt, and the vast down-sweep of the lines.

His hands were cold and he slipped off his gloves a minute to beat them together, but this was hard to do because of the glass of water he was holding. He finished pouring the water in little dribbles around the roots of the olive tree and set down the glass beside the mended flowerpot. But something still remained in his hand, folded into the palm like a crib for a high-school French final, *que je fusse, que tu fusses, qu'il fût,* small and sweat-stuck. He opened his hand and studied the item for some while. A message. From whom, to whom? From grave, to womb. A little packet, sealed, containing 100 mg of LSD/a in sugar.

Sealed?

He remembered, with precision and in order, opening it, swallowing the stuff, the taste of it. He also remembered with equal order and precision where he had been since then and knew that he had not been there yet.

He went over to Jim who was just exhaling the breath he had been inhaling as Lewis began to water the olive tree. Deftly and gently Lewis tucked the packet into Jim's coat pocket.

"Aren't you coming along?" Jim asked, smiling a mild smile.

Lewis shook his head. "Chicken," he murmured. It was hard to explain that he had already come back from the trip he had not made. Besides, Jim wouldn't hear him. He was off where people don't hear and can't answer, walled in.

"Have a good trip," Lewis said.

He got his raincoat (dirty poplin, no fleece lining, hold on, wait)

and went down the stairs and out into the streets. The summer was ending, the season changing. It was raining but not dark yet, and the city wind blew in great cool gusts that smelled of wet earth and forests and the night.

NINE LIVES

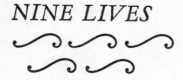

The biologist Gordon Rattray Taylor is innocently responsible for this story. He has a chapter on cloning in his fine book The Biological Time Bomb. *I read that, and then I wrote this.*

It is as near "hard-core" or wiring-diagram science fiction as I ever get; that is, it's a working out of a theme directly extrapolated from contemporary work in one of the quantitative sciences—a what-if story. The theme, however, is developed qualitatively, psychologically. Essentially I am using the scientific element, not as an end in itself, but as a metaphor or symbol, a means of saying something not otherwise expressible.

"Nine Lives" appeared in Playboy *in 1968, under the only pen name I have ever used: U. K. Le Guin. The editors politely asked if they could use the first initial only, and I agreed. It's not surprising that* Playboy *hadn't had its consciousness raised back then, but it is surprising to me to realize how thoughtlessly I went along with them. It was the first (and is the only) time I met with anything I understood as sexual prejudice, prejudice against me as a woman writer, from any editor or publisher; and it seemed so silly, so grotesque, that I failed to see that it was also important.*

Playboy *made a good many minor changes in the story, and these have been kept in reprintings of it under their imprint. I prefer my*

*version of it, and whenever I have had control of reprintings it has
appeared in the version given here, and under my unabridged name.*

She was alive inside but dead outside, her face a black and dun net
of wrinkles, tumors, cracks. She was bald and blind. The tremors
that crossed Libra's face were mere quiverings of corruption. Under-
neath, in the black corridors, the halls beneath the skin, there were
crepitations in darkness, ferments, chemical nightmares that went
on for centuries. "O the damned flatulent planet," Pugh murmured
as the dome shook and a boil burst a kilometer to the southwest,
spraying silver pus across the sunset. The sun had been setting for
the last two days. "I'll be glad to see a human face."

"Thanks," said Martin.

"Yours is human to be sure," said Pugh, "but I've seen it so long
I can't see it."

Radvid signals cluttered the communicator which Martin was
operating, faded, returned as face and voice. The face filled the
screen, the nose of an Assyrian king, the eyes of a samurai, skin
bronze, eyes the color of iron: young, magnificent. "Is that what
human beings look like?" said Pugh with awe. "I'd forgotten."

"Shut up, Owen, we're on."

"Libra Exploratory Mission Base, come in please, this is *Passerine*
launch."

"Libra here. Beam fixed. Come on down, launch."

"Expulsion in seven E-seconds. Hold on." The screen blanked and
sparkled.

"Do they all look like that? Martin, you and I are uglier men
than I thought."

"Shut up, Owen. . . ."

For twenty-two minutes Martin followed the landing craft down
by signal and then through the cleared dome they saw it, small star

in the blood-colored east, sinking. It came down neat and quiet, Libra's thin atmosphere carrying little sound. Pugh and Martin closed the headpieces of their imsuits, zipped out of the dome airlocks, and ran with soaring strides, Nijinsky and Nureyev, toward the boat. Three equipment modules came floating down at four-minute intervals from each other and hundred-meter intervals east of the boat. "Come on out," Martin said on his suit radio, "we're waiting at the door."

"Come on in, the methane's fine," said Pugh.

The hatch opened. The young man they had seen on the screen came out with one athletic twist and leaped down onto the shaky dust and clinkers of Libra. Martin shook his hand, but Pugh was staring at the hatch, from which another young man emerged with the same neat twist and jump, followed by a young woman who emerged with the same neat twist, ornamented by a wriggle, and the jump. They were all tall, with bronze skin, black hair, high-bridged noses, epicanthic fold, the same face. They all had the same face. The fourth was emerging from the hatch with a neat twist and jump. "Martin bach," said Pugh, "we've got a clone."

"Right," said one of them, "we're a tenclone. John Chow's the name. You're Lieutenant Martin?"

"I'm Owen Pugh."

"Alvaro Guillen Martin," said Martin, formal, bowing slightly. Another girl was out, the same beautiful face; Martin stared at her and his eye rolled like a nervous pony's. Evidently he had never given any thought to cloning and was suffering technological shock. "Steady," Pugh said in the Argentine dialect, "it's only excess twins." He stood close by Martin's elbow. He was glad himself of the contact.

It is hard to meet a stranger. Even the greatest extravert meeting even the meekest stranger knows a certain dread, though he may not know he knows it. Will he make a fool of me wreck my image

of myself invade me destroy me change me? Will he be different from me? Yes, that he will. There's the terrible thing: the strangeness of the stranger.

After two years on a dead planet, and the last half year isolated as a team of two, oneself and one other, after that it's even harder to meet a stranger, however welcome he may be. You're out of the habit of difference, you've lost the touch; and so the fear revives, the primitive anxiety, the old dread.

The clone, five males and five females, had got done in a couple of minutes what a man might have got done in twenty: greeted Pugh and Martin, had a glance at Libra, unloaded the boat, made ready to go. They went, and the dome filled with them, a hive of golden bees. They hummed and buzzed quietly, filled up all silences, all spaces with a honey-brown swarm of human presence. Martin looked bewildered at the long-limbed girls, and they smiled at him, three at once. Their smile was gentler than that of the boys, but no less radiantly self-possessed.

"Self-possessed," Owen Pugh murmured to his friend, "that's it. Think of it, to be oneself ten times over. Nine seconds for every motion, nine ayes on every vote. It would be glorious." But Martin was asleep. And the John Chows had all gone to sleep at once. The dome was filled with their quiet breathing. They were young, they didn't snore. Martin sighed and snored, his Hershey-bar-colored face relaxed in the dim afterglow of Libra's primary, set at last. Pugh had cleared the dome and stars looked in, Sol among them, a great company of lights, a clone of splendors. Pugh slept and dreamed of a one-eyed giant who chased him through the shaking halls of Hell.

From his sleeping bag Pugh watched the clone's awakening. They all got up within one minute except for one pair, a boy and a girl, who lay snugly tangled and still sleeping in one bag. As Pugh saw this there was a shock like one of Libra's earthquakes inside him, a

very deep tremor. He was not aware of this and in fact thought he was pleased at the sight; there was no other such comfort on this dead hollow world. More power to them, who made love. One of the others stepped on the pair. They woke and the girl sat up flushed and sleepy, with bare golden breasts. One of her sisters murmured something to her; she shot a glance at Pugh and disappeared in the sleeping bag; from another direction came a fierce stare, from still another direction a voice: "Christ, we're used to having a room to ourselves. Hope you don't mind, Captain Pugh."

"It's a pleasure," Pugh said half truthfully. He had to stand up then wearing only the shorts he slept in, and he felt like a plucked rooster, all white scrawn and pimples. He had seldom envied Martin's compact brownness so much. The United Kingdom had come through the Great Famines well, losing less than half its population: a record achieved by rigorous food control. Black marketeers and hoarders had been executed. Crumbs had been shared. Where in richer lands most had died and a few had thriven, in Britain fewer died and none throve. They all got lean. Their sons were lean, their grandsons lean, small, brittle-boned, easily infected. When civilization became a matter of standing in lines, the British had kept queue, and so had replaced the survival of the fittest with the survival of the fair-minded. Owen Pugh was a scrawny little man. All the same, he was there.

At the moment he wished he wasn't.

At breakfast a John said, "Now if you'll brief us, Captain Pugh— "

"Owen, then."

"Owen, we can work out our schedule. Anything new on the mine since your last report to your Mission? We saw your reports when *Passerine* was orbiting Planet V, where they are now."

Martin did not answer, though the mine was his discovery and project, and Pugh had to do his best. It was hard to talk to them. The same faces, each with the same expression of intelligent interest,

all leaned toward him across the table at almost the same angle. They all nodded together.

Over the Exploitation Corps insigne on their tunics each had a nameband, first name John and last name Chow of course, but the middle names different. The men were Aleph, Kaph, Yod, Gimel, and Samedh; the women Sadhe, Daleth, Zayin, Beth, and Resh. Pugh tried to use the names but gave it up at once; he could not even tell sometimes which one had spoken, for all the voices were alike.

Martin buttered and chewed his toast, and finally interrupted: "You're a team. Is that it?"

"Right," said two Johns.

"God, what a team! I hadn't seen the point. How much do you each know what the others are thinking?"

"Not at all, properly speaking," replied one of the girls, Zayin. The others watched her with the proprietary, approving look they had. "No ESP, nothing fancy. But we think alike. We have exactly the same equipment. Given the same stimulus, the same problem, we're likely to be coming up with the same reactions and solutions at the same time. Explanations are easy—don't even have to make them, usually. We seldom misunderstand each other. It does facilitate our working as a team."

"Christ yes," said Martin. "Pugh and I have spent seven hours out of ten for six months misunderstanding each other. Like most people. What about emergencies, are you as good at meeting the unexpected problem as a nor . . . an unrelated team?"

"Statistics so far indicate that we are," Zayin answered readily. Clones must be trained, Pugh thought, to meet questions, to reassure and reason. All they said had the slightly bland and stilted quality of answers furnished to the Public. "We can't brainstorm as single-tons can, we as a team don't profit from the interplay of varied minds; but we have a compensatory advantage. Clones are drawn

from the best human material, individuals of IIQ ninety-ninth percentile, Genetic Constitution alpha double A, and so on. We have more to draw on than most individuals do."

"And it's multiplied by a factor of ten. Who is—who was John Chow?"

"A genius surely," Pugh said politely. His interest in cloning was not so new and avid as Martin's.

"Leonardo Complex type," said Yod. "Biomath, also a cellist and an undersea hunter, and interested in structural engineering problems and so on. Died before he'd worked out his major theories."

"Then you each represent a different facet of his mind, his talents?"

"No," said Zayin, shaking her head in time with several others. "We share the basic equipment and tendencies, of course, but we're all engineers in Planetary Exploitation. A later clone can be trained to develop other aspects of the basic equipment. It's all training; the genetic substance is identical. We *are* John Chow. But we are differently trained."

Martin looked shell-shocked. "How old are you?"

"Twenty-three."

"You say he died young—had they taken germ cells from him beforehand or something?"

Gimel took over: "He died at twenty-four in an air car crash. They couldn't save the brain, so they took some intestinal cells and cultured them for cloning. Reproductive cells aren't used for cloning, since they have only half the chromosomes. Intestinal cells happen to be easy to despecialize and reprogram for total growth."

"All chips off the old block," Martin said valiantly. "But how can . . . some of you be women. . . ?"

Beth took over: "It's easy to program half the clonal mass back to the female. Just delete the male gene from half the cells and they revert to the basic, that is, the female. It's trickier to go the other

way, have to hook in artificial Y chromosomes. So they mostly clone from males, since clones function best bisexually."

Gimel again: "They've worked these matters of technique and function out carefully. The taxpayer wants the best for his money, and of course clones are expensive. With the cell manipulations, and the incubation in Ngama Placentae, and the maintenance and training of the foster-parent groups, we end up costing about three million apiece."

"For your next generation," Martin said, still struggling, "I suppose you . . . you breed?"

"We females are sterile," said Beth with perfect equanimity. "You remember that the Y chromosome was deleted from our original cell. The males can interbreed with approved singletons, if they want to. But to get John Chow again as often as they want, they just reclone a cell from this clone."

Martin gave up the struggle. He nodded and chewed cold toast. "Well," said one of the Johns, and all changed mood, like a flock of starlings that change course in one wingflick, following a leader so fast that no eye can see which leads. They were ready to go. "How about a look at the mine? Then we'll unload the equipment. Some nice new models in the roboats; you'll want to see them. Right?" Had Pugh or Martin not agreed they might have found it hard to say so. The Johns were polite but unanimous; their decisions carried. Pugh, Commander of Libra Base 2, felt a qualm. Could he boss around this superman/woman-entity-of-ten? and a genius at that? He stuck close to Martin as they suited for outside. Neither said anything.

Four apiece in the three large airjets, they slipped off north from the dome, over Libra's dun rugose skin, in starlight.

"Desolate," one said.

It was a boy and girl with Pugh and Martin. Pugh wondered if these were the two that had shared a sleeping bag last night. No

doubt they wouldn't mind if he asked them. Sex must be as handy as breathing to them. Did you two breathe last night?

"Yes," he said, "it is desolate."

"This is our first time off, except training on Luna." The girl's voice was definitely a bit higher and softer.

"How did you take the big hop?"

"They doped us. I wanted to experience it." That was the boy; he sounded wistful. They seemed to have more personality, only two at a time. Did repetition of the individual negate individuality?

"Don't worry," said Martin, steering the sled, "you can't experience no-time because it isn't there."

"I'd just like to once," one of them said. "So we'd know."

The Mountains of Merioneth showed leprotic in starlight to the east, a plume of freezing gas trailed silvery from a vent-hole to the west, and the sled tilted groundward. The twins braced for the stop at one moment, each with a slight protective gesture to the other. Your skin is my skin, Pugh thought, but literally, no metaphor. What would it be like, then, to have someone as close to you as that? Always to be answered when you spoke; never to be in pain alone. Love your neighbor as you love yourself. . . . That hard old problem was solved. The neighbor was the self: the love was perfect.

And here was Hellmouth, the mine.

Pugh was the Exploratory Mission's E.T. geologist, and Martin his technician and cartographer; but when in the course of a local survey Martin had discovered the U-mine, Pugh had given him full credit, as well as the onus of prospecting the lode and planning the Exploitation Team's job. These kids had been sent out from Earth years before Martin's reports got there and had not known what their job would be until they got here. The Exploitation Corps simply sent out teams regularly and blindly as a dandelion sends out its seed, knowing there would be a job for them on Libra or the next planet out or one they hadn't even heard about yet. The govern-

ment wanted uranium too urgently to wait while reports drifted home across the lightyears. The stuff was like gold, old-fashioned but essential, worth mining extraterrestrially and shipping interstellar. Worth its weight in people, Pugh thought sourly, watching the tall young men and women go one by one, glimmering in starlight, into the black hole Martin had named Hellmouth.

As they went in their homeostatic forehead-lamps brightened. Twelve nodding gleams ran along the moist, wrinkled walls. Pugh heard Martin's radiation counter peeping twenty to the dozen up ahead. "Here's the drop-off," said Martin's voice in the suit intercom, drowning out the peeping and the dead silence that was around them. "We're in a side-fissure, this is the main vertical vent in front of us." The black void gaped, its far side not visible in the headlamp beams. "Last vulcanism seems to have been a couple of thousand years ago. Nearest fault is twenty-eight kilos east, in the Trench. This area seems to be as safe seismically as anything in the area. The big basalt-flow overhead stabilizes all these substructures, so long as it remains stable itself. Your central lode is thirty-six meters down and runs in a series of five bubble caverns northeast. It is a lode, a pipe of very high-grade ore. You saw the percentage figures, right? Extraction's going to be no problem. All you've got to do is get the bubbles topside."

"Take off the lid and let 'em float up." A chuckle. Voices began to talk, but they were all the same voice and the suit radio gave them no location in space. "Open the thing right up. —Safer that way. —But it's a solid basalt roof, how thick, ten meters here? —Three to twenty, the report said. —Blow good ore all over the lot. —Use this access we're in, straighten it a bit and run slider rails for the robos. —Import burros. —Have we got enough propping material? —What's your estimate of total payload mass, Martin?"

"Say over five million kilos and under eight."

"Transport will be here in ten E-months. —It'll have to go pure.

—No, they'll have the mass problem in NAFAL shipping licked by now, remember it's been sixteen years since we left Earth last Tuesday. —Right, they'll send the whole lot back and purify it in Earth orbit. —Shall we go down, Martin?"

"Go on. I've been down."

The first one—Aleph? (Heb., the ox, the leader)—swung onto the ladder and down; the rest followed. Pugh and Martin stood at the chasm's edge. Pugh set his intercom to exchange only with Martin's suit, and noticed Martin doing the same. It was a bit wearing, this listening to one person think aloud in ten voices, or was it one voice speaking the thoughts of ten minds?

"A great gut," Pugh said, looking down into the black pit, its veined and warted walls catching stray gleams of headlamps far below. "A cow's bowel. A bloody great constipated intestine."

Martin's counter peeped like a lost chicken. They stood inside the dead but epileptic planet, breathing oxygen from tanks, wearing suits impermeable to corrosives and harmful radiations, resistant to a 200-degree range of temperatures, tear-proof, and as shock-resistant as possible given the soft vulnerable stuff inside.

"Next hop," Martin said, "I'd like to find a planet that has nothing whatever to exploit."

"You found this."

"Keep me home next time."

Pugh was pleased. He had hoped Martin would want to go on working with him, but neither of them was used to talking much about their feelings, and he had hesitated to ask. "I'll try that," he said.

"I hate this place. I like caves, you know. It's why I came in here. Just spelunking. But this one's a bitch. Mean. You can't ever let down in here. I guess this lot can handle it, though. They know their stuff."

"Wave of the future, whatever," said Pugh.

The wave of the future came swarming up the ladder, swept Martin to the entrance, gabbled at and around him: "Have we got enough material for supports? —If we convert one of the extractor servos to anneal, yes. —Sufficient if we miniblast? —Kaph can calculate stress." Pugh had switched his intercom back to receive them; he looked at them, so many thoughts jabbering in an eager mind, and at Martin standing silent among them, and at Hellmouth and the wrinkled plain. "Settled! How does that strike you as a preliminary schedule, Martin?"

"It's your baby," Martin said.

Within five E-days the Johns had all their material and equipment unloaded and operating and were starting to open up the mine. They worked with total efficiency. Pugh was fascinated and frightened by their effectiveness, their confidence, their independence. He was no use to them at all. A clone, he thought, might indeed be the first truly stable, self-reliant human being. Once adult it would need nobody's help. It would be sufficient to itself physically, sexually, emotionally, intellectually. Whatever he did, any member of it would always receive the support and approval of his peers, his other selves. Nobody else was needed.

Two of the clone stayed in the dome doing calculations and paperwork, with frequent sled trips to the mine for measurements and tests. They were the mathematicians of the clone, Zayin and Kaph. That is, as Zayin explained, all ten had had thorough mathematical training from age three to twenty-one, but from twenty-one to twenty-three she and Kaph had gone on with math while the others intensified study in other specialties, geology, mining, engineering, electronic engineering, equipment robotics, applied atomics, and so on. "Kaph and I feel," she said, "that we're the element of the clone closest to what John Chow was in his singleton lifetime. But of course he was principally in biomath, and they didn't take us far in that."

"They needed us most in this field," Kaph said, with the patriotic priggishness they sometimes evinced.

Pugh and Martin soon could distinguish this pair from the others, Zayin by gestalt, Kaph only by a discolored left fourth fingernail, got from an ill-aimed hammer at the age of six. No doubt there were many such differences, physical and psychological, among them; nature might be identical, nurture could not be. But the differences were hard to find. And part of the difficulty was that they never really talked to Pugh and Martin. They joked with them, were polite, got along fine. They gave nothing. It was nothing one could complain about; they were very pleasant, they had the standardized American friendliness. "Do you come from Ireland, Owen?"

"Nobody comes from Ireland, Zayin."

"There are lots of Irish-Americans."

"To be sure, but no more Irish. A couple of thousand in all the island, the last I knew. They didn't go in for birth control, you know, so the food ran out. By the Third Famine there were no Irish left at all but the priesthood, and they all celibate, or nearly all."

Zayin and Kaph smiled stiffly. They had no experience of either bigotry or irony. "What are you then, ethnically?" Kaph asked, and Pugh replied, "A Welshman."

"Is it Welsh that you and Martin speak together?"

None of your business, Pugh thought, but said, "No, it's his dialect, not mine: Argentinean. A descendant of Spanish."

"You learned it for private communication?"

"Whom had we here to be private from? It's just that sometimes a man likes to speak his native language."

"Ours is English," Kaph said unsympathetically. Why should they have sympathy? That's one of the things you give because you need it back.

"Is Wells quaint?" asked Zayin.

"Wells? Oh, Wales, it's called. Yes, Wales is quaint." Pugh

switched on his rock-cutter, which prevented further conversation by a synapse-destroying whine, and while it whined he turned his back and said a profane word in Welsh.

That night he used the Argentine dialect for private communication. "Do they pair off in the same couples or change every night?"

Martin looked surprised. A prudish expression, unsuited to his features, appeared for a moment. It faded. He too was curious. "I think it's random."

"Don't whisper, man, it sounds dirty. I think they rotate."

"On a schedule?"

"So nobody gets omitted."

Martin gave a vulgar laugh and smothered it. "What about us? Aren't we omitted?"

"That doesn't occur to them."

"What if I proposition one of the girls?"

"She'd tell the others and they'd decide as a group."

"I am not a bull," Martin said, his dark, heavy face heating up. "I will not be judged—"

"Down, down, *machismo*," said Pugh. "Do you mean to proposition one?"

Martin shrugged, sullen. "Let 'em have their incest."

"Incest is it, or masturbation?"

"I don't care, if they'd do it out of earshot!"

The clone's early attempts at modesty had soon worn off, unmotivated by any deep defensiveness of self or awareness of others. Pugh and Martin were daily deeper swamped under the intimacies of its constant emotional-sexual-mental interchange: swamped yet excluded.

"Two months to go," Martin said one evening.

"To what?" snapped Pugh. He was edgy lately, and Martin's sullenness got on his nerves.

"To relief."

In sixty days the full crew of their Exploratory Mission were due back from their survey of the other planets of the system. Pugh was aware of this.

"Crossing off the days on your calendar?" he jeered.

"Pull yourself together, Owen."

"What do you mean?"

"What I say."

They parted in contempt and resentment.

Pugh came in after a day alone on the Pampas, a vast lava plain the nearest edge of which was two hours south by jet. He was tired but refreshed by solitude. They were not supposed to take long trips alone but lately had often done so. Martin stooped under bright lights, drawing one of his elegant masterly charts. This one was of the whole face of Libra, the cancerous face. The dome was otherwise empty, seeming dim and large as it had before the clone came.

"Where's the golden horde?"

Martin grunted ignorance, cross-hatching. He straightened his back to glance round at the sun, which squatted feebly like a great red toad on the eastern plain, and at the clock, which said 18:45. "Some big quakes today," he said, returning to his map. "Feel them down there? Lots of crates were falling around. Take a look at the seismo."

The needle jigged and wavered on the roll. It never stopped dancing here. The roll had recorded five quakes of major intensity back in midafternoon; twice the needle had hopped off the roll. The attached computer had been activated to emit a slip reading, "Epicenter 61' N by 42' 4" E."

"Not in the Trench this time."

"I thought it felt a bit different from usual. Sharper."

"In Base One I used to lie awake all night feeling the ground jump. Queer how you get used to things."

"Go spla if you didn't. What's for dinner?"

"I thought you'd have cooked it."

"Waiting for the clone."

Feeling put upon, Pugh got out a dozen dinnerboxes, stuck two in the Instobake, pulled them out. "All right, here's dinner."

"Been thinking," Martin said, coming to table. "What if some clone cloned itself? Illegally. Made a thousand duplicates—ten thousand. Whole army. They could make a tidy power grab, couldn't they?"

"But how many millions did this lot cost to rear? Artificial placentae and all that. It would be hard to keep secret, unless they had a planet to themselves. . . . Back before the Famines when Earth had national governments, they talked about that: clone your best soldiers, have whole regiments of them. But the food ran out before they could play that game."

They talked amicably, as they used to do.

"Funny," Martin said, chewing. "They left early this morning, didn't they?"

"All but Kaph and Zayin. They thought they'd get the first pay-load above ground today. What's up?"

"They weren't back for lunch."

"They won't starve, to be sure."

"They left at seven."

"So they did." Then Pugh saw it. The air tanks held eight hours' supply.

"Kaph and Zayin carried out spare cans when they left. Or they've got a heap out there."

"They did, but they brought the whole lot in to recharge." Martin stood up, pointing to one of the stacks of stuff that cut the dome into rooms and alleys.

"There's an alarm signal on every imsuit."

"It's not automatic."

Pugh was tired and still hungry. "Sit down and eat, man. That lot can look after themselves."

Martin sat down but did not eat. "There was a big quake, Owen. The first one. Big enough it scared me."

After a pause Pugh sighed and said, "All right."

Unenthusiastically, they got out the two-man sled that was always left for them and headed it north. The long sunrise covered everything in poisonous red jello. The horizontal light and shadow made it hard to see, raised walls of fake iron ahead of them which they slid through, turned the convex plain beyond Hellmouth into a great dimple full of bloody water. Around the tunnel entrance a wilderness of machinery stood, cranes and cables and servos and wheels and diggers and robocarts and sliders and control huts, all slanting and bulking incoherently in the red light. Martin jumped from the sled, ran into the mine. He came out again, to Pugh. "Oh God, Owen, it's down," he said. Pugh went in and saw, five meters from the entrance, the shiny moist, black wall that ended the tunnel. Newly exposed to air, it looked organic, like visceral tissue. The tunnel entrance, enlarged by blasting and double-tracked for robocarts, seemed unchanged until he noticed thousands of tiny spiderweb cracks in the walls. The floor was wet with some sluggish fluid.

"They were inside," Martin said.

"They may be still. They surely had extra air cans—"

"Look, Owen, look at the basalt flow, at the roof, don't you see what the quake did, look at it."

The low hump of land that roofed the caves still had the unreal look of an optical illusion. It had reversed itself, sunk down, leaving a vast dimple or pit. When Pugh walked on it he saw that it too was cracked with many tiny fissures. From some a whitish gas was seeping, so that the sunlight on the surface of the gas pool was shafted as if by the waters of a dim red lake.

"The mine's not on the fault. There's no fault here!"

Pugh came back to him quickly. "No, there's no fault, Martin— Look, they surely weren't all inside together."

Martin followed him and searched among the wrecked machines dully, then actively. He spotted the airsled. It had come down heading south, and stuck at an angle in a pothole of colloidal dust. It had carried two riders. One was half sunk in the dust, but his suit meters registered normal functioning; the other hung strapped onto the tilted sled. Her imsuit had burst open on the broken legs, and the body was frozen hard as any rock. That was all they found. As both regulation and custom demanded, they cremated the dead at once with the laser guns they carried by regulation and had never used before. Pugh, knowing he was going to be sick, wrestled the survivor onto the two-man sled and sent Martin off to the dome with him. Then he vomited and flushed the waste out of his suit, and finding one four-man sled undamaged, followed after Martin, shaking as if the cold of Libra had got through to him.

The survivor was Kaph. He was in deep shock. They found a swelling on the occiput that might mean concussion, but no fracture was visible.

Pugh brought two glasses of food concentrate and two chasers of aquavit. "Come on," he said. Martin obeyed, drinking off the tonic. They sat down on crates near the cot and sipped the aquavit.

Kaph lay immobile, face like beeswax, hair bright black to the shoulders, lips stiffly parted for faintly gasping breaths.

"It must have been the first shock, the big one," Martin said. "It must have slid the whole structure sideways. Till it fell in on itself. There must be gas layers in the lateral rocks, like those formations in the Thirty-first Quadrant. But there wasn't any sign—" As he spoke the world slid out from under them. Things leaped and clattered, hopped and jigged, shouted Ha! Ha! Ha! "It was like this at fourteen hours," said Reason shakily in Martin's voice,

amidst the unfastening and ruin of the world. But Unreason sat up, as the tumult lessened and things ceased dancing, and screamed aloud.

Pugh leaped across his spilt aquavit and held Kaph down. The muscular body flailed him off. Martin pinned the shoulders down. Kaph screamed, struggled, choked; his face blackened. "Oxy," Pugh said, and his hand found the right needle in the medical kit as if by homing instinct; while Martin held the mask he struck the needle home to the vagus nerve, restoring Kaph to life.

"Didn't know you knew that stunt," Martin said, breathing hard.

"The Lazarus Jab, my father was a doctor. It doesn't often work," Pugh said. "I want that drink I spilled. Is the quake over? I can't tell."

"Aftershocks. It's not just you shivering."

"Why did he suffocate?"

"I don't know, Owen. Look in the book."

Kaph was breathing normally and his color was restored; only the lips were still darkened. They poured a new shot of courage and sat down by him again with their medical guide. "Nothing about cyanosis or asphyxiation under 'Shock' or 'Concussion.' He can't have breathed in anything with his suit on. I don't know. We'd get as much good out of *Mother Mog's Home Herbalist....* 'Anal Hemorrhoids,' fy!" Pugh pitched the book to a crate table. It fell short, because either Pugh or the table was still unsteady.

"Why didn't he signal?"

"Sorry?"

"The eight inside the mine never had time. But he and the girl must have been outside. Maybe she was in the entrance and got hit by the first slide. He must have been outside, in the control hut maybe. He ran in, pulled her out, strapped her onto the sled, started for the dome. And all that time never pushed the panic button in his imsuit. Why not?"

"Well, he'd had that whack on his head. I doubt he ever realized the girl was dead. He wasn't in his senses. But if he had been I don't know if he'd have thought to signal us. They looked to one another for help."

Martin's face was like an Indian mask, grooves at the mouth corners, eyes of dull coal. "That's so. What must he have felt, then, when the quake came and he was outside, alone—"

In answer Kaph screamed.

He came off the cot in the heaving convulsions of one suffocating, knocked Pugh right down with his flailing arm, staggered into a stack of crates and fell to the floor, lips blue, eyes white. Martin dragged him back onto the cot and gave him a whiff of oxygen, then knelt by Pugh, who was sitting up, and wiped at his cut cheekbone. "Owen, are you all right, are you going to be all right, Owen?"

"I think I am," Pugh said. "Why are you rubbing that on my face?"

It was a short length of computer tape, now spotted with Pugh's blood. Martin dropped it. "Thought it was a towel. You clipped your cheek on that box there."

"Is he out of it?"

"Seems to be."

They stared down at Kaph lying stiff, his teeth a white line inside dark parted lips.

"Like epilepsy. Brain damage maybe?"

"What about shooting him full of meprobamate?"

Pugh shook his head. "I don't know what's in that shot I already gave him for shock. Don't want to overdose him."

"Maybe he'll sleep it off now."

"I'd like to myself. Between him and the earthquake I can't seem to keep on my feet."

"You got a nasty crack there. Go on, I'll sit up a while."

Pugh cleaned his cut cheek and pulled off his shirt, then paused. "Is there anything we ought to have done—have tried to do— " "They're all dead," Martin said heavily, gently.

Pugh lay down on top of his sleeping bag and one instant later was wakened by a hideous, sucking, struggling noise. He staggered up, found the needle, tried three times to jab it in correctly and failed, began to massage over Kaph's heart. "Mouth-to-mouth," he said, and Martin obeyed. Presently Kaph drew a harsh breath, his heartbeat steadied, his rigid muscles began to relax.

"How long did I sleep?"

"Half an hour."

They stood up sweating. The ground shuddered, the fabric of the dome sagged and swayed. Libra was dancing her awful polka again, her *Totentanz.* The sun, though rising, seemed to have grown larger and redder; gas and dust must have been stirred up in the feeble atmosphere.

"What's wrong with him, Owen?"

"I think he's dying with them."

"Them— But they're all dead, I tell you."

"Nine of them. They're all dead, they were crushed or suffocated. They were all him, he is all of them. They died, and now he's dying their deaths one by one."

"Oh, pity of God," said Martin.

The next time was much the same. The fifth time was worse, for Kaph fought and raved, trying to speak but getting no words out, as if his mouth were stopped with rocks or clay. After that the attacks grew weaker, but so did he. The eighth seizure came at about four-thirty; Pugh and Martin worked till five-thirty doing all they could to keep life in the body that slid without protest into death. They kept him, but Martin said, "The next will finish him." And it did; but Pugh breathed his own breath into the inert lungs, until he himself passed out.

He woke. The dome was opaqued and no light on. He listened and heard the breathing of two sleeping men. He slept, and nothing woke him till hunger did.

The sun was well up over the dark plains, and the planet had stopped dancing. Kaph lay asleep. Pugh and Martin drank tea and looked at him with proprietary triumph.

When he woke Martin went to him: "How do you feel, old man?" There was no answer. Pugh took Martin's place and looked into the brown, dull eyes that gazed toward but not into his own. Like Martin he quickly turned away. He heated food concentrate and brought it to Kaph. "Come on, drink."

He could see the muscles in Kaph's throat tighten. "Let me die," the young man said.

"You're not dying."

Kaph spoke with clarity and precision: "I am nine-tenths dead. There is not enough of me left alive."

That precision convinced Pugh, and he fought the conviction. "No," he said, peremptory. "They are dead. The others. Your brothers and sisters. You're not them, you're alive. You are John Chow. Your life is in your own hands."

The young man lay still, looking into a darkness that was not there.

Martin and Pugh took turns taking the Exploitation hauler and a spare set of robos over to Hellmouth to salvage equipment and protect it from Libra's sinister atmosphere, for the value of the stuff was, literally, astronomical. It was slow work for one man at a time, but they were unwilling to leave Kaph by himself. The one left in the dome did paperwork, while Kaph sat or lay and stared into his darkness and never spoke. The days went by, silent.

The radio spat and spoke: the Mission calling from the ship. "We'll be down on Libra in five weeks, Owen. Thirty-four E-days nine hours I make it as of now. How's tricks in the old dome?"

"Not good, chief. The Exploit team were killed, all but one of them, in the mine. Earthquake. Six days ago."

The radio crackled and sang starsong. Sixteen seconds' lag each way; the ship was out around Planet II now. "Killed, all but one? You and Martin were unhurt?"

"We're all right, chief."

Thirty-two seconds.

"*Passerine* left an Exploit team out here with us. I may put them on the Hellmouth project then, instead of the Quadrant Seven project. We'll settle that when we come down. In any case you and Martin will be relieved at Dome Two. Hold tight. Anything else?"

"Nothing else."

Thirty-two seconds.

"Right then. So long, Owen."

Kaph had heard all this, and later on Pugh said to him, "The chief may ask you to stay here with the other Exploit team. You know the ropes here." Knowing the exigencies of Far Out life, he wanted to warn the young man. Kaph made no answer. Since he had said, "There is not enough of me left alive," he had not spoken a word.

"Owen," Martin said on suit intercom, "he's spla. Insane. Psycho."

"He's doing very well for a man who's died nine times."

"Well? Like a turned-off android is well? The only emotion he has left is hate. Look at his eyes."

"That's not hate, Martin. Listen, it's true that he has, in a sense, been dead. I cannot imagine what he feels. But it's not hatred. He can't even see us. It's too dark."

"Throats have been cut in the dark. He hates us because we're not Aleph and Yod and Zayin."

"Maybe. But I think he's alone. He doesn't see us or hear us, that's the truth. He never had to see anyone else before. He never was alone before. He had himself to see, talk with, live with, nine

other selves all his life. He doesn't know how you go it alone. He must learn. Give him time."

Martin shook his heavy head. "Spla," he said. "Just remember when you're alone with him that he could break your neck one-handed."

"He could do that," said Pugh, a short, soft-voiced man with a scarred cheekbone; he smiled. They were just outside the dome airlock, programming one of the servos to repair a damaged hauler. They could see Kaph sitting inside the great half-egg of the dome like a fly in amber.

"Hand me the insert pack there. What makes you think he'll get any better?"

"He has a strong personality, to be sure."

"Strong? Crippled. Nine-tenths dead, as he put it."

"But he's not dead. He's a live man: John Kaph Chow. He had a jolly queer upbringing, but after all every boy has got to break free of his family. He will do it."

"I can't see it."

"Think a bit, Martin bach. What's this cloning for? To repair the human race. We're in a bad way. Look at me. My IIQ and GC are half this John Chow's. Yet they wanted me so badly for the Far Out Service that when I volunteered they took me and fitted me out with an artificial lung and corrected my myopia. Now if there were enough good sound lads about would they be taking one-lunged short-sighted Welshmen?"

"Didn't know you had an artificial lung."

"I do then. Not tin, you know. Human, grown in a tank from a bit of somebody; cloned, if you like. That's how they make replacement organs, the same general idea as cloning, but bits and pieces instead of whole people. It's my own lung now, whatever. But what I am saying is this, there are too many like me these days and not enough like John Chow. They're trying to raise the

level of the human genetic pool, which is a mucky little puddle since the population crash. So then if a man is cloned, he's a strong and clever man. It's only logic, to be sure."

Martin grunted; the servo began to hum.

Kaph had been eating little; he had trouble swallowing his food, choking on it, so that he would give up trying after a few bites. He had lost eight or ten kilos. After three weeks or so, however, his appetite began to pick up, and one day he began to look through the clone's possessions, the sleeping bags, kits, papers which Pugh had stacked neatly in a far angle of a packing-crate alley. He sorted, destroyed a heap of papers and oddments, made a small packet of what remained, then relapsed into his walking coma.

Two days later he spoke. Pugh was trying to correct a flutter in the tape-player and failing; Martin had the jet out, checking their maps of the Pampas. "Hell and damnation!" Pugh said, and Kaph said in a toneless voice, "Do you want me to do that?"

Pugh jumped, controlled himself, and gave the machine to Kaph. The young man took it apart, put it back together, and left it on the table.

"Put on a tape," Pugh said with careful casualness, busy at another table.

Kaph put on the topmost tape, a chorale. He lay down on his cot. The sound of a hundred human voices singing together filled the dome. He lay still, his face blank.

In the next days he took over several routine jobs, unasked. He undertook nothing that wanted initiative, and if asked to do anything he made no response at all.

"He's doing well," Pugh said in the dialect of Argentina.

"He's not. He's turning himself into a machine. Does what he's programmed to do, no reaction to anything else. He's worse off than when he didn't function at all. He's not human any more."

Pugh sighed. "Well, good night," he said in English. "Good night, Kaph."

"Good night," Martin said; Kaph did not.

Next morning at breakfast Kaph reached across Martin's plate for the toast. "Why don't you ask for it?" Martin said with the geniality of repressed exasperation. "I can pass it."

"I can reach it," Kaph said in his flat voice.

"Yes, but look. Asking to pass things, saying good night or hello, they're not important, but all the same when somebody says something a person ought to answer. . . ."

The young man looked indifferently in Martin's direction; his eyes still did not seem to see clear through to the person he looked toward. "Why should I answer?"

"Because somebody has said something to you."

"Why?"

Martin shrugged and laughed. Pugh jumped up and turned on the rock-cutter.

Later on he said, "Lay off that, please, Martin."

"Manners are essential in small isolated crews, some kind of manners, whatever you work out together. He's been taught that, everybody in Far Out knows it. Why does he deliberately flout it?"

"Do you tell yourself good night?"

"So?"

"Don't you see Kaph's never known anyone but himself?"

Martin brooded and then broke out. "Then by God this cloning business is all wrong. It won't do. What are a lot of duplicate geniuses going to do for us when they don't even know we exist?"

Pugh nodded. "It might be wiser to separate the clones and bring them up with others. But they make such a grand team this way."

"Do they? I don't know. If this lot had been ten average inefficient E.T. engineers, would they all have got killed? What if, when the quake came and things started caving in, what if all those kids

ran the same way, farther into the mine, maybe, to save the one who was farthest in? Even Kaph was outside and went in. . . . It's hypothetical. But I keep thinking, out of ten ordinary confused guys, more might have got out."

"I don't know. It's true that identical twins tend to die at about the same time, even when they have never seen each other. Identity and death, it is very strange. . . ."

The days went on, the red sun crawled across the dark sky, Kaph did not speak when spoken to, Pugh and Martin snapped at each other more frequently each day. Pugh complained of Martin's snoring. Offended, Martin moved his cot clear across the dome and also ceased speaking to Pugh for some while. Pugh whistled Welsh dirges until Martin complained, and then Pugh stopped speaking for a while.

The day before the Mission ship was due, Martin announced he was going over to Merioneth.

"I thought at least you'd be giving me a hand with the computer to finish the rock analyses," Pugh said, aggrieved.

"Kaph can do that. I want one more look at the Trench. Have fun," Martin added in dialect, and laughed, and left.

"What is that language?"

"Argentinean. I told you that once, didn't I?"

"I don't know." After a while the young man added, "I have forgotten a lot of things, I think."

"It wasn't important, to be sure," Pugh said gently, realizing all at once how important this conversation was. "Will you give me a hand running the computer, Kaph?"

He nodded.

Pugh had left a lot of loose ends, and the job took them all day. Kaph was a good co-worker, quick and systematic, much more so than Pugh himself. His flat voice, now that he was talking again, got on the nerves; but it didn't matter, there was only this one

day left to get through and then the ship would come, the old crew, comrades and friends.

During tea break Kaph said, "What will happen if the Explore ship crashes?"

"They'd be killed."

"To you, I mean."

"To us? We'd radio SOS signals and live on half rations till the rescue cruiser from Area Three Base came. Four and a half E-years away it is. We have life support here for three men for, let's see, maybe between four and five years. A bit tight, it would be."

"Would they send a cruiser for three men?"

"They would."

Kaph said no more.

"Enough cheerful speculations," Pugh said cheerfully, rising to get back to work. He slipped sideways and the chair avoided his hand; he did a sort of half-pirouette and fetched up hard against the dome hide. "My goodness," he said, reverting to his native idiom, "what is it?"

"Quake," said Kaph.

The teacups bounced on the table with a plastic cackle, a litter of papers slid off a box, the skin of the dome swelled and sagged. Underfoot there was a huge noise, half sound, half shaking, a sub-sonic boom.

Kaph sat unmoved. An earthquake does not frighten a man who died in an earthquake.

Pugh, white-faced, wiry black hair sticking out, a frightened man, said, "Martin is in the Trench."

"What trench?"

"The big fault line. The epicenter for the local quakes. Look at the seismograph." Pugh struggled with the stuck door of a still-jittering locker.

"Where are you going?"

"After him."

"Martin took the jet. Sleds aren't safe to use during quakes. They go out of control."

"For God's sake man, shut up."

Kaph stood up, speaking in a flat voice as usual. "It's unnecessary to go out after him now. It's taking an unnecessary risk."

"If his alarm goes off, radio me," Pugh said, shut the head-piece of his suit, and ran to the lock. As he went out Libra picked up her ragged skirts and danced a belly dance from under his feet clear to the red horizon.

Inside the dome, Kaph saw the sled go up, tremble like a meteor in the dull red daylight, and vanish to the northeast. The hide of the dome quivered, the earth coughed. A vent south of the dome belched up a slow-flowing bile of black gas.

A bell shrilled and a red light flashed on the central control board. The sign under the light read Suit 2 and scribbled under that, A. G. M. Kaph did not turn the signal off. He tried to radio Martin, then Pugh, but got no reply from either.

When the aftershocks decreased he went back to work and finished up Pugh's job. It took him about two hours. Every half hour he tried to contact Suit 1 and got no reply, then Suit 2 and got no reply. The red light had stopped flashing after an hour.

It was dinnertime. Kaph cooked dinner for one and ate it. He lay down on his cot.

The aftershocks had ceased except for faint rolling tremors at long intervals. The sun hung in the west, oblate, pale red, immense. It did not sink visibly. There was no sound at all.

Kaph got up and began to walk about the messy, half-packed-up, overcrowded, empty dome. The silence continued. He went to the player and put on the first tape that came to hand. It was pure music, electronic, without harmonies, without voices. It ended. The silence continued.

Pugh's uniform tunic, one button missing, hung over a stack of rock samples. Kaph stared at it a while.

The silence continued.

The child's dream: There is no one else alive in the world but me. In all the world.

Low, north of the dome, a meteor flickered.

Kaph's mouth opened as if he were trying to say something, but no sound came. He went hastily to the north wall and peered out into the gelatinous red light.

The little star came in and sank. Two figures blurred the airlock. Kaph stood close beside the lock as they came in. Martin's imsuit was covered with some kind of dust so that he looked raddled and warty like the surface of Libra. Pugh had him by the arm.

"Is he hurt?"

Pugh shucked his suit, helped Martin peel off his. "Shaken up," he said, curt.

"A piece of cliff fell onto the jet," Martin said, sitting down at the table and waving his arms. "Not while I was in it though. I was parked, see, and poking about that carbon-dust area when I felt things humping. So I went out onto a nice bit of early igneous I'd noticed from above, good footing and out from under the cliffs. Then I saw this bit of the planet fall off onto the flyer, quite a sight it was, and after a while it occurred to me the spare aircans were in the flyer, so I leaned on the panic button. But I didn't get any radio reception, that's always happening here during quakes, so I didn't know if the signal was getting through either. And things went on jumping around and pieces of the cliff coming off. Little rocks flying around, and so dusty you couldn't see a meter ahead. I was really beginning to wonder what I'd do for breathing in the small hours, you know, when I saw old Owen buzzing up the Trench in all that dust and junk like a big ugly bat—"

"Want to eat?" said Pugh.

"Of course I want to eat. How'd you come through the quake here, Kaph? No damage? It wasn't a big one actually, was it, what's the seismo say? My trouble was I was in the middle of it.

Old Epicenter Alvaro. Felt like Richter fifteen there—total destruction of planet—"

"Sit down," Pugh said. "Eat."

After Martin had eaten a little his spate of talk ran dry. He very soon went off to his cot, still in the remote angle where he had removed it when Pugh complained of his snoring. "Good night, you one-lunged Welshman," he said across the dome.

"Good night."

There was no more out of Martin. Pugh opaqued the dome, turned the lamp down to a yellow glow less than a candle's light, and sat doing nothing, saying nothing, withdrawn.

The silence continued.

"I finished the computations."

Pugh nodded thanks.

"The signal from Martin came through, but I couldn't contact you or him."

Pugh said with effort, "I should not have gone. He had two hours of air left even with only one can. He might have been heading home when I left. This way we were all out of touch with one another. I was scared."

The silence came back, punctuated now by Martin's long, soft snores.

"Do you love Martin?"

Pugh looked up with angry eyes: "Martin is my friend. We've worked together, he's a good man." He stopped. After a while he said, "Yes, I love him. Why did you ask that?"

Kaph said nothing, but he looked at the other man. His face was changed, as if he were glimpsing something he had not seen before; his voice too was changed. "How can you . . . How do you . . ."

But Pugh could not tell him. "I don't know," he said, "it's practice, partly. I don't know. We're each of us alone, to be sure. What can you do but hold your hand out in the dark?"

Kaph's strange gaze dropped, burned out by its own intensity.

"I'm tired," Pugh said. "That was ugly, looking for him in all that black dust and muck, and mouths opening and shutting in the ground. . . . I'm going to bed. The ship will be transmitting to us by six or so." He stood up and stretched.

"It's a clone," Kaph said. "The other Exploit Team they're bringing with them."

"Is it then?"

"A twelveclone. They came out with us on the *Passerine.*"

Kaph sat in the small yellow aura of the lamp seeming to look past it at what he feared: the new clone, the multiple self of which he was not part. A lost piece of a broken set, a fragment, inexpert at solitude, not knowing even how you go about giving love to another individual, now he must face the absolute, closed self-sufficiency of the clone of twelve; that was a lot to ask of the poor fellow, to be sure. Pugh put a hand on his shoulder in passing. "The chief won't ask you to stay here with a clone. You can go home. Or since you're Far Out maybe you'll come on farther out with us. We could use you. No hurry deciding. You'll make out all right."

Pugh's quiet voice trailed off. He stood unbuttoning his coat, stooped a little with fatigue. Kaph looked at him and saw the thing he had never seen before, saw him: Owen Pugh, the other, the stranger who held his hand out in the dark.

"Good night," Pugh mumbled, crawling into his sleeping bag and half asleep already, so that he did not hear Kaph reply after a pause, repeating, across darkness, benediction.

THINGS

Damon Knight, editor mirabilis, first published this story in a volume of Orbit, *under the title "The End." I don't now remember how we arrived at it, but I suspect he thought that "Things" sounded too much like something you see on the television at one* A.M., *with purple tentacles. But I have gone back to it because—at least after reading the psychomyth—it puts the right emphasis. Things you use; things you possess, and are possessed by; things you build with—bricks, words. You build houses with them, and towns, and causeways. But the buildings fall, the causeways cannot go all the way. There is an abyss, a gap, a last step to be taken.*

On the shore of the sea he stood looking out over the long foam-lines far where vague the Islands lifted or were guessed. There, he said to the sea, there lies my kingdom. The sea said to him what the sea says to everybody. As evening moved from behind his back across the water the foam-lines paled and the wind fell, and very far in the west shone a star perhaps, perhaps a light, or his desire for a light.

He climbed the streets of his town again in late dusk. The shops and huts of his neighbors were looking empty now, cleared out,

cleaned up, packed away in preparation for the end. Most of the people were up at the Weeping in Heights-Hall or down with the Ragers in the fields. But Lif had not been able to clear out and clean up; his wares and belongings were too heavy to throw away, too hard to break, too dull to burn. Only centuries could waste them. Wherever they were piled or dropped or thrown they formed what might have been, or seemed to be, or yet might be, a city. So he had not tried to get rid of his things. His yard was still stacked and piled with bricks, thousands and thousands of bricks of his own making. The kiln stood cold but ready, the barrels of clay and dry mortar and lime, the hods and barrows and trowels of his trade, everything was there. One of the fellows from Scriveners Lane had asked sneering, Going to build a brick wall and hide behind it when that old end comes, man?

Another neighbor on his way up to the Heights-Hall gazed a while at those stacks and heaps and loads and mounds of well-shaped, well-baked bricks all a soft reddish gold in the gold of the afternoon sun, and sighed at last with the weight of them on his heart: Things, things! Free yourself of things, Lif, from the weight that drags you down! Come with us, above the ending world!

Lif had picked up a brick from the heap and put it in place on the stack and smiled in embarrassment. When they were all past he had gone neither up to the Hall nor out to help wreck the fields and kill the animals, but down to the beach, the end of the ending world, beyond which lay only water. Now back in his brickyard hut with the smell of salt in his clothes and his face hot with the sea wind, he still felt neither the Ragers' laughing and wrecking despair nor the soaring and weeping despair of the communicants of the Heights; he felt empty; he felt hungry. He was a heavy little man and the sea wind at the world's edge had blown at him all evening without moving him at all.

Hey, Lif! said the widow from Weavers Lane, which crossed his

street a few houses down, —I saw you coming up the street, and
never another soul since sunset, and getting dark, and quieter than
. . . She did not say what the town was quieter than, but went on,
Have you had your supper? I was about to take my roast out of
the oven, and the little one and I will never eat up all that meat
before the end comes, no doubt, and I hate to see good meat go
to waste.

Well thank you very much, says Lif, putting on his coat again;
and they went down Masons Lane to Weavers Lane through the
dark and the wind sweeping up steep streets from the sea. In the
widow's lamplit house Lif played with her baby, the last born in the
town, a little fat boy just learning how to stand up. Lif stood him up
and he laughed and fell over, while the widow set out bread and hot
meat on the table of heavy woven cane. They sat to eat, even the
baby, who worked with four teeth at a hard hunk of bread. —How
is it you're not up on the Hill or in the fields? asked Lif, and the
widow replied as if the answer sufficed to her mind, Oh, I have the
baby.

Lif looked around the little house which her husband, who had
been one of Lif's bricklayers, had built. —This is good, he said. I
haven't tasted meat since last year some time.

I know, I know! No houses being built any more.

Not a one, he said. Not a wall nor a henhouse, not even repairs.
But your weaving, that's still wanted?

Yes; some of them want new clothes right up to the end. This
meat I bought from the Ragers that slaughtered all my lord's flocks,
and I paid with the money I got for a piece of fine linen I wove for
my lord's daughter's gown that she wants to wear at the end! The
widow gave a little derisive, sympathetic snort, and went on: But
now there's no flax, and scarcely any wool. No more to spin, no
more to weave. The fields burnt and the flocks dead.

Yes, said Lif, eating the good roast meat. Bad times, he said, the worst times.

And now, the widow went on, where's bread to come from, with the fields burnt? And water, now they're poisoning the wells? I sound like the Weepers up there, don't I? Help yourself, Lif. Spring lamb's the finest meat in the world, my man always said, till autumn came and then he'd say roast pork's the finest meat in the world. Come on now, give yourself a proper slice. . . .

That night in his hut in the brickyard Lif dreamed. Usually he slept as still as the bricks themselves but this night he drifted and floated in dream all night to the Islands, and when he woke they were no longer a wish or a guess: like a star as daylight darkens they had become certain, he knew them. But what, in his dream, had borne him over the water? He had not flown, he had not walked, he had not gone underwater like the fish; yet he had come across the grey-green plains and wind-moved hillocks of the sea to the Islands, he had heard voices call, and seen the lights of towns.

He set his mind to think how a man could ride on water. He thought of how grass floats on streams, and saw how one might make a sort of mat of woven cane and lie on it pushing with one's hands: but the great canebrakes were still smoldering down by the stream, and the piles of withies at the basketmaker's had all been burnt. On the Islands in his dream he had seen canes or grasses half a hundred feet high, with brown stems thicker than his arms could reach around, and a world of green leaves spread sunward from the thousand outreaching twigs. On those stems a man might ride over the sea. But no such plants grew in his country nor ever had; though in the Heights-Hall was a knife-handle made of a dull brown stuff, said to come from a plant that grew in some other land, called wood. But he could not ride across the bellowing sea on a knife-handle.

Greased hides might float; but the tanners had been idle now for weeks, there were no hides for sale. He might as well stop looking about for any help. He carried his barrow and his largest hod down to the beach that white windy morning and laid them in the still water of a lagoon. Indeed they floated, deep in the water, but when he leaned even the weight of one hand on them they tipped, filled, sank. They were too light, he thought.

He went back up the cliff and through the streets, loaded the barrow with useless well-made bricks, and wheeled a hard load down. As so few children had been born these last years there was no young curiosity about to ask him what he was doing, though a Rager or two, groggy from last night's wreckfest, glanced sidelong at him from a dark doorway through the brightness of the air. All that day he brought down bricks and the makings of mortar, and the next day, though he had not had the dream again, he began to lay his bricks there on the blustering beach of March with rain and sand handy in great quantities to set his cement. He built a little brick dome, upside down, oval with pointed ends like a fish, all of a single course of bricks laid spiral very cunningly. If a cupful or a barrowful of air would float, would not a brick domeful? And it would be strong. But when the mortar was set, and straining his broad back he overturned the dome and pushed it into the cream of the breakers, it dug deeper and deeper into the wet sand, burrowing down like a clam or a sand flea. The waves filled it, and refilled it when he tipped it empty, and at last a green-shouldered breaker caught it with its white dragging backpull, rolled it over, smashed it back into its elemental bricks and sank them in the restless sodden sand. There stood Lif wet to the neck and wiping salt spray out of his eyes. Nothing lay westward on the sea but wavewrack and rain-clouds. But they were there. He knew them, with their great grasses ten times a man's height, their wild golden fields raked by the sea

wind, their white towns, their white-crowned hills above the sea; and the voices of shepherds called on the hills.

I'm a builder, not a floater, said Lif after he had considered his stupidity from all sides. And he came doggedly out of the water and up the cliff-side path and through the rainy streets to get another barrowload of bricks.

Free for the first time in a week for his fool dream of floating, he noticed now that Leather Street seemed deserted. The tannery was rubbishy and vacant. The craftsmen's shops lay like a row of little black gaping mouths, and the sleeping-room windows above them were blind. At the end of the lane an old cobbler was burning, with a terrible stench, a small heap of new shoes never worn. Beside him a donkey waited, saddled, flicking its ears at the stinking smoke.

Lif went on and loaded his barrow with bricks. This time as he wheeled it down, straining back against the tug of the barrow on the steep streets, swinging all the strength of his shoulders to balance its course on the winding cliff-path down to the beach, a couple of townsmen followed him. Two or three more from Scriveners Lane followed after them, and several more from the streets round the market place, so that by the time he straightened up, the sea foam fizzing on his bare black feet and the sweat cold on his face, there was a little crowd strung out along the deep single track of his barrow over the sand. They had the lounging listless air of Ragers. Lif paid them no heed, though he was aware that the widow of Weavers Lane was up on the cliffs watching with a scared face.

He ran the barrow out into the sea till the water was up to his chest, and tipped the bricks out, and came running in with a great breaker, his banging barrow full of foam.

Already some of the Ragers were drifting away down the beach. A tall fellow from the Scriveners Lane lot lounged by him and said with a little grin, Why don't you throw 'em from the top of the cliff, man?

They'd only hit the sand, said Lif.

And you want to drown 'em. Well good. You know there was some of us thought you was building something down here! They was going to make cement out of you. Keep those bricks wet and cool, man.

Grinning, the Scrivener drifted off, and Lif started up the cliff for another load.

Come for supper, Lif, said the widow at the cliff's top with a worried voice, holding her baby close to keep it from the wind.

I will, he said. I'll bring a loaf of bread, I laid in a couple before the bakers left. He smiled, but she did not. As they climbed the streets together she asked, Are you dumping your bricks in the sea, Lif?

He laughed wholeheartedly and answered yes.

She had a look then that might have been relief and might have been sadness; but at supper in her lamplit house she was quiet and easy as ever, and they ate their cheese and stale bread with good cheer.

Next day he went on carrying bricks down load after load, and if the Ragers watched him they thought him busy on their own kind of work. The slope of the beach out to deep water was gradual, so that he could keep building without ever working above water. He had started at low tide so that his work would never be laid bare. At high tide it was hard, dumping the bricks and trying to lay them in rough courses with the whole sea boiling in his face and thundering over his head, but he kept at it. Towards evening he brought down long iron rods and braced what he had built, for a crosscurrent tended to undermine his causeway about eight feet from its beginning. He made sure that even the tips of the rods were under water at low tide, so that no Rager might suspect an affirmation was being made. A couple of elderly men coming down from a Weeping in the Heights-Hall passed him clanging and battering his empty

barrow up the stone streets in dusk, and gravely smiled upon him. It is well to be free of Things, said one softly, and the other nodded.

Next day, though still he had not dreamed of the Islands again, Lif went on building his causeway. The sand began to shelve off more steeply as he went further. His method now was to stand on the last bit he had built and tip the carefully-loaded barrow from there, and then tip himself off and work, floundering and gasping and coming up and pushing down, to get the bricks levelled and fitted between the pre-set rods; then up again, across the grey sand and up the cliff and bang-clatter through the quiet streets for another load.

Some time that week the widow said, meeting him in his brick-yard, Let me throw 'em over the cliff for you, it'll save you one leg of the trip.

It's heavy work loading the barrow, he said.

Oh, well, said she.

All right, so long as you want to. But bricks are heavy bastards. Don't try to carry many. I'll give you the small barrow. And the little rat here can sit on the load and get a ride.

So she helped him on and off through days of silvery weather, fog in the morning, clear sea and sky all afternoon, and the weeds in crannies of the cliff flowering; there was nothing else left to flower. The causeway ran out many yards from shore now, and Lif had had to learn a skill which no one else had ever learned that he knew of, except the fish. He could float and move himself about on the water or under it, in the very sea, without touching foot or hand to solid earth.

He had never heard that a man could do this thing; but he did not think much about it, being so busy with his bricks, in and out of air and in and out of water all day long, with the foam, the bubbles of water-circled air or air-circled water, all about him, and the fog, and the April rain, a confusion of the elements. Sometimes

he was happy down in the murky green unbreathable world, wrestling strangely willful and weightless bricks among the staring shoals, and only the need of air drove him gasping up into the spray-laden wind.

He built all day long, scrambling up on the sand to collect the bricks that his faithful helper dumped over the cliff's edge for him, load them in his barrow and run them out the causeway that went straight out a foot or two under sea level at low tide and four or five feet under at high, then dump them at the end, dive in, and build; then back ashore for another load. He came up into town only at evening, worn out, salt-bleared and salt-itching, hungry as a shark, to share what food turned up with the widow and her little boy. Lately, though spring was getting on with soft, long, warm evenings, the town was very dark and still.

One night when he was not too tired to notice this he spoke of it, and the widow said, Oh, they're all gone now, I think.

—All? A pause. —Where did they go?

She shrugged. She raised her dark eyes to his across the table and gazed through lamplit silence at him for a time. Where? she said. Where does your sea-road lead, Lif?

He stayed still a while. To the Islands, he answered at last, and then laughed and met her look.

She did not laugh. She only said, Are they there? Is it true, then, there are Islands? Then she looked over at her sleeping baby, and out the open doorway into the darkness of late spring that lay warm in the streets where no one walked and the rooms where no one lived. At last she looked back at Lif, and said to him, Lif, you know, there aren't many bricks left. A few hundred. You'll have to make some more. Then she began to cry softly.

By God! said Lif, thinking of his underwater road across the sea that went for a hundred and twenty feet, and the sea that went on ten thousand miles from the end of it— I'll swim there! Now then,

don't cry, dear heart. Would I leave you and the little rat here by yourselves? After all the bricks you've nearly hit my head with, and all the queer weeds and shellfish you've found us to eat lately, after your table and fireside and your bed and your laughter would I leave you when you cry? Now be still, don't cry. Let me think of a way we can get to the Islands, all of us together.

But he knew there was no way. Not for a brickmaker. He had done what he could do. What he could do went one hundred and twenty feet from shore.

Do you think, he asked after a long time, during which she had cleared the table and rinsed the plates in wellwater that was coming clear again now that the Ragers had been gone many days— Do you think that maybe . . . this . . . He found it hard to say but she stood quiet, waiting, and he had to say it: That this *is* the end?

Stillness. In the one lamplit room and all the dark rooms and streets and the burnt fields and wasted lands, stillness. In the black Hall above them on the hill's height, stillness. A silent air, a silent sky, silence in all places unbroken, unreplying. Except for the far sound of the sea, and, very soft though nearer, the breathing of a sleeping child.

No, the woman said. She sat down across from him and put her hands upon the table, fine hands as dark as earth, the palms like ivory. No, she said, the end will be the end. This is still just the waiting for it.

Then why are we still here—just us?

Oh, well, she said, you had your things—your bricks—and I had the baby. . . .

Tomorrow we must go, he said after a time. She nodded.

Before sunrise they were up. There was nothing at all left to eat, and so when she had put a few clothes for the baby in a bag and had on her warm leather mantle, and he had stuck his knife and

trowel in his belt and put on a warm cloak that had been her husband's, they left the little house, going out into the cold wan light in the deserted streets.

They went downhill, he leading, she following with the sleepy child in a fold of her cloak. He turned neither to the road that led north up the coast nor to the southern road, but went on past the market place and out on the cliff and down the rocky path to the beach. All the way she followed and neither of them spoke. At the edge of the sea he turned.

I'll keep you up in the water as long as we can manage, he said.

She nodded, and said softly, We'll use the road you built, as far as it goes.

He took her free hand and led her into the water. It was cold. It was bitter cold, and the cold light from the east behind them shone on the foam-lines hissing on the sand. When they stepped on the beginning of the causeway the bricks were firm under their feet, and the child had gone back to sleep on her shoulder in a fold of her cloak.

As they went on the buffeting of the waves got stronger. The tide was coming in. The outer breakers wet their clothes, chilled their flesh, drenched their hair and faces. They reached the end of his long work. There lay the beach a little way behind them, the sand dark under the cliff over which stood the silent, paling sky. Around them was wild water and foam. Ahead of them was the unresting water, the great abyss, the gap.

A breaker hit them on its way in to shore and they staggered; the baby, waked by the sea's hard slap, cried, a little wail in the long, cold, hissing mutter of the sea always saying the same thing.

Oh, I can't! cried the mother, but she gripped the man's hand more firmly and came on at his side.

Lifting his head to take the last step from what he had done towards no shore, he saw the shape riding the western water, the

leaping light, the white flicker like a swallow's breast catching the break of day. It seemed as if voices rang over the sea's voice. What is it? he said, but her head was bowed to her baby, trying to soothe the little wail that challenged the vast babbling of the sea. He stood still and saw the whiteness of the sail, the dancing light above the waves, dancing on towards them and towards the greater light that grew behind them.

Wait, the call came from the form that rode the grey waves and danced on the foam, Wait! The voices rang very sweet, and as the sail leaned white above him he saw the faces and the reaching arms, and heard them say to him, Come, come on the ship, come with us to the Islands.

Hold on, he said softly to the woman, and they took the last step.

A TRIP TO THE HEAD

Most people "lead lives of quiet desperation," and some stories start there, too. We were in England and it was November and dark at two in the afternoon and raining and the suitcase containing all my manuscripts had been stolen at the dock in Southampton and I hadn't written anything for months and I couldn't understand the greengrocer and he couldn't understand me and it was desperation— but quiet—stiff upper lip, don't you know. So I sat down and started scribbling words, perfectly hopelessly. Words, words, words. They went on about as far as " 'Try being Amanda,' the other said sourly," and stopped. A year or so later (British Rails, all honor to them, had found my stolen suitcase, we were back home in Oregon, it was raining) I found the scribble, and went on scribbling, and came to the end. I never did find out what the title ought to be—my agent, Virginia Kidd, did that, to my delight.

There is a kind of story which I would describe as a Bung Puller. The writer for one reason or another has been stuck, can't work; and gets started again suddenly, with a pop, and a lot of beer comes leaping out of the keg and foaming all over the floor. This story was definitely a Bung Puller.

"Is this Earth?" he cried, for things had changed abruptly.

"Yes, this is Earth," said the one beside him, "nor are you out of

it. In Zambia men are rolling down hills inside barrels as training for space flight. Israel and Egypt have defoliated each other's deserts. The *Reader's Digest* has bought a controlling interest in the United States of America/General Mills combine. The population of the Earth is increasing by thirty billion every Thursday. Mrs Jacqueline Kennedy Onassis will marry Mao Tse-Tung on Saturday, in search of security; and Russia has contaminated Mars with bread mold."

"Why then," said he, "nothing has changed."

"Nothing much," said the one beside him. "As Jean-Paul Sartre has said in his lovable way, 'Hell is other people.' "

"To Hell with Jean-Paul Sartre. I want to know where I am."

"Well then," said the other, "tell me who you are."

"I'm."

"Well?"

"My name is."

"What?"

He stood, his eyes filling with tears and his knees with palsy, and knew he did not know his name. He was a blank, a cipher, an x. He had a body and all that, but he had no who.

They stood at the edge of a forest, he and the other one. It was a recognizable forest, though rather dingy in the leaf, and damaged at the fringes by weedkiller. A fawn was walking away from them into the forest and as it went its name fell away from it. Something looked back at them with mild eyes from the darkness of the trees before it vanished. "This is England!" cried blank, grasping the floating straw, but the other said, "England sank years ago."

"Sank?"

"Yes. Foundered. Nothing is left now but the topmost fourteen feet of Mt Snowdon, known as the New Welsh Reef."

At this blank also sank. He was crushed. "Oh," he cried on his knees, intending to ask somebody's help, but he could not remember whose help it was one asked. It began with a T, he was almost certain. He began to weep.

The other sat down on the grass beside him and presently put a hand on his shoulder, saying, "Come on now, don't take it so hard."

The kindly voice gave blank some courage. He controlled himself, dried his face on his sleeve, and looked at the other. It was like him, roughly. It was another. However, it had no name either. What good was it?

Shadow came into the eyes as Earth went round on its axis. Shadow slipped eastward and upward into the other's eyes.

"I think," blank said carefully, "that we should move out from the shadow of the, this, here." He gestured to the objects near them, large things, dark below and multitudinously green above, the names of which he could no longer remember. He wondered if each one had a name, or if they were all called by the same name. What about himself and the other, did they share a name in common, or did each have one of his own? "I have a feeling I'll remember better farther away from it, from them," he said.

"Certainly," said the other. "But it won't make as much difference as it used to."

When they came clear away from it into the sunlight, he at once remembered that it was called a forest and that they were called trees. However, he could not recall whether or not each tree had a name of its own. If they did, he did not remember any of them. Perhaps he did not know these trees personally.

"What shall I do," he said, "what shall I do?"

"Well, look here, you can call yourself whatever you please, you know. Why not?"

"But I want to know my *real* name."

"That isn't always easy. But meanwhile you could just take a label, as it were, for ease of reference and conversational purposes. Pick a name, any name!" said the other, and held out a blue box named DISPOSABLE.

"No," said blank proudly, "I'll choose my own."

"Right. But don't you want a kleenex?"

Blank took a kleenex, blew his nose, and said, "I shall call myself . . ." He halted in terror.

The other watched him, mild-eyed.

"How can I say who I am when I can't say what I am?"

"How would you find out what you are?"

"If I had anything— If I did something— "

"That would make you be?"

"Of course it would."

"I never thought of that. Well, then, it doesn't matter what name you're called by; any one will do; it's what you do that counts."

Blank stood up. "I will exist," he stated firmly. "I will call myself Ralph."

Whipcord breeches fitted close on his powerful thighs, the stock rose high on his neck, sweat clung in his thick, curly hair. He tapped his boots with his riding-crop, his back to Amanda, who sat in her old grey dress in the deep shade of the pecan tree. He stood in full sunlight, hot with anger. "You're a fool," he said.

"Why Mr Ralph," came the soft lilting Southern voice, "Ah'm just a little bit stubborn."

"You realize, don't you, that Yankee as I am, I own all the land from here to Weevilville? I own this county! Your farm wouldn't make a peanut-patch for one of my darkies' kitchen gardens!"

"Indeed not. Won't you come sit down in the shade, Mr Ralph? Youah gettin' so hot out theah."

"You proud vixen," he murmured, turning. He saw her, white as a lily in her worn old dress, in the shade of the great old trees: the white lily of the garden. Suddenly he was at her feet, clasping her hands. She fluttered in his powerful grasp. "Oh Mr Ralph," she cried faintly, "what does this mean?"

"I am a man, Amanda, and you are a woman. I never wanted your land. I never wanted anything but you, my white lily, my little rebel! I want you, I want you! Amanda! Say you will be my wife!"

"Ah will," she breathed faintly, bending towards him as a white flower stoops; and their lips met in a long, long kiss. But it did not seem to help at all.

Perhaps it ought to be moved up twenty or thirty years.

"You sick bitch," he muttered, turning. He saw her, stark naked there in the shade, her back against the pecan tree, her knees up. He strode towards her unbuttoning his fly. They coupled in the centipede-infested crabgrass. He bucked like a bronco, she cried ululatingly, *Oooh! Aaah!* Coming coming coming COME wow wow wow CLIMAX!

Now what?

Blank stood at a little distance from the forest and stared disconsolately at the other.

"Am I a man?" he inquired. "Are you a woman?"

"Don't ask me," the other said, morose.

"I thought surely that was the most important thing to establish!"

"Not so damned important."

"You mean it doesn't *matter* if I am a man or a woman?"

"Of course it matters. It matters to me too. It also matters which man and which woman we are or, as the case may be, are not. For instance, what if Amanda was black?"

"But sex."

"Oh, Hell," said the other with a flare of temper, "bristleworms have sex, tree-sloths have sex, Jean-Paul Sartre has sex—what does it prove?"

"Why, sex is real, I mean really real—it's having and acting in its intensest form. When a man takes a woman he proves his being!"

"I see. But what if he's a woman?"

"I was Ralph."

"Try being Amanda," the other said sourly.

There was a pause. Shadows were coming on eastward and upward from the forest over the grass. Small birds cried *jug jug, tereu*.

Blank sat hunched over his knees. The other lay stretched out, making patterns with fallen pine needles, shadowed, sorrowful.

"I'm sorry," blank said.

"No harm done," the other said. "After all, it wasn't real."

"Listen," blank said, leaping up, "I know what's happened! I'm on some kind of trip. I took something, and I'm on a trip, that's it!"

It was. He was on a trip. A canoe trip. He was paddling a small canoe along a long, narrow, dark, shining stretch of water. The roof and walls were of concrete. It was pretty dark. The long lake, or stream, or sewer, slanted upward visibly. He was paddling against the current, uphill. It was hard work, but the canoe kept sliding forward upriver as silently as the black shining water moved back down. He kept his strokes quiet, the paddle entering the water silent as a knife in butter. His large black-and-pearl electric guitar lay on the forward seat. He knew there was somebody behind him, but he didn't say anything. He wasn't allowed to say anything or even look around, so if they didn't keep up that was their lookout, he couldn't be called responsible. He certainly couldn't slow down, the current might get hold of his canoe and pull it right out from under him and then where'd he be? He shut his eyes and kept paddling, silent entry, strong stroke. There was no sound behind him. The water made no sound. The cement made no sound. He wondered if he was actually going forward or only hanging still while the black water ran hellbent beneath. He would never get out to daylight. Out, out—

out. The other didn't even seem to have noticed that blank had been away on a trip, but just lay there making patterns with pine needles, and presently said, "How is your memory?"

Blank searched it to see if it had improved while he was away. There was less in it than before. The cupboard was bare. There was a lot of junk in the cellars and attics, old toys, nursery rhymes, myths,

old wives' tales, but no nourishment for adults, no least scrap of possession, not a crumb of success. He searched and searched like a starving methodical rat. At last he said uncertainly, "I do remember England."

"Why surely. I expect you can even remember Omaha."

"But I mean, I remember being in England."

"Do you?" The other sat up, scattering pinestraw. "You do remember being, then! What a pity England sank."

They were silent again.

"I have lost everything."

There was a darkness in the other's eyes and on the eastern edge of the earth plunging down the steepening slopes of night.

"I'm nobody."

"At least," said the other, "you know you're human."

"Oh, what good's that? with no name, no sex, no nothing? I might as well be a bristleworm or a tree-sloth!"

"You might as well," the other agreed, "be Jean-Paul Sartre."

"I?" said blank, offended. Driven to denial by so nauseous a notion, he stood up and said, "I certainly am not Jean-Paul Sartre. I am myself." And so saying he found himself to be, in fact, himself; his name was Lewis D. Charles and he knew it as well as he knew his own name. There he was.

The forest was there, root and branch.

The other was, however, gone.

Lewis D. Charles looked in the red eye of the west and the dark eye of the east. He shouted aloud, "Come back! Please come back!"

He had gone at it all wrong, backwards. He had found the wrong name. He turned, and without the least impulse of self-preservation plunged into the pathless forest, casting himself away so that he might find what he had cast away.

Under the trees he forgot his name again at once. He also forgot

what he was looking for. What was it he had lost? He went deeper and deeper into shadows, under leaves, eastward, in the forest where nameless tigers burned.

VASTER THAN EMPIRES AND MORE SLOW

Trees again.

As I recall, Robert Silverberg, who first published this story in New Dimensions 1, asked very gently if I would change the title. I could see where a reader about halfway through might find the title all too descriptive of the story itself; but it was too beautiful, and too beautifully apt, to part with, and Mr Silverberg let me keep it. It's from Marvell, "To his Coy Mistress"—

> Our vegetable love should grow
> Vaster than empires, and more slow. . . .

Like "Nine Lives," this is not a psychomyth but a regular science fiction story, developed not for action/adventure, but psychologically. Unless physical action reflects psychic action, unless the deeds express the person, I get very bored with adventure stories; often it seems that the more action there is, the less happens. Obviously my interest is in what goes on inside. Inner space and all that. We all have forests in our minds. Forests unexplored, unending. Each of us gets lost in the forest, every night, alone.

Hidden in the foliage here is a tiny act of homage. The protagonist of "He Who Shapes" by Roger Zelazny, one of the finest science fiction stories I know, is called Charles Render. I christened a syndrome after him.

It was only during the earliest decades of the League that the Earth sent ships out on the enormously long voyages, beyond the pale, over the stars and far away. They were seeking for worlds which had not been seeded or settled by the Founders on Hain, truly alien worlds. All the Known Worlds went back to the Hainish Origin, and the Terrans, having been not only founded but salvaged by the Hainish, resented this. They wanted to get away from the family. They wanted to find somebody new. The Hainish, like tiresomely understanding parents, supported their explorations, and contributed ships and volunteers, as did several other worlds of the League.

All these volunteers to the Extreme Survey crews shared one peculiarity: they were of unsound mind.

What sane person, after all, would go out to collect information that would not be received for five or ten centuries? Cosmic mass interference had not yet been eliminated from the operation of the ansible, and so instantaneous communication was reliable only within a range of 120 lightyears. The explorers would be quite isolated. And of course they had no idea what they might come back to, if they came back. No normal human being who had experienced time-slippage of even a few decades between League worlds would volunteer for a round trip of centuries. The Surveyors were escapists, misfits. They were nuts.

Ten of them climbed aboard the ferry at Smeming Port, and made varyingly inept attempts to get to know one another during the three days the ferry took getting to their ship, *Gum*. Gum is a Cetian nickname, on the order of Baby or Pet. There were two Cetians on the team, two Hainishmen, one Beldene, and five Terrans; the Cetian-built ship was chartered by the Government of Earth. Her motley crew came aboard wriggling through the coupling tube one by one like apprehensive spermatozoa trying to fertilize the universe. The ferry left, and the navigator put *Gum* underway. She flittered for some hours on the edge of space a few hundred million miles from Smeming Port, and then abruptly vanished.

When, after 10 hours 29 minutes, or 256 years, *Gum* reappeared in normal space, she was supposed to be in the vicinity of Star KG–E–96651. Sure enough, there was the gold pinhead of the star. Somewhere within a four-hundred-million-kilometer sphere there was also a greenish planet, World 4470, as charted by a Cetian mapmaker. The ship now had to find the planet. This was not quite so easy as it might sound, given a four-hundred-million-kilometer haystack. And *Gum* couldn't bat about in planetary space at near lightspeed; if she did, she and Star KG-E-96651 and World 4470 might all end up going bang. She had to creep, using rocket propulsion, at a few hundred thousand miles an hour. The Mathematician/Navigator, Asnanifoil, knew pretty well where the planet ought to be, and thought they might raise it within ten E-days. Meanwhile the members of the Survey team got to know one another still better.

"I can't stand him," said Porlock, the Hard Scientist (chemistry, plus physics, astronomy, geology, etc.), and little blobs of spittle appeared on his mustache. "The man is insane. I can't imagine why he was passed as fit to join a Survey team, unless this is a deliberate experiment in noncompatibility, planned by the Authority, with us as guinea pigs."

"We generally use hamsters and Hainish gholes," said Mannon, the Soft Scientist (psychology, plus psychiatry, anthropology, ecology, etc.), politely; he was one of the Hainishmen. "Instead of guinea pigs. Well, you know, Mr Osden is really a very rare case. In fact, he's the first fully cured case of Render's Syndrome—a variety of infantile autism which was thought to be incurable. The great Terran analyst Hammergeld reasoned that the cause of the autistic condition in this case is a supernormal empathic capacity, and developed an appropriate treatment. Mr Osden is the first patient to undergo that treatment, in fact he lived with Dr Hammergeld until he was eighteen. The therapy was completely successful."

"Successful?"

"Why, yes. He certainly is not autistic."

"No, he's intolerable!"

"Well, you see," said Mannon, gazing mildly at the saliva-flecks on Porlock's mustache, "the normal defensive-aggressive reaction between strangers meeting—let's say you and Mr Osden just for example—is something you're scarcely aware of; habit, manners, inattention get you past it; you've learned to ignore it, to the point where you might even deny it exists. However, Mr Osden, being an empath, feels it. Feels his feelings, and yours, and is hard put to say which is which. Let's say that there's a normal element of hostility towards any stranger in your emotional reaction to him when you meet him, plus a spontaneous dislike of his looks, or clothes, or handshake—it doesn't matter what. He feels that dislike. As his autistic defense has been unlearned, he resorts to an aggressive-defense mechanism, a response in kind to the aggression which you have unwittingly projected onto him." Mannon went on for quite a long time.

"Nothing gives a man the right to be such a bastard," Porlock said.

"He can't tune us out?" asked Harfex, the Biologist, another Hainishman.

"It's like hearing," said Olleroo, Assistant Hard Scientist, stooping over to paint her toenails with fluorescent lacquer. "No eyelids on your ears. No Off switch on empathy. He hears our feelings whether he wants to or not."

"Does he know what we're *thinking?*" asked Eskwana, the Engineer, looking round at the others in real dread.

"No," Porlock snapped. "Empathy's not telepathy! Nobody's got telepathy."

"Yet," said Mannon, with his little smile. "Just before I left Hain there was a most interesting report in from one of the recently rediscovered worlds, a hilfer named Rocannon reporting what appears to be a teachable telepathic technique existent among a

mutated hominid race; I only saw a synopsis in the HILF Bulletin, but—" He went on. The others had learned that they could talk while Mannon went on talking; he did not seem to mind, nor even to miss much of what they said.

"Then why does he hate us?" Eskwana said.

"Nobody hates you, Ander honey," said Olleroo, daubing Eskwana's left thumbnail with fluorescent pink. The engineer flushed and smiled vaguely.

"He acts as if he hated us," said Haito, the Coordinator. She was a delicate-looking woman of pure Asian descent, with a surprising voice, husky, deep, and soft, like a young bullfrog. "Why, if he suffers from our hostility, does he increase it by constant attacks and insults? I can't say I think much of Dr Hammergeld's cure, really, Mannon; autism might be preferable. . . ."

She stopped. Osden had come into the main cabin.

He looked flayed. His skin was unnaturally white and thin, showing the channels of his blood like a faded road map in red and blue. His Adam's apple, the muscles that circled his mouth, the bones and ligaments of his wrists and hands, all stood out distinctly as if displayed for an anatomy lesson. His hair was pale rust, like long-dried blood. He had eyebrows and lashes, but they were visible only in certain lights; what one saw was the bones of the eye sockets, the veining of the lids, and the colorless eyes. They were not red eyes, for he was not really an albino, but they were not blue or grey; colors had cancelled out in Osden's eyes, leaving a cold water-like clarity, infinitely penetrable. He never looked directly at one. His face lacked expression, like an anatomical drawing, or a skinned face.

"I agree," he said in a high, harsh tenor, "that even autistic withdrawal might be preferable to the smog of cheap secondhand emotions with which you people surround me. What are you sweating hate for now, Porlock? Can't stand the sight of me? Go practice

some auto-eroticism the way you were doing last night, it improves your vibes. Who the devil moved my tapes, here? Don't touch my things, any of you. I won't have it."

"Osden," said Asnanifoil in his large slow voice, "why *are* you such a bastard?"

Ander Eskwana cowered and put his hands in front of his face. Contention frightened him. Olleroo looked up with a vacant yet eager expression, the eternal spectator.

"Why shouldn't I be?" said Osden. He was not looking at Asnanifoil, and was keeping physically as far away from all of them as he could in the crowded cabin. "None of you constitute, in yourselves, any reason for my changing my behavior."

Harfex, a reserved and patient man, said, "The reason is that we shall be spending several years together. Life will be better for all of us if—"

"Can't you understand that I don't give a damn for all of you?" Osden said, took up his microtapes, and went out. Eskwana had suddenly gone to sleep. Asnanifoil was drawing slipstreams in the air with his finger and muttering the Ritual Primes. "You cannot explain his presence on the team except as a plot on the part of the Terran Authority. I saw this almost at once. This mission is meant to fail," Harfex whispered to the Coordinator, glancing over his shoulder. Porlock was fumbling with his fly-button; there were tears in his eyes. I did tell you they were all crazy, but you thought I was exaggerating.

All the same, they were not unjustified. Extreme Surveyors expected to find their fellow team members intelligent, well-trained, unstable, and personally sympathetic. They had to work together in close quarters and nasty places, and could expect one another's paranoias, depressions, manias, phobias and compulsions to be mild enough to admit of good personal relationships, at least most of the

time. Osden might be intelligent, but his training was sketchy and his personality was disastrous. He had been sent only on account of his singular gift, the power of empathy: properly speaking, of wide-range bioempathic receptivity. His talent wasn't species-specific; he could pick up emotion or sentience from anything that felt. He could share lust with a white rat, pain with a squashed cockroach, and phototropy with a moth. On an alien world, the Authority had decided, it would be useful to know if anything nearby is sentient, and if so, what its feelings towards you are. Osden's title was a new one: he was the team's Sensor.

"What is emotion, Osden?" Haito Tomiko asked him one day in the main cabin, trying to make some rapport with him for once. "What is it, exactly, that you pick up with your empathic sensitivity?"

"Muck," the man answered in his high, exasperated voice. "The psychic excreta of the animal kingdom. I wade through your faeces."

"I was trying," she said, "to learn some facts." She thought her tone was admirably calm.

"You weren't after facts. You were trying to get at me. With some fear, some curiosity, and a great deal of distaste. The way you might poke a dead dog, to see the maggots crawl. Will you understand once and for all that I don't want to be got at, that I want to be left alone?" His skin was mottled with red and violet, his voice had risen. "Go roll in your own dung, you yellow bitch!" he shouted at her silence.

"Calm down," she said, still quietly, but she left him at once and went to her cabin. Of course he had been right about her motives; her question had been largely a pretext, a mere effort to interest him. But what harm in that? Did not that effort imply respect for the other? At the moment of asking the question she had felt at

most a slight distrust of him; she had mostly felt sorry for him, the poor arrogant venomous bastard, Mr No-Skin as Olleroo called him. What did he expect, the way he acted? Love?

"I guess he can't stand anybody feeling sorry for him," said Olleroo, lying on the lower bunk, gilding her nipples.

"Then he can't form any human relationship. All his Dr Hammergeld did was turn an autism inside out. . . ."

"Poor frot," said Olleroo. "Tomiko, you don't mind if Harfex comes in for a while tonight, do you?"

"Can't you go to his cabin? I'm sick of always having to sit in Main with that damned peeled turnip."

"You do hate him, don't you? I guess he feels that. But I slept with Harfex last night too, and Asnanifoil might get jealous, since they share the cabin. It would be nicer here."

"Service them both," Tomiko said with the coarseness of offended modesty. Her Terran subculture, the East Asian, was a puritanical one; she had been brought up chaste.

"I only like one a night," Olleroo replied with innocent serenity. Beldene, the Garden Planet, had never discovered chastity, or the wheel.

"Try Osden, then," Tomiko said. Her personal instability was seldom so plain as now: a profound self-distrust manifesting itself as destructivism. She had volunteered for this job because there was, in all probability, no use in doing it.

The little Beldene looked up, paintbrush in hand, eyes wide. "Tomiko, that was a dirty thing to say."

"Why?"

"It would be vile! I'm not attracted to Osden!"

"I didn't know it mattered to you," Tomiko said indifferently, though she did know. She got some papers together and left the cabin, remarking, "I hope you and Harfex or whoever it is finish by last bell; I'm tired."

Olleroo was crying, tears dripping on her little gilded nipples. She wept easily. Tomiko had not wept since she was ten years old.

It was not a happy ship; but it took a turn for the better when Asnanifoil and his computers raised World 4470. There it lay, a dark-green jewel, like truth at the bottom of a gravity well. As they watched the jade disc grow, a sense of mutuality grew among them. Osden's selfishness, his accurate cruelty, served now to draw the others together. "Perhaps," Mannon said, "he was sent as a beating-gron. What Terrans call a scapegoat. Perhaps his influence will be good after all." And no one, so careful were they to be kind to one another, disagreed.

They came into orbit. There were no lights on nightside, on the continents none of the lines and clots made by animals who build.

"No men," Harfex murmured.

"Of course not," snapped Osden, who had a viewscreen to himself, and his head inside a polythene bag. He claimed that the plastic cut down on the empathic noise he received from the others. "We're two lightcenturies past the limit of the Hainish Expansion, and outside that there are no men. Anywhere. You don't think Creation would have made the same hideous mistake twice?"

No one was paying him much heed; they were looking with affection at that jade immensity below them, where there was life, but not human life. They were misfits among men, and what they saw there was not desolation, but peace. Even Osden did not look quite so expressionless as usual; he was frowning.

Descent in fire on the sea; air reconnaissance; landing. A plain of something like grass, thick, green, bowing stalks, surrounded the ship, brushed against extended viewcameras, smeared the lenses with a fine pollen.

"It looks like a pure phytosphere," Harfex said. "Osden, do you pick up anything sentient?"

They all turned to the Sensor. He had left the screen and was

pouring himself a cup of tea. He did not answer. He seldom answered spoken questions.

The chitinous rigidity of military discipline was quite inapplicable to these teams of mad scientists; their chain of command lay somewhere between parliamentary procedure and peck-order, and would have driven a regular service officer out of his mind. By the inscrutable decision of the Authority, however, Dr Haito Tomiko had been given the title of Coordinator, and she now exercised her prerogative for the first time. "Mr Sensor Osden," she said, "please answer Mr Harfex."

"How could I 'pick up' anything from outside," Osden said without turning, "with the emotions of nine neurotic hominids pullulating around me like worms in a can? When I have anything to tell you, I'll tell you. I'm aware of my responsibility as Sensor. If you presume to give me an order again, however, Coordinator Haito, I'll consider my responsibility void."

"Very well, Mr. Sensor. I trust no orders will be needed henceforth." Tomiko's bullfrog voice was calm, but Osden seemed to flinch slightly as he stood with his back to her, as if the surge of her suppressed rancor had struck him with physical force.

The biologist's hunch proved correct. When they began field analyses they found no animals even among the microbiota. Nobody here ate anybody else. All life-forms were photosynthesizing or saprophagous, living off light or death, not off life. Plants: infinite plants, not one species known to the visitors from the house of Man. Infinite shades and intensities of green, violet, purple, brown, red. Infinite silences. Only the wind moved, swaying leaves and fronds, a warm soughing wind laden with spores and pollens, blowing the sweet pale-green dust over prairies of great grasses, heaths that bore no heather, flowerless forests where no foot had ever walked, no eye had ever looked. A warm, sad world, sad and serene. The Surveyors, wandering like picnickers over sunny plains

of violet filicaliformes, spoke softly to each other. They knew their voices broke a silence of a thousand million years, the silence of wind and leaves, leaves and wind, blowing and ceasing and blowing again. They talked softly; but being human, they talked.

"Poor old Osden," said Jenny Chong, Bio and Tech, as she piloted a helijet on the North Polar Quadrating run. "All that fancy hi-fi stuff in his brain and nothing to receive. What a bust."

"He told me he hates plants," Olleroo said with a giggle.

"You'd think he'd like them, since they don't bother him like we do."

"Can't say I much like these plants myself," said Porlock, looking down at the purple undulations of the North Circumpolar Forest. "All the same. No mind. No change. A man alone in it would go right off his head."

"But it's all alive," Jenny Chong said. "And if it lives, Osden hates it."

"He's not really so bad," Olleroo said, magnanimous. Porlock looked at her sidelong and asked, "You ever slept with him, Olleroo?"

Olleroo burst into tears and cried, "You Terrans are obscene!"

"No she hasn't," Jenny Chong said, prompt to defend. "Have you, Porlock?"

The chemist laughed uneasily: ha, ha, ha. Flecks of spittle appeared on his mustache.

"Osden can't bear to be touched," Olleroo said shakily. "I just brushed against him once by accident and he knocked me off like I was some sort of dirty . . . thing. We're all just things, to him."

"He's evil," Porlock said in a strained voice, startling the two women. "He'll end up shattering this team, sabotaging it, one way or another. Mark my words. He's not fit to live with other people!"

They landed on the North Pole. A midnight sun smouldered over low hills. Short, dry, greenish-pink bryoform grasses stretched away

in every direction, which was all one direction, south. Subdued by the incredible silence, the three Surveyors set up their instruments and set to work, three viruses twitching minutely on the hide of an unmoving giant.

Nobody asked Osden along on runs as pilot or photographer or recorder, and he never volunteered, so he seldom left base camp. He ran Harfex's botanical taxonomic data through the onship computers, and served as assistant to Eskwana, whose job here was mainly repair and maintenance. Eskwana had begun to sleep a great deal, twenty-five hours or more out of the thirty-two-hour day, dropping off in the middle of repairing a radio or checking the guidance circuits of a helijet. The Coordinator stayed at base one day to observe. No one else was home except Poswet To, who was subject to epileptic fits; Mannon had plugged her into a therapy-circuit today in a state of preventive catatonia. Tomiko spoke reports into the storage banks, and kept an eye on Osden and Eskwana. Two hours passed.

"You might want to use the 860 microwaldoes in sealing that connection," Eskwana said in his soft, hesitant voice.

"Obviously!"

"Sorry. I just saw you had the 840's there—"

"And will replace them when I take the 860's out. When I don't know how to proceed, Engineer, I'll ask your advice."

After a minute Tomiko looked round. Sure enough, there was Eskwana sound asleep, head on the table, thumb in his mouth.

"Osden."

The white face did not turn, he did not speak, but conveyed impatiently that he was listening.

"You can't be unaware of Eskwana's vulnerability."

"I am not responsible for his psychopathic reactions."

"But you are responsible for your own. Eskwana is essential to our work here, and you're not. If you can't control your hostility, you must avoid him altogether."

Osden put down his tools and stood up. "With pleasure!" he said in his vindictive, scraping voice. "You could not possibly imagine what it's like to experience Eskwana's irrational terrors. To have to share his horrible cowardice, to have to cringe with him at everything!"

"Are you trying to justify your cruelty towards him? I thought you had more self-respect." Tomiko found herself shaking with spite. "If your empathic power really makes you share Ander's misery, why does it never induce the least compassion in you?"

"Compassion," Osden said. "Compassion. What do you know about compassion?"

She stared at him, but he would not look at her.

"Would you like me to verbalize your present emotional affect regarding myself?" he said. "I can do so more precisely than you can. I'm trained to analyze such responses as I receive them. And I do receive them."

"But how can you expect me to feel kindly towards you when you behave as you do?"

"What does it matter how I *behave,* you stupid sow, do you think it makes any difference? Do you think the average human is a well of loving-kindness? My choice is to be hated or to be despised. Not being a woman or a coward, I prefer to be hated."

"That's rot. Self-pity. Every man has—"

"But I am not a man," Osden said. "There are all of you. And there is myself. I am *one.*"

Awed by that glimpse of abysmal solipsism, she kept silent a while; finally she said with neither spite nor pity, clinically, "You could kill yourself, Osden."

"That's your way, Haito," he jeered. "I'm not depressive, and *seppuku* isn't my bit. What do you want me to do here?"

"Leave. Spare yourself and us. Take the aircar and a data-feeder and go do a species count. In the forest; Harfex hasn't even started the forests yet. Take a hundred-square-meter forested area, any-

where inside radio range. But outside empathy range. Report in at 8 and 24 o'clock daily."

Osden went, and nothing was heard from him for five days but laconic all-well signals twice daily. The mood at base camp changed like a stage-set. Eskwana stayed awake up to eighteen hours a day. Poswet To got out her stellar lute and chanted the celestial harmonies (music had driven Osden into a frenzy). Mannon, Harfex, Jenny Chong, and Tomiko all went off tranquillizers. Porlock distilled something in his laboratory and drank it all by himself. He had a hangover. Asnanifoil and Poswet To held an all-night Numerical Epiphany, that mystical orgy of higher mathematics which is the chief pleasure of the religious Cetian soul. Olleroo slept with everybody. Work went well.

The Hard Scientist came towards base at a run, laboring through the high, fleshy stalks of the graminiformes. "Something—in the forest—" His eyes bulged, he panted, his mustache and fingers trembled. "Something big. Moving, behind me. I was putting in a benchmark, bending down. It came at me. As if it was swinging down out of the trees. Behind me." He stared at the others with the opaque eyes of terror or exhaustion.

"Sit down, Porlock. Take it easy. Now wait, go through this again. You *saw* something—"

"Not clearly. Just the movement. Purposive. A—an—I don't know what it could have been. Something self-moving. In the trees, the arboriformes, whatever you call 'em. At the edge of the woods."

Harfex looked grim. "There is nothing here that could attack you, Porlock. There are not even microzoa. There *could not* be a large animal."

"Could you possibly have seen an epiphyte drop suddenly, a vine come loose behind you?"

"No," Porlock said. "It was coming down at me, through the branches, fast. When I turned it took off again, away and upward.

It made a noise, a sort of crashing. If it wasn't an animal, God knows what it could have been! It was big—as big as a man, at least. Maybe a reddish color. I couldn't see, I'm not sure."

"It was Osden," said Jenny Chong, "doing a Tarzan act." She giggled nervously, and Tomiko repressed a wild feckless laugh. But Harfex was not smiling.

"One gets uneasy under the arboriformes," he said in his polite, repressed voice. "I've noticed that. Indeed that may be why I've put off working in the forests. There's a hypnotic quality in the colors and spacing of the stems and branches, especially the helically-arranged ones; and the spore-throwers grow so regularly spaced that it seems unnatural. I find it quite disagreeable, subjectively speaking. I wonder if a stronger effect of that sort mightn't have produced a hallucination. . . ?"

Porlock shook his head. He wet his lips. "It was there," he said. "Something. Moving with purpose. Trying to attack me from behind."

When Osden called in, punctual as always, at 24 o'clock that night, Harfex told him Porlock's report. "Have you come on anything at all, Mr Osden, that could substantiate Mr Porlock's impression of a motile, sentient life-form, in the forest?"

Ssss, the radio said sardonically. "No. Bullshit," said Osden's unpleasant voice.

"You've been actually inside the forest longer than any of us," Harfex said with unmitigable politeness. "Do you agree with my impression that the forest ambiance has a rather troubling and possibly hallucinogenic effect on the perceptions?"

Ssss. "I'll agree that Porlock's perceptions are easily troubled. Keep him in his lab, he'll do less harm. Anything else?"

"Not at present," Harfex said, and Osden cut off.

Nobody could credit Porlock's story, and nobody could discredit it. He was positive that something, something big, had tried to

attack him by surprise. It was hard to deny this, for they were on an alien world, and everyone who had entered the forest had felt a certain chill and foreboding under the "trees." ("Call them trees, certainly," Harfex had said. "They really are the same thing, only, of course, altogether different.") They agreed that they had felt uneasy, or had had the sense that something was watching them from behind.

"We've got to clear this up," Porlock said, and he asked to be sent as a temporary Biologist's Aide, like Osden, into the forest to explore and observe. Olleroo and Jenny Chong volunteered if they could go as a pair. Harfex sent them all off into the forest near which they were encamped, a vast tract covering four-fifths of Continent D. He forbade side-arms. They were not to go outside a fifty-mile half-circle, which included Osden's current site. They all reported in twice daily, for three days. Porlock reported a glimpse of what seemed to be a large semi-erect shape moving through the trees across the river; Olleroo was sure she had heard something moving near the tent, the second night.

"There are no animals on this planet," Harfex said, dogged.

Then Osden missed his morning call.

Tomiko waited less than an hour, then flew with Harfex to the area where Osden had reported himself the night before. But as the helijet hovered over the sea of purplish leaves, illimitable, impenetrable, she felt a panic despair. "How can we find him in this?"

"He reported landing on the riverbank. Find the aircar; he'll be camped near it, and he can't have gone far from his camp. Species-counting is slow work. There's the river."

"There's his car," Tomiko said, catching the bright foreign glint among the vegetable colors and shadows. "Here goes, then."

She put the ship in hover and pitched out the ladder. She and Harfex descended. The sea of life closed over their heads.

As her feet touched the forest floor, she unsnapped the flap of her holster; then glancing at Harfex, who was unarmed, she left the gun untouched. But her hand kept coming back up to it. There was no sound at all, as soon as they were a few meters away from the slow, brown river, and the light was dim. Great boles stood well apart, almost regularly, almost alike; they were soft-skinned, some appearing smooth and others spongy, grey or greenish-brown or brown, twined with cable-like creepers and festooned with epiphytes, extending rigid, entangled armfuls of big, saucer-shaped, dark leaves that formed a roof-layer twenty to thirty meters thick. The ground underfoot was springy as a mattress, every inch of it knotted with roots and peppered with small, fleshy-leaved growths.

"Here's his tent," Tomiko said, cowed at the sound of her voice in that huge community of the voiceless. In the tent was Osden's sleeping bag, a couple of books, a box of rations. We should be calling, shouting for him, she thought, but did not even suggest it; nor did Harfex. They circled out from the tent, careful to keep each other in sight through the thick-standing presences, the crowding gloom. She stumbled over Osden's body, not thirty meters from the tent, led to it by the whitish gleam of a dropped notebook. He lay face down between two huge-rooted trees. His head and hands were covered with blood, some dried, some still oozing red.

Harfex appeared beside her, his pale Hainish complexion quite green in the dusk. "Dead?"

"No. He's been struck. Beaten. From behind." Tomiko's fingers felt over the bloody skull and temples and nape. "A weapon or a tool . . . I don't find a fracture."

As she turned Osden's body over so they could lift him, his eyes opened. She was holding him, bending close to his face. His pale lips writhed. A deathly fear came into her. She screamed aloud two or three times and tried to run away, shambling and stumbling

into the terrible dusk. Harfex caught her, and at his touch and the sound of his voice, her panic decreased. "What is it? What is it?" he was saying.

"I don't know," she sobbed. Her heartbeat still shook her, and she could not see clearly. "The fear—the . . . I panicked. When I saw his eyes."

"We're both nervous. I don't understand this—"

"I'm all right now, come on, we've got to get him under care."

Both working with senseless haste, they lugged Osden to the riverside and hauled him up on a rope under his armpits; he dangled like a sack, twisting a little, over the glutinous dark sea of leaves. They pulled him into the helijet and took off. Within a minute they were over open prairie. Tomiko locked onto the homing beam. She drew a deep breath, and her eyes met Harfex's.

"I was so terrified I almost fainted. I have never done that."

"I was . . . unreasonably frightened also," said the Hainishman, and indeed he looked aged and shaken. "Not so badly as you. But as unreasonably."

"It was when I was in contact with him, holding him. He seemed to be conscious for a moment."

"Empathy? . . . I hope he can tell us what attacked him."

Osden, like a broken dummy covered with blood and mud, half lay as they had bundled him into the rear seats in their frantic urgency to get out of the forest.

More panic met their arrival at base. The ineffective brutality of the assault was sinister and bewildering. Since Harfex stubbornly denied any possibility of animal life they began speculating about sentient plants, vegetable monsters, psychic projections. Jenny Chong's latent phobia reasserted itself and she could talk about nothing except the Dark Egos which followed people around behind their backs. She and Olleroo and Porlock had been summoned back to base; and nobody was much inclined to go outside.

Osden had lost a good deal of blood during the three or four hours he had lain alone, and concussion and severe contusions had put him in shock and semi-coma. As he came out of this and began running a low fever he called several times for "Doctor," in a plaintive voice: "Doctor Hammergeld . . ." When he regained full consciousness, two of those long days later, Tomiko called Harfex into his cubicle.

"Osden: can you tell us what attacked you?"

The pale eyes flickered past Harfex's face.

"You were attacked," Tomiko said gently. The shifty gaze was hatefully familiar, but she was a physician, protective of the hurt. "You may not remember it yet. Something attacked you. You were in the forest—"

"Ah!" he cried out, his eyes growing bright and his features contorting. "The forest—in the forest—"

"What's in the forest?"

He gasped for breath. A look of clearer consciousness came into his face. After a while he said, "I don't know."

"Did you see what attacked you?" Harfex asked.

"I don't know."

"You remember it now."

"I don't know."

"All our lives may depend on this. You must tell us what you saw!"

"I don't know," Osden said, sobbing with weakness. He was too weak to hide the fact that he was hiding the answer, yet he would not say it. Porlock, nearby, was chewing his pepper-colored mustache as he tried to hear what was going on in the cubicle. Harfex leaned over Osden and said, "You *will* tell us—" Tomiko had to interfere bodily.

Harfex controlled himself with an effort that was painful to see. He went off silently to his cubicle, where no doubt he took a double or triple dose of tranquillizers. The other men and women, scat-

tered about the big frail building, a long main hall and ten sleeping-cubicles, said nothing, but looked depressed and edgy. Osden, as always, even now, had them all at his mercy. Tomiko looked down at him with a rush of hatred that burned in her throat like bile. This monstrous egotism that fed itself on others' emotions, this absolute selfishness, was worse than any hideous deformity of the flesh. Like a congenital monster, he should not have lived. Should not be alive. Should have died. Why had his head not been split open?

As he lay flat and white, his hands helpless at his sides, his colorless eyes were wide open, and there were tears running from the corners. He tried to flinch away. "Don't," he said in a weak hoarse voice, and tried to raise his hands to protect his head. "Don't!"

She sat down on the folding-stool beside the cot, and after a while put her hand on his. He tried to pull away, but lacked the strength.

A long silence fell between them.

"Osden," she murmured, "I'm sorry. I'm very sorry. I will you well. Let me will you well, Osden. I don't want to hurt you. Listen, I do see now. It was one of us. That's right, isn't it. No, don't answer, only tell me if I'm wrong; but I'm not. . . . Of course there are animals on this planet. Ten of them. I don't care who it was. It doesn't matter, does it. It could have been me, just now. I realize that. I didn't understand how it is, Osden. You can't see how difficult it is for us to understand. . . . But listen. If it were love, instead of hate and fear . . . Is it never love?"

"No."

"Why not? Why should it never be? Are human beings all so weak? That is terrible. Never mind, never mind, don't worry. Keep still. At least right now it isn't hate, is it? Sympathy at least, concern, well-wishing. You do feel that, Osden? Is it what you feel?"

"Among . . . other things," he said, almost inaudibly.

"Noise from my subconscious, I suppose. And everybody else in the room . . . Listen, when we found you there in the forest, when I tried to turn you over, you partly wakened, and I felt a horror of you. I was insane with fear for a minute. Was that your fear of me I felt?"

"No."

Her hand was still on his, and he was quite relaxed, sinking towards sleep, like a man in pain who has been given relief from pain. "The forest," he muttered; she could barely understand him. "Afraid."

She pressed him no further, but kept her hand on his and watched him go to sleep. She knew what she felt, and what therefore he must feel. She was confident of it: there is only one emotion, or state of being, that can thus wholly reverse itself, polarize, within one moment. In Great Hainish indeed there is one word, *ontá,* for love and for hate. She was not in love with Osden, of course, that was another kettle of fish. What she felt for him was *ontá,* polarized hate. She held his hand and the current flowed between them, the tremendous electricity of touch, which he had always dreaded. As he slept the ring of anatomy-chart muscles around his mouth relaxed, and Tomiko saw on his face what none of them had ever seen, very faint, a smile. It faded. He slept on.

He was tough; next day he was sitting up, and hungry. Harfex wished to interrogate him, but Tomiko put him off. She hung a sheet of polythene over the cubicle door, as Osden himself had often done. "Does it actually cut down your empathic reception?" she asked, and he replied, in the dry, cautious tone they were now using to each other, "No."

"Just a warning, then."

"Partly. More faith-healing. Dr Hammergeld thought it worked. . . . Maybe it does, a little."

There had been love, once. A terrified child, suffocating in the tidal rush and battering of the huge emotions of adults, a drowning child, saved by one man. Taught to breathe, to live, by one man. Given everything, all protection and love, by one man. Father/Mother/God: no other. "Is he still alive?" Tomiko asked, thinking of Osden's incredible loneliness, and the strange cruelty of the great doctors. She was shocked when she heard his forced, tinny laugh. "He died at least two and a half centuries ago," Osden said. "Do you forget where we are, Coordinator? We've all left our little families behind. . . ."

Outside the polythene curtain the eight other human beings on World 4470 moved vaguely. Their voices were low and strained. Eskwana slept; Poswet To was in therapy; Jenny Chong was trying to rig lights in her cubicle so that she wouldn't cast a shadow.

"They're all scared," Tomiko said, scared. "They've all got these ideas about what attacked you. A sort of ape-potato, a giant fanged spinach, I don't know. . . . Even Harfex. You may be right not to force them to see. That would be worse, to lose confidence in one another. But why are we all so shaky, unable to face the fact, going to pieces so easily? Are we really all insane?"

"We'll soon be more so."

"Why?"

"There *is* something." He closed his mouth, the muscles of his lips stood out rigid.

"Something sentient?"

"A sentience."

"In the forest?"

He nodded.

"What is it, then—?"

"The fear." He began to look strained again, and moved restlessly. "When I fell, there, you know, I didn't lose consciousness

at once. Or I kept regaining it. I don't know. It was more like being paralyzed."

"You were."

"I was on the ground. I couldn't get up. My face was in the dirt, in that soft leaf mold. It was in my nostrils and eyes. I couldn't move. Couldn't see. As if I was in the ground. Sunk into it, part of it. I knew I was between two trees even though I never saw them. I suppose I could feel the roots. Below me in the ground, down under the ground. My hands were bloody, I could feel that, and the blood made the dirt around my face sticky. I felt the fear. It kept growing. As if they'd finally *known* I was there, lying on them there, under them, among them, the thing they feared, and yet part of their fear itself. I couldn't stop sending the fear back, and it kept growing, and I couldn't move, I couldn't get away. I would pass out, I think, and then the fear would bring me to again, and I still couldn't move. Any more than they can."

Tomiko felt the cold stirring of her hair, the readying of the apparatus of terror. "They: who are they, Osden?"

"They, it—I don't know. The fear."

"What is he talking about?" Harfex demanded when Tomiko reported this conversation. She would not let Harfex question Osden yet, feeling that she must protect Osden from the onslaught of the Hainishman's powerful, over-repressed emotions. Unfortunately this fueled the slow fire of paranoid anxiety that burned in poor Harfex, and he thought she and Osden were in league, hiding some fact of great importance or peril from the rest of the team.

"It's like the blind man trying to describe the elephant. Osden hasn't seen or heard the . . . the sentience, any more than we have."

"But he's felt it, my dear Haito," Harfex said with just-suppressed rage. "Not empathically. On his skull. It came and knocked him down and beat him with a blunt instrument. Did he not catch *one* glimpse of it?"

"What would he have seen, Harfex?" Tomiko asked, but he would not hear her meaningful tone; even he had blocked out that comprehension. What one fears is alien. The murderer is an outsider, a foreigner, not one of us. The evil is not in me!

"The first blow knocked him pretty well out," Tomiko said a little wearily, "he didn't see anything. But when he came to again, alone in the forest, he felt a great fear. Not his own fear, an empathic effect. He is certain of that. And certain it was nothing picked up from any of us. So that evidently the native life-forms are not all insentient."

Harfex looked at her a moment, grim. "You're trying to frighten me, Haito. I do not understand your motives." He got up and went off to his laboratory table, walking slowly and stiffly, like a man of eighty not of forty.

She looked round at the others. She felt some desperation. Her new, fragile, and profound interdependence with Osden gave her, she was well aware, some added strength. But if even Harfex could not keep his head, who of the others would? Porlock and Eskwana were shut in their cubicles, the others were all working or busy with something. There was something queer about their positions. For a while the Coordinator could not tell what it was, then she saw that they were all sitting facing the nearby forest. Playing chess with Asnanifoil, Olleroo had edged her chair around until it was almost beside his.

She went to Mannon, who was dissecting a tangle of spidery brown roots, and told him to look for the pattern-puzzle. He saw it at once, and said with unusual brevity, "Keeping an eye on the enemy."

"What enemy? What do *you* feel, Mannon?" She had a sudden hope in him as a psychologist, on this obscure ground of hints and empathies where biologists went astray.

"I feel a strong anxiety with a specific spatial orientation. But I

am not an empath. Therefore the anxiety is explicable in terms of the particular stress-situation, that is, the attack on a team member in the forest, and also in terms of the total stress-situation, that is, my presence in a totally alien environment, for which the archetypical connotations of the word 'forest' provide an inevitable metaphor."

Hours later Tomiko woke to hear Osden screaming in nightmare; Mannon was calming him, and she sank back into her own dark-branching pathless dreams. In the morning Eskwana did not wake. He could not be roused with stimulant drugs. He clung to his sleep, slipping farther and farther back, mumbling softly now and then until, wholly regressed, he lay curled on his side, thumb at his lips, gone.

"Two days; two down. Ten little Indians, nine little Indians . . ." That was Porlock.

"And you're the next little Indian," Jenny Chong snapped. "Go analyze your urine, Porlock!"

"He is driving us all insane," Porlock said, getting up and waving his left arm. "Can't you feel it? For God's sake, are you all deaf and blind? Can't you feel what he's doing, the emanations? It all comes from him—from his room there—from his mind. He is driving us all insane with fear!"

"Who is?" said Asnanifoil, looming precipitous and hairy over the little Terran.

"Do I have to say his name? Osden, then. Osden! Osden! Why do you think I tried to kill him? In self-defense! To save all of us! Because you won't see what he's doing to us. He's sabotaged the mission by making us quarrel, and now he's going to drive us all insane by projecting fear at us so that we can't sleep or think, like a huge radio that doesn't make any sound, but it broadcasts all the time, and you can't sleep, and you can't think. Haito and Harfex

are already under his control but the rest of you can be saved. I had to do it!"

"You didn't do it very well," Osden said, standing half-naked, all rib and bandage, at the door of his cubicle. "I could have hit myself harder. Hell, it isn't me that's scaring you blind, Porlock, it's out there—there, in the woods!"

Porlock made an ineffectual attempt to assault Osden; Asnanifoil held him back, and continued to hold him effortlessly while Mannon gave him a sedative shot. He was put away shouting about giant radios. In a minute the sedative took effect, and he joined a peaceful silence to Eskwana's.

"All right," said Harfex. "Now, Osden, you'll tell us what you know and all you know."

Osden said, "I don't know anything."

He looked battered and faint. Tomiko made him sit down before he talked.

"After I'd been three days in the forest, I thought I was occasionally receiving some kind of affect."

"Why didn't you report it?"

"Thought I was going spla, like the rest of you."

"That, equally, should have been reported."

"You'd have called me back to base. I couldn't take it. You realize that my inclusion in the mission was a bad mistake. I'm not able to coexist with nine other neurotic personalities at close quarters. I was wrong to volunteer for Extreme Survey, and the Authority was wrong to accept me."

No one spoke; but Tomiko saw, with certainty this time, the flinch in Osden's shoulders and the tightening of his facial muscles, as he registered their bitter agreement.

"Anyhow, I didn't want to come back to base because I was curious. Even going psycho, how could I pick up empathic affects when there was no creature to emit them? They weren't bad, then.

Very vague. Queer. Like a draft in a closed room, a flicker in the corner of your eye. Nothing really."

For a moment he had been borne up on their listening: they heard, so he spoke. He was wholly at their mercy. If they disliked him he had to be hateful; if they mocked him he became grotesque; if they listened to him he was the storyteller. He was helplessly obedient to the demands of their emotions, reactions, moods. And there were seven of them, too many to cope with, so that he must be constantly knocked about from one to another's whim. He could not find coherence. Even as he spoke and held them, somebody's attention would wander: Olleroo perhaps was thinking that he wasn't un-attractive, Harfex was seeking the ulterior motive of his words, Asnanifoil's mind, which could not be long held by the concrete, was roaming off towards the eternal peace of number, and Tomiko was distracted by pity, by fear. Osden's voice faltered. He lost the thread. "I . . . I thought it must be the trees," he said, and stopped.

"It's not the trees," Harfex said. "They have no more nervous system than do plants of the Hainish Descent on Earth. None."

"You're not seeing the forest for the trees, as they say on Earth," Mannon put in, smiling elfinly; Harfex stared at him. "What about those root-nodes we've been puzzling about for twenty days—eh?"

"What about them?"

"They are, indubitably, connections. Connections among the trees. Right? Now let's just suppose, most improbably, that you knew nothing of animal brain-structure. And you were given one axon, or one detached glial cell, to examine. Would you be likely to discover what it was? Would you see that the cell was capable of sentience?"

"No. Because it isn't. A single cell is capable of mechanical response to stimulus. No more. Are you hypothesizing that individual arboriformes are 'cells' in a kind of brain, Mannon?"

"Not exactly. I'm merely pointing out that they are all inter-connected, both by the root-node linkage and by your green epiphytes

in the branches. A linkage of incredible complexity and physical extent. Why, even the prairie grass-forms have those root-connectors, don't they? I know that sentience or intelligence isn't a thing, you can't find it in, or analyze it out from, the cells of a brain. It's a function of the connected cells. It is, in a sense, the connection: the connectedness. It doesn't exist. I'm not trying to say it exists. I'm only guessing that Osden might be able to describe it."

And Osden took him up, speaking as if in trance. "Sentience without senses. Blind, deaf, nerveless, moveless. Some irritability, response to touch. Response to sun, to light, to water, and chemicals in the earth around the roots. Nothing comprehensible to an animal mind. Presence without mind. Awareness of being, without object or subject. Nirvana."

"Then why do you receive fear?" Tomiko asked in a low voice.

"I don't know. I can't see how awareness of objects, of others, could arise: an unperceiving response . . . But there was an uneasiness, for days. And then when I lay between the two trees and my blood was on their roots—" Osden's face glittered with sweat. "It became fear," he said shrilly, "only fear."

"If such a function existed," Harfex said, "it would not be capable of conceiving of a self-moving, material entity, or responding to one. It could no more become aware of us than we can 'become aware' of Infinity."

" 'The silence of those infinite expanses terrifies me,' " muttered Tomiko. "Pascal was aware of Infinity. By way of fear."

"To a forest," Mannon said, "we might appear as forest fires. Hurricanes. Dangers. What moves quickly is dangerous, to a plant. The rootless would be alien, terrible. And if it is mind, it seems only too probable that it might become aware of Osden, whose own mind is open to connection with all others so long as he's conscious, and who was lying in pain and afraid within it, actually inside it. No wonder it was afraid—"

"Not 'it,'" Harfex said. "There is no being, no huge creature, no person! There could at most be only a function— "

"There is only a fear," Osden said.

They were all still a while, and heard the stillness outside.

"Is that what I feel all the time coming up behind me?" Jenny Chong asked, subdued.

Osden nodded. "You all feel it, deaf as you are. Eskwana's the worst off, because he actually has some empathic capacity. He could send if he learned how, but he's too weak, never will be anything but a medium."

"Listen, Osden," Tomiko said, "you can send. Then send to it— the forest, the fear out there—tell it that we won't hurt it. Since it has, or is, some sort of affect that translates into what we feel as emotion, can't you translate back? Send out a message, We are harmless, we are friendly."

"You must know that nobody can emit a false empathic message, Haito. You can't send something that doesn't exist."

"But we don't intend harm, we are friendly."

"Are we? In the forest, when you picked me up, did you feel friendly?"

"No. Terrified. But that's—it, the forest, the plants, not my own fear, isn't it?"

"What's the difference? It's all you felt. Can't you see," and Osden's voice rose in exasperation, "why I dislike you and you dislike me, all of you? Can't you see that I retransmit every negative or aggressive affect you've felt towards me since we first met? I return your hostility, with thanks. I do it in self-defense. Like Porlock. It is self-defense, though; it's the only technique I developed to replace my original defense of total withdrawal from others. Unfortunately it creates a closed circuit, self-sustaining and self-reinforcing. Your initial reaction to me was the instinctive antipathy to a cripple; by now of course it's hatred. Can you fail to see my point? The forest-

mind out there transmits only terror, now, and the only message I can send it is terror, because when exposed to it I can feel nothing except terror!"

"What must we do, then?" said Tomiko, and Mannon replied promptly, "Move camp. To another continent. If there are plant-minds there, they'll be slow to notice us, as this one was; maybe they won't notice us at all."

"It would be a considerable relief," Osden observed stiffly. The others had been watching him with a new curiosity. He had re-vealed himself, they had seen him as he was, a helpless man in a trap. Perhaps, like Tomiko, they had seen that the trap itself, his crass and cruel egotism, was their own construction, not his. They had built the cage and locked him in it, and like a caged ape he threw filth out through the bars. If, meeting him, they had offered trust, if they had been strong enough to offer him love, how might he have appeared to them?

None of them could have done so, and it was too late now. Given time, given solitude, Tomiko might have built up with him a slow resonance of feeling, a consonance of trust, a harmony; but there was no time, their job must be done. There was not room enough for the cultivation of so great a thing, and they must make do with sympathy, with pity, the small change of love. Even that much had given her strength, but it was nowhere near enough for him. She could see in his flayed face now his savage resentment of their curiosity, even of her pity.

"Go lie down, that gash is bleeding again," she said, and he obeyed her.

Next morning they packed up, melted down the sprayform hangar and living quarters, lifted *Gum* on mechanical drive and took her halfway round World 4470, over the red and green lands, the many warm green seas. They had picked out a likely spot on Continent G: a prairie, twenty thousand square kilos of windswept

graminiformes. No forest was within a hundred kilos of the site, and there were no lone trees or groves on the plain. The plant-forms occurred only in large species-colonies, never intermingled, except for certain tiny ubiquitous saprophytes and spore-bearers. The team sprayed holomeld over structure forms, and by evening of the thirty-two-hour day were settled in to the new camp. Eskwana was still asleep and Porlock still sedated, but everyone else was cheerful. "You can breathe here!" they kept saying.

Osden got on his feet and went shakily to the doorway; leaning there he looked through twilight over the dim reaches of the swaying grass that was not grass. There was a faint, sweet odor of pollen on the wind; no sound but the soft, vast sibilance of wind. His bandaged head cocked a little, the empath stood motionless for a long time. Darkness came, and the stars, lights in the windows of the distant house of Man. The wind had ceased, there was no sound. He listened.

In the long night Haito Tomiko listened. She lay still and heard the blood in her arteries, the breathing of sleepers, the wind blowing, the dark veins running, the dreams advancing, the vast static of stars increasing as the universe died slowly, the sound of death walking. She struggled out of her bed, fled the tiny solitude of her cubicle. Eskwana alone slept. Porlock lay straitjacketed, raving softly in his obscure native tongue. Olleroo and Jenny Chong were playing cards, grim-faced. Poswet To was in the therapy niche, plugged in. Asnanifoil was drawing a mandala, the Third Pattern of the Primes. Mannon and Harfex were sitting up with Osden.

She changed the bandages on Osden's head. His lank, reddish hair, where she had not had to shave it, looked strange. It was salted with white, now. Her hands shook as she worked. Nobody had yet said anything.

"How can the fear be here too?" she said, and her voice rang flat and false in the terrific silence.

"It's not just the trees; the grasses too . . ."

"But we're twelve thousand kilos from where we were this morning, we left it on the other side of the planet."

"It's all one," Osden said. "One big green thought. How long does it take a thought to get from one side of your brain to the other?"

"It doesn't think. It isn't thinking," Harfex said, lifelessly. "It's merely a network of processes. The branches, the epiphytic growths, the roots with those nodal junctures between individuals: they must all be capable of transmitting electrochemical impulses. There are no individual plants, then, properly speaking. Even the pollen is part of the linkage, no doubt, a sort of windborne sentience, connecting overseas. But it is not conceivable. That all the biosphere of a planet should be one network of communications, sensitive, irrational, immortal, isolated. . . ."

"Isolated," said Osden. "That's it! That's the fear. It isn't that we're motile, or destructive. It's just that we are. We are other. There has never been any other."

"You're right," Mannon said, almost whispering. "It has no peers. No enemies. No relationship with anything but itself. One alone forever."

"Then what's the function of its intelligence in species-survival?"

"None, maybe," Osden said. "Why are you getting teleological, Harfex? Aren't you a Hainishman? Isn't the measure of complexity the measure of the eternal joy?"

Harfex did not take the bait. He looked ill. "We should leave this world," he said.

"Now you know why I always want to get out, get away from you," Osden said with a kind of morbid geniality. "It isn't pleasant, is it—the other's fear. . . ? If only it were an animal intelligence. I can get through to animals. I get along with cobras and tigers; superior intelligence gives one the advantage. I should have been used in a zoo, not on a human team. . . . If I could get through to

the damned stupid potato! If it wasn't so overwhelming . . . I still pick up more than the fear, you know. And before it panicked it had a—there was a serenity. I couldn't take it in, then, I didn't realize how big it was. To know the whole daylight, after all, and the whole night. All the winds and lulls together. The winter stars and the summer stars at the same time. To have roots, and no enemies. To be entire. Do you see? No invasion. No others. To be whole . . ."

He had never spoken before, Tomiko thought.

"You are defenseless against it, Osden," she said. "Your personality has changed already. You're vulnerable to it. We may not all go mad, but you will, if we don't leave."

He hesitated, then he looked up at Tomiko, the first time he had ever met her eyes, a long, still look, clear as water.

"What's sanity ever done for me?" he said, mocking. "But you have a point, Haito. You have something there."

"We should get away," Harfex muttered.

"If I gave in to it," Osden mused, "could I communicate?"

"By 'give in,'" Mannon said in a rapid, nervous voice, "I assume that you mean, stop sending back the empathic information which you receive from the plant-entity: stop rejecting the fear, and absorb it. That will either kill you at once, or drive you back into total psychological withdrawal, autism."

"Why?" said Osden. "Its message is *rejection*. But my salvation is rejection. It's not intelligent. But I am."

"The scale is wrong. What can a single human brain achieve against something so vast?"

"A single human brain can perceive pattern on the scale of stars and galaxies," Tomiko said, "and interpret it as Love."

Mannon looked from one to the other of them; Harfex was silent.

"It'd be easier in the forest," Osden said. "Which of you will fly me over?"

"When?"

"Now. Before you all crack up or go violent."

"I will," Tomiko said.

"None of us will," Harfex said.

"I can't," Mannon said. "I . . . I am too frightened. I'd crash the jet."

"Bring Eskwana along. If I can pull this off, he might serve as a medium."

"Are you accepting the Sensor's plan, Coordinator?" Harfex asked formally.

"Yes."

"I disapprove. I will come with you, however."

"I think we're compelled, Harfex," Tomiko said, looking at Osden's face, the ugly white mask transfigured, eager as a lover's face.

Olleroo and Jenny Chong, playing cards to keep their thoughts from their haunted beds, their mounting dread, chattered like scared children. "This thing, it's in the forest, it'll get you— "

"Scared of the dark?" Osden jeered.

"But look at Eskwana, and Porlock, and even Asnanifoil— "

"It can't hurt you. It's an impulse passing through synapses, a wind passing through branches. It is only a nightmare."

They took off in a helijet, Eskwana curled up still sound asleep in the rear compartment, Tomiko piloting, Harfex and Osden silent, watching ahead for the dark line of forest across the vague grey miles of starlit plain.

They neared the black line, crossed it; now under them was darkness.

She sought a landing place, flying low, though she had to fight her frantic wish to fly high, to get out, get away. The huge vitality of the plant-world was far stronger here in the forest, and its panic beat in immense dark waves. There was a pale patch ahead, a bare

knoll-top a little higher than the tallest of the black shapes around it; the not-trees; the rooted; the parts of the whole. She set the helijet down in the glade, a bad landing. Her hands on the stick were slippery, as if she had rubbed them with cold soap.

About them now stood the forest, black in darkness.

Tomiko cowered and shut her eyes. Eskwana moaned in his sleep. Harfex's breath came short and loud, and he sat rigid, even when Osden reached across him and slid the door open.

Osden stood up; his back and bandaged head were just visible in the dim glow of the control panel as he paused stooping in the doorway.

Tomiko was shaking. She could not raise her head. "No, no, no, no, no, no, no," she said in a whisper. "No. No. No."

Osden moved suddenly and quietly, swinging out of the doorway, down into the dark. He was gone.

I am coming! said a great voice that made no sound.

Tomiko screamed. Harfex coughed; he seemed to be trying to stand up, but did not do so.

Tomiko drew in upon herself, all centered in the blind eye in her belly, in the center of her being; and outside that there was nothing but the fear.

It ceased.

She raised her head; slowly unclenched her hands. She sat up straight. The night was dark, and stars shone over the forest. There was nothing else.

"Osden," she said, but her voice would not come. She spoke again, louder, a lone bullfrog croak. There was no reply.

She began to realize that something had gone wrong with Harfex. She was trying to find his head in the darkness, for he had slipped down from the seat, when all at once, in the dead quiet, in the dark rear compartment of the craft, a voice spoke. "Good," it said.

It was Eskwana's voice. She snapped on the interior lights and

saw the engineer lying curled up asleep, his hand half over his mouth.

The mouth opened and spoke. "All well," it said.

"Osden—"

"All well," said the soft voice from Eskwana's mouth.

"Where are you?"

Silence.

"Come back."

A wind was rising. "I'll stay here," the soft voice said.

"You can't stay—"

Silence.

"You'd be alone, Osden!"

"Listen." The voice was fainter, slurred, as if lost in the sound of wind. "Listen. I will you well."

She called his name after that, but there was no answer. Eskwana lay still. Harfex lay stiller.

"Osden!" she cried, leaning out the doorway into the dark, wind-shaken silence of the forest of being. "I will come back. I must get Harfex to the base. I will come back, Osden!"

Silence and wind in leaves.

They finished the prescribed survey of World 4470, the eight of them; it took them forty-one days more. Asnanifoil and one or another of the women went into the forest daily at first, searching for Osden in the region around the bare knoll, though Tomiko was not in her heart sure which bare knoll they had landed on that night in the very heart and vortex of terror. They left piles of supplies for Osden, food enough for fifty years, clothing, tents, tools. They did not go on searching; there was no way to find a man alone, hiding, if he wanted to hide, in those unending labyrinths and dim corridors vine-entangled, root-floored. They might have passed within arm's reach of him and never seen him.

But he was there; for there was no fear any more.

Rational, and valuing reason more highly after an intolerable experience of the immortal mindless, Tomiko tried to understand rationally what Osden had done. But the words escaped her control. He had taken the fear into himself, and, accepting, had transcended it. He had given up his self to the alien, an unreserved surrender, that left no place for evil. He had learned the love of the Other, and thereby had been given his whole self. —But this is not the vocabulary of reason.

The people of the Survey team walked under the trees, through the vast colonies of life, surrounded by a dreaming silence, a brooding calm that was half aware of them and wholly indifferent to them. There were no hours. Distance was no matter. Had we but world enough and time . . . The planet turned between the sunlight and the great dark; winds of winter and summer blew fine, pale pollen across the quiet seas.

Gum returned after many surveys, years, and lightyears, to what had several centuries ago been Smeming Port. There were still men there, to receive (incredulously) the team's reports, and to record its losses: Biologist Harfex, dead of fear, and Sensor Osden, left as a colonist.

THE STARS BELOW

The popular notion of science fiction, I guess, is of a story that takes some possible or impossible technological gimmick-of-the-future—Soylent Green, the time machine, the submarine—and makes hay out of it. There certainly are science fiction stories which do just that, but to define science fiction by them is a bit like defining the United States as Kansas.

Writing "The Stars Below," I thought I knew what I was doing. As in the early story "The Masters," I was telling a story not about a gimmick or device or hypothesis, but about science itself—the idea of science. And about what happens to the idea of science when it meets utterly opposed and powerful ideas, embodied in government, as when seventeenth-century astronomy ran up against the Pope, or genetics in the 1930s ran up against Stalin. But all this was cast as a psychomyth, a story outside real time, past or future, in part to generalize it, and in part because I was also using science as a synonym for art. What happens to the creative mind when it is driven underground?

That was the question, and I thought I knew my answer. It all seemed straightforward, a mere allegory, really. But you don't go exploring the places underground all that easily. The symbols you thought were simple equivalences, signs, come alive, and take on meanings you did not intend and cannot explain. Long after I wrote the story I came on a passage in Jung's On the Nature of the Psyche:

"We would do well to think of ego-consciousness as being sur-rounded by a multitude of little luminosities. . . . Introspective intuitions . . . capture the state of the unconscious: The star-strewn heavens, stars reflected in dark water, nuggets of gold or golden sand scattered in black earth." And he quotes from an alchemist, "Seminate aurum in terram albam foliatam"—the precious metal strewn in the layers of white clay.

Perhaps this story is not about science, or about art, but about the mind, my mind, any mind, that turns inward to itself.

The wooden house and outbuildings caught fire fast, blazed up, burned down, but the dome, built of lathe and plaster above a drum of brick, would not burn. What they did at last was heap up the wreckage of the telescopes, the instruments, the books and charts and drawings, in the middle of the floor under the dome, pour oil on the heap, and set fire to that. The flames spread to the wooden beams of the big telescope frame and to the clockwork mechanisms. Villagers watching from the foot of the hill saw the dome, whitish against the green evening sky, shudder and turn, first in one direc-tion then in the other, while a black and yellow smoke full of sparks gushed from the oblong slit: an ugly and uncanny thing to see.

It was getting dark, stars were showing in the east. Orders were shouted. The soldiers came down the road in single file, dark men in dark harness, silent.

The villagers at the foot of the hill stayed on after the soldiers had gone. In a life without change or breadth a fire is as good as a festival. They did not climb the hill, and as the night grew full dark they drew closer together. After a while they began to go back to their villages. Some looked back over their shoulders at the hill, where nothing moved. The stars turned slowly behind the black beehive of the dome, but it did not turn to follow them.

About an hour before daybreak a man rode up the steep zigzag, dismounted by the ruins of the workshops, and approached the dome on foot. The door had been smashed in. Through it a reddish haze of light was visible, very dim, coming from a massive support-beam that had fallen and had smoldered all night inward to its core. A hanging, sour smoke thickened the air inside the dome. A tall figure moved there and its shadow moved with it, cast upward on the murk. Sometimes it stooped, or stopped, then blundered slowly on.

The man at the door said: "Guennar! Master Guennar!"

The man in the dome stopped still, looking towards the door. He had just picked up something from the mess of wreckage and half-burnt stuff on the floor. He put this object mechanically into his coat pocket, still peering at the door. He came towards it. His eyes were red and swollen almost shut, he breathed harshly in gasps, his hair and clothes were scorched and smeared with black ash.

"Where were you?"

The man in the dome pointed vaguely at the ground.

"There's a cellar? That's where you were during the fire? By God! Gone to ground! I knew it, I knew you'd be here." Bord laughed, a little crazily, taking Guennar's arm. "Come on. Come out of there, for the love of God. There's light in the east already."

The astronomer came reluctantly, looking not at the grey east but back up at the slit in the dome, where a few stars burned clear. Bord pulled him outside, made him mount the horse, and then, bridle in hand, set off down the hill leading the horse at a fast walk.

The astronomer held the pommel with one hand. The other hand, which had been burned across the palm and fingers when he picked up a metal fragment still red-hot under its coat of cinders, he kept pressed against his thigh. He was not conscious of doing so, or of the pain. Sometimes his senses told him, "I am on horseback," or, "It's getting lighter," but these fragmentary messages made no

sense to him. He shivered with cold as the dawn wind rose, rattling the dark woods by which the two men and the horse now passed in a deep lane overhung by teasel and briar; but the woods, the wind, the whitening sky, the cold were all remote from his mind, in which there was nothing but a darkness shot with the reek and heat of burning.

Bord made him dismount. There was sunlight around them now, lying long on rocks above a river valley. There was a dark place, and Bord urged him and pulled him into the dark place. It was not hot and close there but cold and silent. As soon as Bord let him stop he sank down, for his knees would not bear; and he felt the cold rock against his seared and throbbing hands.

"Gone to earth, by God!" said Bord, looking about at the veined walls, marked with the scars of miners' picks, in the light of his lanterned candle. "I'll be back; after dark, maybe. Don't come out. Don't go farther in. This is an old adit, they haven't worked this end of the mine for years. May be slips and pitfalls in these old tunnels. Don't come out! Lie low. When the hounds are gone, we'll run you across the border."

Bord turned and went back up the adit in darkness. When the sound of his steps had long since died away, the astronomer lifted his head and looked around him at the dark walls and the little burning candle. Presently he blew it out. There came upon him the earth-smelling darkness, silent and complete. He saw green shapes, ocherous blots drifting on the black; these faded slowly. The dull, chill black was balm to his inflamed and aching eyes, and to his mind.

If he thought, sitting there in the dark, his thoughts found no words. He was feverish from exhaustion and smoke inhalation and a few slight burns, and in an abnormal condition of mind; but perhaps his mind's workings, though lucid and serene, had never been normal. It is not normal for a man to spend twenty years grinding

lenses, building telescopes, peering at stars, making calculations, lists, maps and charts of things which no one knows or cares about, things which cannot be reached, or touched, or held. And now all he had spent his life on was gone, burned. What was left of him might as well be, as it was, buried.

But it did not occur to him, this idea of being buried. All he was keenly aware of was a great burden of anger and grief, a burden he was unfit to carry. It was crushing his mind, crushing out reason. And the darkness here seemed to relieve that pressure. He was accustomed to the dark, he had lived at night. The weight here was only rock, only earth. No granite is so hard as hatred and no clay so cold as cruelty. The earth's black innocence enfolded him. He lay down within it, trembling a little with pain and with relief from pain, and slept.

Light waked him. Count Bord was there, lighting the candle with flint and steel. Bord's face was vivid in the light: the high color and blue eyes of a keen huntsman, a red mouth, sensual and obstinate. "They're on the scent," he was saying. "They know you got away."

"Why . . . " said the astronomer. His voice was weak; his throat, like his eyes, was still smoke-inflamed. "Why are they after me?"

"Why? Do you still need telling? To burn you alive, man! For heresy!" Bord's blue eyes glared through the steadying glow of the candle.

"But it's gone, burned, all I did."

"Aye, the earth's stopped, all right, but where's their fox? They want their fox! But damned if I'll let them get you."

The astronomer's eyes, light and wide-set, met his and held. "Why?"

"You think I'm a fool," Bord said with a grin that was not a smile, a wolf's grin, the grin of the hunted and the hunter. "And I am one. I was a fool to warn you. You never listened. I was a fool to listen

to you. But I liked to listen to you. I liked to hear you talk about the stars and the courses of the planets and the ends of time. Who else ever talked to me of anything but seed corn and cow dung? Do you see? And I don't like soldiers and strangers, and trials and burnings. Your truth, their truth, what do I know about the truth? Am I a master? Do I know the courses of the stars? Maybe you do. Maybe they do. All I know is you have sat at my table and talked to me. Am I to watch you burn? God's fire, they say; but you said the stars are the fires of God. Why do you ask me that, 'Why?' Why do you ask a fool's question of a fool?"

"I am sorry," the astronomer said.

"What do you know about men?" the count said. "You thought they'd let you be. And you thought I'd let you burn." He looked at Guennar through the candlelight, grinning like a driven wolf, but in his blue eyes there was a glint of real amusement. "We who live down on the earth, you see, not up among the stars . . ."

He had brought a tinderbox and three tallow candles, a bottle of water, a ball of peas-pudding, a sack of bread. He left soon, warning the astronomer again not to venture out of the mine.

When Guennar woke again a strangeness in his situation troubled him, not one which would have worried most people hiding in a hole to save their skins, but most distressing to him: he did not know the time.

It was not clocks he missed, the sweet banging of the church bells in the villages calling to morning and evening prayer, the delicate and willing accuracy of the timepieces he used in his observatory and on whose refinement so many of his discoveries had depended; it was not the clocks he missed, but the great clock.

Not seeing the sky, one cannot know the turning of the earth. All the processes of time, the sun's bright arch and the moon's phases,

the planet's dance, the wheeling of the constellations around the pole star, the vaster wheeling of the seasons of the stars, all these were lost, the warp on which his life was woven.

Here there was no time.

"O my God," Guennar the astronomer prayed in the darkness under ground, "how can it offend you to be praised? All I ever saw in my telescopes was one spark of your glory, one least fragment of the order of your creation. You could not be jealous of that, my Lord! And there were few enough who believed me, even so. Was it my arrogance in daring to describe your works? But how could I help it, Lord, when you let me see the endless fields of stars? Could I see and be silent? O my God, do not punish me any more, let me rebuild the smaller telescope. I will not speak, I will not publish, if it troubles your holy Church. I will not say anything more about the orbits of the planets or the nature of the stars. I will not speak, Lord, only let me see!"

"What the devil, be quiet, Master Guennar. I could hear you halfway up the tunnel," said Bord, and the astronomer opened his eyes to the dazzle of Bord's lantern. "They've called the full hunt up for you. Now you're a necromancer. They swear they saw you sleeping in your house when they came, and they barred the doors; but there's no bones in the ashes."

"I was asleep," Guennar said, covering his eyes. "They came, the soldiers. . . . I should have listened to you. I went into the passage under the dome. I left a passage there so I could go back to the hearth on cold nights, when it's cold my fingers get too stiff, I have to go warm my hands sometimes." He spread out his blistered, blackened hands and looked at them vaguely. "Then I heard them overhead. . . ."

"Here's some more food. What the devil, haven't you eaten?"

"Has it been long?"

"A night and a day. It's night now. Raining. Listen, Master:

there's two of the black hounds living at my house now. Emissaries of the Council, what the devil, I had to offer hospitality. This is my county, they're here, I'm the count. It makes it hard for me to come. And I don't want to send any of my people here. What if the priests asked them, 'Do you know where he is? Will you answer to God you don't know where he is?' It's best they don't know. I'll come when I can. You're all right here? You'll stay here? I'll get you out of here and over the border when they've cleared away. They're like flies now. Don't talk aloud like that. They might look into these old tunnels. You should go farther in. I will come back. Stay with God, Master."

"Go with God, count."

He saw the color of Bord's blue eyes, the leap of shadows up the rough-hewn roof as he took up the lantern and turned away. Light and color died as Bord, at the turning, put out the lantern. Guennar heard him stumble and swear as he groped his way.

Presently Guennar lighted one of his candles and ate and drank a little, eating the staler bread first, and breaking off a piece of the crusted lump of peas-pudding. This time Bord had brought him three loaves and some salt meat, two more candles and a second skin bottle of water, and a heavy duffle cloak. Guennar had not felt cold. He was wearing the coat he always wore on cold nights in the observatory and very often slept in, when he came stumbling to bed at dawn. It was a good sheepskin, filthy from his rummagings in the wreckage in the dome and scorched at the sleeve-ends, but it was as warm as ever, and was like his own skin to him. He sat inside it eating, gazing out through the sphere of frail yellow candlelight to the darkness of the tunnel beyond. Bord's words, "You should go farther in," were in his mind. When he was done eating he bundled up the provisions in the cloak, took up the bundle in one hand and the lighted candle in the other, and set off down the side-tunnel and then the adit, down and inward.

After a few hundred paces he came to a major cross-tunnel, off which ran many short leads and some large rooms or stopes. He turned left, and presently passed a big stope in three levels. He entered it. The farthest level was only about five feet under the roof, which was still well timbered with posts and beams. In a corner of the backmost level, behind an angle of quartz intrusion which the miners had left jutting out as a supporting buttress, he made his new camp, setting out the food, water, tinderbox, and candles where they would come under his hand easily in the dark, and laying the cloak as a mattress on the floor, which was of a rubbly, hard clay. Then he put out the candle, already burned down by a quarter of its length, and lay down in the dark.

After his third return to that first side-tunnel, finding no sign that Bord had come there, he went back to his camp and studied his provisions. There were still two loaves of bread, half a bottle of water, and the salt meat, which he had not yet touched; and four candles. He guessed that it might have been six days since Bord had come, but it might have been three, or eight. He was thirsty, but dared not drink, so long as he had no other supply.

He set off to find water.

At first he counted his paces. After a hundred and twenty he saw that the timbering of the tunnel was askew, and there were places where the rubble fill had broken through, half filling the passage. He came to a winze, a vertical shaft, easy to scramble down by what remained of the wooden ladder, but after it, in the lower level, he forgot to count his steps. Once he passed a broken pick handle; farther on he saw a miner's discarded headband, a stump of candle still stuck in the forehead socket. He dropped this into the pocket of his coat and went on.

The monotony of the walls of hewn stone and planking dulled his mind. He walked on like one who will walk forever. Darkness followed him and went ahead of him.

His candle burning short spilled a stream of hot tallow on his fingers, hurting him. He dropped the candle, and it went out.

He groped for it in the sudden dark, sickened by the reek of its smoke, lifting his head to avoid that stink of burning. Before him, straight before him, far away, he saw the stars.

Tiny, bright, remote, caught in a narrow opening like the slot in the observatory dome: an oblong full of stars in blackness.

He got up, forgetting about the candle, and began to run towards the stars.

They moved, dancing, like the stars in the telescope field when the clockwork mechanism shuddered or when his eyes were very tired. They danced, and brightened.

He came among them, and they spoke to him.

The flames cast queer shadows on the blackened faces and brought queer lights out of the bright, living eyes.

"Here, then, who's that? Hanno?"

"What were you doing up that old drift, mate?"

"Hey, who is that?"

"Who the devil, stop him—"

"Hey, mate! Hold on!"

He ran blind into the dark, back the way he had come. The lights followed him and he chased his own faint, huge shadow down the tunnel. When the shadow was swallowed by the old dark and the old silence came again he still stumbled on, stooping and groping so that he was oftenest on all fours or on his feet and one hand. At last he dropped down and lay huddled against the wall, his chest full of fire.

Silence, dark.

He found the candle end in the tin holder in his pocket, lighted it with the flint and steel, and by its glow found the vertical shaft not fifty feet from where he had stopped. He made his way back up to his camp. There he slept; woke and ate, and drank the last of his water; meant to get up and go seeking water again; fell asleep, or

into a doze or daze, in which he dreamed of a voice speaking to him.

"There you are. All right. Don't startle. I'll do you no harm. I said it wasn't no knocker. Who ever heard of a knocker as tall as a man? Or who ever seen one, for that matter. They're what you *don't* see, mates, I said. And what we did see was a man, count on it. So what's he doing in the mine, said they, and what if he's a ghost, one of the lads that was caught when the house of water broke in the old south adit, maybe, come walking? Well then, I said, I'll go see that. I never seen a ghost yet, for all I heard of them. I don't care to see what's not meant to be seen, like the knocker folk, but what harm to see Temon's face again, or old Trip, haven't I seen 'em in dreams, just the same, in the ends, working away with their faces sweating same as life? Why not? So I come along. But you're no ghost, nor miner. A deserter you might be, or a thief. Or are you out of your wits, is that it, poor man? Don't fear. Hide if you like. What's it to me? There's room down here for you and me. Why are you hiding from the light of the sun?"

"The soldiers . . . "

"I thought so."

When the old man nodded, the candle bound to his forehead set light leaping over the roof of the stope. He squatted about ten feet from Guennar, his hands hanging between his knees. A bunch of candles and his pick, a short-handled, finely shaped tool, hung from his belt. His face and body, beneath the restless star of the candle, were rough shadows, earth-colored.

"Let me stay here."

"Stay and welcome! Do I own the mine? Where did you come in, eh, the old drift above the river? That was luck to find that, and luck you turned this way in the crosscut, and didn't go east instead. Eastward this level goes on to the caves. There's great caves there; did you know it? Nobody knows but the miners. They opened up the caves before I was born, following the old lode that lay along

here sunward. I seen the caves once, my dad took me, you should see this once, he says. See the world underneath the world. A room there was no end to. A cavern as deep as the sky, and a black stream falling into it, falling and falling till the light of the candle failed and couldn't follow it, and still the water was falling on down into the pit. The sound of it came up like a whisper without an end, out of the dark. And on beyond that there's other caves, and below. No end to them, maybe. Who knows? Cave under cave, and glittering with the barren crystal. It's all barren stone, there. And all worked out, here, years ago. It's a safe enough hole you chose, mate, if you hadn't come stumbling in on us. What was you after? Food? A human face?"

"Water."

"No lack of that. Come on, I'll show you. Beneath here in the lower level there's all too many springs. You turned the wrong direction. I used to work down there, with the damned cold water up to my knees, before the vein ran out. A long time ago. Come on."

The old miner left him in his camp, after showing him where the spring rose and warning him not to follow down the watercourse, for the timbering would be rotted and a step or sound might bring the earth down. Down there all the timbers were covered with a deep glittering white fur, saltpeter perhaps, or a fungus: it was very strange, above the oily water. When he was alone again Guennar thought he had dreamed that white tunnel full of black water, and the visit of the miner. When he saw a flicker of light far down the tunnel, he crouched behind the quartz buttress with a great wedge of granite in his hand: for all his fear and anger and grief had come down to one thing here in the darkness, a determination that no man would lay hand on him. A blind determination, blunt and heavy as a broken stone, heavy in his soul.

It was only the old man coming, with a hunk of dry cheese for him.

He sat with the astronomer, and talked. Guennar ate up the cheese, for he had no food left, and listened to the old man talk. As he listened the weight seemed to lift a little, he seemed to see a little farther in the dark.

"You're no common soldier," the miner said, and he replied, "No, I was a student once," but no more, because he dared not tell the miner who he was. The old man knew all the events of the region; he spoke of the burning of the Round House on the hill, and of Count Bord. "He went off to the city with them, with these black-gowns, to be tried, they do say, to come before their council. Tried for what? What did he ever do but hunt boar and deer and foxen? Is it the council of the foxen trying him? What's it all about, this snooping and soldiering and burning and trying? Better leave honest folk alone. The count was honest, as far as the rich can be, a fair landlord. But you can't trust them, none of such folk. Only down here. You can trust the men who go down into the mine. What else has a man got down here but his own hands and his mates' hands? What's between him and death, when there's a fall in the level or a winze closes and he's in the blind end, but their hands, and their shovels, and their will to dig him out? There'd be no silver up there in the sun if there wasn't trust between us down here in the dark. Down here you can count on your mates. And nobody comes but them. Can you see the owner in his lace, or the soldiers, coming down the ladders, coming down and down the great shaft into the dark? Not them! They're brave at tramping on the grass, but what good's a sword and shouting in the dark? I'd like to see 'em come down here. . . ."

The next time he came another man was with him, and they brought an oil lamp and a clay jar of oil, as well as more cheese, bread, and some apples. "It was Hanno thought of the lamp," the

old man said. "A hempen wick it is, if she goes out blow sharp and she'll likely catch up again. Here's a dozen candles, too. Young Per swiped the lot from the doler, up on the grass."

"They all know I'm here?"

"*We* do," the miner said briefly. "*They* don't."

Some time after this, Guennar returned along the lower, west-leading level he had followed before, till he saw the miners' candles dance like stars; and he came into the stope where they were working. They shared their meal with him. They showed him the ways of the mine, and the pumps, and the great shaft where the ladders were and the hanging pulleys with their buckets; he sheered off from that, for the wind that came sucking down the great shaft smelled to him of burning. They took him back and let him work with them. They treated him as a guest, as a child. They had adopted him. He was their secret.

There is not much good spending twelve hours a day in a black hole in the ground all your life long if there's nothing there, no secret, no treasure, nothing hidden.

There was the silver, to be sure. But where ten crews of fifteen had used to work these levels and there had been no end to the groan and clatter and crash of the loaded buckets going up on the screaming winch and the empties banging down to meet the trammers running with their heavy carts, now one crew of eight men worked: men over forty, old men, who had no skill but mining. There was still some silver there in the hard granite, in little veins among the gangue. Sometimes they would lengthen an end by one foot in two weeks.

"It was a great mine," they said with pride.

They showed the astronomer how to set a gad and swing the sledge, how to go at granite with the finely balanced and sharp-pointed pick, how to sort and "cob," what to look for, the rare bright branchings of the pure metal, the crumbling rich rock of

the ore. He helped them daily. He was in the stope waiting for them when they came, and spelled one or another on and off all day with the shovel work, or sharpening tools, or running the ore-cart down its grooved plank to the great shaft, or working in the ends. There they would not let him work long; pride and habit forbade it. "Here, leave off chopping at that like a woodcutter. Look: this way, see?" But then another would ask him, "Give me a blow here, lad, see, on the gad, that's it."

They fed him from their own coarse meager meals.

In the night, alone in the hollow earth, when they had climbed the long ladders up "to grass" as they said, he lay and thought of them, their faces, their voices, their heavy, scarred, earth-stained hands, old men's hands with thick nails blackened by bruising rock and steel; those hands, intelligent and vulnerable, which had opened up the earth and found the shining silver in the solid rock. The silver they never held, never kept, never spent. The silver that was not theirs.

"If you found a new vein, a new lode, what would you do?"

"Open her, and tell the masters."

"Why tell the masters?"

"Why, man! We gets paid for what we brings up! D'you think we does this damned work for love?"

"Yes."

They all laughed at him, loud, jeering laughter, innocent. The living eyes shone in their faces blackened with dust and sweat.

"Ah, if we could find a new lode! The wife would keep a pig like we had once, and by God I'd swim in beer! But if there's silver they'd have found it; that's why they pushed the workings so far east. But it's barren there, and worked out here, that's the short and long of it."

Time stretched behind him and ahead of him like the dark drifts and crosscuts of the mine, all present at once, wherever he with his

small candle might be among them. When he was alone now the astronomer often wandered in the tunnels and the old stopes, knowing the dangerous places, the deep levels full of water, adept at shaky ladders and tight places, intrigued by the play of his candle on the rock walls and faces, the glitter of mica that seemed to come from deep inside the stone. Why did it sometimes shine out that way? as if the candle found something far within the shining broken surface, something that winked in answer and occulted, as if it had slipped behind a cloud or an unseen planet's disc.

"There are stars in the earth," he thought. "If one knew how to see them."

Awkward with the pick, he was clever with machinery; they admired his skill, and brought him tools. He repaired pumps and windlasses; he fixed up a lamp on a chain for "young Per" working in a long narrow deadend, with a reflector made from a tin candle-holder beaten out into a curved sheet and polished with fine rock-dust and the sheepskin lining of his coat. "It's a marvel," Per said. "Like daylight. Only, being behind me, it don't go out when the air gets bad, and tell me I should be backing out for a breath."

For a man can go on working in a narrow end for some time after his candle has gone out for lack of oxygen.

"You should have a bellows rigged there."

"What, like I was a forge?"

"Why not?"

"Do ye ever go up to the grass, nights?" asked Hanno, looking wistfully at Guennar. Hanno was a melancholy, thoughtful, soft-hearted fellow. "Just to look about you?"

Guennar did not answer. He went off to help Bran with a timbering job; the miners did all the work that had once been done by crews of timberers, trammers, sorters, and so on.

"He's deathly afraid to leave the mine," Per said, low.

"Just to see the stars and get a breath of the wind," Hanno said, as if he was still speaking to Guennar.

One night the astronomer emptied out his pockets and looked at the stuff that had been in them since the night of the burning of the observatory: things he had picked up in those hours which he now could not remember, those hours when he had groped and stumbled in the smoldering wreckage, seeking . . . seeking what he had lost. . . . He no longer thought of what he had lost. It was sealed off in his mind by a thick scar, a burn-scar. For a long time this scar in his mind kept him from understanding the nature of the objects now ranged before him on the dusty stone floor of the mine: a wad of papers scorched all along one side; a round piece of glass or crystal; a metal tube; a beautifully worked wooden cogwheel; a bit of twisted blackened copper etched with fine lines; and so on, bits, wrecks, scraps. He put the papers back into his pocket, without trying to separate the brittle half-fused leaves and make out the fine script. He continued to look at and occasionally to pick up and examine the other things, especially the piece of glass.

This he knew to be the eyepiece of his ten-inch telescope. He had ground the lens himself. When he picked it up he handled it delicately, by the edges, lest the acid of his skin etch the glass. Finally he began to polish it clean, using a wisp of fine lambswool from his coat. When it was clear, he held it up and looked at and through it at all angles. His face was calm and intent, his light wide-set eyes steady.

Tilted in his fingers, the telescope lens reflected the lamp flame in one bright tiny point near the edge and seemingly beneath the curve of the face, as if the lens had kept a star in it from the many hundred nights it had been turned toward the sky.

He wrapped it carefully in the wisp of wool and made a place for it in the rock niche with his tinderbox. Then he took up the other things one by one.

During the next weeks the miners saw their fugitive less often while they worked. He was off a great deal by himself: exploring the deserted eastern regions of the mine, he said, when they asked him what he did.

"What for?"

"Prospecting," he said with the brief, wincing smile that gave him a very crazy look.

"Oh, lad, what do you know about that? She's all barren there. The silver's gone; and they found no eastern lode. You might be finding a bit of poor ore or a vein of tinstone, but nothing worth the digging."

"How do you know what's in the earth, in the rock under your feet, Per?"

"I know the signs, lad. Who should know better?"

"But if the signs are hidden?"

"Then the silver's hidden."

"Yet you know it is there, if you knew where to dig, if you could see into the rock. And what else is there? You find the metal, because you seek it, and dig for it. But what else might you find, deeper than the mine, if you sought, if you knew where to dig?"

"Rock," said Per. "Rock, and rock, and rock."

"And then?"

"And then? Hellfire, for all I know. Why else does it get hotter as the shafts go deeper? That's what they say. Getting nearer hell."

"No," the astronomer said, clear and firm. "No. There is no hell beneath the rocks."

"What is there, then, underneath it all?"

"The stars."

"Ah," said the miner, floored. He scratched his rough, tallow-clotted hair, and laughed. "There's a poser," he said, and stared at Guennar with pity and admiration. He knew Guennar was mad, but the size of his madness was a new thing to him, and admirable. "Will you find 'em then, the stars?"

"If I learn how to look," Guennar said, so calmly that Per had no response but to heft his shovel and get back to loading the cart.

One morning when the miners came down they found Guennar still sleeping, rolled up in the battered cloak Count Bord had given him, and by him a strange object, a contraption made of silver tubing, tin struts and wires beaten from old headlamp-sockets, a frame of pick handles carefully carved and fitted, cogged wheels, a bit of twinkling glass. It was elusive, makeshift, delicate, crazy, intricate.

"What the devil's that?"

They stood about and stared at the thing, the lights of their headlamps centering on it, a yellow beam sometimes flickering over the sleeping man as one or another glanced at him.

"He made it, sure."

"Sure enough."

"What for?"

"Don't touch it."

"I wasn't going to."

Roused by their voices, the astronomer sat up. The yellow beams of the candles brought his face out white against the dark. He rubbed his eyes and greeted them.

"What would that be, lad?"

He looked troubled or confused when he saw the object of their curiosity. He put a hand on it protectively, yet he looked at it himself without seeming to recognize it for a while. At last he said, frowning and speaking in a whisper, "It's a telescope."

"What's that?"

"A device that makes distant things clear to the eye."

"How come?" one of the miners asked, baffled. The astronomer answered him with growing assurance. "By virtue of certain properties of light and lenses. The eye is a delicate instrument, but it is blind to half the universe—far more than half. The night sky is

black, we say: between the stars is void and darkness. But turn the telescope-eye on that space between the stars, and lo, the stars! Stars too faint and far for the eye alone to see, rank behind rank, glory beyond glory, out to the uttermost boundaries of the universe. Beyond all imagination, in the outer darkness, there is light: a great glory of sunlight. I have seen it. I have seen it, night after night, and mapped the stars, the beacons of God on the shores of darkness. And here too there is light! There is no place bereft of the light, the comfort and radiance of the creator spirit. There is no place that is outcast, outlawed, forsaken. There is no place left dark. Where the eyes of God have seen, there light is. We must go farther, we must look farther! There is light if we will see it. Not with eyes alone, but with the skill of the hands and the knowledge of the mind and the heart's faith is the unseen revealed, and the hidden made plain. And all the dark earth shines like a sleeping star."

He spoke with that authority which the miners knew belonged by rights to the priests, to the great words priests spoke in the echoing churches. It did not belong here, in the hole where they grubbed their living, in the words of a crazy fugitive. Later on, one talking to another, they shook their heads, or tapped them. Per said, "The madness is growing in him," and Hanno said, "Poor soul, poor soul!" Yet there was not one of them who did not, also, believe what the astronomer had told them.

"Show me," said old Bran, finding Guennar alone in a deep eastern drift, busy with his intricate device. It was Bran who had first followed Guennar, and brought him food, and led him back to the others.

The astronomer willingly stood aside and showed Bran how to hold the device pointing downward at the tunnel floor, and how to aim and focus it, and tried to describe its function and what Bran might see: all hesitantly, since he was not used to explaining to the

ignorant, but without impatience when Bran did not understand.

"I don't see nothing but the ground," the old man said after a long and solemn observation with the instrument. "And the little dust and pebbles on it."

"The lamp blinds your eyes, perhaps," the astronomer said with humility. "It is better to look without light. I can do it because I have done it for so long. It is all practice—like placing the gads, which you always do right, and I always do wrong."

"Aye. Maybe. Tell me what you see—" Bran hesitated. He had not long ago realized who Guennar must be. Knowing him to be a heretic made no difference but knowing him to be a learned man made it hard to call him "mate" or "lad." And yet here, and after all this time, he could not call him Master. There were times when, for all his mildness, the fugitive spoke with great words, gripping one's soul, times when it would have been easy to call him Master. But it would have frightened him.

The astronomer put his hand on the frame of his mechanism and replied in a soft voice, "There are . . . constellations."

"What's that, constellations?"

The astronomer looked at Bran as if from a great way off, and said presently, "The Wain, the Scorpion, the Sickle by the Milky Way in summer, those are constellations. Patterns of stars, gatherings of stars, parenthoods, semblances . . ."

"And you see those here, with this?"

Still looking at him through the weak lamplight with clear brooding eyes, the astronomer nodded, and did not speak, but pointed downward, at the rock on which they stood, the hewn floor of the mine.

"What are they like?" Bran's voice was hushed.

"I have only glimpsed them. Only for a moment. I have not learned the skill; it is a somewhat different skill. . . . But they are there, Bran."

Often now he was not in the stope where they worked, when they came to work, and did not join them even for their meal, though they always left him a share of food. He knew the ways of the mine now better than any of them, even Bran, not only the "living" mine but the "dead" one, the abandoned workings and exploratory tunnels that ran eastward, ever deeper, towards the caves. There he was most often; and they did not follow him.

When he did appear amongst them and they talked with him, they were more timid with him, and did not laugh.

One night as they were all going back with the last cartload to the main shaft, he came to meet them, stepping suddenly out of a crosscut to their right. As always he wore his ragged sheepskin coat, black with the clay and dirt of the tunnels. His fair hair had gone grey. His eyes were clear. "Bran," he said, "come, I can show you now."

"Show me what?"

"The stars. The stars beneath the rock. There's a great constellation in the stope on the old fourth level, where the white granite cuts down through the black."

"I know the place."

"It's there: underfoot, by that wall of white rock. A great shining and assembly of stars. Their radiance beats up through the darkness. They are like the faces of dancers, the eyes of angels. Come and see them, Bran!"

The miners stood there, Per and Hanno with backs braced to hold the cart from rolling: stooped men with tired, dirty faces and big hands bent and hardened by the grip of shovel and pick and sledge. They were embarrassed, compassionate, impatient.

"We're just quitting. Off home to supper. Tomorrow," Bran said.

The astronomer looked from one face to another and said nothing.

Hanno said in his hoarse gentle voice, "Come up with us, for this once, lad. It's dark night out, and likely raining; it's November now; no soul will see you if you come and sit at my hearth, for once, and eat hot food, and sleep beneath a roof and not under the heavy earth all by yourself alone!"

Guennar stepped back. It was as if a light went out, as his face went into shadow. "No," he said. "They will burn out my eyes."

"Leave him be," said Per, and set the heavy ore-cart moving towards the shaft.

"Look where I told you," Guennar said to Bran. "The mine is not dead. Look with your own eyes."

"Aye. I'll come with you and see. Good night!"

"Good night," said the astronomer, and turned back to the side-tunnel as they went on. He carried no lamp or candle; they saw him one moment, darkness the next.

In the morning he was not there to meet them. He did not come. Bran and Hanno sought him, idly at first, then for one whole day. They went as far down as they dared, and came at last to the entrance of the caves, and entered, calling sometimes, though in the great caverns even they, miners all their lives, dared not call aloud because of the terror of the endless echoes in the dark.

"He has gone down," Bran said. "Down farther. That's what he said. Go farther, you must go farther, to find the light."

"There is no light," Hanno whispered. "There was never light here. Not since the world's creation."

But Bran was an obstinate old man, with a literal and credulous mind; and Per listened to him. One day the two went to the place the astronomer had spoken of, where a great vein of hard light granite that cut down through the darker rock had been left untouched, fifty years ago, as barren stone. They re-timbered the roof of the old stope where the supports had weakened, and began to

dig, not into the white rock but down, beside it; the astronomer had left a mark there, a kind of chart or symbol drawn with candle-black on the stone floor. They came on silver ore a foot down, beneath the shell of quartz; and under that—all eight of them working now—the striking picks laid bare the raw silver, the veins and branches and knots and nodes shining among broken crystals in the shattered rock, like stars and gatherings of stars, depth below depth without end, the light.

THE FIELD OF VISION

I hardly know what to say about "The Field of Vision"; it is a sort of sublimated temper tantrum. An indignant Letter to the Editor. A raspberry.

Shelley was kicked out of Oxford—I think the story is unauthenticated, but who cares—because he painted a sign on the end wall of a dead-end alley: THIS WAY TO HEAVEN. I feel that every now and then his sign needs repainting.

I saw Eternity the other night
Like a great Ring of pure and endless light. . . .

—Henry Vaughan, 1621–1695

Reports from Psyche XIV came in regularly, all routine, until just before their return window opened. Then all at once Commander Rogers radioed that they had left surface, had rejoined the ship, and were commencing departure procedures—82 hours 18 minutes early. Houston of course demanded explanations, but Psyche's answers were erratic. The 220-second answer lag didn't help. Psyche kept breaking contact. Once Rogers said, "We have got to bring her home now if we're going to do it at all," apparently in answer to Houston's questions, but the next thing was Hughes asking for a reading, and then something about a dosage. The sun was noisy

and reception was very bad. The voice transmission ceased without sign-off.

The automatic information feed from the ship continued. Departure was normal. Normal reports came in during the twenty-six days of flight which the astronauts spent in drugged sleep on HKL and I.V. hookups. There was no medical monitor on Psyche missions. The only link with the crew was voice contact. When they did not call in on Day 2, the long tension at Houston tightened to despair.

The onboard automatics, directed by the ground crew, had just about established Psyche's re-entry course when the dead speakers suddenly said in Hughes's voice, "Houston, can you give me readings. Optical interference here." They tried to direct him, but the one attempt he made at a manual correction was disastrous, and took ground control five hours to compensate. They told him hands off, they'd bring in the ship. Almost immediately after that they lost voice contact again.

The great pale parachutes opened above the grey Pacific, roses slowly falling out of heaven. The speed-burnt ship screamed steam, plunging; popped back up and rocked, quiet, on the long deep swells. Ground control had done a beautiful job. She was down within a half-kilo of the *California*. Helicopters hovered, rafts assembled, the ship was stabilized, the hatch was opened. Nobody scrambled out.

They went in and brought them out.

Commander Rogers was in his flight seat, still strapped down and plugged into the HKL and I.V.s. He had been dead about ten days, and it was clear why the others had not opened his suit.

Captain Temski seemed physically unhurt, but dazed and bewildered. He did not speak, or respond to instructions. They had to manhandle him to haul him out of the ship, though he put up no active resistance.

Dr Hughes was in a state of collapse, but fully conscious; he appeared to be blind.

"Please . . ."

"Can you see anything?"

"Yes! Please let me have the blindfold."

"Do you see this light I'm showing? What color is it, Dr Hughes?"

"All colors, white, it's too bright."

"Will you point towards it, please?"

"It's everywhere. It's too bright."

"The room's quite dark, Dr Hughes. Now, will you open your eyes again, please."

"It isn't dark."

"Mmmh. Possible supersensitivity here. All right now, how about that? Dark enough for you?"

"Make it dark!"

"No, keep your hands down, please. Take it easy. All right, we'll put the compresses back on."

The struggling man relaxed as soon as his eyes were covered, and lay still, breathing hard. His narrow face, framed in a month's growth of dark beard, was oiled with sweat. "I'm sorry," he said.

"We'll try again later on when you've rested."

"Will you open your eyes, please. The room's quite dark."

"Why do you tell me that when it's *not* dark?"

"Dr Hughes, I can hardly make out your face; I've got the faintest red illumination on my scope—nothing else. Can you see me?"

"No! I can't see for the light!"

The doctor increased the illumination until he could see Hughes's face, the clenched jaw, the open, dazzled, frightened eyes.

"There, does that make it any darker?" he asked with the sarcasm of helplessness.

"No!" Hughes shut his eyes; he had gone dead white. "Get dizzy," he muttered, "the whirling," then he gasped for breath and began to vomit.

Hughes was unmarried and had no immediate kin. His closest friend was known to be Bernard Decelis. They had trained together; Decelis had been specialist on Psyche XII, the mission that had discovered the City of Mars, as Hughes was on XIV. They flew Decelis to the debriefing station in Pasadena and instructed him to go in and talk with his friend. The conversation was of course recorded.

D. *Hullo, Gerry. Decelis.*

H. *Barnie?*

D. *How you doing?*

H. *Fine. You been OK?*

D. *Sure. No picnic, was it?*

H. *How's Gloria?*

D. *Fine, just fine.*

H. *She got past "Aunt Rhody" yet?*

D. *[laughs] Oh, Christ, yeah. She can play "Greensleeves" now. At least she calls it "Greensleeves."*

H. *What have they got you in this dump for?*

D. *To see you.*

H. *Wish I could return the compliment.*

D. *You will. Listen. I've been assured by three different oculists, or whatever the hell they are, opthamollywhoggers, eye-doctors here, that there is absolutely nothing wrong with your eyes. Three opthamacadamizers and a neurologist, in fact. It's a sort of chorus they have. But they sure as hell seem sure of it.*

H. *So what's wrong is my brain, evidently.*

D. *In the sense of a crossed connection, maybe.*

H. *What about Joe Temski?*

D. *I don't know. Haven't seen him.*

H. *What did they tell you about him?*

D. *They didn't have a chorus line worked out for him. Just said he's inclined to be withdrawn.*

H. *Withdrawn! Jesus, I'll say so. Like a rock is withdrawn.*

D. *Temski? That joker?*

H. *It started with him.*

D. *What did?*

H. *At the site. He stopped answering.*

D. *What happened?*

H. *Just that. He stopped answering. Stopped talking. Stopped noticing. Dwight thought it was cafard. Is that what they're still calling it?*

D. *It's mentioned as one possibility. Was there anything special happened, there at the site?*

H. *We found the room.*

D. *The room, yeah. That all came back on your reports. I've seen them, and some of the holos you brought back with you. Fantastic. What the hell is it, Gerry?*

H. *I don't know.*

D. *Is it a construct?*

H. *I don't know. What's the whole City?*

D. *It was built, made; it must have been.*

H. *How do you know, how can you tell, when you don't know what made it? Is a seashell "made"? If you didn't know, if you didn't have any background and couldn't assume any likeness, and you looked at a seashell and a ceramic ashtray, could you tell, could you say which was "made"? And what for? What does it mean? Or what about a ceramic seashell? Or a paper-wasp's nest? Or a geode?*

D. *Yeah, OK. But what about those things, that . . . arrangement that you call "pigeonholes" in the reports? I saw the holos.*

What did you make of them?

H. *What did you make of them?*

D. *I don't know. They're weird. I thought of running the spatial arrangements through a computer, looking for meaningful pattern. . . . You don't think much of that.*

H. *No. Fine. Only what are you going to program for "meaning"?*

D. *Mathematical relationships. Any kind of geometrical pattern, regularity, code. I don't know. What was the place like, Gerry?*

H. *I don't know.*

D. *You were in there a lot?*

H. *All the time, after we found it.*

D. *That's where you noticed this kind of eye trouble you've got? How did it start?*

H. *Things going out of focus. Like eye strain. It was worse outside the room. Came on over several days. I could still make things out all right when we were taking the ML up to the ship. But getting worse. There'd be these flashes of light, left my depth perception all screwed up, I'd get dizzy. Dwight and I set up the course, one or the other of us was functioning most of the time. But he was getting kind of wild. Didn't want to use the radio, wouldn't touch the onboard computer.*

D. *What was . . . wrong with him?*

H. *I don't know. When I told him about my eyes he said he'd been having something like shaking fits. I said we'd better get the hell up to the ship while we could. He said OK, because Joe was really beginning to not function. Before we even launched he started having some kind of seizures, like epilepsy—Dwight, I mean. When he came out of one he was shaky, but he seemed rational. He took us up OK, but as soon as we docked in he went into another fit, and they kept getting longer. He started hallucinating in between them. I gave him some tranquillizers*

and strapped him in; it was wearing him out. When I took the
sleep, I don't know, he could have been dead already then.

D. *No, he died in the sleep. About ten days out from Earth.*

H. *They didn't tell me that.*

D. *There wasn't anything you could have done, Gerry.*

H. *I don't know. Those attacks he had, they were like overloads.*
Like all his fuses blew. Burned him out. He talked, while he
was in them. Sort of in bursts, like barking—as if he was trying
to say a whole sentence at once. Epileptics don't talk, do they,
when they're having a seizure?

D. *I don't know. Epilepsy's so well controlled now you don't hear*
much about it. They catch the tendency, and cure it first. If
Rogers had had the tendency . . .

H. *Yeah. He never would have been in the program. Christ, he'd*
had six months in space.

D. *What had you had—six days?*

H. *Like you. One Moon hop.*

D. *It isn't that, then. Do you think . . .*

H. *What?*

D. *Some kind of virus?*

H. *Space plague? Martian fever? Mysterious ancient spores*
madden astronauts?

D. *All right, it sounds dumb. But look, the room had been sealed.*
And it does sound like all of you—

H. *Dwight gets a cortical overcharge, Joe goes catatonic, I start*
seeing things. What's the connection?

D. *Nervous system.*

H. *Why different symptoms in each of us?*

D. *Well, drugs affect people differently—*

H. *Do you think we found some kind of God damned Martian*
psychogenic mushrooms in there? There isn't anything there,
it's dead, like all the rest of Mars. You know, you've been there!

> There aren't any God damned germs or viruses, there's no life
> there, no life.

D. *But there may have been—*

H. *What makes you think so?*

D. *The room you found. The City we found.*

H. *City! For Christ's sake, Barnie, you talk like some damned pop
journalist, you know damned well the whole thing is a set of
mud concretions for all we can tell. There's no way to tell. It's
too old, conditions are too different, we have no context. We
don't understand, we can't understand, it's something the
human mind is outside of. Cities, rooms, all that—we're just
analogizing, trying to make sense in our terms. But it's not in
our terms. There is no sense. I can see that now. That's the only
thing I can see!*

D. *See what, Gerry?*

H. *What I see when I open my eyes!*

D. *What?*

H. *Everything that isn't there and doesn't make sense. Oh—I—*

D. *Here, come on. Take it easy. Look, it'll be OK. It's going to
be OK, Gerry, you'll be OK.*

H. *[unclear] light, and the [unclear] try to see what I touch and
I can't, I don't understand and I can't [unclear]*

D. *Hang on. I'm right here. Take it easy, old man.*

Hughes, who had entered the space program from astrophysics,
came with a very good record, in fact a brilliant one. This troubled
many of his military superiors, to whom high intelligence was a
code word for instability and insubordination. His performance had
been solid and his behavior irreproachable; but now it was frequently
recalled that he was, after all, an intellectual.

Temski was harder to explain. He was a crack test pilot, an Air

Force captain, and a baseball fan, but now his behavior was even more aberrant than Hughes's.

All Temski did was sit. He was capable of looking after himself, and did so. That is, when he was hungry and food was present, he ate some with his fingers; when he had to relieve himself, he went to a corner and did so; when he was sleepy, he lay down on the floor and slept. The rest of the time he sat. He was in good physical condition and quite calm. Nothing said to him produced the slightest reaction, nor did he take any interest in anything that went on. His wife was brought in to see him in hopes of producing a response. She was taken away weeping after five minutes.

Since Temski wouldn't respond, and Rogers, being dead, couldn't respond, it was quite natural to look upon Hughes as being, somehow, responsible.

There was nothing wrong with him except a case of something like hysterical blindness, so it was to be expected that he should answer questions rationally and explain precisely what had happened. This, however, he could not, or would not, do.

A psychiatric consultant was brought in, a distinguished New York doctor called Shapir. He was requested to work with both Temski and Hughes. It was of course unthinkable to admit that the mission had been a failure (the word "disaster" was not even mentioned), but a couple of rumors had leaked out to the press despite all security precautions. Irresponsible journalists demanded to know why the crew of Psyche XIV was being held incommunicado, and claimed the "right" of the American people to "know," etc. It had been necessary to issue a statement concerning a new health test being run on astronauts who had spent over fifteen days in space, due to Commander Rogers's unexpected and tragic death from heart failure, and to have a whole new series of articles written for the papers concerning plans for a "Little America" dome city on Mars, to maintain a positive attitude in the public. The real people of course knew that the rest of the Psyche program was in jeopardy;

and they instructed Dr Shapir to diagnose and cure the astronauts with all deliberate speed.

Shapir talked with Hughes for half an hour about the food in the hospital, Cal Tech, and the latest Chinese report on their Alpha Centauri probe, all very relaxed and trivial. Then he said, "What is it you see, when you open your eyes?"

Hughes, who was up and dressed now, sat silent for a while. Opaque goggles covered his eyes entirely, giving him the arrogant, staring look of people who affect dark glasses. "Nobody's asked that," he said.

"Didn't the oculists?"

"Yes, I guess Kray did. Early on. Before they decided I was a mental case."

"What did you tell him?"

"It's hard to describe. The point is, it's indescribable. At first it was things going out of focus, going transparent, going away. Then the light. Too much light. Like overexposing a film, bleaching everything out. But with that, a kind of whirling. Changing positions and relationships, changing perspectives, constant transformation. It made me get dizzy. My eyes kept sending signals to my inner ears, I guess. Like that inner-ear disease, only in reverse. Doesn't it foul up your spatial orientation?"

"Ménière's syndrome, I think it's called, yes, it does. Especially on stairs and slopes."

"It's as if I was looking from a great height, or . . . up at a great height. . . ."

"Heights ever worry you?"

"Hell no. They don't even mean anything to me. What's up and down, in space? No, see, I'm not giving you the picture. There is no picture. I've been trying to look more, to learn to . . . how to see . . . it's not much good."

There was a pause. "That takes courage," said Shapir.

"What do you mean?" the astronaut said sharply.

"Well . . . To have the sensory input which is most important to the conscious mind—sight—reporting non-existent and incomprehensible things, in flagrant contradiction with all other sensory input—your touch, your hearing, your sense of balance, and so on—to have that going on, every time you try to open your eyes, and not only to live with it but to attempt to investigate it . . . It doesn't sound easy."

"So mostly I keep my eyes shut," Hughes said, dour. "Like a damned see-no-evil monkey."

"When you do have your eyes open, and you look towards some object you know is there—your own hand, for instance—what do you see?"

" 'A blooming, buzzing confusion.' "

"William James," Shapir said with satisfaction. "What was he talking about—how a baby perceives the world, eh?" He had a pleasant voice with a mild, glancing quality to it, non-percussive; one could not imagine him scolding or yelling. He nodded several times, thinking out the implications of what Hughes had said. "To learn how to see, you said. To learn. That's how you feel about it?"

Hughes hesitated, then said with a sudden, marked increase of trust, "I have to. What else can I do? Apparently I'm never going to be able to—to see the way I used to, the way other people do, again. But I still do *see*. Only I don't understand what I see, it doesn't make sense. There are no outlines, no distinctions, even between nearer and farther. There *is* something there—only I can't say that, because there aren't any *things*. No forms. Instead of forms, I see transformations—transfigurations. Does that make any sense at all?"

"I think it does," Shapir said, "only it's enormously difficult to put a direct experience into words. And when the experience is new, unique, overwhelming . . ."

"And irrational. That's it." Hughes spoke now with real gratitude. "If only I could show it to you," he said wistfully.

The two astronauts were being kept on the tenth floor of a big military hospital in Maryland now. They were not permitted to leave that floor, and anyone who visited it still spent ten days in quarantine before he rejoined the outer world: the Martian plague theory was currently on top. At Shapir's insistence, Hughes was allowed to go up to the roof garden of the hospital (after which the elevator was elaborately sterilized and roped off for three days).

They demanded that Hughes wear a surgical mask; and Shapir had asked him not to wear his goggles. Docile, he went up the elevator with his mouth and nose covered, his eyes uncovered, but tightly shut.

The change from the dusk of the elevator to the hot smoggy sunlight of July on the open roof did not, as far as Shapir could see, affect those shut eyes. Hughes did not screw them tighter against the flooding light, though he raised his face to it as if he felt the heat pleasant on his skin, and took a deep breath through the binding gauze.

"I haven't been outside since March," he said.

It was true, of course. He had been in a spacesuit or in a hospital room, breathing canned or conditioned air.

"Have you got your compass bearings?" Shapir asked.

"Not the faintest. It makes me feel blinder, being outdoors. Afraid to walk off the edge." Hughes had refused assistance coming through the corridors and in the elevator, feeling his way adeptly with his hands, and now despite his joke about falling off he began to explore the roof garden. He was exhilarated: an active man released from long confinement. Shapir watched him, brooding. The low furniture was a hazard to him but he learned at once how to feel for it; he had tactile intelligence; there was grace in his movements, even as he blundered in blindness.

"Will you open your eyes?" Shapir said in his glancing, reluctant voice.

Hughes stopped. "All right," he said; but he turned towards

Shapir, and his right hand came up gropingly. Shapir came forward and let that hand take his arm.

The grip of it tightened, as Hughes opened his eyes. Then Hughes let go, and took a step away, stretching out both his arms. A cry broke from him. He reached forward and upward, his head back, his eyes wide open, staring at the empty sky. "Oh, my God!" he whispered, and dropped, like a man hit by a sledgehammer.

Psychiatric counselling session, 18 July. S. Shapir, Geraint Hughes.

S. *Hello. Sidney. . . . I won't stay long. Listen, that wasn't such a bright idea of mine. The roof. I'm sorry. I had no idea. But no right, either. . . . Would you rather I left?*

H. No.

S. *All right . . . I'm getting stir-crazy myself. Need a good walk. I walk a good deal, usually. About two miles to my office and the same back. Then I add detours. Whatever they say, New York is a beautiful town to walk in. If you know how to pick your route. Listen, I have a queer story about Joe Temski. Not a story, just a queer fact, actually. Did you know that they have written on his record that he is "functionally deaf"?*

H. *Deaf?*

S. *Yes, deaf. Well, you know, I began to wonder. I go in and talk to Joe, you know, touch him, try to make eye contact, any kind of contact, to get through. No go. I've had patients tell me in so many words, "I can't hear you." A metaphor. But what if it isn't a metaphor? It happens sometimes with little kids, they're called retarded and it turns out they've got thirty, sixty, eighty percent hearing dysfunction. Well, maybe Joe really can't hear me. Just like you can't see me.*

H. *[pause of forty seconds] Do you mean he's hearing things? Listening?*

S. *It's possible.*

H. [*pause of twenty seconds*] *You can't shut your ears.*

S. *That's what I thought, too. It could be rough, couldn't it? Well, what I thought was, what about trying to shut them for him? Put earplugs in his ears.*

H. *He still wouldn't be able to hear you.*

S. *No, but he wouldn't be distracted. If you had to watch your light show all the time, you wouldn't be able to pay much attention to me or anything else, right? Maybe it's like that with Joe. Maybe there's this noise drowning out everything else for him.*

H. [*pause of twenty seconds*] *It would be more than noise.*

S. *I don't suppose you want to talk about . . . on the roof. . . . No, all right.*

H. *You'd like to know what I saw, wouldn't you?*

S. *Sure I would. But in your own time.*

H. *Yeah, I've got so much else to do here besides talk to you. All the books I can read and the beautiful women I can look at. You know damned well I'll tell you eventually, because I haven't got anybody else to talk to.*

S. *Oh, hell, Geraint.* [*pause of ten seconds*]

H. *Shit. I'm sorry, Sidney. If I didn't have you to talk to, I'd have cracked completely. I know that. You're very patient with me.*

S. *Whatever you saw, up there, disturbs you. That's one reason why I want to know what it was. But what the hell, if you can handle it alone, do. That's the idea, after all. My curiosity is my problem, not yours! Listen. Let's forget talking. Let me read you this article in* Science. *Your Colonel Wood gave it to me, said you might be interested. I was. It's on what they found inside the Argentinian meteorite. The authors are suggesting we go comb the Meteor Belt for remnants of a trans-stellar fleet that came to grief in our solar system about six hundred million*

years ago. They would have landed on Mars first, of course. Are
these guys nuts?

H. I don't know. Read the article.

Temski slept heavily, and it was easy for Shapir to insert ordinary
wax plugs like those insomniacs use into his ears while he was
asleep. When Temski woke he did nothing unusual at first. He sat
up, yawned, stretched, scratched, looked lazily around to see if any-
thing to eat was handy, in that serene way which Shapir privately
felt was altogether unlike any psychotic behavior he had ever seen,
and in fact unlike any human behavior he had ever seen. Temski
reminded him of a healthy, poised, contented, tame animal. Not a
chimpanzee; something milder, more contemplative, an orang,
maybe.

But the orang began to feel uncomfortable.

Temski looked around, left and right, nervous. Perhaps he was
not looking but moving his head trying to find the vanished sounds.
The lost chord, Shapir thought. Temski grew more and more
disturbed and alert. He got up, still turning his head restlessly. He
looked across the room. For the first time in seventeen days of daily
contact, he saw Shapir.

His handsome face was now contorted with anxiety or bewilder-
ment.

"Where," he said, "where— "

His hands, groping at his ears to find the cause of silence, found
the earplugs and removed one. That was enough. "Ah," he said, and
stood still. His eyes were still directed towards Shapir, but he did not
see him. His face relaxed.

Later attempts were more successful. Though bewildered at first,
Temski was cooperative while artificially deafened, and responded
readily to Shapir's attempts to communicate with him by touch, by
sign, and finally by writing. After the fifth such session, Temski

consented to longer sessions involving the use of a drug which would deaden his auditory nerve endings for about five hours at a time.

During the second of these long periods he asked to see Hughes. Shapir had already been instructed to let the two astronauts talk together if possible; there was a feeling that this might elicit more information, if they talked freely together. It was necessary for Hughes to write, since Temski was artificially deafened; as he knew touch typing he carried on his part of the dialogue on a portable typewriter. Not all the material found in the wastebasket, however, could be successfully collated in to the tape of Temski's spoken conversation. The two men mostly discussed the return journey and Commander Rogers's illness and death, which Temski could not recall; Hughes described all this as he had done before without new information. They did not talk about the "room" (Site D) or their respective disabilities, except as follows:

T. *It's not inside, is it?*

H. *If it was, earplugs wd improve yr reception*

T. *It's real, then.*

H. *Hell yes*

T. *See, when they first stuck those plugs in my ears, when I woke up and there was this silence, I was really spooked. It took me a long time to come back from where I'd been. And I didn't much want to come back. But when Shapir began telling me how long it had been, and I realized this was Earth, you know, that's what spooked me—I thought, maybe all this has been some sort of, like, hallucination. You know. Jesus, have I been off my chump? That scared me. Like I was two different people. But I began to put it together, to see that it wasn't a split, but a . . .*

H. *Change*

T. *Exactly, it changed me, it had changed me. It's real. Because*

*when I can hear, that's what I hear. And when you can see,
that's what you see. Right? In other words, it is real. We have
to be artificially blinded and made deaf to not hear it and see it.
That's it, isn't it?*

[*Hughes's typed responses for the following section were not
identifiable in the wastebasket material.*]

H.

T. *Oh, no. Beautiful. It took me a long time, at least I know now
it was a long time, to begin to get it. At first it didn't make any
sense, Jesus, it scared the balls off me at first. You or Dwight
would say something, and there'd be this kind of chords all
around your voice, like rainbows around a prism so you can't
even see the prism—yeah, that's what it's like for you, isn't it?
It's the same, only this is with hearing, it's like everything turns
into this music, only it isn't music, it's . . . At first like I said I
didn't know how to hear it. I thought it was something wrong
with my suit radio! Jesus! [laughs] I couldn't follow the pat-
terns, you know, the modulations, like, the transformations.
It was all so different. But you learn. The more you listen the
more you hear. I wish you could hear it. You know, you tell me
it's two months since we left Mars, and so on, and shit, I believe
you, but it doesn't matter. It really doesn't matter—does it,
Gerry?*

H.

T. *I wish I could see it, the way you do. It must be tremendous.
But I'll tell you, I'm glad they pull me out of it like this, every
day now. I think it's meant to be that way. I was kind of, I
don't know, swamped, overwhelmed, it's too much. We're not
built right, not quite strong enough, maybe. At least at first.
Can't take it all at once. What I'd like to try to do while I'm out
of touch is try to write some of it down.*

H.

T. *No, I don't. But it wouldn't have to be music. See, it isn't music, that's just like a way of describing it because it's beautiful. I think I could get it into words just as well. Maybe better. To say what it means.*

H.

T. *Afraid of what?*

Bernard Decelis and his wife called Hughes every couple of days on the telephone, though they were prevented by the quarantine from coming to see him. On the 27th of July Hughes and Decelis had a significant conversation concerning the so-called room, site D of the Psyche XIV survey. Decelis said, "If I don't get on the Sixteen team and *see* that damned place, I'll flip."

"Seeing is believing," Hughes remarked. He was not as excitable as he had been earlier, tending to be terse and rather bitter.

"Listen, Gerry. Was there ever machinery in those pigeonholes?"

"No."

"Hah! There's a definite answer! I thought you wouldn't assert anything about Site D except its incomprehensibility to the human mind. You softening up?"

"No. Learning."

"Learning what?"

"How to see."

After a pause Decelis asked cautiously, "See what?"

"Site D. Since it's all I can see."

"You mean, that's what you—when your eyes are open— "

"No." Hughes spoke wearily and with reluctance. "It's more complex than that. I don't see Site D. I see . . . the world in the light cast by Site D. . . . A new light. The man you ought to ask is Joe Temski. Or, listen, did you ever run the pigeonholes through Algie, like you said?"

"I had trouble setting up the program."

"I'll bet you did," Hughes said with a short laugh. "Send the stuff on up here. I'll set it up. Blindfolded."

Temski came into Hughes's room, radiant. "Gerry," he said, "I've got it."

"Got what?"

"I've got it together. I heard you. No, I wasn't lip-reading. Say something with your back turned. Go on!"

"Ptomaine poisoning."

" 'Ptomaine poisoning.' —OK? See, I'm hearing you. But I haven't lost the music. I've got it all together!"

Blue-eyed and fair, Temski was ordinarily a handsome man; now he was magnificent. Hughes could not see him (though the spy camera in the ventilator grille could and did), but he heard the vibration of his voice, and was moved, and frightened.

"Take off your blinkers, Gerry," the gentle, vibrant voice said.

Hughes shook his head.

"You can't sit in the dark inside yourself forever. Come out. You can't choose blindness, Gerry."

"Why can't I?"

"Not after you've seen the light."

"What light?"

"The light, the word, the truth we have been taught to perceive and to know," Temski said, with the gentleness of utter certainty, and a warmth in his voice, a warmth like sunlight.

"Get out," Hughes said. "Get out, Temski!"

Twelve weeks had passed since Psyche XIV splashdown. Nobody on the debriefing staff had come down with any symptoms more alarming than boredom. Hughes was no worse, and Temski was now completely recovered. It could be safely assumed that whatever had affected the crew of Psyche XIV, it had not been an infection

vectored by a virus, spore, bacterium, or other physical agent. The hypothesis accepted tentatively and with various reservations by the majority, including Dr Shapir, was that something in the arrangement of the elements constituting the "room," Site D, had, during their prolonged and intense study of the site, caused a degree of brain-wave disruption in all three men, analogous to the brain-function disturbance caused by strobe lights at certain frequencies, etc. Precisely what elements of the "room" were involved was not yet known, though the holographs were being examined intensively by experts. Psyche XV was to make a still more thorough investigation of the site, taking due precautions to protect and monitor the astronauts.

These suspect elements of Site D were so numerous and so intricately interrelated that it was very hard for a single mind to attempt to arrange or order them. Some Martianologists were sure the peculiar properties of the "room" were only a geological accident, and that all the "room" had to "tell" us was the kind of information furnished so concisely and beautifully by the strata of rocks, the rings of a tree, the lines of a spectrum. Others were as convinced that intelligent beings had built the City, and that in studying it we might learn something of their nature and the way their minds worked—those unimaginable minds of six hundred million years ago (for the radioactive-decay dating of the site was absolutely definite now). The job of doing so, however, was daunting. T. A. Newman of the Smithsonian Institution put it well: "Archaeologists are used to getting a lot of information out of very simple things—potsherds, bits of flint, a wall here, a grave there. But what if all we had of an ancient civilization was a very complicated thing, complicated in more than a technological sense—let's say, one copy of Shakespeare's *Hamlet*. Now let's assume that the achaeologists who find this copy of *Hamlet* are not humanoid, don't have books, don't have plays, don't speak, write, or think at all as we do. What

are they going to make of that little physical artifact, the evident complexity and purposefulness of it, the repetition of certain elements and the non-repetition of others, the semi-regularity of line lengths, and so on? How are they going to read *Hamlet?*"

To those who accepted the *"Hamlet* theory," the obvious first step was to employ computers, and a number of them had been set to work analyzing the various elements of Site D: the spacing, size, depth, and configurations of the "pigeonholes," the proportions of the first, middle, and third "subchambers," the extraordinary acoustical properties of the "room" as a whole, and so on. None of these programs had as yet produced any sure evidence of conscious planning or rational pattern; none, that is, except the program set up by Decelis and Hughes on NASA's new Algebraic V, which had certainly got results, though they could not be called rational. Indeed, that print-out had given a shudder to the NASA brass, and a good laugh to those few scientists to whom Decelis had shown it before it was suppressed as being probably a fraud and certainly an embarrassment. The entire print-out read as follows:

RUN

PIGEONHOLES SITE D MARS SECTOR NINE

DECELIS HUGHES

GOD

GOOD GOD GOD GOOD YOU ARE GOD

RESET

RESET TOTALITY COMPREHENSION NONSENSE

PERCEIVE NONSENSE NO SENSE REAL GOOD GOD

PERCEIVE RECEIVE DIRECTIONS DIRECTION

PROCEED INFORM UNINFORMED

GOD GOD GOD GOD GOD GOD

END RUN

Shapir came in to find Hughes lying on his bed, as he now did most of the time, wearing his black goggles. He looked white and ill.

"I think you've been overdoing it."

Hughes did not answer.

Shapir sat down. "They're sending me back to New York," he said presently.

Hughes did not answer.

"Temski's been released, you know. He's on his way to Florida now. With his wife. I can't find out what they plan for you. I asked . . ." After a long pause he completed the sentence. "I asked for another two weeks here with you. No go."

"It's all right," Hughes said.

"I want to keep in touch with you, Geraint. Obviously we can't write letters. But there's the phone. And tapes; I'm leaving a cassette recorder here with you. When you want to talk, please call me. If you can't get me, talk to the recorder. It's not the same, but—"

"You're a very good man, Sidney," Hughes said gently. "I wish. . . ." After a minute he sat up. He reached up to his face and took off the black goggles. They fitted so closely around his eye sockets that it took him a little while to get them off. When they were off he lowered his hands, and looked across the room, directly at Shapir. His eyes, the pupils enlarged by long privation of light, were almost as dark as the goggles.

"I see you," he said. "Hide and seek. I spy. You're It. Do you want to know what I see?"

"Yes," Shapir said softly.

"A blot. A shadow. An incompleteness, a rudiment, an obstruction. Something completely unimportant. You see, it doesn't do any *good* to be a good man, even . . ."

"And when you look at yourself?"

"The same. Just the same. A hindrance, a triviality. A blot on the field of vision."

"The field of vision. What is the field of vision?"

"What do you think?" Hughes said, very quietly and wearily. "What is true vision of? Reality, of course. I have been re-programmed to perceive reality, to see the truth. I see God." He sank his face into his hands, covering his eyes. "I was a thinking man," he said. "I tried to be a rational man. But what good's reason, when you can *see* the truth? Seeing is believing. . . ." He looked up again at Shapir, his dark eyes both piercing and unseeing. "If you want a real explanation, go ask Joe Temski. He's keeping quiet now; he's biding his time. But he's the one who can tell you. And he will, when his time comes. He can translate what he hears—translate it into words. It's harder to do with visual perceptions. Mystics have always had trouble putting their visions into words; except the ones that got the Word, that heard the Voice. They usually got right up and acted, didn't they? Temski will act. But I will not. I refuse. I will not preach. I will not be a missionary."

"A missionary?"

"Don't you see? Don't you see that's what the 'room' is? A training center, a briefing room, a— "

"A religious center? A church?"

"Well, in a way. A place where you are taught to see God, and hear God, and know God. And love God. A conversion center. A place where you're converted! And then you want to go out and preach the knowledge of God to the others—to the heathen. Because now you know how blind they are, and how easy it is to see. No, not just a church; a mission. The Mission. And you learn the

Mission, and you come out of it with the Mission. They weren't explorers. They were missionaries, bearing the truth, bringing it to the other races and the future races, all the poor damned heathens living in the outer darkness. They knew the answer, and they wanted us all to know the answer. Nothing else matters, once you've learned the answer. It doesn't matter if you're a good man or a bad one, if I'm an intelligent man or a fool. Nothing about us matters except that we are trivial vehicles of the great truth. The earth doesn't matter, the stars don't matter, death doesn't matter, nothing is anything. Only God is."

"An alien god?"

"Not a god. God—the one true God, immanent in all things. Everywhere, forever. I have learned to see God. All I have to do is open my eyes, and I see the Face of God. And I'd give all my life just to see one human face again, to see a tree, just a tree, a chair— a plain wooden chair, ordinary— They can keep their God, they can keep their Light. I want the world back. I want questions, not the answer. I want my own life back, and my own death!"

On the recommendation of the Army psychiatrist who took over the case of Geraint Hughes after Shapir was dismissed, Hughes was moved to a military hospital for the insane. As he was generally a quiet and cooperative patient he was not kept under strict supervision, and after eleven months of confinement he unfortunately carried out a successful suicide attempt, slashing his wrists with a spoon-handle which he had stolen from the mess hall and sharpened by rubbing against the bed frame. It is an interesting fact that he killed himself on the day the Psyche XV Mission started back to Earth from Mars, bringing the documents and records which, as interpreted by the First Apostle, now form the first chapters of the Revelation of the Ancients, the sacred texts of the holy and universal

Church of God, bringer of light to the heathen, sole vehicle of the One Eternal Truth.

> O fools (said I) thus to prefer dark night
> Before true light. . . .
> But as I did their madness so discuss
> One whisper'd thus,
> *This Ring the Bride-groome did for none provide*
> *But for his bride.*

DIRECTION OF THE ROAD

The tree stands just south of the McMinnville bypass on Oregon State Highway 18. It lost a major limb last year, but still looks grand. We drive past it several times a year, and it has never failed to uphold Relativity with dignity and the skill of long practice.

They did not use to be so demanding. They never hurried us into anything more than a gallop, and that was rare; most of the time it was just a jigjog foot-pace. And when one of them was on his own feet, it was a real pleasure to approach him. There was time to accomplish the entire act with style. There he'd be, working his legs and arms the way they do, usually looking at the road, but often aside at the fields, or straight at me: and I'd approach him steadily but quite slowly, growing larger all the time, synchronizing the rate of approach and the rate of growth perfectly, so that at the very moment that I'd finished enlarging from a tiny speck to my full size—sixty feet in those days—I was abreast of him and hung above him, loomed, towered, overshadowed him. Yet he would show no fear. Not even the children were afraid of me, though often they kept their eyes on me as I passed by and started to diminish.

Sometimes on a hot afternoon one of the adults would stop me right there at our meeting-place, and lie down with his back against

mine for an hour or more. I didn't mind in the least. I have an excellent hill, good sun, good wind, good view; why should I mind standing still for an hour or an afternoon? It's only a relative stillness, after all. One need only look at the sun to realize how fast one is going; and then, one grows continually—especially in summer. In any case I was touched by the way they would entrust themselves to me, letting me lean against their little warm backs, and falling sound asleep there between my feet. I liked them. They have seldom lent us Grace as do the birds; but I really preferred them to squirrels.

In those days the horses used to work for them, and that too was enjoyable from my point of view. I particularly liked the canter, and got quite proficient at it. The surging and rhythmical motion accompanied shrinking and growing with a swaying and swooping, almost an illusion of flight. The gallop was less pleasant. It was jerky, pounding: one felt tossed about like a sapling in a gale. And then, the slow approach and growth, the moment of looming-over, and the slow retreat and diminishing, all that was lost during the gallop. One had to hurl oneself into it, cloppety-cloppety-cloppety! and the man usually too busy riding, and the horse too busy running, even to look up. But then, it didn't happen often. A horse is mortal, after all, and like all the loose creatures grows tired easily; so they didn't tire their horses unless there was urgent need. And they seemed not to have so many urgent needs, in those days.

It's been a long time since I had a gallop, and to tell the truth I shouldn't mind having one. There was something invigorating about it, after all.

I remember the first motorcar I saw. Like most of us, I took it for a mortal, some kind of loose creature new to me. I was a bit startled, for after a hundred and thirty-two years I thought I knew all the local fauna. But a new thing is always interesting, in its

trivial fashion, so I observed this one with attention. I approached it at a fair speed, about the rate of a canter, but in a new gait, suitable to the ungainly looks of the thing: an uncomfortable, bouncing, rolling, choking, jerking gait. Within two minutes, before I'd grown a foot tall, I knew it was no mortal creature, bound or loose or free. It was a making, like the carts the horses got hitched to. I thought it so very ill-made that I didn't expect it to return, once it gasped over the West Hill, and I heartily hoped it never would, for I disliked that jerking bounce.

But the thing took to a regular schedule, and so, perforce, did I. Daily at four I had to approach it, twitching and stuttering out of the West, and enlarge, loom-over, and diminish. Then at five back I had to come, poppeting along like a young jackrabbit for all my sixty feet, jigging and jouncing out of the East, until at last I got clear out of sight of the wretched little monster and could relax and loosen my limbs to the evening wind. There were always two of them inside the machine: a young male holding the wheel, and behind him an old female wrapped in rugs, glowering. If they ever said anything to each other I never heard it. In those days I overheard a good many conversations on the road, but not from that machine. The top of it was open, but it made so much noise that it overrode all voices, even the voice of the song-sparrow I had with me that year. The noise was almost as vile as the jouncing.

I am of a family of rigid principle and considerable self-respect. The Quercian motto is "Break but bend not," and I have always tried to uphold it. It was not only personal vanity, but family pride, you see, that was offended when I was forced to jounce and bounce in this fashion by a mere making.

The apple trees in the orchard at the foot of the hill did not seem to mind; but then, apples are tame. Their genes have been tampered with for centuries. Besides, they are herd creatures; no orchard tree can really form an opinion of its own.

I kept my own opinion to myself.

But I was very pleased when the motorcar ceased to plague us. All month went by without it, and all month I walked at men and trotted at horses most willingly, and even bobbed for a baby on its mother's arm, trying hard though unsuccessfully to keep in focus.

Next month, however—September it was, for the swallows had left a few days earlier—another of the machines appeared, a new one, suddenly dragging me and the road and our hill, the orchard, the fields, the farmhouse roof, all jigging and jouncing and racketing along from East to West; I went faster than a gallop, faster than I had ever gone before. I had scarcely time to loom, before I had to shrink right down again.

And the next day there came a different one.

Yearly then, weekly, daily, they became commoner. They became a major feature of the local Order of Things. The road was dug up and re-metalled, widened, finished off very smooth and nasty, like a slug's trail, with no ruts, pools, rocks, flowers, or shadows on it. There used to be a lot of little loose creatures on the road, grasshoppers, ants, toads, mice, foxes, and so on, most of them too small to move for, since they couldn't really see one. Now the wise creatures took to avoiding the road, and the unwise ones got squashed. I have seen all too many rabbits die in that fashion, right at my feet. I am thankful that I am an oak, and that though I may be wind-broken or uprooted, hewn or sawn, at least I cannot, under any circumstances, be squashed.

With the presence of many motorcars on the road at once, a new level of skill was required of me. As a mere seedling, as soon as I got my head above the weeds, I had learned the basic trick of going two directions at once. I learned it without thinking about it, under the simple pressure of circumstances on the first occasion that I saw a walker in the East and a horseman facing him in the West.

I had to go two directions at once, and I did so. It's something we trees master without real effort, I suppose. I was nervous, but I succeeded in passing the rider and then shrinking away from him while at the same time I was still jigjogging towards the walker, and indeed passed him (no looming, back in those days!) only when I had got quite out of sight of the rider. I was proud of myself, being very young, that first time I did it; but it sounds more difficult than it really is. Since those days of course I had done it innumerable times, and thought nothing about it; I could do it in my sleep. But have you ever considered the feat accomplished, the skill involved, when a tree enlarges, simultaneously yet at slightly different rates and in slightly different manners, for each one of forty motorcar drivers facing two opposite directions, while at the same time diminishing for forty more who have got their backs to it, meanwhile remembering to loom over each single one at the right moment: and to do this minute after minute, hour after hour, from daybreak till nightfall or long after?

For my road had become a busy one; it worked all day long under almost continual traffic. It worked, and I worked. I did not jounce and bounce so much any more, but I had to run faster and faster: to grow enormously, to loom in a split second, to shrink to nothing, all in a hurry, without time to enjoy the action, and without rest: over and over and over.

Very few of the drivers bothered to look at me, not even a seeing glance. They seemed, indeed, not to see any more. They merely stared ahead. They seemed to believe that they were "going somewhere." Little mirrors were affixed to the front of their cars, at which they glanced to see where they had been; then they stared ahead again. I had thought that only beetles had this delusion of Progress. Beetles are always rushing about, and never looking up. I had always had a pretty low opinion of beetles. But at least they let me be.

I confess that sometimes, in the blessed nights of darkness with no moon to silver my crown and no stars occluding with my branches, when I could rest, I would think seriously of escaping my obligation to the general Order of Things: of *failing to move.* No, not seriously. Half-seriously. It was mere weariness. If even a silly, three-year-old, female pussy willow at the foot of the hill accepted her responsibility, and jounced and rolled and accelerated and grew and shrank for each motorcar on the road, was I, an oak, to shirk? Noblesse oblige, and I trust I have never dropped an acorn that did not know its duty.

For fifty or sixty years, then, I have upheld the Order of Things, and have done my share in supporting the human creatures' illusion that they are "going somewhere." And I am not unwilling to do so. But a truly terrible thing has occurred, which I wish to protest.

I do not mind going two directions at once; I do not mind growing and shrinking simultaneously; I do not mind moving, even at the disagreeable rate of sixty or seventy miles an hour. I am ready to go on doing all these things until I am felled or bulldozed. They're my job. But I do object, passionately, to being made eternal.

Eternity is none of my business. I am an oak, no more, no less. I have my duty, and I do it; I have my pleasures, and enjoy them, though they are fewer, since the birds are fewer, and the wind's foul. But, long-lived though I may be, impermanence is my right. Mortality is my privilege. And it has been taken from me.

It was taken from me on a rainy evening in March last year.

Fits and bursts of cars, as usual, filled the rapidly moving road in both directions. I was so busy hurtling along, enlarging, looming, diminishing, and the light was failing so fast, that I scarcely noticed what was happening until it happened. One of the drivers of one of the cars evidently felt that his need to "go somewhere" was exceptionally urgent, and so attempted to place his car in front of the car in front of it. This maneuver involves a temporary slanting of

the Direction of the Road and a displacement onto the far side, the side which normally runs the other direction (and may I say that I admire the road very highly for its skill in executing such maneuvers, which must be difficult for an unliving creature, a mere making). Another car, however, happened to be quite near the urgent one, and facing it, as it changed sides; and the road could not do anything about it, being already overcrowded. To avoid impact with the facing car, the urgent car totally violated the Direction of the Road, swinging it round to North-South in its own terms, and so forcing me to leap directly at it. I had no choice. I had to move, and move fast—eighty-five miles an hour. I leapt: I loomed enormous, larger than I have ever loomed before. And then I hit the car.

I lost a considerable piece of bark, and, what's more serious, a fair bit of cambium layer; but as I was seventy-two feet tall and about nine feet in girth at the point of impact, no real harm was done. My branches trembled with the shock enough that a last-year's robin's nest was dislodged and fell; and I was so shaken that I groaned. It is the only time in my life that I have ever said anything out loud.

The motorcar screamed horribly. It was smashed by my blow, squashed, in fact. Its hinder parts were not much affected, but the forequarters knotted up and knurled together like an old root, and little bright bits of it flew all about and lay like brittle rain.

The driver had no time to say anything; I killed him instantly.

It is not this that I protest. I had to kill him. I had no choice, and therefore have no regret. What I protest, what I cannot endure, is this: as I leapt at him, he saw me. He looked up at last. He saw me as I have never been seen before, not even by a child, not even in the days when people looked at things. He saw me whole, and saw nothing else—then, or ever.

He saw me under the aspect of eternity. He confused me with

eternity. And because he died in that moment of false vision, because it can never change, I am caught in it, eternally.

This is unendurable. I cannot uphold such an illusion. If the human creatures will not understand Relativity, very well; but they must understand Relatedness.

If it is necessary to the Order of Things, I will kill drivers of cars, though killing is not a duty usually required of oaks. But it is unjust to require me to play the part, not of the killer only, but of death. For I am not death. I am life: I am mortal.

If they wish to see death visibly in the world, that is their business, not mine. I will not act Eternity for them. Let them not turn to the trees for death. If that is what they want to see, let them look into one another's eyes and see it there.

THE ONES WHO WALK
AWAY FROM OMELAS

(Variations on a theme by William James)

The central idea of this psychomyth, the scapegoat, turns up in Dostoyevsky's Brothers Karamazov, *and several people have asked me, rather suspiciously, why I gave the credit to William James. The fact is, I haven't been able to re-read Dostoyevsky, much as I loved him, since I was twenty-five, and I'd simply forgotten he used the idea. But when I met it in James's "The Moral Philosopher and the Moral Life," it was with a shock of recognition. Here is how James puts it:*

Or if the hypothesis were offered us of a world in which Messrs. Fourier's and Bellamy's and Morris's utopias should all be outdone, and millions kept permanently happy on the one simple condition that a certain lost soul on the far-off edge of things should lead a life of lonely torment, what except a specifical and independent sort of emotion can it be which would make us immediately feel, even though an impulse arose within us to clutch at the happiness so offered, how hideous a thing would be its enjoyment when deliberately accepted as the fruit of such a bargain?

The dilemma of the American conscience can hardly be better stated. Dostoyevsky was a great artist, and a radical one, but his early social radicalism reversed itself, leaving him a violent reactionary. Whereas the American James, who seems so mild, so naïvely gentlemanly—look how he says "us," assuming all his readers are

as decent as himself!—was, and remained, and remains, a genuinely radical thinker. Directly after the "lost soul" passage he goes on,

All the higher, more penetrating ideals are revolutionary. They present themselves far less in the guise of effects of past experience than in that of probable causes of future experience, factors to which the environment and the lessons it has so far taught us must learn to bend.

The application of those two sentences to this story, and to science fiction, and to all thinking about the future, is quite direct. Ideals as "the probable causes of future experience"—that is a subtle and an exhilarating remark!

Of course I didn't read James and sit down and say, Now I'll write a story about that "lost soul." It seldom works that simply. I sat down and started a story, just because I felt like it, with nothing but the word "Omelas" in mind. It came from a road sign: Salem (Oregon) backwards. Don't you read road signs backwards? POTS. WOLS nerdlihc. Ocsicnarf Nas . . . Salem equals schelomo equals salaam equals Peace. Melas. O melas. Omelas. Homme hélas. "Where do you get your ideas from, Ms Le Guin?" From forgetting Dostoyevsky and reading road signs backwards, naturally. Where else?

With a clamor of bells that set the swallows soaring, the Festival of Summer came to the city Omelas, bright-towered by the sea. The rigging of the boats in harbor sparkled with flags. In the streets between houses with red roofs and painted walls, between old moss-grown gardens and under avenues of trees, past great parks and public buildings, processions moved. Some were decorous: old people in long stiff robes of mauve and grey, grave master workmen,

quiet, merry women carrying their babies and chatting as they walked. In other streets the music beat faster, a shimmering of gong and tambourine, and the people went dancing, the procession was a dance. Children dodged in and out, their high calls rising like the swallows' crossing flights over the music and the singing. All the processions wound towards the north side of the city, where on the great water-meadow called the Green Fields boys and girls, naked in the bright air, with mud-stained feet and ankles and long, lithe arms, exercised their restive horses before the race. The horses wore no gear at all but a halter without bit. Their manes were braided with streamers of silver, gold, and green. They flared their nostrils and pranced and boasted to one another; they were vastly excited, the horse being the only animal who has adopted our ceremonies as his own. Far off to the north and west the mountains stood up half encircling Omelas on her bay. The air of morning was so clear that the snow still crowning the Eighteen Peaks burned with white-gold fire across the miles of sunlit air, under the dark blue of the sky. There was just enough wind to make the banners that marked the racecourse snap and flutter now and then. In the silence of the broad green meadows one could hear the music winding through the city streets, farther and nearer and ever approaching, a cheerful faint sweetness of the air that from time to time trembled and gathered together and broke out into the great joyous clanging of the bells.

Joyous! How is one to tell about joy? How describe the citizens of Omelas?

They were not simple folk, you see, though they were happy. But we do not say the words of cheer much any more. All smiles have become archaic. Given a description such as this one tends to make certain assumptions. Given a description such as this one tends to look next for the King, mounted on a splendid stallion and surrounded by his noble knights, or perhaps in a golden litter

borne by great-muscled slaves. But there was no king. They did not use swords, or keep slaves. They were not barbarians. I do not know the rules and laws of their society, but I suspect that they were singularly few. As they did without monarchy and slavery, so they also got on without the stock exchange, the advertisement, the secret police, and the bomb. Yet I repeat that these were not simple folk, not dulcet shepherds, noble savages, bland utopians. They were not less complex than us. The trouble is that we have a bad habit, encouraged by pedants and sophisticates, of considering happiness as something rather stupid. Only pain is intellectual, only evil interesting. This is the treason of the artist: a refusal to admit the banality of evil and the terrible boredom of pain. If you can't lick 'em, join 'em. If it hurts, repeat it. But to praise despair is to condemn delight, to embrace violence is to lose hold of everything else. We have almost lost hold; we can no longer describe a happy man, nor make any celebration of joy. How can I tell you about the people of Omelas? They were not naïve and happy children—though their children were, in fact, happy. They were mature, intelligent, passionate adults whose lives were not wretched. O miracle! but I wish I could describe it better. I wish I could convince you. Omelas sounds in my words like a city in a fairy tale, long ago and far away, once upon a time. Perhaps it would be best if you imagined it as your own fancy bids, assuming it will rise to the occasion, for certainly I cannot suit you all. For instance, how about technology? I think that there would be no cars or helicopters in and above the streets; this follows from the fact that the people of Omelas are happy people. Happiness is based on a just discrimination of what is necessary, what is neither necessary nor destructive, and what is destructive. In the middle category, however—that of the unnecessary but undestructive, that of comfort, luxury, exuberance, etc.—they could perfectly well have central heating, subway trains, washing machines, and all kinds of marve-

lous devices not yet invented here, floating light-sources, fuelless
power, a cure for the common cold. Or they could have none of
that: it doesn't matter. As you like it. I incline to think that people
from towns up and down the coast have been coming in to Omelas
during the last days before the Festival on very fast little trains and
double-decked trams, and that the train station of Omelas is actually
the handsomest building in town, though plainer than the magnifi-
cent Farmers' Market. But even granted trains, I fear that Omelas so
far strikes some of you as goody-goody. Smiles, bells, parades, horses,
bleh. If so, please add an orgy. If an orgy would help, don't hesitate.
Let us not, however, have temples from which issue beautiful nude
priests and priestesses already half in ecstasy and ready to copulate
with any man or woman, lover or stranger, who desires union with
the deep godhead of the blood, although that was my first idea. But
really it would be better not to have any temples in Omelas—at least,
not manned temples. Religion yes, clergy no. Surely the beautiful
nudes can just wander about, offering themselves like divine soufflés
to the hunger of the needy and the rapture of the flesh. Let them
join the processions. Let tambourines be struck above the copulations,
and the glory of desire be proclaimed upon the gongs, and (a not
unimportant point) let the offspring of these delightful rituals be
beloved and looked after by all. One thing I know there is none
of in Omelas is guilt. But what else should there be? I thought at
first there were no drugs, but that is puritanical. For those who like
it, the faint insistent sweetness of *drooz* may perfume the ways of the
city, *drooz* which first brings a great lightness and brilliance to the
mind and limbs, and then after some hours a dreamy languor, and
wonderful visions at last of the very arcana and inmost secrets of the
Universe, as well as exciting the pleasure of sex beyond all belief;
and it is not habit-forming. For more modest tastes I think there
ought to be beer. What else, what else belongs in the joyous city? The
sense of victory, surely, the celebration of courage. But as we did

without clergy, let us do without soldiers. The joy built upon success-ful slaughter is not the right kind of joy; it will not do; it is fearful and it is trivial. A boundless and generous contentment, a mag-nanimous triumph felt not against some outer enemy but in com-munion with the finest and fairest in the souls of all men everywhere and the splendor of the world's summer: this is what swells the hearts of the people of Omelas, and the victory they celebrate is that of life. I really don't think many of them need to take *drooz*.

Most of the processions have reached the Green Fields by now. A marvelous smell of cooking goes forth from the red and blue tents of the provisioners. The faces of small children are amiably sticky; in the benign grey beard of a man a couple of crumbs of rich pastry are entangled. The youths and girls have mounted their horses and are beginning to group around the starting line of the course. An old woman, small, fat, and laughing, is passing out flowers from a basket, and tall young men wear her flowers in their shining hair. A child of nine or ten sits at the edge of the crowd, alone, playing on a wooden flute. People pause to listen, and they smile, but they do not speak to him, for he never ceases playing and never sees them, his dark eyes wholly rapt in the sweet, thin magic of the tune.

He finishes, and slowly lowers his hands holding the wooden flute.

As if that little private silence were the signal, all at once a trumpet sounds from the pavilion near the starting line: imperious, melan-choly, piercing. The horses rear on their slender legs, and some of them neigh in answer. Sober-faced, the young riders stroke the horses' necks and soothe them, whispering, "Quiet, quiet, there my beauty, my hope. . . ." They begin to form in rank along the starting line. The crowds along the racecourse are like a field of grass and flowers in the wind. The Festival of Summer has begun.

Do you believe? Do you accept the festival, the city, the joy? No? Then let me describe one more thing.

In a basement under one of the beautiful public buildings of Omelas, or perhaps in the cellar of one of its spacious private homes, there is a room. It has one locked door, and no window. A little light seeps in dustily between cracks in the boards, secondhand from a cobwebbed window somewhere across the cellar. In one corner of the little room a couple of mops, with stiff, clotted, foul-smelling heads, stand near a rusty bucket. The floor is dirt, a little damp to the touch, as cellar dirt usually is. The room is about three paces long and two wide: a mere broom closet or disused tool room. In the room a child is sitting. It could be a boy or a girl. It looks about six, but actually is nearly ten. It is feeble-minded. Perhaps it was born defective, or perhaps it has become imbecile through fear, malnutrition, and neglect. It picks its nose and occasionally fumbles vaguely with its toes or genitals, as it sits hunched in the corner farthest from the bucket and the two mops. It is afraid of the mops. It finds them horrible. It shuts its eyes, but it knows the mops are still standing there; and the door is locked; and nobody will come. The door is always locked; and nobody ever comes, except that sometimes— the child has no understanding of time or interval—sometimes the door rattles terribly and opens, and a person, or several people, are there. One of them may come in and kick the child to make it stand up. The others never come close, but peer in at it with frightened, disgusted eyes. The food bowl and the water jug are hastily filled, the door is locked, the eyes disappear. The people at the door never say anything, but the child, who has not always lived in the tool room, and can remember sunlight and its mother's voice, sometimes speaks. "I will be good," it says. "Please let me out. I will be good!" They never answer. The child used to scream for help at night, and cry a good deal, but now it only makes a kind of whining, "eh-haa, eh-haa," and it speaks less and less often. It is so thin there are no calves to its legs; its belly protrudes; it lives on a half-bowl of corn meal and grease a day. It is naked. Its buttocks and thighs are a mass of festered sores, as it sits in its own excrement continually.

They all know it is there, all the people of Omelas. Some of them have come to see it, others are content merely to know it is there. They all know that it has to be there. Some of them understand why, and some do not, but they all understand that their happiness, the beauty of their city, the tenderness of their friendships, the health of their children, the wisdom of their scholars, the skill of their makers, even the abundance of their harvest and the kindly weathers of their skies, depend wholly on this child's abominable misery.

This is usually explained to children when they are between eight and twelve, whenever they seem capable of understanding; and most of those who come to see the child are young people, though often enough an adult comes, or comes back, to see the child. No matter how well the matter has been explained to them, these young spectators are always shocked and sickened at the sight. They feel disgust, which they had thought themselves superior to. They feel anger, outrage, impotence, despite all the explanations. They would like to do something for the child. But there is nothing they can do. If the child were brought up into the sunlight out of that vile place, if it were cleaned and fed and comforted, that would be a good thing, indeed; but if it were done, in that day and hour all the prosperity and beauty and delight of Omelas would wither and be destroyed. Those are the terms. To exchange all the goodness and grace of every life in Omelas for that single, small improvement: to throw away the happiness of thousands for the chance of the happiness of one: that would be to let guilt within the walls indeed.

The terms are strict and absolute; there may not even be a kind word spoken to the child.

Often the young people go home in tears, or in a tearless rage, when they have seen the child and faced this terrible paradox. They may brood over it for weeks or years. But as time goes on they begin to realize that even if the child could be released, it would not get

much good of its freedom: a little vague pleasure of warmth and food, no doubt, but little more. It is too degraded and imbecile to know any real joy. It has been afraid too long ever to be free of fear. Its habits are too uncouth for it to respond to humane treatment. Indeed, after so long it would probably be wretched without walls about it to protect it, and darkness for its eyes, and its own excrement to sit in. Their tears at the bitter injustice dry when they begin to perceive the terrible justice of reality, and to accept it. Yet it is their tears and anger, the trying of their generosity and the acceptance of their helplessness, which are perhaps the true source of the splendor of their lives. Theirs is no vapid, irresponsible happiness. They know that they, like the child, are not free. They know compassion. It is the existence of the child, and their knowledge of its existence, that makes possible the nobility of their architecture, the poignancy of their music, the profundity of their science. It is because of the child that they are so gentle with children. They know that if the wretched one were not there snivelling in the dark, the other one, the flute-player, could make no joyful music as the young riders line up in their beauty for the race in the sunlight of the first morning of summer.

Now do you believe in them? Are they not more credible? But there is one more thing to tell, and this is quite incredible.

At times one of the adolescent girls or boys who go to see the child does not go home to weep or rage, does not, in fact, go home at all. Sometimes also a man or woman much older falls silent for a day or two, and then leaves home. These people go out into the street, and walk down the street alone. They keep walking, and walk straight out of the city of Omelas, through the beautiful gates. They keep walking across the farmlands of Omelas. Each one goes alone, youth or girl, man or woman. Night falls; the traveler must pass down village streets, between the houses with yellow-lit windows, and on out into the darkness of the fields. Each alone, they go west

or north, towards the mountains. They go on. They leave Omelas, they walk ahead into the darkness, and they do not come back. The place they go towards is a place even less imaginable to most of us than the city of happiness. I cannot describe it at all. It is possible that it does not exist. But they seem to know where they are going, the ones who walk away from Omelas.

THE DAY BEFORE
THE REVOLUTION

In memoriam Paul Goodman, 1911–1972

My novel The Dispossessed *is about a small worldful of people who call themselves Odonians. The name is taken from the founder of their society, Odo, who lived several generations before the time of the novel, and who therefore doesn't get into the action—except implicitly, in that all the action started with her.*

Odonianism is anarchism. Not the bomb-in-the-pocket stuff, which is terrorism, whatever name it tries to dignify itself with; not the social-Darwinist economic "libertarianism" of the far right; but anarchism, as prefigured in early Taoist thought, and expounded by Shelley and Kropotkin, Goldman and Goodman. Anarchism's principal target is the authoritarian State (capitalist or socialist); its principal moral-practical theme is cooperation (solidarity, mutual aid). It is the most idealistic, and to me the most interesting, of all political theories.

To embody it in a novel, which had not been done before, was a long and hard job for me, and absorbed me totally for many months. When it was done I felt lost, exiled—a displaced person. I was very grateful, therefore, when Odo came out of the shadows and across the gulf of Probability, and wanted a story written, not about the world she made, but about herself.

This story is about one of the ones who walked away from Omelas.

The speaker's voice was as loud as empty beer-trucks in a stone street, and the people at the meeting were jammed up close, cobble-stones, that great voice booming over them. Taviri was somewhere on the other side of the hall. She had to get to him. She wormed and pushed her way among the dark-clothed, close-packed people. She did not hear the words, nor see the faces: only the booming, and the bodies pressed one behind the other. She could not see Taviri, she was too short. A broad black-vested belly and chest loomed up, block-ing her way. She must get through to Taviri. Sweating, she jabbed fiercely with her fist. It was like hitting stone, he did not move at all, but the huge lungs let out right over her head a prodigious noise, a bellow. She cowered. Then she understood that the bellow had not been at her. Others were shouting. The speaker had said something, something fine about taxes or shadows. Thrilled, she joined the shouting— "Yes! Yes!" —and shoving on, came out easily into the open expanse of the Regimental Drill Field in Parheo. Overhead the evening sky lay deep and colorless, and all around her nodded the tall weeds with dry, white, close-floreted heads. She had never known what they were called. The flowers nodded above her head, swaying in the wind that always blew across the fields in the dusk. She ran among them, and they whipped lithe aside and stood up again swaying, silent. Taviri stood among the tall weeds in his good suit, the dark grey one that made him look like a professor or a play-actor, harshly elegant. He did not look happy, but he was laughing, and saying something to her. The sound of his voice made her cry, and she reached out to catch hold of his hand, but she did not stop, quite. She could not stop. "Oh, Taviri," she said, "it's just on there!" The queer sweet smell of the white weeds was heavy as she went on. There were thorns, tangles underfoot, there were slopes, pits. She feared to fall, to fall, she stopped.

Sun, bright morning-glare, straight in the eyes, relentless. She had forgotten to pull the blind last night. She turned her back on

the sun, but the right side wasn't comfortable. No use. Day. She sighed twice, sat up, got her legs over the edge of the bed, and sat hunched in her nightdress looking down at her feet.

The toes, compressed by a lifetime of cheap shoes, were almost square where they touched each other, and bulged out above in corns; the nails were discolored and shapeless. Between the knob-like anklebones ran fine, dry wrinkles. The brief little plain at the base of the toes had kept its delicacy, but the skin was the color of mud, and knotted veins crossed the instep. Disgusting. Sad, depressing. Mean. Pitiful. She tried on all the words, and they all fit, like hideous little hats. Hideous: yes, that one too. To look at oneself and find it hideous, what a job! But then, when she hadn't been hideous, had she sat around and stared at herself like this? Not much! A proper body's not an object, not an implement, not a belonging to be admired, it's just you, yourself. Only when it's no longer you, but yours, a thing owned, do you worry about it— Is it in good shape? Will it do? Will it last?

"Who cares?" said Laia fiercely, and stood up.

It made her giddy to stand up suddenly. She had to put out her hand to the bed-table, for she dreaded falling. At that she thought of reaching out to Taviri, in the dream.

What had he said? She could not remember. She was not sure if she had even touched his hand. She frowned, trying to force memory. It had been so long since she had dreamed about Taviri; and now not even to remember what he had said!

It was gone, it was gone. She stood there hunched in her nightdress, frowning, one hand on the bed-table. How long was it since she had thought of him—let alone dreamed of him—even thought of him, as "Taviri"? How long since she had said his name?

Asieo said. When Asieo and I were in prison in the North. Before I met Asieo. Asieo's theory of reciprocity. Oh yes, she talked about him, talked about him too much no doubt, maundered, dragged him

in. But as "Asieo," the last name, the public man. The private man was gone, utterly gone. There were so few left who had even known him. They had all used to be in jail. One laughed about it in those days, all the friends in all the jails. But they weren't even there, these days. They were in the prison cemeteries. Or in the common graves.

"Oh, oh my dear," Laia said out loud, and she sank down onto the bed again because she could not stand up under the remembrance of those first weeks in the Fort, in the cell, those first weeks of the nine years in the Fort in Drio, in the cell, those first weeks after they told her that Asieo had been killed in the fighting in Capitol Square and had been buried with the Fourteen Hundred in the lime-ditches behind Oring Gate. In the cell. Her hands fell into the old position on her lap, the left clenched and locked inside the grip of the right, the right thumb working back and forth a little pressing and rubbing on the knuckle of the left first finger. Hours, days, nights. She had thought of them all, each one, each one of the Fourteen Hundred, how they lay, how the quicklime worked on the flesh, how the bones touched in the burning dark. Who touched him? How did the slender bones of the hand lie now? Hours, years.

"Taviri, I have never forgotten you!" she whispered, and the stupidity of it brought her back to morning light and the rumpled bed. Of course she hadn't forgotten him. These things go without saying between husband and wife. There were her ugly old feet flat on the floor again, just as before. She had got nowhere at all, she had gone in a circle. She stood up with a grunt of effort and disapproval, and went to the closet for her dressing gown.

The young people went about the halls of the House in becoming immodesty, but she was too old for that. She didn't want to spoil some young man's breakfast with the sight of her. Besides, they had grown up in the principle of freedom of dress and sex and all

the rest, and she hadn't. All she had done was invent it. It's not the same.

Like speaking of Asieo as "my husband." They winced. The word she should use as a good Odonian, of course, was "partner." But why the hell did she have to be a good Odonian?

She shuffled down the hall to the bathrooms. Mairo was there, washing her hair in a lavatory. Laia looked at the long, sleek, wet hank with admiration. She got out of the House so seldom now that she didn't know when she had last seen a respectably shaven scalp, but still the sight of a full head of hair gave her pleasure, vigorous pleasure. How many times had she been jeered at, *Longhair, Longhair,* had her hair pulled by policemen or young toughs, had her hair shaved off down to the scalp by a grinning soldier at each new prison? And then had grown it all over again, through the fuzz, to the frizz, to the curls, to the mane. . . . In the old days. For God's love, couldn't she think of anything today but the old days?

Dressed, her bed made, she went down to commons. It was a good breakfast, but she had never got her appetite back since the damned stroke. She drank two cups of herb tea, but couldn't finish the piece of fruit she had taken. How she had craved fruit as a child badly enough to steal it; and in the Fort—oh, for God's love stop it! She smiled and replied to the greetings and friendly inquiries of the other breakfasters and big Aevi who was serving the counter this morning. It was he who had tempted her with the peach, "Look at this, I've been saving it for you," and how could she refuse? Anyway she had always loved fruit, and never got enough; once when she was six or seven she had stolen a piece off a vendor's cart in River Street. But it was hard to eat when everyone was talking so excitedly. There was news from Thu, real news. She was inclined to discount it at first, being wary of enthusiasms, but after she had read the article in the paper, and read between the lines of it, she thought, with a strange kind of certainty, deep but

cold, Why, this is it; it has come. And in Thu, not here. Thu will break before this country does; the Revolution will first prevail there. As if that mattered! There will be no more nations. And yet it did matter somehow, it made her a little cold and sad—envious, in fact. Of all the infinite stupidities. She did not join in the talk much, and soon got up to go back to her room, feeling sorry for herself. She could not share their excitement. She was out of it, really out of it. It's not easy, she said to herself in justification, laboriously climbing the stairs, to accept being out of it when you've been in it, in the center of it, for fifty years. Oh, for God's love. Whining!

She got the stairs and the self-pity behind her, entering her room. It was a good room, and it was good to be by herself. It was a great relief. Even if it wasn't strictly fair. Some of the kids in the attics were living five to a room no bigger than this. There were always more people wanting to live in an Odonian House than could be properly accommodated. She had this big room all to herself only because she was an old woman who had had a stroke. And maybe because she was Odo. If she hadn't been Odo, but merely the old woman with a stroke, would she have had it? Very likely. After all, who the hell wanted to room with a drooling old woman? But it was hard to be sure. Favoritism, elitism, leader-worship, they crept back and cropped out everywhere. But she had never hoped to see them eradicated in her lifetime, in one generation; only Time works the great changes. Meanwhile this was a nice, large, sunny room, proper for a drooling old woman who had started a world revolution.

Her secretary would be coming in an hour to help her despatch the day's work. She shuffled over to the desk, a beautiful, big piece, a present from the Nio Cabinetmakers' Syndicate because somebody had heard her remark once that the only piece of furniture she had ever really longed for was a desk with drawers and enough room on top . . . damn, the top was practically covered with papers with notes clipped to them, mostly in Noi's small clear handwriting: Urgent. —Northern Provinces. —Consult w/R. T.?

Her own handwriting had never been the same since Asieo's death. It was odd, when you thought about it. After all, within five years after his death she had written the whole *Analogy*. And there were those letters, which the tall guard with the watery grey eyes, what was his name, never mind, had smuggled out of the Fort for her for two years. *The Prison Letters* they called them now, there were a dozen different editions of them. All that stuff, the letters which people kept telling her were so full of "spiritual strength"— which probably meant she had been lying herself blue in the face when she wrote them, trying to keep her spirits up—and the *Analogy* which was certainly the solidest intellectual work she had ever done, all of that had been written in the Fort in Drio, in the cell, after Asieo's death. One had to do something, and in the Fort they let one have paper and pens. . . . But it had all been written in the hasty, scribbling hand which she had never felt was hers, not her own like the round, black scrollings of the manuscript of *Society Without Government,* forty-five years old. Taviri had taken not only her body's and her heart's desire to the quicklime with him, but even her good clear handwriting.

But he had left her the Revolution.

How brave of you to go on, to work, to write, in prison, after such a defeat for the Movement, after your partner's death, people had used to say. Damn fools. What else had there been to do? Bravery, courage—what was courage? She had never figured it out. Not fearing, some said. Fearing yet going on, others said. But what could one do but go on? Had one any real choice, ever?

To die was merely to go on in another direction.

If you wanted to come home you had to keep going on, that was what she meant when she wrote "True journey is return," but it had never been more than an intuition, and she was farther than ever now from being able to rationalize it. She bent down, too suddenly, so that she grunted a little at the creak in her bones, and began to root in a bottom drawer of the desk. Her hand came on an age-

292 The Wind's Twelve Quarters

softened folder and drew it out, recognizing it by touch before
sight confirmed: the manuscript of *Syndical Organization in Revolu-
tionary Transition.* He had printed the title on the folder and
written his name under it, Taviri Odo Asieo, IX 741. There was an
elegant handwriting, every letter well-formed, bold, and fluent. But
he had preferred to use a voiceprinter. The manuscript was all in
voiceprint, and high quality too, hesitancies adjusted and idiosyn-
crasies of speech normalized. You couldn't see there how he had
said "o" deep in his throat as they did on the North Coast. There
was nothing of him there but his mind. She had nothing of him at
all except his name written on the folder. She hadn't kept his letters,
it was sentimental to keep letters. Besides, she never kept anything.
She couldn't think of anything that she had ever owned for more
than a few years, except this ramshackle old body, of course, and
she was stuck with that. . . .

Dualizing again. "She" and "it." Age and illness made one dualist,
made one escapist; the mind insisted, *It's not me, it's not me.* But it
was. Maybe the mystics could detach mind from body, she had always
rather wistfully envied them the chance, without hope of emulating
them. Escape had never been her game. She had sought for freedom
here, now, body and soul.

First self-pity, then self-praise, and here she still sat, for God's
love, holding Asieo's name in her hand, why? Didn't she know his
name without looking it up? What was wrong with her? She raised
the folder to her lips and kissed the handwritten name firmly and
squarely, replaced the folder in the back of the bottom drawer, shut
the drawer, and straightened up in the chair. Her right hand
tingled. She scratched it, and then shook it in the air, spitefully. It
had never quite got over the stroke. Neither had her right leg, or
right eye, or the right corner of her mouth. They were sluggish, in-
ept, they tingled. They made her feel like a robot with a short
circuit.

And time was getting on, Noi would be coming, what had she been doing ever since breakfast?

She got up so hastily that she lurched, and grabbed at the chair-back to make sure she did not fall. She went down the hall to the bathroom and looked in the big mirror there. Her grey knot was loose and droopy, she hadn't done it up well before breakfast. She struggled with it a while. It was hard to keep her arms up in the air. Amai, running in to piss, stopped and said, "Let me do it!" and knotted it up tight and neat in no time, with her round, strong, pretty fingers, smiling and silent. Amai was twenty, less than a third of Laia's age. Her parents had both been members of the Movement, one killed in the insurrection of '60, the other still recruiting in the South Provinces. Amai had grown up in Odonian Houses, born to the Revolution, a true daughter of anarchy. And so quiet and free and beautiful a child, enough to make you cry when you thought: this is what we worked for, this is what we meant, this is it, here she is, alive, the kindly, lovely future.

Laia Asieo Odo's right eye wept several little tears, as she stood between the lavatories and the latrines having her hair done up by the daughter she had not borne; but her left eye, the strong one, did not weep, nor did it know what the right eye did.

She thanked Amai and hurried back to her room. She had noticed, in the mirror, a stain on her collar. Peach juice, probably. Damned old dribbler. She didn't want Noi to come in and find her with drool on her collar.

As the clean shirt went on over her head, she thought, What's so special about Noi?

She fastened the collar-frogs with her left hand, slowly.

Noi was thirty or so, a slight, muscular fellow with a soft voice and alert dark eyes. That's what was special about Noi. It was that simple. Good old sex. She had never been drawn to a fair man or a fat one, or the tall fellows with big biceps, never, not even when

she was fourteen and fell in love with every passing fart. Dark, spare, and fiery, that was the recipe. Taviri, of course. This boy wasn't a patch on Taviri for brains, nor even for looks, but there it was: she didn't want him to see her with dribble on her collar and her hair coming undone.

Her thin, grey hair.

Noi came in, just pausing in the open doorway—my God, she hadn't even shut the door while changing her shirt! She looked at him and saw herself. The old woman.

You could brush your hair and change your shirt, or you could wear last week's shirt and last night's braids, or you could put on cloth of gold and dust your shaven scalp with diamond powder. None of it would make the slightest difference. The old woman would look a little less, or a little more, grotesque.

One keeps oneself neat out of mere decency, mere sanity, awareness of other people.

And finally even that goes, and one dribbles unashamed.

"Good morning," the young man said in his gentle voice.

"Hello, Noi."

No, by God, it was *not* out of mere decency. Decency be damned. Because the man she had loved, and to whom her age would not have mattered—because he was dead, must she pretend she had no sex? Must she suppress the truth, like a damned puritan authoritarian? Even six months ago, before the stroke, she had made men look at her and like to look at her; and now, though she could give no pleasure, by God she could please herself.

When she was six years old, and Papa's friend Gadeo used to come by to talk politics with Papa after dinner, she would put on the gold-colored necklace that Mama had found on a trash heap and brought home for her. It was so short that it always got hidden under her collar where nobody could see it. She liked it that way. She knew she had it on. She sat on the doorstep and listened to

them talk, and knew that she looked nice for Gadeo. He was dark, with white teeth that flashed. Sometimes he called her "pretty Laia." "There's my pretty Laia!" Sixty-six years ago.

"What? My head's dull. I had a terrible night." It was true. She had slept even less than usual.

"I was asking if you'd seen the papers this morning."

She nodded.

"Pleased about Soinehe?"

Soinehe was the province in Thu which had declared its secession from the Thuvian State last night.

He was pleased about it. His white teeth flashed in his dark, alert face. Pretty Laia.

"Yes. And apprehensive."

"I know. But it's the real thing, this time. It's the beginning of the end of the Government in Thu. They haven't even tried to order troops into Soinehe, you know. It would merely provoke the soldiers into rebellion sooner, and they know it."

She agreed with him. She herself had felt that certainty. But she could not share his delight. After a lifetime of living on hope because there is nothing but hope, one loses the taste for victory. A real sense of triumph must be preceded by real despair. She had un-learned despair a long time ago. There were no more triumphs. One went on.

"Shall we do those letters today?"

"All right. Which letters?"

"To the people in the North," he said without impatience.

"In the North?"

"Parheo, Oaidun."

She had been born in Parheo, the dirty city on the dirty river. She had not come here to the capital till she was twenty-two and ready to bring the Revolution. Though in those days, before she and the others had thought it through, it had been a very green and puerile

revolution. Strikes for better wages, representation for women. Votes and wages—Power and Money, for the love of God! Well, one does learn a little, after all, in fifty years.

But then one must forget it all.

"Start with Oaidun," she said, sitting down in the armchair. Noi was at the desk ready to work. He read out excerpts from the letters she was to answer. She tried to pay attention, and succeeded well enough that she dictated one whole letter and started on another. "Remember that at this stage your brotherhood is vulnerable to the threat of . . . no, to the danger . . . to . . ." She groped till Noi suggested, "The danger of leader-worship?"

"All right. And that nothing is so soon corrupted by power-seeking as altruism. No. And that nothing corrupts altruism—no. O for God's love you know what I'm trying to say, Noi, you write it. They know it too, it's just the same old stuff, why can't they read my books!"

"Touch," Noi said gently, smiling, citing one of the central Odonian themes.

"All right, but I'm tired of being touched. If you'll write the letter I'll sign it, but I can't be bothered with it this morning." He was looking at her with a little question or concern. She said, irritable, "There is something else I have to do!"

When Noi had gone she sat down at the desk and moved the papers about, pretending to be doing something, because she had been startled, frightened, by the words she had said. She had nothing else to do. She never had had anything else to do. This was her work: her lifework. The speaking tours and the meetings and the streets were out of reach for her now, but she could still write, and that was her work. And anyhow if she had had anything else to do, Noi would have known it; he kept her schedule, and tactfully

reminded her of things, like the visit from the foreign students this afternoon.

Oh, damn. She liked the young, and there was always something to learn from a foreigner, but she was tired of new faces, and tired of being on view. She learned from them, but they didn't learn from her; they had learnt all she had to teach long ago, from her books, from the Movement. They just came to look, as if she were the Great Tower in Rodarred, or the Canyon of the Tulaevea. A phenomenon, a monument. They were awed, adoring. She snarled at them: Think your own thoughts! —That's not anarchism, that's mere obscurantism. —You don't think liberty and discipline are incompatible, do you?— They accepted their tongue-lashing meekly as children, gratefully, as if she were some kind of All-Mother, the idol of the Big Sheltering Womb. She! She who had mined the shipyards at Seissero, and had cursed Premier Inoilte to his face in front of a crowd of seven thousand, telling him he would have cut off his own balls and had them bronzed and sold as souvenirs, if he thought there was any profit in it—she who had screeched, and sworn, and kicked policemen, and spat at priests, and pissed in public on the big brass plaque in Capitol Square that said HERE WAS FOUNDED THE SOVEREIGN NATION STATE OF A–IO ETC ETC, psssssssss to all that! And now she was everybody's grandmama, the dear old lady, the sweet old monument, come worship at the womb. The fire's out, boys, it's safe to come up close.

"No, I won't," Laia said out loud. "I will not." She was not self-conscious about talking to herself, because she always had talked to herself. "Laia's invisible audience," Taviri had used to say, as she went through the room muttering. "You needn't come, I won't be here," she told the invisible audience now. She had just decided what it was she had to do. She had to go out. To go into the streets.

It was inconsiderate to disappoint the foreign students. It was

erratic, typically senile. It was unOdonian. Psssssss to all that. What was the good working for freedom all your life and ending up without any freedom at all? She would go out for a walk.

"What is an anarchist? One who, choosing, accepts the responsibility of choice."

On the way downstairs she decided, scowling, to stay and see the foreign students. But then she would go out.

They were very young students, very earnest: doe-eyed, shaggy, charming creatures from the Western Hemisphere, Benbili and the Kingdom of Mand, the girls in white trousers, the boys in long kilts, warlike and archaic. They spoke of their hopes. "We in Mand are so very far from the Revolution that maybe we are near it," said one of the girls, wistful and smiling: "The Circle of Life!" and she showed the extremes meeting, in the circle of her slender, dark-skinned fingers. Amai and Aevi served them white wine and brown bread, the hospitality of the House. But the visitors, unpresumptuous, all rose to take their leave after barely half an hour. "No, no, no," Laia said, "stay here, talk with Aevi and Amai. It's just that I get stiff sitting down, you see, I have to change about. It has been so good to meet you, will you come back to see me, my little brothers and sisters, soon?" For her heart went out to them, and theirs to her, and she exchanged kisses all round, laughing, delighted by the dark young cheeks, the affectionate eyes, the scented hair, before she shuffled off. She was really a little tired, but to go up and take a nap would be a defeat. She had wanted to go out. She would go out. She had not been alone outdoors since—when? Since winter! before the stroke. No wonder she was getting morbid. It had been a regular jail sentence. Outside, the streets, that's where she lived.

She went quietly out the side door of the House, past the vegetable patch, to the street. The narrow strip of sour city dirt had been beautifully gardened and was producing a fine crop of beans and *ceëa,* but Laia's eye for farming was unenlightened. Of course it had

been clear that anarchist communities, even in the time of transition, must work towards optimal self-support, but how that was to be managed in the way of actual dirt and plants wasn't her business. There were farmers and agronomists for that. Her job was the streets, the noisy, stinking streets of stone, where she had grown up and lived all her life, except for the fifteen years in prison.

She looked up fondly at the façade of the House. That it had been built as a bank gave peculiar satisfaction to its present occupants. They kept their sacks of meal in the bomb-proof money-vault, and aged their cider in kegs in safe deposit boxes. Over the fussy columns that faced the street carved letters still read, "National Investors and Grain Factors Banking Association." The Movement was not strong on names. They had no flag. Slogans came and went as the need did. There was always the Circle of Life to scratch on walls and pavements where Authority would have to see it. But when it came to names they were indifferent, accepting and ignoring whatever they got called, afraid of being pinned down and penned in, unafraid of being absurd. So this best known and second oldest of all the cooperative Houses had no name except The Bank.

It faced on a wide and quiet street, but only a block away began the Temeba, an open market, once famous as a center for black-market psychogenics and teratogenics, now reduced to vegetables, secondhand clothes, and miserable sideshows. Its crapulous vitality was gone, leaving only half-paralyzed alcoholics, addicts, cripples, hucksters, and fifth-rate whores, pawnshops, gambling dens, fortune-tellers, body-sculptors, and cheap hotels. Laia turned to the Temeba as water seeks its level.

She had never feared or despised the city. It was her country. There would not be slums like this, if the Revolution prevailed. But there would be misery. There would always be misery, waste, cruelty. She had never pretended to be changing the human condition, to be Mama taking tragedy away from the children so they won't hurt

themselves. Anything but. So long as people were free to choose, if they chose to drink flybane and live in sewers, it was their business. Just so long as it wasn't the business of Business, the source of profit and the means of power for other people. She had felt all that before she knew anything; before she wrote the first pamphlet, before she left Parheo, before she knew what "capital" meant, before she'd been farther than River Street where she played rolltaggie kneeling on scabby knees on the pavement with the other six-year-olds, she had known it: that she, and the other kids, and her parents, and their parents, and the drunks and whores and all of River Street, were at the bottom of something—were the foundation, the reality, the source. But will you drag civilization down into the mud? cried the shocked decent people, later on, and she had tried for years to explain to them that if all you had was mud, then if you were God you made it into human beings, and if you were human you tried to make it into houses where human beings could live. But nobody who thought he was better than mud would understand. Now, water seeking its level, mud to mud, Laia shuffled through the foul, noisy street, and all the ugly weakness of her old age was at home. The sleepy whores, their lacquered hair-arrangements dilapidated and askew, the one-eyed woman wearily yelling her vegetables to sell, the half-wit beggar slapping flies, these were her countrywomen. They looked like her, they were all sad, disgusting, mean, pitiful, hideous. They were her sisters, her own people.

She did not feel very well. It had been a long time since she had walked so far, four or five blocks, by herself, in the noise and push and striking summer heat of the streets. She had wanted to get to Koly Park, the triangle of scruffy grass at the end of the Temeba, and sit there for a while with the other old men and women who always sat there, to see what it was like to sit there and be old; but it was too far. If she didn't turn back now, she might get a dizzy spell, and she had a dread of falling down, falling down and having

to lie there and look up at the people come to stare at the old woman in a fit. She turned and started home, frowning with effort and self-disgust. She could feel her face very red, and a swimming feeling came and went in her ears. It got a bit much, she was really afraid she might keel over. She saw a doorstep in the shade and made for it, let herself down cautiously, sat, sighed.

Nearby was a fruit-seller, sitting silent behind his dusty, withered stock. People went by. Nobody bought from him. Nobody looked at her. Odo, who was Odo? Famous revolutionary, author of *Community, The Analogy,* etc. etc. She, who was she? An old woman with grey hair and a red face sitting on a dirty doorstep in a slum, muttering to herself.

True? Was that she? Certainly it was what anybody passing her saw. But was it she, herself, any more than the famous revolutionary, etc., was? No. It was not. But who was she, then?

The one who loved Taviri.

Yes. True enough. But not enough. That was gone; he had been dead so long.

"Who am I?" Laia muttered to her invisible audience, and they knew the answer and told it to her with one voice. She was the little girl with scabby knees, sitting on the doorstep staring down through the dirty golden haze of River Street in the heat of late summer, the six-year-old, the sixteen-year-old, the fierce, cross, dream-ridden girl, untouched, untouchable. She was herself. Indeed she had been the tireless worker and thinker, but a blood clot in a vein had taken that woman away from her. Indeed she had been the lover, the swimmer in the midst of life, but Taviri, dying, had taken that woman away with him. There was nothing left, really, but the foundation. She had come home; she had never left home. "True voyage is return." Dust and mud and a doorstep in the slums. And beyond, at the far end of the street, the field full of tall dry weeds blowing in the wind as night came.

"Laia! What are you doing here? Are you all right?"

One of the people from the House, of course, a nice woman, a bit fanatical and always talking. Laia could not remember her name though she had known her for years. She let herself be taken home, the woman talking all the way. In the big cool common room (once occupied by tellers counting money behind polished counters supervised by armed guards) Laia sat down in a chair. She was unable just as yet to face climbing the stairs, though she would have liked to be alone. The woman kept on talking, and other excited people came in. It appeared that a demonstration was being planned. Events in Thu were moving so fast that the mood here had caught fire, and something must be done. Day after tomorrow, no, tomorrow, there was to be a march, a big one, from Old Town to Capitol Square—the old route. "Another Ninth Month Uprising," said a young man, fiery and laughing, glancing at Laia. He had not even been born at the time of the Ninth Month Uprising, it was all history to him. Now he wanted to make some history of his own. The room had filled up. A general meeting would be held here, tomorrow, at eight in the morning. "You must talk, Laia."

"Tomorrow? Oh, I won't be here tomorrow," she said brusquely. Whoever had asked her smiled, another one laughed, though Amai glanced round at her with a puzzled look. They went on talking and shouting. The Revolution. What on earth had made her say that? What a thing to say on the eve of the Revolution, even if it was true.

She waited her time, managed to get up and, for all her clumsiness, to slip away unnoticed among the people busy with their planning and excitement. She got to the hall, to the stairs, and began to climb them one by one. "The general strike," a voice, two voices, ten voices were saying in the room below, behind her. "The general strike," Laia muttered, resting for a moment on the landing. Above, ahead, in her room, what awaited her? The private stroke. That

was mildly funny. She started up the second flight of stairs, one by one, one leg at a time, like a small child. She was dizzy, but she was no longer afraid to fall. On ahead, on there, the dry white flowers nodded and whispered in the open fields of evening. Seventy-two years and she had never had time to learn what they were called.

DATE DUE

JAN 1 9 1978		
JUL 1 0 1978		
NOV 16 '78		
FEB 5 1979		
SE 14 '83		
JA 2 '84		
FE 16 '84		
MY '86		
GAYLORD		PRINTED IN U.S.A.